Praise for *The Scandalous Life of a True Lady*

"Another winner from an author who writes with a light touch and a kindly understanding of human nature. Barbara Metzger is a true artist with a palette of words." —Romance Reviews Today

"[Has] witty, spicy dialogue and intelligent characters." —*Romantic Times*

"[Contains Barbara Metzger's] trademark situational comedy and witty repartee . . . fans of Ms. Metzger won't want to miss this story." —Rakehell

"Barbara Metzger creates a treasure with *The Scandalous Life of a True Lady*." —Manic Readers

"Metzger's cup of imagination seems to overflow. Stellar!" —Huntress Book Reviews

**Raves for
Barbara Metzger's Other Romances**

"Funny and touching—what a joy!" —Edith Layton

"Metzger's gift for re-creating the flavor and ambience of the period shines here, and the antics of her dirty-dish villains, near-villains, and starry-eyed lovers are certain to entertain."

—*Publishers Weekly* (starred review)

"Metzger presents an extraordinary book that commands the reader's attention and lingers in the mind long after the last page is turned."

—*Booklist* (starred review)

"The complexities of both story and character contribute much to its richness. Like life, this book is much more exciting when the layers are peeled back and savored." —*Affaire de Coeur*

"A true tour de force. . . . A very satisfying read." —The Best Reviews

Also by Barbara Metzger

The Wicked Ways of a True Hero

Barbara Metzger

A SIGNET ECLIPSE BOOK

SIGNET ECLIPSE
Published by New American Library, a division of
Penguin Group (USA) Inc., 375 Hudson Street,
New York, New York 10014, USA
Penguin Group (Canada), 90 Eglinton Avenue East, Suite 700, Toronto,
Ontario M4P 2Y3, Canada (a division of Pearson Penguin Canada Inc.)
Penguin Books Ltd., 80 Strand, London WC2R 0RL, England
Penguin Ireland, 25 St. Stephen's Green, Dublin 2,
Ireland (a division of Penguin Books Ltd.)
Penguin Group (Australia), 250 Camberwell Road, Camberwell, Victoria 3124,
Australia (a division of Pearson Australia Group Pty. Ltd.)
Penguin Books India Pvt. Ltd., 11 Community Centre, Panchsheel Park,
New Delhi - 110 017, India
Penguin Group (NZ), 67 Apollo Drive, Rosedale, North Shore 0632,
New Zealand (a division of Pearson New Zealand Ltd.)
Penguin Books (South Africa) (Pty.) Ltd., 24 Sturdee Avenue,
Rosebank, Johannesburg 2196, South Africa

Penguin Books Ltd., Registered Offices:
80 Strand, London WC2R 0RL, England

First published by Signet Eclipse, an imprint of New American Library,
a division of Penguin Group (USA) Inc.

First Printing, March 2009
10 9 8 7 6 5 4 3 2 1

For Chris,
because she loves books and dogs

Chapter One

The end was near, inevitable and inescapable. All men had to meet their fates. Like all men, Daniel Stamfield protested his imminent demise.

"Great gods, I'm not ready!" he shouted, his fist raised to the heavens.

The gods, great or small, did not answer, but his companion cringed farther back on her side of the bed.

Daniel did not notice. He leaped from the bed, bare as the day he was born, and charged to the dressing table. He grabbed the bottle there—brandy or gin or spice-scented cologne; he didn't care which. He ignored the nearby glass just as he ignored Miss White's mew of distress when he raised the bottle to his mouth and took a long swallow. Then another. The liquor could not change the outcome, nor delay it. Being dead drunk on judgment day wasn't such a wise act, either, he realized, which only reminded him.

"Dead. I'm a dead man." He went back to the bed, as if sinking into the downy mattress, pulling the covers over his head and Miss White closer to his cold body, could save him. "I'm too young to die. Not even thirty. I thought I had more time."

Don't all men think that?

The note was still on the bed, though, where he'd tossed it after the manservant brought the damn thing. On a silver tray, no less. Daniel stared at it now—the expensive stationery, the flowing script, his name on the front of the folded sheet, the familiar seal on the back. His blue-eyed glare couldn't make the missive disappear, this death warrant, this end of his carefree days, this letter from his mother.

"They're in Town," he told Miss White, "expecting me to play the beau for my sister's come-out." He looked longingly back at the bottle on the table, then at the window overlooking the alley, as if escape lay in that direction. There was no escape, Daniel knew, not anywhere in London. "I wrote that Susanna was too young to make her curtsies at court. I said she and Mother should come to Town before next Christmas to shop, to take in the theater and visit the lending libraries. A few tea parties and morning calls to Mother's old friends, especially those with daughters Susanna's age. I'd take her to Astley's Amphitheatre to see the trick riding. Susanna would like that. I did at her age."

Daniel still enjoyed visits to the circus, but now he went more to admire the bareback riders in their tights and short spangled skirts. He groaned at the memory that would be just that, a fond, forlorn dream, now that his family was in Town. "A short visit would have been fine—a chance for Susanna to see the metropolis and pick up a bit of Town bronze and perhaps make some new friends before facing the marriage mart next year. A week or two, that's what I told them. Did anyone listen to me, the head of the family? No, damn it. They are here now, here for the whole blasted spring Season. Weeks. Months. Maybe into summer. An eternity of balls and routs, masquerades and presentations and operas. Balls," he repeated, with a different meaning.

No more bachelor days, wagering and wenching and lying abed, when he found his way home at daybreak or later. No more race meets or prizefights or tavern brawls. No more comfortable clothes, either. He grimaced at the loose shirt he pulled over his head, the baggy Cossack trousers he dragged on. They'd soon be gone, along with the opera dancers and actresses and serving girls.

The spotted kerchief he knotted at his throat felt like a noose. "Gads, they'll expect me to wear satin knee breeches and starched neckcloths." He could feel the rash already. And that was the least of his itches.

Some men came home from war with wounds or scars or medals. Daniel Stamfield had come home with a rash. Like all the men of his family, Daniel had a gift—or curse, depending on how one felt. Somehow they could all tell truth from lies. His uncle the Earl of Royce heard discordant notes. His cousin Rex, the Royce heir, saw scarlet. Harry, his other cousin, from the wrong side of the blanket, tasted bitter lies on his tongue. Daniel? His curse wasn't subtle or private. That would have been too easy, too comfortable for a man who already stuck out like a sore thumb because of his overlarge, ungainly size. A sore thumb? He'd be happy with that. Instead he got itchy toes, itchy ears, bright red splotches on his neck, his face, his hands. Worst of all, a lot of lies, continuous lies, blatant lies, gave him a rash on his private parts. That was how he'd been thrown out of Almack's his first time at the hallowed hall of propriety. He'd scratched his arse. What if Susanna was denied vouchers for that sacred altar to the matchmaking deities because of him?

Hell, he would die at the first Venetian breakfast from all the polite mistruths and insincere flatteries the beau monde mouthed. His mother and sister would die, too, of embarrassment. Susanna's Season would be ruined, a debacle, a disgrace. No gentleman would marry her. Sweet little Sukey'd be an old maid at seventeen, all because of him and his sensitive skin. He should have stayed in the army, no matter the cost. Perhaps he had time to reenlist. So what if the war with France was over and that madman Napoleon was finally defeated? There was bound to be a battle somewhere, some way he could prove useful. More useful than he'd be to poor Susanna.

All the Royce descendants were invaluable to the government, in necessarily secret service to their country. They'd be burned as witches or warlocks if anyone suspected their hidden talent, or ostracized as charlatans. Mind readers? The devil! Truth knowers? Bosh. So they worked behind the scenes, disguising their gift as wisdom, wit, and uncanny luck.

Uncle Royce advised the courts. Harry used to run a spy network. Rex worked with Bow Street after he was wounded in the Peninsular War, after Daniel left the army. Together Rex and Daniel had been the dreaded Inquisitors, the intelligence officers in charge of gathering information from captured enemy officers. Daniel's size alone intimidated their prisoners. Their unfailing results terrified everyone else, even their superiors. Since only a select few could know of the family trait, the War Office let stand the rumors that the Inquisitors were torturers, immoral brutes. They were despised by friend and foe alike, despite the countless English lives they saved. Daniel had constant rashes.

He came home when his father died, relieved to have an excuse to leave the army and his ugly but important employment. The life of a country squire, or a town buck, was just as filled with falsehoods, though, and boredom to boot. Then came the guilt over leaving Rex to serve the country by himself, until the fool got shot.

Daniel had sworn to look after his cousin and best friend. He'd failed. He'd lied, which was the worst thing a Royce relative could do. When Rex turned into a morose, hermitlike cripple, Daniel turned into a libertine, a wastrel, a gambler, a drunk. He threw himself into whatever debauchery London offered, along with its other dregs and demimondaines. So what if his new companions lied and cheated? Their haunts were usually too dark for anyone to notice Daniel's spots, and half his neighbors itched just as badly, from lice or fleas or bedbugs. Women were paid to please, and Daniel paid them more not to pretend any tender feelings or passion. His size and reputation protected him from the dangers of the night, and his mighty fists protected him from anyone stupid enough to try in the shadows.

Then Rex came to London as a favor to his father and got involved with solving crimes. The clunch almost got himself killed again for his efforts, but he actually liked working with Bow Street's investigators. Rex tried to drag Daniel out of the gambling dens and into his detective work, but Daniel was having none of it. Damn, did they think the suspects were going to confess when they knew they'd be hanged or deported? No, the scum told lies on top of lies, and Daniel got more rashes.

Even Harry, the earl's illegitimate son, tried to enlist Daniel in his sanctioned skulduggery, uncovering blackmailers and traitors and revolutionaries in the government. Were there no honest politicians?

Both of his cousins wanted Daniel to continue their work in Parliament or the police precincts. Uncle Royce offered him a magistrate's position, so he could use his gift in the courts. England needed him, they all said. He should be working, they all said, for the good of king and country.

Daniel'd said no. He was not interested in their noble missions, their self-righteous sacrifices, not when he could enjoy a redheaded wench and a bottle of wine. He'd served his country; he'd done his share. So no, he would not mingle among the gentlemen who ruled the kingdom, to listen for their lies. No, he would not preside over the courts where bewigged barristers spewed prevarications to save their clients. No, he would not sit at some battered desk to hear scurvy felons falsely plead their innocence. No, he would not need a tin of talcum powder on his posterior every day.

"No chance of saying no to my mother," he told Miss White, his voice full of regret and resignation. He might be brave, and full of brawn if not brains, but she was his mother. She was also Lady Cora Stamfield, née Royce, daughter of the former earl, sister to the current Lord Royce, widow of one of the largest landholders in the eastern shires. Formidable in her own right, she ran Stamfield Manor and the rest of the parish, as well. Mostly, though, for years now she'd asked for nothing from Daniel but his happiness. She

was not one for rants and recriminations, only stead-
fast love and loyalty to her only son. He knew she
worried while he was with the army, and more so
while he wallowed in London's pleasures. Sowing his
oats, she'd called it, and she waited for him to reap
his harvest and come home. He hadn't, except for
short visits. So how could he refuse her request to join
her and Susanna at Royce House?

"Now she remembers I am the man of the family,
when she thinks she needs me."

Daniel wouldn't be the head of the household if the
earl came to Town, nor would his presence be required.
Mother was staying at the earl's mansion in Mayfair,
after all, and Lord and Lady Royce held enough power
in London to oversee seven debutante balls. But the
earl and his countess were recently reunited and enjoying their life in the country. Rex, Viscount Rexford,
that is, had enough countenance and connections to
aid Lady Cora and Susanna, too, but he was the proud
father of twins, with another child due soon. He would
never leave his beloved Amanda and their brood to
take over escort duties. Even Harry would have done
in a pinch, now that he was recognized in polite society. The former master spy, though, was also deliri-
ously happily wed, traveling on honeymoon, showing
off his beautiful bride to relatives, inspecting his new
estate, and awaiting his first child.

"Like rabbits, that's what they both are," Daniel
said as he pulled on his scuffed boots. "And curse
them all for not being here when I need them. I'd
rather face the blasted French cannons on my own
than the *ton* without a friend at my back."

Miss White made a soft sound of commiseration, or
protest at being ignored. She was here, wasn't she?

Daniel sat beside her on the bed, gathering her close. "I am sorry, puss. I know you'd stand by me, but it will never do. You wouldn't be welcome at Royce House, you know. You're a beauty, my pet, but not of their elevated, rarefied world. No more than I am, but I have no choice. You'll be happier here." He looked around at the comfortable rooms he'd taken over from Harry, above McCann's Club. No one cared what time he came or went, in what condition, or with which companion. The service was excellent, the food ample, and the company undemanding. He'd miss it, the freedom, the camaraderie, the easy acceptance of who and what he was, with no demands that he become anything else. But his mother wanted him to reside with the family, likely to be at their beck and call. "I'll miss you most of all, my dear, but you'll do. You already rule the kitchens here, so you won't go hungry, and Harry will return soon and take you up again."

He gave Miss White one last kiss on the top of her silky head, then stood and brushed her white cat hairs off his coat. That was the least he could do for his beloved mother, present a neat appearance on this first day. She'd be disappointed in him soon enough. Like everyone else in the family already was.

Chapter Two

"Shall I walk your horse, sir?" the young groom asked when he took the reins from Daniel outside Royce House. "Or will you be staying a bit?"

Condemned men seldom got to choose. "I'm afraid I'm here for life. That is, as long as my mother wishes."

The boy sighed with understanding. "My mum makes me go to church every week, and she's back at Stamfield Manor."

That locale was looking more appealing. Sheep and cows didn't force a chap into cravats or cotillions. Corn didn't tell fibs. Then Daniel noticed the groom was standing as far from the huge bay gelding—big enough to carry Daniel's weight—as the reins allowed.

"Old Gideon won't give you any trouble," he told the boy. "All he wants is fresh hay, plenty of oats, and as little exertion as he can manage." In fact, Gideon, at least, would be happy here. The stables were bound to be cleaner, brighter, and better attended than the cramped quarters the bay was used to. Horses at Royce House were treated better than some of the guests. No one would eye him with the sneer the butler was giving Daniel right now from the opened doors of the earl's town house.

The man was new since Daniel had been here last, likely hired for the Season while the countess's regular majordomo was with her in the country. This fellow looked as if he'd gone to the same buttling school as every other starched-up, supercilious, elitist servant of society's upper class. That was the school where they were taught to take their standing from the family they served, to look down on ordinary mortals, and to stick a poker up their—

"Ah," the man said now, the corners of his mouth raised the barest fraction. "You must be Mr. Stamfield. Lady Cora did say she was expecting you. Welcome to Royce House."

He held out his immaculate white-gloved hand. Daniel had no idea why—not that he was averse to shaking a servant's hand, but even in his recent milieu, that was odd. Perhaps the chap was waiting for Daniel's hat, which he'd lost months ago in a blindfolded race.

His gloves? Daniel wore the plaguey things only in the depths of winter, and misplaced them more often than not.

A cane? An affectation of the swells on the strut.

A riding crop? Gideon went his own pace, so why bother?

Surely the prig could not be waiting for a gratuity, not at Daniel's mother's own residence, where the butler hadn't done a thing for her son yet, and looked like he never would if he had his druthers.

The servant's nostrils flared in haughty disdain. "Your card, sir. So I might carry it to Lady Cora."

There was only so much sacrifice Daniel was willing to make for his mother. Taking manure from a stiff-rumped toad was not on the list. Daniel grabbed the

much smaller man by the shoulders—padded shoulders at that—and lifted him right off his feet. "What
is your name?" he demanded.

"D-Dobbson, sir."

"Well, Duhdobbson, if I am going to live here, we
need to come to terms. My terms. No damn calling
cards, no punctilious rituals, no sticking your beak up
at me or my ways."

"Yes, sir. You are fine just as you are. A perfect
gentleman. A credit to Royce House and the earldom.
My pleasure to serve you, Mr. Stamfield."

Daniel could feel the welts rising on the back of his
neck, but wouldn't give the butler the satisfaction of
seeing him scratch on the street. He set the man back
on his own feet. "And no blasted lies!"

"I'll just go announce you to Lady Cora." Dobbson
took one look at Daniel, still looming close enough
for another application of brute force, and stepped
back, out of range. He straightened his disordered tailcoat, patted his powdered wig to ensure it was properly situated, and said, "I'm sure my lady would rather
you surprise her. You'll announce yourself, shall
you?"

There was no need, for Lady Cora was at the open
door, her arms held wide to welcome her son. While
they embraced, before he could apologize for picking
on someone smaller, older, weaker, and of lesser rank,
his mother whispered, "I've been wishing to box that
man's ears all morning. Thank you, dear. Lady Royce
hired him, don't you know. Dear Margaret always was
a countess to her toenails."

Daniel smiled. His mother might be all fancified in
silks and jewels befitting Lady Cora—she even sported
a turban—but she was still plain Mrs. Stamfield who

had hugs for him and Rex no matter how much dirt two grubby schoolboys trailed into her clean house, or what trouble they'd caused in the neighborhood. Judging from the spread waiting in the morning room, she still knew how much fuel a body as large as Daniel's needed, and how he loved raspberry tarts. Surely she'd understand his loathing of polite society and his total unsuitability to take his place there. He pleaded his case over tea and tarts in the sun-filled parlor.

His doting parent looked at him over the rim of her cup. "Nonsense. You can be a perfect gentleman when you wish. I raised you myself, didn't I? And your father might have been a country squire, but he would have been just as comfortable at the king's court."

"The king is mad," Daniel muttered, realizing he was getting nowhere but to the last raspberry tart. So he reminded her about the fiasco at Almack's, and any number of other social solecisms he'd committed, and might in the future. Hell, he'd been thrown out of more bars and brothels than he could recall, but those were not tales for his mother's ears. "I won't be any help to you getting Susanna established, you know. I never attend the *ton* parties or associate with anyone respectable enough to be considered a suitable *parti* for a gently bred female, much less their mamas. No one you'd care to know sends me invites anymore."

Lady Cora set down her teacup and raised her chin. "I assure you, the Stamfield name is enough to gain my daughter entry to all the best homes. If not, the Royce connection certainly is. No one would wish to insult the earl or the countess."

Lud, no. Aunt Royce was the starchiest female Daniel had ever known. She made the Almack's patronesses look and sound like cockney charwomen.

"There. You see, with Aunt Royce's backing, you do not need me."

"Of course I do. We cannot go about with servants as our only escorts. What would people think, that Susanna is unprotected? Why, every rake and fortune hunter would believe they could take advantage of a young lady with no one to hold them to account."

His little sister? Daniel choked on the last bite of pastry, and wished he had something besides tea to wash down the bad taste left in his mouth. "I'd thrash anyone who dared show her the least insult."

His mother smiled fondly. "Exactly. Not that you will, of course. But the possibility is enough to discourage anyone going beyond the line of what is proper. And you must be present and available to refuse honorable but unwanted suitors, also. You cannot expect Susanna to handle those awkward proposals. Or me. Heavens, no."

His mother could handle any number of callow youths, and give them biscuits and advice, besides. "They all are unwanted," he grumbled, eyeing the empty platter. "Susanna is too young."

"Nonsense. I was her age when I met your father. In this very room, in fact. He came to call with one of his friends I'd danced with. I knew he was the man for me as soon as I saw him. You have his strong build, you know, and his gentleness. I felt cherished just sitting beside him. Of course my father was here, too, to inspect and reject unacceptable callers. Anyone with dishonorable intentions would never have come through the front door."

Her father was the Royce who got headaches from lies. Of course he'd send any scoundrels to perdition. "Dobbson can simply dismiss the undesirables. A proper London butler always knows wheat from chaff. If Aunt Royce hired him, he is bound to have the same haughty demeanor to set down any pretensions."

"He is a servant, dear. You are Susanna's brother."

"And as her brother, I say she is too young to be speaking of suitors and proposals. Doesn't she want to attend a few parties first? At home?"

"She has been attending the local assemblies for a year now without settling on any of the neighbor lads."

Daniel snorted. "I should think not. The miller's sons and the apothecary's assistant? Or does she dance with that young curate with no chin?"

"The curate is of a good family, with a promising future, but now you understand why we came to London," Lady Cora said. She smiled as if Daniel were back in the schoolroom and had given the proper answer during a geography lesson.

He was still at sea. "No, I do not understand why you and she could not have waited until she knows her own mind better. It's not as if some heavy-handed patriarch is going to arrange a match for her, willy-nilly, like in olden times. Nowadays a female should be mature enough to make such important decisions for herself. Susanna is still an infant."

His mother shook her head, then removed the heavy turban, revealing still-shiny black hair untouched by gray. "She wants what every woman wants: a home of her own. A handsome man by her side. Babies."

"Great gods, she is a child herself!"

"She is almost eighteen. And no one claims she

should marry immediately. A respectable courtship takes months, for the young people to know their own minds, as you said. And for that first infatuation to ripen into lasting affection, if it is going to. The wedding itself can take almost a full year to plan properly. Why, you were born when I was not much older than Susanna is now." Lady Cora smiled, remembering. "You did arrive a bit early, I must admit. Long engagements are such a trial when you are in love."

"Mother!" The notion of his baby sister with a man was bad enough. But his parents anticipating their vows? Lord, he needed something stronger than tea in a fragile cup. He looked around, but did not see any decanters or bottles. Just one more reason he wished he were back in his rented rooms.

His mother was lost in her own musings. "You might wish to consider starting your own nursery, you know. I've never pressed you, but it wouldn't hurt you to look around at the other debutantes while we are out and about."

"Those simpering little twits in pastel ruffles? What would I want with one of them?"

"Babies," she firmly stated. "A son to inherit the manor. A daughter to cuddle."

More responsibility. Daniel shuddered, remembering Rex's twin infants. They had put the girl in Daniel's arms at the church christening. He was her godfather, after all—an honor, everyone said. Why they couldn't have made him the boy's godparent instead of Harry, he did not know. He could teach a lad to ride and shoot—no, Harry was better at both, and he supposed Rex was thinking Daniel could fend off those rakes and fortune hunters better, with his size.

But a female? A tiny, red-faced female? Why, he'd

broken out in a sweat fearing he'd crush her in his big, clumsy paws. Or get her dirty in that trailing white lacy thing she wore. Or make her cry. That would be the worst. No, misplacing her like he did his gloves would be worse. Jupiter, a baby girl of his own?

"I'll, ah, be content with Rex's hatchlings. And Harry's."

"Well, I won't be, you gudgeon. I want grandchildren of my own. Yours and Susanna's."

Daniel used his napkin to dab at the bead of sweat he could feel forming on his forehead. Then he tried to speak softly, without shouting or foul language. "I am not in the petticoat line, Mother."

She patted her own lips with her napkin, barely hiding her smile. "That is not what we hear in the country."

Now he did shout: "Those are not ladies, and we shall not speak of my private affairs!" He winced at the last word, stood, and strode to the hall. Dobbson was waiting there, as Daniel knew he would be, likely taking in every embarrassing word. Dash it, a good butler would have anticipated the need for stronger sustenance when discussing weddings and babies. "Brandy. Now."

When Daniel sat across from his mother again, she was already compiling mental matchmaking lists; he could tell by the speculative gleam in her eyes. He kept his voice lowered in case Dobbson was on his way back. "I tell you, I am not ready to marry."

"Of course not. A gentleman never is, until he can't wait for the day."

Daniel ignored that bit of feminine illogic. "Besides, no female in her right mind would have me."

"Piffle. You are handsome—"

"Not nearly as good-looking as Harry. Or Rex before he was scarred."

"Bosh. You three are like peas in a pod with your black hair and bright blue eyes." She preened a bit. "The same as mine. And Royce's, although my brother has gone sadly gray. I say you are the best-looking of the lot, although that may be a mother's prejudice speaking. You are certainly better built than either of your cousins."

He had to laugh. "Well built for a bull, you mean. A delicate female would cringe in fear of being trampled." But he had lost some of the recently gained weight, boxing at Jackson's, fencing with Harry before he left Town.

His mother was not finished. "You are easily able to support a wife in elegant fashion."

"My pockets aren't half as deep as Rex's."

"Few men's are. Not every miss can wed into an earldom, and you're better off than most wellborn bachelors. Better connected, at any rate."

"I may be gentry-born, but women look for a title. The vultures crave a 'lady' in front of their name."

His mother raised one eyebrow. "I didn't require a title from your father."

"Of course not, you had one of your own. My apologies, Mother, but I am not husband material, so set aside your schemes. My reputation alone—"

"You were a war hero, an aid to the Crown."

"You are forgetting the last few years. Accept it, dear Mother. I simply am not one of your Town beaux. I am a disgrace. My manners are rough, my language crude, my wardrobe built for comfort rather than style.

I eat and drink too much, and I'd rather use my fists than spar with words. I am too clumsy to dance and have no conversation fit for a lady's parlor."

"We are having a conversation right now, and you have not uttered one foul word."

He did now, but under his breath. "Mother, listen to me. You must not make me part of Susanna's Season. I'll only disappoint you."

She stood and came to touch his cheek. "I have never, ever been disappointed in you."

Daniel waited for the rash to appear. Nothing happened, no itch, no welts. His mother spoke the truth. He was lost. Ditched. Trapped. Netted and gutted.

"And I shan't be now."

His mother loved him, just the way he was. Then she proceeded to make him over in the image she kept in her heart, a perfect gentleman, squire, and escort. Dobbson returned in time to be consulted about hiring a valet, which tailor to patronize, what style of haircut would look best.

Daniel took the glass from the tray Dobbson held; then he took the decanter, too.

Dobbson glanced down. "And boots."

Daniel started to say there was nothing wrong with his boots, but gave up in favor of savoring his uncle's excellent brandy. He'd forgotten the earl had connections with the smugglers around Dover, part of controlling the flow of information, gold, and spies to France in the war.

Lady Cora sent Dobbson off for paper and pencil, to compose a list. "It wouldn't hurt for you to practice a bit with Susanna's dance instructor, either, Daniel."

Daniel refilled his glass.

His mother moved the decanter. "You will have to dance with both girls at our own balls, but you'll also need to lead them out if no one else offers. They must not appear to be wallflowers, you know."

"Our own balls? Girls? They?"

"Oh, did I forget to mention that Susanna thought she'd feel more at ease if she had a friend with her?"

He scowled at his mother, who was pouring out another cup of tea, so she did not notice. "Somehow that tiny item escaped your letters. I do not need another silly, frilly chit to look after. Let her own brother play duenna."

"I'm afraid she has no brother, dear. And before you can shout loudly enough for her to hear upstairs, her father is not in Town. Nor is she the least bit silly."

Daniel narrowed his eyes. "Just who is this friend of Susanna's you've dragged to Town?"

"Miss Corisande Abbott."

The crystal brandy goblet slammed down onto the table. "Send her home. I won't have that female here."

"Need I remind you this is not your house? This is my brother's home and I invited her, as is my right. Nay, my duty. Corisande is my goddaughter, named after me, as you well know. Her dear departed mother and I were best friends. It is my responsibility to see her launched into society."

"Your responsibility should be to your own daughter. That female can be only a bad influence on Susanna with her wild ways, if her reputation doesn't get you all banned from society. Hell, I thought my name was besmirched enough."

His mother set her teacup down with a decidedly unladylike clatter. "Corisande was young and made a mistake. What, three years ago? Thanks to you and her father, no one knows anything about that unfortunate incident."

"You know. I know. The deuce, I helped her father track her and that dastard Snelling down after they ran off. Mother, when we found her, she was in bed with her lover! Yes, I made certain he would never speak her name again, but not even you and the vaunted Royce name can foist soiled goods off on some unsuspecting suitor."

"Corisande swears the, ah, act was never consummated."

Daniel swallowed the last of the brandy in his glass. "And you believe her? A wanton jade who disobeyed her father, stole the household money, and lied to everyone in three counties?"

Lady Cora's sapphire blue eyes pierced her son's similar ones. "You can ask her yourself."

Daniel might as well start itching now. "As if she would tell the truth. As if I could ask a female if her maidenhead is intact. Devil take it, ma'am, she is not a fit companion for my sister!"

"Susanna loves her as dearly as I do. And Miss Corisande Abbott shall have no difficulty attracting suitors. She is the only child of a wealthy landowner. She is well educated, with pleasing looks and manners. Her dowry is respectable, and her reputation is unsullied to everyone but you. I wish to see her well established, and so I shall. She is my god-daughter."

Daniel glared at the woman, who sat so straight,

stirring her tea as if they were discussing the latest play at Drury Lane. "She is a whore."

Lady Cora glared right back at him. "Do you recall what I said about your never disappointing me?" She reached for the decanter and poured a dollop of brandy into her teacup. "I take it back."

Chapter Three

Dobbson cleared his throat before coming into the room with the writing supplies.

"You heard nothing," Lady Cora said, an order, not a question.

"Not a thing, my lady." The butler bowed, avoiding looking at Daniel, who was scratching his ear.

"Lies on top of lies. That is what I hate most about this damned place," Daniel said when Dobbson bowed himself out of the room. Then he grabbed the decanter back before his sweet, loving, gentle mother could finish the brandy. He was about to bring the bottle to his lips, ignoring his glass and his parent's *tsk*, when the door opened again.

"We found your sewing basket, Lady Cora. It was packed with the—oh."

The woman in the doorway was taller than Daniel remembered. She must have continued growing since he'd seen her last. She was no longer the angry, frightened child of three years ago, but a woman. Her hair was the same light brown, but neatly braided into a coronet now, not trailing down her shoulders in wanton disarray. She was a lot prettier than he remembered, but her face had been flushed and swollen from crying then, from her father's tirade as he dragged her out of the room, leaving her lover for Daniel to deal with.

His glance lowered, then widened. She was a woman grown, all right. "Your bodice is too low. People will think you are fast."

"Daniel!" his mother shouted.

Miss Abbott gasped and went pale. Then all the color she'd lost rushed back, starting at the top of her nearly nonexistent bodice, Daniel noted, and up her neck to her high-boned cheeks. She raised the sewing basket to block his rude stare.

"Daniel," his mother repeated, this time in a wail. It was his turn to blush scarlet for his words and his ogling. Instead of apologizing for insulting a female he hardly knew, in his own mother's parlor no less, he turned to the instigator of the whole sorry scene. "Now you see why you'd do better without me, Mother. I told you I am not fit for the drawing room."

Then his sister skipped past Miss Abbott, ran toward him, and kissed his cheek. "You are acting like a looby, Daniel. Low necklines are all the thing. Mine is even lower than Corie's."

By gad, it was. While his sister had their mother's slight stature, dark hair, and blue eyes, she'd inherited some of their father's heft, all in one place, it appeared. Lord, did it appear. He looked around for a lap throw to toss over her shoulders. Lord knew a napkin wouldn't cover enough. "When the devil did you get bos—that is, when did you get so beautiful?"

Susanna showed her dimples and kissed him again. "Amanda says my bust is my best feature, and Simone assured me all the ladies are lowering their necklines."

Rex's wife, Amanda, had been imprisoned for a

murder charge; Harry's Simone was a half Gypsy who'd hired herself out as his mistress. Those were the two women whose example innocent little Susanna was following? Heaven help them all.

"Only ladybirds show their, ah, attributes so blatantly," he insisted.

Susanna laughed again. "How would you know what proper females wear, brother? I doubt you've been near one since the twins' christening. I do know for a fact that no gentleman dresses like you, for I made sure to observe every one we passed on our way through London. And I've been watching out the window."

Which statement sent their mother's gaze skyward. "We did send for the fashion magazines from London, Daniel, to be certain of the styles."

"You wouldn't want us to appear as dowds on our first day here, would you?" Susanna wrinkled her charming, upturned nose. "Well, perhaps you wouldn't know the difference. But no matter. Dobbson will have you well in hand before dinner, I'd wager, so we'll all be bang up to the nines. That's the phrase Rex said when we showed him our new gowns. Oh, Daniel, don't purse your lips the way my old governess used to."

And Rex was spending all the time he could spare from his growing family among the criminal class. "Fine, I'll look like an overstuffed sausage and you'll look like Haymarket ware and sound like a pickpocket."

Susanna turned to their mother. "I told you he'd turn all stuffy and stiff. All reformed rakes do. Simone says Harry's a pattern card of virtue now."

Lud, Harry'd had at least ten disguises and aliases.

Daniel hoped he'd never been as underhanded. "I am not a rake. And I am not reformed. That is, I have nothing to reform from."

He scratched his ear again. His mother rubbed her eye, but Susanna just smiled. To think he used to find her dimples charming. Now the brat was saying, "Well, I'd say you owe our guest an apology. You remember Miss Abbott, don't you, Daniel? I am so happy she agreed to come to Town with us. Otherwise I wouldn't know a soul. And she's read all the guidebooks and knows what museums and cathedrals we must see."

Daniel groaned. He supposed they'd expect him to escort them there, too. Besides, he could never trust this pair loose in London. Reluctantly, but knowing he had no choice, he bowed in the older girl's direction. "My regrets, Miss Abbott, for my wayward tongue. I warned my mother how it would be. She'd do better with Dobbson as escort. Or my horse."

She didn't smile. Too bad, that. Daniel thought she'd be more beautiful with her lips softened, if it were possible for a female to be any prettier.

Instead she bobbed a slight curtsy in acknowledgment of his apology and said, "How do you do, Mr. Stamfield."

Susanna clucked her tongue. "Oh, we are all family here," she insisted. "There is no need for such formality in our own home. You should use your first names."

Before Daniel could say how improper that would be—lud, was he truly reformed already, caring about the conventions?—Miss Abbott placed the sewing basket in his mother's lap and said, "I'll go finish the unpacking, shall I, and leave you to your reunion?" She nodded in his direction. "Until dinner, Mr. Stamfield."

Now, there was a setdown worthy of a duchess. And a rear view as she left the room worthy of a dockside dolly-mop. Daniel decided he wasn't reformed at all. Not by half.

"Dinner!" His mother jumped up, scattering her notepaper and overturning the work basket, but taking her teacup with her. "I forgot to tell Cook that she needs to prepare for a man's hearty appetite. She'll be thrilled to cook for someone not watching her figure."

Which was a not-so-subtle reminder that he was staring after Miss Abbott and her graceful exit. A looby indeed! Now his wits and his manners had both gone begging.

Susanna stayed on in the parlor, gathering up the yarns and needles while Daniel restacked the notepapers. "You needn't look so stricken," she told her brother, misunderstanding the cause of his dismay. "It won't be so bad; you'll see. We'll have a good time."

Trying to avoid being caught in a seductress's spell? For his sister's sake, he asked, "Am I supposed to enjoy looking over your prospective suitors while they look down your gown? Or inspecting the statues in the museum? Both are as appealing. Dash it, Sukey, you're too young to wed. I told Mother, but she won't listen." He handed her a thimble that had rolled in his direction.

"Oh, you don't need to be concerned with my beaux. I'm not on the lookout for a husband."

He felt not so much as a goose bump, so she was telling the truth. "Then why the devil did you come to London?"

"Why, to see the sights. To dance the night away, to attend the theater and three balls and two dinners, all in the same night!"

"That sounds like one of the rings of Dante's *Inferno*."

"It sounds delightful after the quietude of Stamfield. Nothing ever happens there. No one new ever visits, as you well know. You never stay above a week or two yourself, so how can you blame me for wanting to see more of the world? To expand my horizons, as it were, before I do marry and start breeding? I could be stuck in the shires forever then. Not that I dislike the country. I don't think I will ever get used to the noise or the foul air in the city, but the change is exciting."

Daniel bent down to pick up a small gold scissors in the shape of a bird that had fallen under the end table. "I suppose you have a point."

"Besides, how am I to find Mother a lover in the country?"

He stood so fast he cracked his head on the end of the table. A point? Too bad the embroidery scissors' point was too short to pierce his heart. "A lover? Mother?"

"Well, I suppose she could marry if she wants. After all, it's not like Mother to want to live in sin, ostracized by all the neighbors."

His mother, a fallen woman? Daniel could not picture it, so he chose the safer course—for anyone else—marriage. "Does she want to remarry? She and Father were so close, I never thought she'd look at another man."

"Think of it now, Daniel. Mother put off her mourning gowns a full year ago, and burned them; she was that glad to be out of dark, dreary colors. Why shouldn't she find another companion?"

"If she wants a companion, we can hire some dried-up old prune like your last governess. Or I could send for one of those impoverished Stamfield great-aunts who get passed from relative to relative like unwanted wedding gifts."

"Do not be so buffle-headed. I don't mean a paid companion or an old relict. I meant company for her, a special someone of her own. I'll marry and move away eventually, to who knows where. You never come home, and when you do, you'll likely be bringing a bride with you. Your wife will want to manage the house in her own way, without a mother-in-law looking over her shoulder. I know I would. And you'll want your privacy, at least at first. So what is Mother to do? Become one of those itinerant old ladies, battening on whichever relation is closest? Or set up an establishment of her own, and devote her life to Good Deeds?"

"She could raise dogs."

Susanna took the scissors from him and shoved it into a ball of yarn. "Why should she spend the rest of her life alone? She is still young and attractive, don't you think?"

He recalled his mother's appearance, but as an objective judge this time, not as her loving son. Whichever way he saw her, Lady Cora was a handsome woman. Her face was unlined, her figure still trim, her Royce black hair and blue eyes still a stunning combination. Moreover, he knew she had a tidy fortune in her own name, and a dragon's horde of jewels. She was just as competent to manage a gentleman's household as a farmstead, and kept abreast of current news and politics. In other words, she'd make some lucky man a damned good wife. "Mother is lovely, of course, but has she said that's what she wants? She told me she wants grandchildren."

"Our babies won't keep her company on long winter nights."

"If not dogs, she could raise cats. I know of one who—"

Susanna tapped her foot. "Daniel, I am not suggesting Mother find another Grand Passion like she had with Papa. But why not a petit passion? With someone whose company and conversation she can enjoy. And caresses. I know she misses—"

Daniel was not about to discuss whatever Susanna thought their mother missed in the marriage bed, not with his unfledged sister. "What about Miss Abbott?" he hurried to ask before Susanna could expound on pleasures she should know nothing about. "Are you looking for a lover for her, too?"

"A lover for an unmarried lady? Do not be vulgar, Daniel. If Corie wants a husband, that's what she shall have: her pick of the finest gentlemen in all of England, for that is what she deserves."

She deserved to be tarred and feathered, but he did not say it. "She must be over twenty years of age by now. Why is she not married already?"

"I think she was disappointed in love at a young age, although she never speaks of it. She has let slip that her father never approves of any of her suitors. His own grandfather was a baron, after all. He considers commoners beneath his daughter."

More like finding her beneath one of them, Daniel thought. Lord Abbott was acting just as he ought, keeping his wayward daughter from ensnaring an unsuspecting gent.

Susanna was going on, as she re-wound a skein of silk threads. "Mother suspects he does not want to part with her dowry, but we never say that to Corie, although everyone knows Squire Abbott is not an easy man. He almost refused to let her come to London with us, until Mother shamed him by offering to pay all of Corie's expenses. I still think the only reason he agreed was that he wanted Corie gone while he courts Mrs. Rivendale."

"The admiral's young widow?" The brazen female had expressed interest in Daniel the last time he was at the manor. She'd even placed her hand on his thigh under the tablecloth at one dinner. He'd left before the dessert course.

"Yes, Alberta Rivendale, the neighborhood's favorite topic of gossip. They say the admiral did not leave her in sufficient funds, and she is constantly looking to feather her nest with a new pigeon to pluck. They also say that Squire Abbott still hopes to father an heir, and Mrs. Rivendale is barely thirty."

"You shouldn't be spreading such tales around, you know. Ain't ladylike."

Susanna made a very unladylike sound. "Hogswallow. If I don't listen to gossip, how am I to learn anything? Besides, that's another reason it's important for Corie to find a match soon. If her father does produce a son, she will not be such an heiress. Not that any of them are in line for the title, of course; the current baron has a large family of sons. But Squire's lands are unentailed. Corie would get it all. If her father reweds, with or without a son, she would not wish to share her home with the likes of Mrs. Rivendale."

"I should think not." And Abbott was a fool for thinking of taking on another woman of easy virtue.

Susanna picked up the last skein of thread. "That's it, then."

"Yes, that's it, all right."

She meant the sewing supplies. Daniel meant his life, his freedom, his days of caring about nothing but finding the next female, the next bottle, the next card game. Now he found himself with three women to shepherd, protect, and get settled. This was no game; it was their future, their security, their becoming some other poor fool's responsibility.

Damn, he had to make sure all three of them found husbands before they found lovers. He had to arrange marriages for a scheming minx, a manipulative matchmaker, and a proven light-skirts—while staying out of parson's mousetrap himself. Had he ever been dealt a worse hand?

He cursed his father for dying young, his mother for thinking young, his sister for being young, and Miss Corisande Abbott for being beautiful.

Chapter Four

The front door beckoned. Daniel thought about bolting out into the street and never returning, except Dobbson stood there, waiting to show him to the room set aside for his use. Or else Dobbson was waiting for Daniel to prove unworthy of the Royce House address by turning craven. So he cursed the butler, too.

And his shiny shoes.

Then he saw the chambers assigned to him. His whole suite at McCann's could fit in the sitting room here. He had his own bathing room, a dressing room, and a bed finally big enough for his size. A fire burned in the grate; decanters paraded along a side table with a tin of biscuits, a wheel of cheese, a bowl of fruit. Now Daniel felt like Gideon must, in his new stall. The surroundings were unfamiliar, but they sure as the devil were tempting.

"You'll wish to change," Dobbson suggested from the doorway. He appeared ready to flee if Daniel took umbrage at his pointing out that the gentleman's attire was fit for swilling at a pig trough, not milady's dinner table.

Daniel did not wish to change at all, his clothes, his manners, his way of life. His mother and her charges could take him the way he was, casual dress and all. But a footman was filling a tub—as well proportioned as the bed—with hot water and fragrant soaps. Daniel could not pass that up, nor could he face putting his same shirt, yesterday's shirt, back on afterward. He doubted he had a cleaner one at his rooms, though. Laundry was a haphazard affair at McCann's.

Dobbson cleared his throat. "I took the liberty of laying out evening attire for you, until a valet is hired to oversee your apparel."

"I have no formal wear."

But the dressing room was filled. The neatly hung coats and trousers looked the right size, too. A crisp white shirt lay over a chair. "How . . . ?"

"Lady Cora said she feared you might not have time to, ah, pack your Town wardrobe, so she brought a few things from home, I understand."

He didn't keep anything at Stamfield Manor but an old hunting jacket. So these must have belonged to his father, who'd been as large as Daniel.

His guess was confirmed when Dobbson held up a dark frock coat and a nankeen waistcoat. "These are a bit dated, but they'll do until you can visit your tailor."

What did he need with a tailor when he had this many changes of suits and shirts? Now he did not have to stand for fittings or bother with choosing colors and styles. He blessed his mother's thrifty ways. And her ways of knowing that her son was like a brick when it came to fashion. Which was to say oblivious and uncaring. So long as the clothes were comfortable, Daniel would have worn a toga. His father wouldn't have, though, so he was safe to pass society's inspection.

"The bootboy will do his best with your, ah, shoes

while you bathe." Dobbson could not bring himself to call Daniel's battered footwear boots. "I have unpacked a pair of pumps for now, in hopes they will fit."

He left, but returned in a moment with a glass of wine and a cigar instead of the shoes. Maybe the old stick wasn't half as rigid as he seemed. Maybe he realized that keeping Daniel content could save his own skin.

There was a lot to be said about luxury, but "Aah" seemed all Daniel could manage as he lowered himself into the bath. Opulence softened a man, but it also felt damned good. He lay back in the tub for once, not cramped and hunched over. The cigar cast a soft haze over his head; the wine spread a soft glow inside his head.

"Aah," he said again. This dutiful-gentleman hogwash mightn't be so bad after all. He could tolerate living like a king for a few weeks, which was all it should take to get the three of them married off. He counted Susanna, despite what he'd said about her being too young. With her talk of lovers and longing, she'd be better off with a ring on her finger, before she went skipping merrily down the primrose path. Besides, if she stayed unwed, they'd only have to go through this same rigmarole next year, and the one after that. He sank lower in the hot water.

No, better to get the marriage business all done in one fell swoop. Susanna was a lively little thing, with a bosom to catch any man's eye and a dowry to please the fussiest family. She'd take, and have her pick of the bachelor crop. Her intended had to be someone who would appreciate her, of course. He'd treat her

like the princess she was, or else. Daniel could see
to that.

His mother posed a thornier problem, not that she
wasn't a rose in her own right. She needed a chap still
in his prime, but not one needing heirs, or a mother
for his unmannered brats. And not one who needed
her fortune to pull himself out of River Tick. Daniel
wasn't having any loose screw batten on his mother,
or on his own income, either. He could see her as a
grand London hostess, helping further a politician's
career or a financier's connections. The problem was,
Daniel did not know any rulers of state or industry.
The earl and his countess were bound to, though. Daniel would write to his aunt and uncle in the morning.

That left Corisande Abbott. He heartily wished
they'd left her home.

Well, now that she was here, she was definitely
beautiful enough to turn heads. If Susanna was right,
that she wanted to escape her father's household, she
had the face to do it. Daniel couldn't blame her for
wanting to try, now that he thought about it. And after
he had a few more sips of Uncle's excellent vintage to
help mellow his notions.

The girl couldn't be comfortable at home knowing
her own father was ashamed of her. Daniel could well
understand that feeling of being the black sheep of
the family.

Nor was the squire a pleasant sort to start with, just
as Susanna had reminded him. Daniel recalled him
thundering up to Stamfield Manor that fateful day,
demanding Lady Cora Stamfield reveal the whereabouts of his wayward daughter and her ne'er-do-well
soldier. Daniel was home on leave, by chance, and

stopped Squire Abbott from rampaging through the house to search or threatening his mother and sister. Daniel knew his mother wasn't lying when she said she didn't know the girl's plans. He suspected Susanna did by her playing least in sight, but was not about to let a raging parent, one brandishing his dueling pistol and a nasty-looking knife, frighten his little sister. Instead, Daniel offered to send riders out to the nearby inns and tollbooths, to see which road the eloping pair took north, to Gretna.

· Daniel couldn't refuse the distraught man's plea for help when a messenger returned with the information they needed, and a description of Snelling's hired coach. Abbott cursed and ranted the entire way about his family's disgrace, the dastard's future as a eunuch, his daughter's deceit. Daniel developed a headache, and a bit of pity for the girl, that her father never worried about her safety, or whether she'd been misled or mistreated by a hardened rake. Then he saw her in the rogue's bed, and all pity disappeared.

Still, if the squire had such an uncaring nature, and a nasty temper to boot, Daniel could understand Miss Abbott's grabbing at the opportunity Lady Cora offered. Fortunately for his own two-week plan, their neighbor couldn't be so picky about her chosen escape route now. Daniel supposed he should think of the unfortunate intended as her mate, not simply a victim. He did not care, only that the man had honorable intentions, and was respectable enough to pass muster with the girl's father, even if that meant snaring a title.

No, if Miss Abbott was determined to find a husband, Daniel would not stand in her way. He wasn't the one who had to lie to the gullible fool about how she'd ridden astride as a youngster, or suffered a fall, to explain why her virginity was not intact. Meanwhile, the more he thought about it, and the more wine he sipped, on top of the brandy he'd had earlier, the more likely it seemed the female could find a fiancé before she fell from grace again. After all, keeping to the straight and narrow was in her own best interests. The least hint of scandal would destroy any chances of making a match or staying at Royce House. The thought relieved Daniel's mind. Now he didn't have to worry about the wench leading Susanna astray.

He could do it, get them engaged if not wed before the end of the month. The women were all pretty, wellborn, and well funded, so why not? Matchmaking couldn't be all that hard; the highborn biddies at Almack's did it all the time. A few introductions, a few whispers in the right ears, and he'd be back in his comfortable digs before Miss White could scratch behind her ears. It might even be fun to watch chaps try to avoid the clutches of three determined women. How he and Rex would laugh at the idea, if his cousin ever came to Town. Damn, he missed his old playmate.

He'd miss a few of the elegancies of an earl's house, too, though, like the warmed towels Dobbson brought, the offer to shave him. The staff at McCann's—which was three steps above the previous dive he'd inhabited—were usually efficient, but too busy. Their main occupation was serving the wealthy patrons in the dining room or the game rooms. That was where the club made its money and the servants made their gratuities. And since the manager was a foster brother of Harry's, Daniel was living there free. He couldn't complain or make demands.

"Shall I tie your neckcloth for you, sir?"

Damn. He couldn't wait to get out of here. Three yards of starched white linen at his throat? Three females at an earl's dinner table? Three kinds of misery.

He shoved the offending article away. "I don't wear the nuisances. I'll just tie my kerchief around my neck again."

"Kerchief? That spotted item? I mistook it for a nose wipe and sent it to the poorhouse with the rest of your clothes."

"My Cossack trousers? My favorite jacket?"

Daniel had no choice but to act like a sniveling schoolboy or let Dobbson wrap and tuck and pull and brush until the butler deemed him ready. The man actually cracked a smile. "Ah, now, that's more like it."

Now he looked more like his father, off to join his father's women. Damn.

When he reached the drawing room, he saw that the women had changed their ensembles, also. Susanna was bursting out of a pink gown this time, but Miss Abbott had a bit of gauze stuck in her bodice top. A fichu, Daniel thought they called it. The effect quite ruined the view, but he was glad to see she was taking on the role of modest young lady. That was what a gentleman wanted in a wife, not in a mistress. Her gown had none of the ruffles and ribbons Susanna's sported—lud, he'd find a better dressmaker for the chit if it killed him—but suited her taller, willowy figure better. Miss Abbott's gown was the color of daffodils, emphasizing the sunny streaks in her hair. Custom permitted her to wear more vivid colors than an ingenue now that she was twenty years old and nearly on the shelf in some eyes. Blind eyes, he decided.

Lady Cora's blue eyes glowed at her son's new appearance, making him feel churlish about his reluctance to don proper dress. His mother was too polite to mention the transformation from vagabond to gentleman, but Susanna did not hesitate.

"Now we won't be ashamed to be seen with you. When a real valet takes you in hand, you might even be as handsome as Har—ooph!"

Lady Cora kicked her and immediately led the way to the dining room. Once there, she made sure no awkward silences occurred, speaking of the neighborhood news, the Rexford infants, and the earl's health. Then she launched into her proposed schedule for the coming Season—at least three months of it—and whom she should call on first to ensure their invitations to the most important functions. The depth of her planning made the War Office strategy look like child's play.

It made the roast beef taste like rotten cabbage to Daniel.

Susanna added to his indigestion by burbling about every guidebook recommendation she wanted to see. Luckily, the circus was high on her list. They could go tomorrow evening before all the shopping was done, she urged, because no one who mattered could see her there in her village-made clothes.

Daniel agreed. "But only if you keep a shawl over your shoulders. I want to enjoy the show, not worry about your catching a chill."

He was proud he remembered his table etiquette, which fork to use, not to wipe his mouth on his sleeve,

to speak to the guests on either side of him. So he
tried to be polite. "What about you, Miss Abbott? Do
you enjoy fancy horsemanship? You are welcome to
come with us, of course."

When she looked up from her plate, he saw that
her eyes were green. Not grass green, but more like
soft moss, with gold flecks. She seemed torn. He could
almost hear her mind working, reasoning that a visit
to the circus meant being his guest, being in his company. She refused. "Thank you, but I have letters to
write. I wish to see if any of my schoolmates are in
Town."

Daniel's toes started itching, damn the borrowed
shoes, and damn the female for fibbing. And for dis-
missing him so handily. He was laughed at, on occasion. Tossed out of bedrooms, frequently. But treated
so disdainfully, as if he was the one who'd gone beyond the line during the aborted elopement? Never.

Surely, he thought, moving the peas around on his
plate, the woman couldn't hold the rescue against him.
That worm Snelling would have taken her money and
left her to starve at the first chance, or crawl back to
her family. Daniel had done her a favor, by George.
And he'd taken a lot of satisfaction rearranging Snelling's nose, along with her life. He thought he'd heard
the slug had died in the war, but Miss Abbott wasn't
blaming him for that, was she? Of course Snelling
mightn't have reached the front lines so quickly without Daniel dragging him to the troopships and using
his influence to see him reassigned.

She ought to thank him. Instead she pointedly spoke
to his mother and Susanna, but not him. He thought
she'd go hungry rather than ask him to pass a dish.
He passed them, anyway. The woman was too thin,

especially next to Susanna. No man wanted to take a sickly looking woman to wife.

Later, Lady Cora suggested an early bedtime, since they had appointments from morning until late in the afternoon. Susanna needed to rest, her mother said, so she looked her best at the circus.

For the horses? Daniel just shook his head.

Both younger ladies agreed. They were weary from all the packing and traveling and noisy inns that could not compare with Royce House for comfort.

"I think I'll toddle off to McCann's, then," Daniel told them. "See if any mail has arrived, that kind of thing."

"But you will return?" His mother was a master of turning a question into a declaration.

"I thought I might stay there except when you need me. The attention is excellent here, and I haven't tasted such food in ages, but my friends—"

"I need you here, now. I simply won't feel safe in London without you nearby."

This from the woman who lived on an estate an hour's drive to the nearest neighbor. Daniel almost laughed, except he could sense another losing battle.

"There is too much crime in the city," Lady Cora went on, "too many robberies. Why, we could be murdered in our sleep."

"And Daniel is going to rescue us?" Susanna giggled. "Only if he wakes up. You know what a sound sleeper he is, Mother. And he snores. That is why you put him down that guest corridor. But do not fret. Dobbson sleeps with a blunderbuss, he told me. And Corie and I can keep fireplace pokers next to our beds."

Miss Abbott looked as if her spine was as stiff as that poker.

"What do you think, Miss Abbott? Will you feel more secure with a man in the house?"

"I believe there are a score of male servants sleeping in the attic, near the kitchen, and at the stable mews. They should prove sufficient deterrent to any marauders."

"Ah, but they are servants. Would you trust your safety to hired staff, with no true loyalty to new employers?"

"I trust no man. I trust my safety to the small pistol I keep under my pillow. And yes, I do know how to use it."

Was that a threat? Daniel couldn't tell if it was personal, or she truly disliked all males.

"This talk of guns and pokers is bound to give me nightmares, I swear," Lady Cora said. "Daniel, I require your presence at breakfast, by which time Dobbson will have made appointments for you with a tailor and a boot maker and a hiring agency for a valet. You'll want to interview the man yourself, won't you?"

"What do I know of valets? They're all finicky sorts, from what I have seen. Just find me a man who doesn't talk much. There's less chance of false flattery and those other toadying lies. And thanks to your foresight, I have enough trappings to see me through your visit, so I don't need to see the tailor."

"Nonsense. You'll go. We rise at seven. Country hours, you know. We'll start sleeping in when we start attending balls and such. For now, we have too much to accomplish in too little time."

"Seven? In the morning? I might as well sleep here, then," he said, irritated. "I'll gather up my things and return in a bit. I'll try to be quiet so not to wake you."

"Just don't come back foxed and falling down, singing bawdy tunes, like you did on your last visit home," his loving sister said.

Here he'd been concentrating on his table manners for nothing. He was still a great clumsy clod, with his own kin making him look like a snoring sot in front of Miss Abbott.

Miss Abbott was sneering, as if she knew he was going to get drunk, find a woman, lose his purse. That was her idea of a how a man spent his time. It was Daniel's usual way, too, as a matter of fact, but that wasn't the point. What was, was how much harder he'd have to work to see her wed. First he worried about her morals, but now he feared she was a moralizing shrew. She did not even try to hide her disdain or disapproval. The devil take the woman, for no man in his right mind would.

On the other hand, if he couldn't roll the dice or spin the wheel all night, a chap needed a good challenge.

Chapter Five

The dumb ox was gone. Good. Now Miss Corisande Abbott could relax.

"I am sorry to delay the cleanup, Mr. Dobbson," she said, lingering over her tea when the other ladies went upstairs to bed. "I know how hard the servants have worked today with all the unloading and such. I'll bring my cup to the kitchen myself."

"Very thoughtful of you, miss. Good night."

She knew, however, that Dobbson would never seek out his own bed until the parlor was tidied, the fires extinguished, and the doors locked, so she did not intend to stay down here long. As particular as he was, the watchful butler must already be in a pother over Mr. Stamfield. Well, so was she.

The beast was gone for the night, thank goodness, into who knew what den of iniquity and depravity. Corie decided to pour a little of Lord Royce's brandy into her tea, the way she'd seen Lady Cora do. If anyone deserved a little tonic for her nerves, she did.

Corie thought she'd done fairly well as a well-mannered guest, considering how her stomach was in knots, her head was aching, and her fingers were itching to pick up the nearest heavy object and bash the oaf over the head. She feared she'd never stop bashing, either, and wouldn't that be poor repayment to her dear godmother?

Not that Daniel Stamfield didn't deserve a good thrashing, she considered while she took the pins out of her hair to relieve the headache. He did, by someone larger, stronger, and more prone to violence than she. No one could hate him more. The cur had stolen her dreams three years ago, and in so doing had blighted her life. That was the past, but now he could destroy her future, also. He had the means to take away her last chance to have a life of her own, out from under her father's thumb.

Daniel Stamfield was mean enough to do it, too. He took pleasure in inflicting pain. In two minutes, according to the maid who helped her dress, he'd manhandled Mr. Dobbson. Corie was not surprised. Just look at the blackguard's history: His army career was dubious at best, barbaric at worst; he'd almost murdered poor Francis Snelling, a total stranger to him; since then, he had been in too many barroom brawls for the servants to count. Tavern keepers were said to hide the breakables when he came—and hide their daughters, too. She'd wager he was one of those nasty little boys who tore the wings off butterflies. His mother would never say so, naturally.

Stamfield already treated Corie like a fallen woman, finding fault with her neckline, telling his mother to send her home, that she'd be a poor influence on Susanna, inviting her to the circus as an afterthought, obviously a reluctant courtesy. She'd leave his house if she had one other place, anywhere, to go. She'd start the letters to old friends as soon as she went up to her room. She was not hopeful, since they had not kept in touch, not after their lives diverged so widely. Her friends were wed, with growing families, while she was a virtual prisoner in her father's house. She doubted they'd invite a near stranger into their homes, but she had to try.

Lord knew, she felt unwelcome here in *his* house, even though the earl owned it and Lady Cora had invited her. Stamfield was the host now, Lady Cora's man of the family, her escort, her protector. Ha! Corie tossed her gloves to the ground.

The lummox was more liable to bring the house down around their ears, and Corie's opportunities with it. If he created another scandal, knocked over the punch bowl or started a brawl at Almack's, told the prince regent he was too fat to sit a horse or Lady Jersey she talked too much, or caused any of a hundred catastrophes an oversized, ready-fisted drunkard could cause, Lady Cora would flee back to the country. Corie's one and only Season would come to an abrupt end.

That could happen, anyway. In his cups, out of spite, or to warn off his fellow bachelors, Stamfield might repeat what he knew of her elopement. Her father had decided Corie was not fit to be any man's wife. Perhaps Stamfield felt the same. Corie fully intended to tell her side of the story to a suitor, but only after he proposed and she accepted. If he chose to renege, then he was not the kind of man she wished to wed.

Before then, before a gentleman cared enough for her to offer for her hand, no one could know about her disgrace. One word of the old scandal, one hint she was no better than she ought to be, and she'd be an outcast. Even if Lady Cora's standing, or the countess's, was enough to keep Corie on the invitations lists, there would be sly glances, innuendos, unwanted advances from every young rake and old rogue who thought she'd be open to illicit offers. What there wouldn't be were honest marriage proposals.

She knew there was no chance Stamfield could forget her past. His attitude proved it. She'd be forever branded a scarlet woman in his paltry mind, the same as in her father's. Neither one of them could understand—or care—that all she ever wanted was a life of her own.

She wasn't wishing for a duke or even a baronet or a Golden Ball. Just a nice man, a quiet man, an even-tempered man with a small income in case her father did not relinquish her dowry. He'd own a small house, with a spot for a garden, for children to play. That wasn't asking for the sun and the moon, was it? Only a distant star.

She'd make that man a good wife, she swore. She'd show him the respect she could not feel for her sire, or for men of Daniel Stamfield's ilk. She'd keep his house, keep her vows, and be grateful for whatever affection they shared. They'd have a good life together, this kind and gentle stranger and she, raising children, taking their places in neighborhood society, growing old. That was her dream, anyway.

If Daniel Stamfield did not steal her chances again.

She sipped at the brandy-laced tea. Honestly, she preferred it plain, but considered the spirits to be medicinal. While she drank, she kicked her slippers off and tried to think of a plan, somewhere to go if staying here proved untenable. She loved Lady Cora too much to remain at Royce House if her presence distressed the dear woman or hindered Susanna's success.

The invitation from her godmother had been a blessing, the only one her father could not refuse. Oth-

erwise, Corie had to wait until she was five and twenty
to come into her mother's money. There was not a
lot of it, but enough to help her find a way to escape,
even if she had to become a governess or a lady's
companion.

Five more years with a parent who despised her?
Five years with Alberta Rivendale or some other trollop her father dragged home to beget him a son? Five
years of not being permitted to spend a night with
Susanna, to accept a house party invitation, to have
an allowance of her own lest she use it to finance
another elopement?

With whom would she elope? Her father made certain Corie had no beaux. Francis was dead—and he'd
turned coward at the first stop, trying to jump out the
window rather than face her father.

Susanna thought Squire Abbott meant only to keep
Corie's dowry in his own coffers by discouraging callers and keeping Corie close to home. Either that or
he was too used to having an unpaid housekeeper to
let her go. Of course Susanna could not know about
the elopement . . . unless her brother told her.

Lady Cora did know. True lady that she was, she
said Corie was older and wiser now, and would never
let a scoundrel take advantage of her innocence again,
so they never needed to speak of the past. She seemed
to understand without words the unhappy situation
that was Corie's existence, so she never talked about
that, either, until she had the chance to change things.
She'd stood up to Corie's father then—something few
men ever did—and refused to take no for an answer.
When he turned down her written invitation to have
Corie join her and Susanna in London, she called in
person. When Abbott's butler said the squire was not

at home, she approached him after church, in front of the vicar and half the congregation. Every inch a noblewoman, she berated him for not doing his fatherly duty by securing his daughter's future. How dare he think of bringing a young bride into his house without finding Corie a home of her own? Corie was not growing younger, Lady Cora reminded him and whoever managed to listen. His dear departed wife would *not* be resting in peace if her baby turned into an old maid. Then she offered to finance Corie's entire Season, appealing to Abbott's so miserly nature.

Now that she thought about it, Corie supposed her clothes, her food, the very postage for the letters she wrote, were all charged to the Stamfield purse, not Lady Cora's personal accounts. Good grief, was it Mr. Stamfield's money paying for this visit? If so, Lady Cora's son had another reason to resent her presence, as if he needed another one. Suddenly she felt warm, so she tugged the scratchy lace fichu away from her neck and shoulders.

Now the man was making her sweat! Lord, how could she set her mind to finding a husband when she had to keep looking over her shoulder to see if he was nearby, scowling at her, ready to frighten off any prospective suitors? She could never relax when any loose-lipped utterance from the bumbling sot could destroy the rest of her life, too. As for having fun, sharing Susanna's joy in the coming Season, well, that was out of the question now, thanks to slimy Daniel Stamfield.

How could Lady Cora love the muckworm? Didn't she see he was churlish and crude? Corie forced herself to acknowledge he did clean up nicely, in a rough-and-tumble, hulking way. Of course he was too big to make a woman feel comfortable, even in the trappings of a gentleman. The threat of violence was always in his size.

He did have beautiful eyes, she admitted, brighter and a more intense blue than Lady Cora's or Susanna's, with thicker black lashes. The effect of those sapphire eyes was ruined by a broken nose from some fight or other. His lips were full and nicely formed, she supposed. Some women might find them appealing. Some women kept pet pigs, too.

Stamfield's finest quality, from what she'd seen or heard of him, was he was loyal to his family and kind to his mother. He'd come to his cousins' aid whenever they asked it of him, and now he'd answered Lady Cora's call. Everyone knew he'd rather visit some sordid gaming hell than dance at a debutante ball. He much preferred smoke and ale to punch and perfume, the company of light-skirts to that of ladies. Yet here he was, dutiful son, devoted brother. Corie clutched that thought to her bosom, like a lifeline. He wouldn't bring disgrace on them. His love for his family wouldn't let him, and that just might save her.

He doted on Susanna, who was as unlike him as chalk from cheese. Bright and sunny, she did not have a drop of venom in her. Mischief, yes, but never malice. Stamfield obviously adored her. He said he would not press her to wed, nor urge a gentleman of his choice on her. He'd never force her to marry a man she could not love. The decision was hers, he promised, when she was ready. Stamfield wouldn't do anything to ruin his sister's chances.

That calmed Corie's rattled nerves. Or else the brandy did. Another drop or two and maybe she'd be able to sleep, to look forward to tomorrow, to new gowns, a new start. Finally her fate was in her own hands. Daniel Stamfield's ham-sized hands were not, metaphorically, around her throat.

Why, she might even manage to find other redeeming qualities in him, if she tried hard enough. He might be a gambler, but he hadn't lost his fortune or mortgaged his ancestral home, the way many other sprigs of society did. He wasn't a dandy, that was for sure, puffed up in his own conceit and padded shoulders. Nor was he a sports-mad Corinthian, spending all his time and money on highbred horses. According to her maid, who heard it from the footman, who played dice with the groom, his mount was a placid plug, good for nothing but to carry Stamfield's extra weight.

She supposed he was no worse than any other town buck out for his own selfish pleasure. The difference was Lady Cora's son chose seedier environs to do his hell raking. McCann's Club entertained men with lesser titles and fortunes than White's or Boodle's. It also had women dealers, women patrons, women allowed in private rooms upstairs.

Stamfield wasn't a seducer of innocents, not that she ever heard. Corie would have heard, too, because there was nothing servants loved as much as gossip about their betters acting like beasts. Nor was his name linked to any highborn wives or willing widows, the way so many so-called gentlemen's were. No, his name was dragged through bordellos, not the boudoirs of the beau monde. Did that make him worse or better than other men? Corie did not know or care. It made no difference, anyway. All men were fools.

Yet Lady Cora thought her son was nearly perfect. A mother's love truly must be blind.

Corie thought of her own mother, resting in peace

or not these many years, and how Corie's life might have been far different had her mother lived. Or not. Mrs. Abbott did not have the backbone of a Lady Cora. Mama believed it was a woman's lot to suffer, ever since the Garden of Eden in her precious Bible. A female was a husband's property, his vassal, his inferior. A wife should not complain, either, for it was a man's right to rule his kingdom. Mama had tried to teach her daughter to be accepting of her place in life, just as Mrs. Squire Abbott accepted dying of neglect and a broken heart.

Corie could not do it, meekly follow her father's dictates. She could not marry the sick old man her father had chosen for her just so she'd be a widow soon, and he'd have control of her rich inheritance. She could not accept someone like Mrs. Rivendale as her stepmother, becoming nursemaid to another woman's infants. She could not, would not, let Daniel Stamfield steal this chance for a better life.

Resolved, Corie decided to go to bed, to be ready to face the next day and whatever came. She thought she would take her cup upstairs with her, refilled with lukewarm tea and a dash of brandy, in case she could not fall asleep.

So there she was, barefoot and gloveless, with her hair trailing down her back, her gown disordered, and one hand holding a brandy decanter. Which was, of course, when Nemesis knocked.

Chapter Six

Daniel did not knock. The door was open, and he was coming in only to wish his mother good night. Instead of his mother or his sister, he found Miss Abbott, alone, and looking like the wanton she was. He almost looked around to see if she had a man—a footman or a groom, even—hidden in the window seat or behind the sofa. He couldn't take his eyes off her, though. He couldn't think straight. Hell, he could hardly breathe, but he had to say something, or she'd know him for the great looby he was.

"I see you are making yourself at home," he said, which was possibly the worst he could have uttered, other than "Please take off the rest of your clothes so I can die a happy man."

Corie set down the bottle. Her chin came up. "Lady Cora said I might."

Damn, that was not what he meant, not entirely. "Of course. Guest and all. Her goddaughter. I, uh, meant no offense."

Maybe not this time, Corie told herself, but his continued stare was insult enough, as if he was mentally undressing the rest of her. She cursed at herself for removing the lace filling from her neckline, right where he was gawking, then cursed at him for not being a gentleman. She couldn't do anything about her hair, her shoes, or the missing fichu, but she still wore layers of firmly laced fabric, thank heavens. She did try to hide her bare hands in her skirts. "I thought you were out," she said, as if that explained her dishabille in the drawing room.

"I needed to write a few letters myself."

He'd unknotted his neckcloth, too, so it was draped around his broad shoulders. His hair was mussed as if he'd drawn his fingers through it in concentration, leading Corie to wonder if the dolt could spell. His coat was unbuttoned, and his waistcoat was missing altogether. He wore his scuffed boots, with an attempt at polish on them now, instead of the old-fashioned buckle shoes he'd worn to dinner. Somehow he looked better in this disarray than tightly trussed in what she understood to be his father's clothes.

No, he looked like he'd just left a lady's bedchamber. Corie was mortified by such wayward thoughts, and hoped the dim candlelight could hide her blushes. Embarrassed, she couldn't think of anything to say that wouldn't reinforce his belief she was a shameless hussy, battening on his mother's generosity.

An awkward silence fell. He kept staring at her hair and the place where her modesty wrap had been and her bare toes, the unmannered boor. No matter that she kept looking at his broad shoulders and bare neck. What, did he think she was a doxy to be inspected before purchase? She refused to walk back to where her slippers waited beside her chair, to sit and lace their ribbons in front of him like a doxy in truth.

She recalled the decanter. "Would you like a glass?"

Daniel swallowed the lump in his throat. Damn, he'd

warned his mother he couldn't make conversation with proper women, and here was the proof. They all looked at him like he'd clambered out from under a rock, the way Miss Corisande Abbott was grimacing at him now. "No. That is, yes. Just the thing. Um, there's a chill in here. Deuced good taste in liquor, my uncle."

Lady Cora had hinted the brandy and other bottles in the vast wine cellar might be contraband. Coming from the coast, Corie knew all about smuggling. "I don't suppose any of it has seen an excise label."

Daniel shrugged.

No wonder he seemed as tongue-tied as she did, Corie thought. She'd practically labeled his uncle, an adviser to the throne and the high courts, as a criminal. Anything he said could incriminate the earl. She was an idiot.

She found a glass, but couldn't decide how high to fill it. The last thing she wanted was to make Mr. Stamfield inebriated, or make him linger over his drink. She poured a tiny amount and brought it to him, then nervously picked up the fichu and twisted it in her hands.

Instead of drinking it all at once as she expected, he took a slow sip. Then he put the glass down.

Was he going to attack her? He was a beast who already considered her a fallen woman. And he was breathing heavily. Corie looked around for a possible weapon.

Daniel looked around for a possible escape.

They both said they ought to be going, at the same time, but neither made a move toward the door.

Another silence filled the room.

Corie did not want to leave before him, not when she'd have to collect her hairpins and shoes and the gloves she'd tossed across the room. Heavens, she could not leave her apparel strewn around the parlor for the maids to find in the morning, or Mr. Dobbson now. Speculation would fly like a swarm of wasps.

Daniel did not want to leave before her, to wonder all night if she was seducing old Dobbson in the dark. "I, uh, wanted to apologize again for my earlier words. You are welcome here if—"

"If?" There was ice in the word.

Daniel did not know how to politely phrase his condition, so he picked up the white lace gloves he spotted on the floor. Instead of bringing them to her, he stared at the wispy things as if they had answers, or eloquence. They were simply spotless and tiny. He couldn't imagine a sillier accessory, for they'd never keep her hands warm or dry. They'd only get in the way of any delicate work, as far as he could see, so their only purpose was to fulfill another of society's stupid conventions. Like how a man's and woman's skin should never touch, like how he shouldn't be alone in the room with an unmarried female of expectations. He almost choked on the ramifications if a stranger saw them like this, their clothing disordered, their hair loose. Lord, she had wondrous hair, with golden sparks among the browns, thick and wavy, far past her shoulders. If only . . .

Corie twisted the fichu some more. The poor thing would be unwearable in another minute. "If you are worried about the money, I will be able to repay you eventually, or if I marry, my husband shall, from my dowry. Or I can economize and not allow Lady Cora to purchase half the gowns she feels I need."

"No, it's not the money. I'm not a squeeze penny like your father." He almost bit his lip. Now he was belittling the girl's sire. For all he knew, she was devoted to the squire. He was her own father, after all.

"Then 'if' what? If I don't stay long, if I do not insist on your company at every turn? Believe me, Mr. Stamfield, I would far rather take my maid or a footman on errands or walks."

"If . . . if you behave yourself," he blurted. "And if you don't bring disgrace to my mother and sister."

"Disgrace? Behave? Me?"

"Well, your past, you know. Your reputation."

The fichu ripped in half, Corie was torturing it so. Too bad it wasn't the dastard's heart she had between her hands. What did he think, that she would tie her garters in public or arrange secret trysts with her lovers in dark, empty rooms?

This was a dark, empty room, with no chaperone in sight. Bother! Corie had taken enough insult from this uncouth creature in his oversized body and underused brain. Forgetting he was her host and Lady Cora's darling, forgetting she was a lady, whether he believed it or not, she tossed the balled-up remnants of the fichu in his face. "You speak of my reputation, sirrah, when it is your own that will bring us down? It is not I who has been living in the London stews, associating with cutpurses and crossing sweeps. I do not get into brawls." Then she listened to her own words and clasped her hands behind her back lest she strike him.

Now he raised his glass and drained the contents. "I do not run off with penniless soldiers."

"No, you run off with prostitutes."

"You see? Talk like that isn't befitting a true lady. My sister should never hear such words."

"Then she should not hear the tittle-tattle about her brother, for that is what is said. You never seemed to care about that, that your family would hear reports of your profligate ways."

"My ways are no worse than any other gentleman's." Not very, anyway.

"Well, I say you are no gentleman to be calling me names, when I have nearly been living the life of a cloistered nun. But here you are, wearing your father's shoes, drinking your uncle's wine, letting your mother run your estate."

"You forgot I am living in my cousin's rooms," he added drily.

"Rooms located over a disreputable gaming club."

"I object to that. There's nothing disreputable about McCann's. They run honest tables and don't water the wine."

Corie overrode his protest by stamping her bare foot. "Susanna says that before your cousins pulled you out of your drunken stupor, you lived in low dives. You were nothing but a miserable, hotheaded drunk. For all I know, you still are, except in better surroundings." She pointedly put the stopper back in the decanter. "You're afraid doors will be shut to us because of me? Without your mother, you could not get through half the entry halls in Mayfair without a battering ram."

"I was never a miserable drunk," he interrupted. "I was quite content, in fact." From what he could remember, anyway. He'd done his best to forget the war and Rex's wounds. "There was no fishwife carping at me."

Corie was too incensed to care that her voice was raised, as was her ire. Her nerves were too frazzled with worry. Her plans were too crucial to leave to this buffoon. "Maybe someone should have shouted at you. Maybe your mother should have come and dragged you home and knocked some sense into that thick skull of yours. You are a blot on your name, a useless stain."

He scowled at her. "Not entirely useless. I was a soldier, recall."

"Do not tell me how you served your country. Susanna is full of tales of your heroism. Rot! You resigned from the army years ago after conduct unbecoming of an officer or gentleman. You managed to help Rexford rescue Amanda, and help Mr. Harry Harmon solve his secret intrigues, but now you are back to doing nothing for anyone. Susanna told me your uncle asked you to serve as magistrate, or stand for a place in the Commons, but no, you chose to stay a feckless barbarian, with no occupation, no concern for anyone but yourself."

If she were a man, she'd be on the floor by now. If she were the kind of woman Daniel was used to, she'd still be on the floor after he kissed her to shut her up. That was what he hated about real ladies. A fellow couldn't thrash them or tumble them. Hell, it wasn't even polite to shout at one of the delicate blossoms. He yelled anyway. "I care for my family, dash it. That's why I don't want you here. And you don't know anything about my career in the army."

"And you do not know anything about my elopement, but that didn't keep you from leaping to conclusions and passing judgment."

"I know all I need to know."

"Then I know all I need to know!"

"Snelling did not kidnap you, did he? You went willingly, packing a trunk, taking blunt from the family coffers."

"You think I stole funds? That was my own purse, what I'd saved from the household allowance and my pin money. Ah, but you never asked for the truth, did you? Did you ask my dear father about the sick old man he bartered me to? How Sir Neville thought a virgin could cure him of the pox? The raddled old ghoul paid my father for my hand. My loving sire thought Sir Neville would die soon and leave me a wealthy widow. Only I'd never see a groat of it, would I? While I was still underage, my finances would be controlled by my father, especially if I contracted the disease. I was seventeen, Mr. Stamfield. Seventeen! Snelling would have been better. Anyone would have been better. I would have married—" She almost said "you," but no, she'd never have tied herself for life to another violent, domineering man. "I would have married a stranger. But you had to ride to the gallant defense of British maidenhood and a man's right to sell his own daughter."

Daniel knew she spoke the truth because he'd have been itching like mad over such a faradiddle otherwise. He knew Abbott was a loose screw, but this was beyond any moral standard of decency. Seventeen. Bloody hell.

"You should have come to my mother."

"What could she have done? No laws were broken."

"But why did you pick that cur Snelling?"

Corie looked at her empty cup with longing, but did not refill it. "The lieutenant needed money desperately. And he was a gentleman who happened to be handsome, attentive, and available."

"He was a known gambler and a womanizer. He would have made you a wretched husband."

"Do you think I didn't know that? I was young, not

ignorant of the world or the local gossip. He was better than pox-ridden Sir Neville, who is still alive, by the way, only blind and raving and kept in the attics by his servants. I'd have been married to a lunatic right now if I hadn't run off."

"Why didn't your father go on with the match once you were home?"

"Because Sir Neville was at our house for the cursed wedding when I left. He wouldn't have me. He assumed I was no longer a virgin." She laughed, without humor. "Can you believe it? That filthy old man wouldn't have me. And Snelling was gone, thanks to you, my father's hero." She laughed again. "Some kind of hero, almost killing a man half your size."

Now Daniel was angry, at Abbott, Sir Neville, and Snelling, but mostly at this virago who was shredding his character along with her apparel. "I never wanted to be a hero. Not in the army; that was Rex's idea, and he is scarred for life. It's dirty and dangerous, and deuced uncomfortable. And not in the law or politics, either. Harry had to stage his own death to avoid assassination. Another man did get killed in his stead, did you know that? Do you think Harry will ever forget or forgive himself? That other poor soul was a hero, saving Harry's life. And he's dead."

Corie stared at her bare toes, peeking out from her hem. "I did not know."

"And you do not know why I choose to enjoy myself instead of dying for some cause that will not make a difference to anyone."

"Some things are worth dying for. Freedom, your loved ones. Pride."

"No, pride is not worth dying for. Do you know how many gentlemen have died over a slight to their honor? I say a good bout of fisticuffs ought to settle anything."

"That is easy for you to say, since you'd always have the advantage. Where is the pride in that?" Corie glanced again at the decanter. Now she understood where Dutch courage came from. She would never have spoken to such a large, intimidating, angry gentleman with such vehemence, such vitriol, on her own. Somehow she was no longer afraid of speaking her mind to this man, despite his size and reputation. Filled with spirits or not, she was certain he would not hurt her, not with his mother in calling distance. So she decided to continue, to relieve her own pent-up hostility.

"Just what do you consider worth living for? Your own pleasure? Losing yourself in drink so you do not have to think of your empty existence?" Her lip curled in a sneer. "I refuse to be insulted by an immoral care-for-naught. You, sir, are nothing but a wastrel."

That was true, too. Daniel did not want to hear the words, so he fought back. "And you are still a fallen woman."

She glared at him, gold sparks flashing in her green eyes. "No, I am not."

Daniel paused to wait for the rash. It never came. Did that mean she was untouched, or simply untouched by scandal? Truth was a strange thing. He thought about asking, but the hellcat was still on a rant.

"You and your stupid assumptions, using the stupid labels of a stupid society. Stupid, stupid, stupid!" She poked him in the chest with each imprecation. Then she recalled she needed this man's cooperation. "London does not know about me and Snelling. He is dead,

Sir Neville is a bedlamite, my father has too much pride, and your mother loves me too much. No one else knows what happened that night. Will you tell them?"

"Gads, you really think I am some kind of cad, don't you?" He'd thought about blackmailing her with the threat, so she'd leave, but her question still hurt. "That would reflect poorly on my mother."

"And your sister," she added, for good measure.

He shrugged. "And my aunt and uncle, for having you in their house."

"And Dobbson, who wants so badly to be butler to the cream of society."

"We mustn't forget the servants."

She could almost smile now.

Daniel did smile back, stepped past her, trying not to notice when she cringed at his closeness, and raised the decanter. He poured more spirits into his own glass, then a drop or two into her teacup. "I propose a treaty. We shall both agree to try to scrape through these next weeks with dignity and grace." He handed her the cup, then raised his glass in a toast.

Corie took the cup, but hesitated. "And we can forget the past?"

"Both of our pasts."

They clicked their drinks together and he said, "To the future." Except he'd still wonder about Snelling and what happened at that inn.

"Did you love him?"

"I wanted to. He was handsome in a scarlet uniform, and made me feel beautiful. I thought he was noble to rescue me, brave to take on my father's wrath. He proved as faithless as every other man, as cruel as my father, as paltry as you."

So the treaty was an end to hostility, Daniel understood, not a friendship. He felt a twinge of regret, but he wasn't one to dwell on what he couldn't change. He was tempted to seal the pact with a kiss, to see if that might change her opinion. He wanted to know if her lips were as soft as they looked, or as prim as Miss Corisande Abbott pretended. He knew he'd get slapped, but who said he wasn't brave? Or stupid.

Chapter Seven

She did not slap him. That would have stung a bit, she supposed, because she was not a small woman.

She cried. Her tears pierced him through the heart.

She hadn't stepped back when he closed the short distance between them. She stiffened a little, but nothing worse. He realized she always cringed when he got too close, which angered him enough that he wanted to show her he could be trusted not to stomp on her feet every time.

She did not scream when he was inches away, or pound his chest with her fists, or race toward the door. She just stared at him as if he'd sprouted horns and a tail. She looked confused, surprised, horrified—he couldn't tell which, and who was thinking, anyway?—as Daniel bent his head. He meant only to brush his lips against hers, just for an instant. But she was looking at him, her mouth open, so he opened his, too.

In the back of his mind, where he might have one, seldom-used wit left, he realized that her being tall for a woman meant he didn't get a crick in his neck from bending over, or in his knees from crouching down. And her skin was as soft as a rose petal, and her scent was lilacs, and she tasted of brandy and tea and sweet woman. That last ounce of sense went flying to his fingertips, which stroked her bare shoulders.

The instant might have lasted forever, or been a blink of the eye. Miss Abbott made a low sound in her throat. He sure as hell hoped the tiny murmur had been one of pleasure, because that kiss had been sweeter than any he'd stolen, shared, or bought in all his years. He stepped back to see.

That was not pleasure he read on her face.

"Hell, are you crying? Did I hurt you? Sometimes I forget my own strength. Clumsy ox, you know. Everyone knows." He babbled like one of those French officers, expecting to be tortured if they didn't tell all their secrets.

Miss Abbott sniffled. She didn't raise her eyes to him. She made that sound again, the one that might have been arousal, but was a smothered sob. "No."

Daniel was relieved. Except when he tipped her chin up, he could see that she was still crying, with great round tears rolling down her cheeks. Gallons of guilt, they looked to him. He wasn't sure how, but he knew the deluge was his fault.

"It—it was only a kiss." And maybe a pet or two. "I'm sorry. I really am."

She brushed a tear away with her hand. She looked as red and swollen as Daniel started to feel for the lie he'd just spoken. He wasn't sorry at all.

He knew he was wrong. Great gods, did kisses come much more wrong than accosting a woman with a dicey past who was trying to land a husband? Assaulting a guest in his mother's parlor? He was ready to apologize, but in his heart, he was not sorry. Or wouldn't be if her lips stopped trembling and her shoulders stopped shaking.

"It . . . it wasn't only a kiss," she said, sniffling again.

"And an embrace. It's not as if I touched—or squeezed your—that is, it wasn't much more than a kiss."

Another tear rolled down her cheek. Daniel wished he had the coat he'd worn to dinner, with the handkerchief carefully tucked in the inside pocket by Dobbson. He picked up a piece of the gauzy thing she'd tossed at him instead, the one that was tucked into her neckline earlier. The scrap wasn't good for anything else but rags now. He held it out.

She ignored it, his excuses, and him. She turned away to find a napkin near her teacup. She wiped her eyes and blew her nose, not all that delicately.

When she appeared done, he addressed her back. "I thought it was fairly nice, myself, certainly not bad enough to cry over. I can do better if you—"

"It was what it meant," she said on a near wail.

The kiss meant nothing but that he was male, maybe with too much brandy, wine, and port in him, and she was beautiful. "Uh, what do you think it meant?"

Now she turned to him, looking up through watery eyes. "That I am open to such improper advances. That I can be kissed and clasped like—like a tavern wench." She sobbed again. "That you think I am a loose woman."

"Dash it, don't cry. It's nothing like that. The problem is, I am not a gentleman. You said it yourself: I'm a cad and a wastrel. I told my mother I shouldn't be here, shouldn't be accompanying her for the Season. I'm not fit for polite company. No gentleman would have forced himself on you, taken liberties without leave, made you cry with brutish attentions."

She gave one last sniff. "It wasn't so bad, I suppose."

Not so bad? Now his amour propre was suffering. "Hmph."

"It was almost nice. Nicer than most."

Daniel was still insulted. "Oh, now you're an expert? First you say you are not a highflier. Next you are comparing kisses."

"I have not had as many kisses as most women my age, if you must know. My father watches me too carefully since . . . well, since I saw you last. I have not kissed as many gentlemen as Susanna, I'd warrant, and she is three years younger. She practices with every boy in the neighborhood. There's always a dark corner or a secluded garden or an unlighted path at dinner parties or assemblies."

He growled. "Great gods, what is my mother thinking, to let her sneak off like that?"

Corie sat down on the chair, reaching for the hairpins she'd left on the end table. "She is thinking your sister should know more of men, so she can judge them better than I did."

Daniel tried not to watch her gather the honeyed waves back and start twisting them into a bun. "You judge a man by his sense of honor, his bank account, his seat on a horse—anything, dash it, but his kisses!"

Corie paused in her braiding. "Why? She won't be sleeping with his ledger books."

And he wouldn't be sleeping tonight, thinking about running his fingers through those long, silky curls. "Because a man doesn't stop at kisses, if he thinks he doesn't have to. Next thing you know, her hair is down, your slippers are missing—no, that's not right."

Corie let her hair fall loose down her shoulders

again. "No, that is not right. I think a woman should know what she is getting, and if she'll like it. Marriage is more than sharing a house and a name."

"But too many stolen kisses can ruin a gal's reputation as fast as a fart. I suppose I can't say that, either. This is London now, not the country, where everyone knows you and accepts a bit of hoydenish behavior. Both of you have to watch your steps here, where every action is scrutinized and dissected, looking for scandal. No kissing, do you hear?"

Corie looked around, afraid Dobbson would hear from the butler's pantry near the front door.

"I am not Susanna. And you must know your sister is not fast—she is just young and experimenting. I've had less than a handful of kisses since Lieutenant Snelling, discounting a few under the mistletoe, in public. For once and for all, I am not a trollop."

"I could tell. You do not kiss like an experienced woman."

Instead of being reassured by his agreement, Corie was annoyed at his words, the same way Daniel's pride had been pricked. Her brow puckered into furrows. "I do not kiss right? You said it was nice. Did you lie?"

"I never lie. That is, seldom. It was a lovely kiss. For a novice."

"Oh." Corie could not decide whether to be pleased Stamfield finally accepted her innocence, or to be irritated he found her less desirable than his demireps.

She gathered the hairpins on the table into a neater pile, missing the twinkle in his eye when he said, "Perhaps I caught you by surprise. That must be it."

"Yes, I was surprised. I never thought you would. That is, I did not think you liked me or found me the least attractive."

To prove her wrong, he had to kiss her again.

She kept her mouth closed, her back rigid, instead of going all soft and warm in his arms. He stepped back.

This time she did slap him. "I am not a whore!"

The slap only reinforced what he already knew. He shook his head, as if that might get his brain working again. "Zeus, I should not be doing this."

"I am a lady."

He nodded. "Right. My mother's goddaughter. My sister's bosom bow. A guest in my house. It will not happen again."

"It better not." She gripped one of the hairpins like a weapon.

"I had a shade too much to drink, don't you know."

"No, I cannot imagine anyone drinking a dent in his honor. Saying you are in your cups is merely an excuse for immoral behavior." She shoved her feet into her slippers and stood up. "You really are no gentleman. I was right to consider you a cad, and a drunk, too."

"Oh, I'd have kissed you stone sober."

She pretended not to see his smile. "You are reprehensible."

"I told my mother I was." Somehow his mood was brightened just knowing Miss Abbott wasn't a flirt. In fact, he was downright cheerful she'd proved virtuous. "I wish you could convince my mother of that, so she releases me back to my life of decadence and debauchery. Then you can go husband hunting in peace."

She sat down again, knowing she had to lace the ribbons on her shoes or she'd trip instead of making a grand exit. "Is it so wrong to look for a match?"

Daniel went to add more coals to the fire. "Ask the

fox how he feels with a pack of slavering dogs chasing after him."

"If he's been raiding the henhouse, Reynard has no one to blame but himself."

"But what if he's been minding his foxish business, smelling the flowers, digging a nice little burrow for himself?"

"Then he'd be lonely. And dirty and hungry. I do feel sorry for the poor fox, of course, but the London Season is not a blood sport. Gentlemen can always get away."

"That's how much you know. You haven't met a determined mama yet, one of those who is ready to arrange a compromising situation just to trap a match for her homely daughter."

"But women are not the only pursuers."

Daniel wiped his hands on his father's trousers. "No, there are fortune hunters aplenty who need to line their pockets with a substantial dowry. I'm not saying that's right, either. Some chaps don't need the blunt; they need to fill their nurseries, to ensure their successions."

"They need a broodmare, in other words."

He shrugged. "If not for the money or the heirs, I'd wager, few men would marry."

One slipper was tied, without showing too much of her ankle. She looked up. "You do not believe in love?"

"Of course I do. I've seen it in Rex and Harry, haven't I? Moonstruck, both of them. They were lucky, that's all."

Corie thought about how lucky their wives were. She sighed. "A woman has fewer choices. It's not like I can study for the law or the church, or go into trade.

Marriage is my only option. I cannot return to my father's house."

"What if you can't find a man to love?"

"I shall still wed if I receive an honorable proposal, and hope for love to follow. If no respectable man offers for me this Season, I'll sell my jewelry, my pearls and a diamond set from my mother. I'll live on that until I find a suitor, or a position as a lady's companion."

"Without references?"

"Your mother could write me recommendations. She might know of a post for me with one of her friends."

"My mother would pay someone to wed you, rather than see you go into service. That is no life for a lady. You'd be miserable."

She looked at him, her eyes narrowed. "Then what do you suggest I become? A courtesan?"

"You'd have no lack of offers." He held up his hand before the prickly female could take affront again, or cry. "No insult intended. But don't worry; plenty of swells with good intentions will be interested. I'd make book on that."

She sighed again. "Until they hear about Snelling."

He bent down to take her foot in his hand to tie the ribbons around her ankle. "They won't hear of it from me. I will forget about Snelling."

"And we'll forget this night ever happened."

He couldn't forget.

She shouldn't forget.

Dobbson sure as hell wouldn't forget.

"Ahem. Your horse is waiting, Mr. Stamfield." The butler was staring at the wall over their heads, at a painting of some Greek gods cavorting. His lip was curled, as if he'd found Daniel and Corie cavorting.

"I was, ah, bidding Miss Abbott good night."

Dobbson's gaze slid to the floor, where Daniel was kneeling, one of Miss Abbott's delicate feet in his hands. Then he looked at Daniel's cheeks, which were red from the slap, and red from the lies.

Daniel rubbed at the back of his neck. "I suppose I had too many strawberries at dinner. They always make my skin erupt, don't you know."

"Me, too," Corie said, to explain her own suddenly scarlet complexion.

Dobbson offered to tell Cook to leave strawberries off the menu from now on. Not that he recalled a single one at the table.

"No, no," Daniel said, "I love them. I'll just eat less next time."

Dobbson looked at the nearby brandy decanter, then at Miss Abbott's trailing hair. "Restraint would be advisable."

"Quite. I'll be on my way, then." Daniel turned to salute her hand. She was too busy picking up more hairpins to offer it.

She did say, "Good night, Mr. Stamfield. Thank you for the advice about London. I am sure it will be valuable."

"I'm sure it will," Dobbson murmured.

The butler's hand went out when they reached the front door. This time there was no mistake. Daniel placed a silver coin in it.

"A bit more valuable than that, I'd say."

A gold coin found its way from Daniel's pocket to Dobbson's. "You will not say a word to anyone, not my mother, not the servants, not at the pubs where other butlers gather and gossip about their employers."

"Speak about my betters? Never."

Oddly enough, Daniel felt no telltale itch. Most likely the powdered prig did not think anyone was better than him. "Nothing happened."

Dobbson peered at him by the light of the dim lamp in the hallway. "Did you just have more strawberries?"

"The lady was relaxing, damn it, her shoes off and hair down, when I stepped into the parlor. I thought my mother might still be making lists and plans. I merely passed a few pleasantries with Miss Abbott."

"And very pleasant they must have been." Somehow he had Corie's lace gloves in his hand.

Daniel took one menacing step in Dobbson's direction, snatched the gloves away, and shook his fist under the man's chin. "Dash it, nothing happened!"

"Quite right. What would happen, between a gentleman and his mother's houseguest?"

Nothing. Not ever.

And now Daniel's feet itched at his own lie.

Chapter Eight

Daniel could not forget, not even with a bottle or two of McCann's finest at his table. He couldn't go up to his former rooms to consider that kiss, those words, that other kiss. Not that he was a man much given to cogitation about females, feelings, or his own future, but Miss White might have some good advice.

Miss White, however, was ensconced as queen of the kitchen, and not moving. Daniel's rooms had been reallocated to a Harrison cousin who was going to earn his rent by keeping the establishment's books. What went unspoken by Harrison, the manager, was that Daniel did nothing for the club but add a mite to the house's gambling bank. Daniel's things got packed and carried out, the manager reported, by three servants from Royce House and two helpful footmen from the club. Most likely while Daniel was at dinner, pleading his case to at least sleep at McCann's.

He was right about the gaming establishment being a better place for him, for all it mattered to his mother. He did not belong at the earl's house, with proper gentlefolk who expected proper behavior.

So he sat in the public rooms of McCann's, where

the noise was too loud to hear oneself think, yet Miss Abbott's words rang out in his head. Not how she found the kiss "Almost nice. Nicer than most," but words like "cad," "wastrel," "drunkard."

His mother wouldn't say it. The uppity butler might think it, but he wouldn't dare say it. Miss Abbott had more backbone than any man Daniel knew, to say it to his face.

If the wine wasn't enough to muddle his head so he could ignore those barbs, maybe a woman was. He smiled at one of the pretty females who played at the tables but plied another trade when her luck was out. He thought he might have bedded her a time or two, but devil take it if he could remember her name.

She swayed toward his table, so obviously she was not offended by his come-hither glance, or averse to spending time with him, which was a happy change. Not that he had a bad reputation with the girls here. He paid well, and more if they didn't pretend. He tried to be gentle and polite, and some were even impressed by his size. He mightn't have a title or a great fortune or a silver tongue, but he did have size. That counted in some circles, if not in Miss Abbott's.

His mother's guest seemed to admire industry and sacrifice and abstinence. Well, she wasn't going to find her perfect match at any rout party in Mayfair. No puritans attended those affairs. She'd do better to set her sights on a blasted good-deed missionary. In some distant jungle.

He set his sights on the ample endowments at his eye level when—Jenny? Janie? Julie?—leaned over, so he could see her charms up close.

"Can I interest you in a private game, Danny?"

She smelled of cheap perfume and gin. The dingy lace on her gown hung limply, and her hair was an improbable red. Her eyes were blue, but dull, with not much intelligence behind them, only greed. He wondered if she had dreams for a better future, like Miss Abbott. Damn.

"Not tonight, love. But here." He tossed a coin her way. "Play a hand on me. Maybe your luck will change."

His luck was definitely on holiday tonight. He even lost at cards.

"My mind's not on the game," he told his fellow players as he tossed in his latest losing hand. Lord Morgan Babcock and his nephew Jeremy had asked Daniel to make up a table with Jeremy's younger friend, a Mr. Clarence Haversmith, who was new on the Town. That way, Lord Morgan explained, young Haversmith wouldn't get fleeced by any Captain Sharps. The Babcocks would take the lad's money gladly, but honestly. Daniel had no heart for trying to lose to the greenhead.

"Maybe you'll be luckier at love," Lord Morgan said, winking at the plump blonde who was trying to get Daniel's attention. Betty? Bonnie? Bunny?

The female draping herself across Daniel's shoulders had nothing to do with love. He tucked a coin down her gown and sent her off. "I've had enough of females for the night."

"Never thought to hear you say it, old man," said Jeremy, who already had a brunette in his lap. Daniel was fairly certain her name was Katherine. Or Kathleen. "What ails you?"

"I know." Lord Morgan called for another bottle, although his hand was none too steady as he tried to light a cigar. "Heard your womenfolk came to Town to take in the sights. That's enough to put any man off his game."

Jeremy's brunette feigned insult to her gender by pouting. She looked like a squirrel with an acorn in each cheek.

"The blazes, you say. I came to London to avoid my family. A houseful of women, don't you know." Young Clarence was counting up his remaining coins, to see if he could afford the services of one of the serving girls, who, Jeremy had informed him, were cleaner than any street-corner prostitute, but less expensive than the women at the fancy houses of convenience.

Jeremy laughed. "You came to Town because you've been thrown out of every school they could find for you. They're paying you to keep far from the neighborhood before you get another one of the dairymaids with child."

Daniel took a better look at the young man. Clarence didn't appear old enough to shave, much less litter the countryside with bastards. He did look stupid enough, though, with his neckcloth tied so high he couldn't turn his head, and wearing two rings on each hand. He was a pigeon waiting to be plucked, all right.

Lord Morgan coughed on his own cigar smoke. "That's it, then? Your ladies are here to visit? Don't worry; they'll spend all their days and half your blunt shopping. You won't have to do a thing but play least in sight."

"It's worse. They're here to launch my sister into society."

Young Clarence murmured condolences. "Gads, I

suppose you'll be expected to trot after her like a sheepdog."

Jeremy said a word that had even the brunette clucking her tongue. "Presentations and debutante balls, hell. I wouldn't be in your shoes if they offered me a knighthood."

"What, for your whoring?" His uncle turned to Daniel, after another bout of coughing that turned into wheezing. "You've just the one sister, I recall, so you'll be done with the nonsense soon. And they're doing it up right, firing the gel off from Royce House and all. You shouldn't have any difficulty. Still, I don't envy you, Stamfield."

The way Daniel saw it, Susanna would be trouble enough. "It's worse. They brought a neighbor to keep Susanna company. My mother's goddaughter."

"Lud, playing escort to two females on the marriage mart at once. Have another drink, my boy. You'll need it."

Daniel sighed. "It's worse still. My mother might be interested in remarrying."

They all lifted their glasses to Daniel, that he survive the Season.

"My sympathies, Stamfield." Lord Morgan wheezed again, then had another drink to clear his throat. He spilled some of it down his shirtfront without noticing. "Poor lad. Living with my late wife was bad enough, but three women?"

Young Clarence had five sisters at home, along with his mother, grandmother, and two maiden great-aunts. None of the sisters was old enough to be presented anytime soon. The youngest was still in leading strings.

No wonder the lad kicked over the traces, Daniel thought. What he said was, "You are lucky to be away from there." He had another glass of wine. "I wish I'd thought to leave Town before they arrived. The colonies, maybe. Or India. Somewhere too far for them to call me home."

Jeremy Babcock now had two females on his lap. "The way you're acting—no women, no cards—they must be antidotes." He looked at the empty plates beside Daniel. "If you stopped eating, I'd really worry. What is it? Spots? Squints? Stutters? Or are they all shrews? Something's got you in the doldrums that they'll never find husbands."

Daniel sat up straighter, instead of slouching in his chair. "That's my family you're speaking of. Not a fault among them," he declared loyally, then hoped he didn't break out in spots himself.

"No offense, old man. But if they don't look or sound like they belong in a barnyard, you have no problem, not with the Royce connections behind them. My sister's got a behind like a sow and a laugh like a donkey. We'll never get her off our hands. My mother's been trying for seven years."

Jeremy had jug-handle ears, a hooked nose, and no eyelashes to speak of. If Babcock's sister looked anything like him, they'd have to try for another seven.

Daniel thought of Susanna in her grown-up gown and what showed out of it. "My sister is bound to be a toast. She's young, but she doesn't simper or giggle or put on any of those debutante airs. She's clever, too, but not bookish."

Jeremy looked too interested, so Daniel quickly

changed the subject. "And my mother is a fine-looking woman."

"Then what's the problem with them? No dowry?"

"Of course my sister is well dowered. I'd make certain of that, if my father hadn't. M'mother has a handsome fortune of her own, not that I'd discuss it with outsiders."

"Bound to be common knowledge as soon as the servants get to gossiping," Lord Morgan said. "They always know."

Jeremy had his hand up the brunette's skirts, but his mind was still on Daniel's problem. "If your relations are passable, then it must be the neighbor girl who has you blue-deviled. Who is she? Anybody we'd know?"

Daniel lowered his voice. "A countryman named Abbott is her sire. There's a barony in the distant family."

Lord Morgan whistled, which brought on a gasp for air. "She don't look like him, does she?"

Daniel thought about lying, but if he called Corie prune-faced, his tongue was liable to swell up and choke him to death on the lie. "Hell, no. Miss Abbott's a diamond of the first water, I'd say. That's if you like tall, outspoken females who are a bit on the prim side."

Jeremy screwed up his face like- the wine had soured. He was short. "Doesn't sound the least appealing. Not like you, my little Jewel."

The brunette giggled. The blonde slapped his shoulder. "What about me, Jeremy? Aren't I a jewel, too?"

"That's her name, you peagoose," Jeremy explained.

The older man interrupted his nephew's messy ménage à trois to ask, "Nasty temper like her father?"

Daniel recalled Corie's tears. "Not that I've seen, but they just arrived this morning. She's no shy young miss, though. Miss Corisande Abbott is older than my sister. Near twenty."

"And still on the shelf? I'd worry, too. What, is she one of those particular females holding out for a prince?"

Daniel thought she'd take any man with two arms, two legs, and a marriage license. "I don't know. I believe her father didn't approve of any of her suitors."

"Abbott ain't like to put much in the gal's dowry, either. Cheap bastard. He'd likely demand a fortune in settlements, too."

"I wouldn't know," Daniel replied, determined to find out in the morning, so he could tell anyone who asked. Dobbson was certain to have the information, or his mother.

No one spoke for a minute or two while Lord Morgan wheezed, Jeremy breathed heavily, and Clarence Haversmith drooled over the redhead who refilled his glass.

"So are you interested?" Lord Morgan wanted to know.

Now Daniel choked on the smoke, or the idea. "In Miss Abbott? Hell, no. I'm not ready for leg shackles."

"Abbott's girl is, you say? Must be, if your mother is bringing her out." Lord Morgan blew a smoke ring. "Abbott's got no other heirs. Maybe I'll pop round and give her a look."

Lord Morgan? Hell, he had to be nearing sixty. "Great gods, she's too young for you. She could be your granddaughter!"

The older man shook his head. "I didn't start as young as our Clarence, here. M'daughter, maybe. But a man don't want an older female for his second wife. What's the point in that? And I've already got an heir, raising sheep and babies in Yorkshire. The thing is, a fellow gets lonely sometimes. He wants someone to look after him in his dotage, and look good on his arm before then."

"I doubt her father would ever consider such a match." Daniel sure as hell wouldn't, if he was in charge of sorting through Miss Abbott's offers. Damn, was he? He'd have to ask his mother that, too.

Lord Morgan was thinking. "Word is, he almost accepted Sir Neville a few years ago. Nasty piece of work, that."

Daniel did not comment. The less said about Sir Neville, the better. He almost held his breath, waiting to hear what else the older man might remember.

"I'd say she made a lucky escape. They say Sir Neville is queer as Dick's hatband."

Daniel relaxed, but only for an instant, until Jeremy Babcock spoke up.

"If Uncle is too old, maybe I'll do. I've got no title, but I am in Dun territory. Marriage to a rich wife seems my only option. Don't suppose you'd consider me for your sis—"

"No."

"So I might have to attend a few of those balls myself. Look over Miss Abbott, see how tall she is."

"I'm tall," Clarence piped up, his voice nearly cracking in his excitement. "Maybe she'll pick me. I'll have an estate someday, and she can help my mother take care of the infants and the old aunties."

"She is too old for you," Jeremy advised. "No man wants to look like a babe to his bride."

"Then what about your sister, Stamfield? You said she's pretty, and clever. Mum would be happy to have someone take over the household books. And add to the family coffers, don't you know."

That idea was just as repugnant.

Lord Morgan was still thinking, now that he had the notion of finding a helpmeet in his later years. "You say your mother might consider getting married again?"

Oh, Lord. "I am not sure. She and my father were close."

"You should convince her. Give her something to think about besides your own prospects and shortcomings. Yes, I might drop round."

Jeremy paused in petting his paramours. "And I, I suppose. One never knows where a woman's fancy takes her."

"Me, too," Clarence added. "My mum would want me to try. What day are the ladies receiving?"

The day hell froze over and the devil went ice-skating, if Daniel had his way. "That has not yet been determined," he said. "But these are ladies, remember, not bits of muslin."

"Of course. A gentleman don't marry the other kind."

Gentlemen? They were mongrels who should stay in their dark alleys, in the smoke and stench of their own foul kind. They had no business coming into the light where beauty and goodness and innocence shone, not these curs with their hangdog desires.

Lord Morgan wanted a nurse; Jeremy sought a wife's money to finance his own profligacy; Clarence Haversmith needed a nanny. Not one of them was good enough for a decent female like Daniel's mother, his sister, or Miss Abbott. They were gamblers and womanizers and drunkards, too old, too young, too worldly, too green, too jaded, too self-centered.

They were too much like Daniel.

Chapter Nine

Corie shouldn't forget. That was what she told herself as she put on her nightgown and brushed out her hair. She should not forget about Snelling, and she should not forget about Daniel Stamfield's kiss, no matter what they agreed was best to do.

Otherwise, she might be tempted to make the same mistakes over again. Not that she'd elope with another fortune hunter, of course, but she had to remember that men were not trustworthy. Not even the handsome ones. Especially not the handsome ones, with their tousled hair and bright blue eyes and boyishly awkward manners. They were the worst. And the most tempting.

Men were interested in two things from women: money and pleasure. And children, if they needed them. Snelling had wanted her money, with no use for heirs, but he'd have the other, too, as a bonus. She doubted Daniel Stamfield needed her dowry, not the way Lady Cora was spending money. And he was not ready for children, by his own admission. So all he wanted from Corie was what only a husband should have.

He had no other reason to kiss her, surely not love at first sight. He had no right to kiss her, but, heavens, he kissed divinely. Of course he did, she told herself. A man known to be a womanizer had to please the women he was pursuing.

Unless he was paying them. Daniel Stamfield was known to patronize brothels, where, she supposed, no one cared if a gentleman kissed like an angel, as long as his pockets were deep. She wondered about those women, and if he cared for them, if he even knew their names. And if they dreamed of a husband of their own, too.

He was a libertine, she reminded herself. No matter how he kissed, or held her so tenderly, or tied the ribbons on her slipper with such care, her foot cradled like a dove in his big hands. He made her feel something she did not want to feel, not for him.

He almost made her forget—not about needing a husband, not about her little house and garden—but to be afraid of such a large, hard-drinking man. He was known to be mean and cruel and rough, yet he had not been rough with her at all, even when she'd shouted at him, called him names, slapped him. Gracious, many men would have struck her back. He'd been gentle. Far gentler than she.

She shouldn't forget what she'd shouted at him, that she was a lady. Not a courtesan, not one of his paid companions. She'd become a lady's maid before she became any man's mistress, if she couldn't become a bride.

She plaited her hair and tied the heavy night braid with a ribbon, then decided to start her letters. The sooner she found another place to stay, the better. She sat at the desk in the corner of the lovely room, all floral prints and soft spring colors. She'd miss seeing spring in the gardens at home, her escape from

the ugliness at her father's house. She wouldn't go
back, so she had to keep her goals in mind.

Dear Annabelle, she wrote. *I know you'll be surprised to hear from your old schoolmate after three
years, but I am in London, staying with Lady Cora
Stamfield at Royce House. I was wondering how you
are, and your family? Perhaps I might pay a morning
call? Please tell me when is convenient.*

Dear Caroline . . .

Dear Lady Elizabeth . . .

What the devil was the married name of that girl
with the crossed eyes? If she could find a match, so
could Corie.

Daniel appeared at the breakfast table only a little
late and only a little bleary-eyed. Corie hardly noticed
because she kept her own darkly shadowed eyes firmly
on her sweet roll and chocolate so she did not have to
face the man who'd figured in her thoughts all night. If
he winked at her or made any comment about anything personal whatsoever, she'd go out and sell her
diamonds today. He didn't. Daniel said good morning;
then he went about filling his plate from the serving
dishes.

Susanna hardly noticed either one of them, chirping
about the plans for the day and the gowns she would
order from the modiste.

"Not so low in front or I'm not paying for them,"
Daniel announced at large, addressing himself to his
kippers and eggs. And ham and rashers and toast and
steak.

Susanna stuck her tongue out at him, but her mother
said they'd see what Madame Journet advised. She was

the most highly recommended dressmaker in Mayfair, and dressed all the young debutantes.

"And half the demimondaines," Daniel put in, around a swallow of coffee. "I asked."

"Surely she will know the difference, dear."

"Hmm," he said, helping himself to half the crock of jam for his toast. "We'll see. That is, if we see too much, I'm not letting you out of the house."

"Mother!" Susanna wailed, ready to toss her napkin at her brother.

"By the way, dear," Lady Cora told Daniel, deflecting the siblings, "Dobbson found you a valet. Lord Carruthers moved to the country and Monsieur Deauville refuses to go with him."

"You hired me a fu—" He paused at his mother's throat-clearing cough. "Fussy Frenchman? We went to war with those ba—"

She cleared her throat again, enough that Corie offered to pour some more tea.

"Those basket-scramblers."

"And we won, and now the war is over. Besides, I do believe Monsieur Deauville fled Napoleon's France for the same reasons we fought them. He was on our side and seemed quite eager to serve one of our finest."

"Until he hears what my position was."

"He knows all about you. You are quite, ah, famous, dear. And he knows your, ah, style, also. You and Lord Carruthers stayed together one sennight for a horse meet. He looks upon you as a challenge."

"That's enough to make a man lose his appetite." Daniel pushed his plate aside.

Corie had to hide her smile, but Susanna laughed. "You've eaten everything on the table."

"I believe Deauville is going through your wardrobe right now, to see what you'll need from the tailor this morning. Your appointment at Weston's is at ten."

"I am not going to any blo-blowhard haberdasher."

"Good, then you can accompany us and help Susanna decide on gowns you will approve."

"What time was that appointment with the tailor?"

The visit to the dressmaker was a joy for Corie, who seldom got to purchase more than one new gown a season, and that made up by the same village seamstress who'd made her girlhood pinafores.

Madame Journet had bolts upon bolts of stunning fabrics, softest silks, lustrous satins, sheer laces. Corie had a whole palette of colors to choose from, not just the debutante's pastels. The fashions Madame recommended were more sophisticated than she showed Susanna and more suited to a taller woman. They'd show off Corie's graceful figure and elegant bearing without trying to make her look younger than her years. Miss Abbott had style, Madame Journet pronounced, and all her assistants taking measurements and fitting half-completed gowns nodded their agreement.

Lady Cora ordered twice as many gowns as Corie thought she needed, with the same number for Susanna and herself. She was tired of dressing like a church-committee woman, she said, or someone's mother.

Madame Journet could not promise, but she would try her best to have them each one ball gown by next week, several day gowns sooner.

*   *   *

The visit to the tailor wasn't half bad. They served wine and biscuits. Two other acquaintances were there, so they wagered on how many pins the assistant fitter dropped. Once he was measured, Daniel gave Deauville's list to the proprietor, said, "Nothing tight, nothing stiff, nothing foppish," and paid in full.

"Of course, Mr. Stamfield. Would you like these tomorrow?"

The ladies took scraps of fabric to the shoemaker, to match scores of shoes, slippers, and boots to the gowns they'd ordered.

Daniel went to the boot maker, had his feet outlined for a pattern, and said he needed day shoes, night shoes, and boots. And if they pinched, he'd throw them through the shop window. Again, he knew several of the other customers. One was on his way to the glover, so Daniel went with him, after a stop to ease their thirst.

Susanna needed six pairs of white gloves, some long, some short, some in between, some with buttons, some without. Corie found three pairs of the lace mitts she preferred, and one pair of gold satin to match the ball gown they'd ordered. Lady Cora decided she could use a full dozen in different colors, since she hadn't replenished her wardrobe since putting off her black gloves. The girls also needed leather riding gloves, in case some gentleman asked them to ride in the park.

Daniel let a pretty shopgirl trace his hands and coo over their size. "Ooh, and I bet your feet are big, too."

He'd misplaced his list somewhere, so he told her to make up whatever a gent needed, and a few for getting lost.

The hatmaker was a different matter. He tried on several, decided he looked like a hackney driver or a chimney sweep, and bought one black evening top hat to carry under his arm when a chapeau was de rigueur.

The ladies visited four millinery establishments and tried on nearly every headpiece in all four shops. They bought toques and turbans and tiaras and some bonnets that matched nothing at all but looked so good they had to have them. They bought straw and satin hats, ones with wide brims, ruched brims, and coal-scuttle brims, military-style shakos and jockey caps to go with their new habits. That was a start, anyway.

Without his list, Daniel had no idea how many stockings, waistcoats, or shirts he needed from the haberdasher. So he'd let his new valet select them.

Cravats? Be damned if he'd waste his time feeling different lengths of linen to see which was smoothest. Let Deauville pick them, too, and if they irritated Daniel's neck, then he could get rid of them and the Frenchman. He'd take a handful of spotted kerchiefs along with him, though. Red, yellow, whatever was handiest.

No, he was not going to order nightshirts. Bad enough he'd be fettered during the day; he refused to be strangled in bed.

It was barely eleven. What else was he supposed to do? Daniel decided to think about his mother's instructions over a meal. He stopped into a coffee shop he knew that did up steak and kidney pie just the way he liked it. He sat with some friends who were going to engage in a fencing match, so he went along with them to Antonio's.

Biggersley declared he was far the better fencer, and Daniel didn't get a single itch, so he bet on him. He won.

After a few celebratory drinks with Biggersley, a few of the chaps went over to Tattersall's to look at horses. None was up to Gideon's size, so Daniel bought a pretty chestnut mare for his sister, even though he didn't think that was on his list.

"I thought you said your sister had black hair and blue eyes," Clarence Haversmith said after overhearing Daniel's conversation. "She'd look better on a gray or a black."

The young man in his high shirt collar and waspwaisted coat was at Tatt's looking for a town hack, most likely something showy and beyond his capabilities, Daniel thought. Daniel mightn't know as much about horseflesh as Rex or Harry, but he knew a sound beast when he saw it, and the one the grooms were parading in front of the buffle-headed boy was not.

He also knew when the auctioneer was lying about the horse's age, disposition, and stamina, so directed young Haversmith elsewhere.

They found a nice-looking bay that seemed a sweet goer. And a dainty black mare for Susanna. He'd keep the pretty chestnut in case Miss Abbott wanted to ride with them. That was only polite, wasn't it?

Clarence was so grateful for the advice and assistance that he invited Daniel to take the midday meal at his rooming house. His landlady was cooking a goose for Clarence's birthday.

The goose was excellent, and so was the cake. And since it was the boy's birthday and Lord Morgan and Jeremy Babcock were away at a bachelor house party, he invited Clarence to Astley's that evening. Clarence would meet Susanna sooner or later, anyway, Daniel reasoned, at one party or another. Better the two green-as-grass infants met now, under Daniel's watchful eye. He'd make certain his sister knew Clarence for what he was, a likable lad with six sisters in Sussex, and a penchant for dairymaids. The would-be rake couldn't get up to any mischief with Susanna, not with Daniel seated between them. And if Miss Abbott changed her mind and came along, too, another gentleman would make the outing less awkward.

There, he'd accomplished everything he ought. And he still had time before dinner for a trot around the park to see if any new ladybirds had taken roost. After that, he stopped in to visit Miss White at McCann's kitchens, and sample some of the cook's dishes. While he was at the club, Harrison needed help removing a drunken viscount, and Lord Chaverford needed a whist partner. Both raised a thirst, but Daniel ordered ale instead of something stronger, since he'd need his wits about him to chaperone his sister and a boy who couldn't keep his trousers closed. And Miss Abbott.

Lord, the days were long when one woke up so early.

The ladies had time for a quick reviving cup of tea between milliners, for they still had to visit corsetieres, feather merchants, fan makers, and ribbon sellers. How could they forget ribbons? And the bargains at the Emporium were so excellent, they sent the carriage home to unload the day's purchases so there would be room for the ladies. After a quick ride through the park, just to see what other women were wearing, they went back to the shops.

They barely had time for a much-needed rest before they had to change for dinner.

Heavens, the days were never long enough!

Chapter Ten

"Monsieur attends the circus this evening, *oui*?" The new valet studied the clothing Daniel had laid out on the bed. So far the man had been quiet, carefully folding and putting away all of Daniel's purchases. Daniel would have dumped them all on a chair, in their wrapped parcels, until he needed a new pair of stockings or such. Deauville's system was definitely more efficient.

The gentleman's gentleman wasn't one of those effete man milliners or fussy sobersides. He was older than Daniel, nearly his height, but a bit heavier in weight, especially in the middle. He wore his hair long, in a queue, and had one gold tooth to replace one he'd lost fleeing his homeland. He had ambitions of purchasing another gold tooth to fill a second gap, this one from a losing prizefight, which helped decide him to go into service.

Daniel thought they'd rub along well together. Then he came out of the bathing room in nothing but a towel to see the man pointing at his clothes for the evening as if they were a knot of vipers, about to strike.

Daniel looked at the offending apparel. He saw nothing wrong with his yellow Cossack trousers brought from McCann's or the brand-new yellow spotted handkerchief. They matched, didn't they?

"*Oui*. That is, yes, the circus."

"Ah, but I thought Monsieur was escorting his sister to the circus, not performing in it as a clown."

Daniel wore the blue Bath superfine coat and biscuit-colored pantaloons the man handed him. And a cravat. He refused the diamond stickpin, the beaver hat he was certain he never ordered, and the gloves that, again, were not what he recalled buying.

The valet straightened Daniel's sleeve and stood back, nodding his approval. "Now everyone will see that Mademoiselle has a gentleman to protect her."

Daniel flexed his muscles, half to see if the coat seams would split, and half to show Deauville that he did not need to dress like a coxcomb to guard his sister.

"A gentleman, not a coal hauler," Deauville said.

Daniel went down to dinner before his new valet ended up needing a few more false teeth.

Lady Cora kissed his cheek. "I must be the luckiest mother in England."

Susanna clapped her hands. "And I must be the luckiest sister. Now the evening is perfect." She was so excited she couldn't eat dinner. "Just think, new gowns, a new horse, my first night out in London, with an escort every woman would envy."

Miss Abbott yawned. She was far too exhausted from the day's outing to go with them, she said. She would stay home to keep Lady Cora company, she said. And he was far too handsome, she did not say.

Daniel had no trouble eating, only in swallowing

his disappointment. He thought he'd be relieved. He wasn't. He thought she'd notice his new haircut. She didn't. He thought she did not matter one whit.

She did.

The Royce House carriage stopped to fetch Clarence Haversmith at his lodgings. He bounded into the coach to sit across from Daniel and his sister, almost as excited as Susanna about this night's entertainment. He was dressed in yellow Cossack trousers that billowed around his spindly legs, a spotted kerchief, a cerulean coat that was tighter than Daniel's and padded at the shoulders, and a puce waistcoat crisscrossed with ribbons and fob chains. And rings, a lot of rings.

Disgruntled, Daniel asked, "Lud, who dressed you, Haversmith? A blind pirate?"

Clarence looked crestfallen, noticing Daniel's sober colors. "But—but it's all the rage. M'tailor said this was perfect for the circus."

Susanna scowled at her brother. "I think he looks magnificent."

"As do you, Miss Stamfield. Your brother did not do you justice. Your hair, those wondrous eyes. Even by the carriage lamps I can see your—"

"I told you that gown was still too low-cut," Daniel groused. He was annoyed with Susanna's clothes, Haversmith's clothes, and his own clothes. He was more annoyed that he was even thinking about fardling clothes! So he grew more aggravated as he listened to Clarence Haversmith pour the butter boat over Susanna, and watched the little peagoose lap it up.

"Don't go getting starry-eyed over the sweet talk," he warned her. "Master Haversmith has seven sisters in Suffolk."

"Actually, that's five in Norfolk, Mr. Stamfield."

"And eight old aunties."

"That's three, if you count Grandmama, but she never leaves her room." He tapped his head. "Empty in the attics, don't you know."

Daniel did not mention the pregnant dairymaid, but he meant to ask the lad about that later, to see if he was doing the decent thing by her. Daniel knew many men did nothing but walk away, leaving the unfortunate woman to bear the babe and her shame alone and often in poverty. He doubted Haversmith would marry the girl, but a real gentleman helped find—or fund—a husband among his tenants or villagers. At worst, he'd pay for a foster family for the infant, and an education if it was a boy. Uncle Royce had done everything for his illegitimate son except take Harry into his own home. Any fornicator who did less was the true bastard and no gentleman. He was not fit to touch a decent female's hem, much less share a carriage and a night out and empty flattery.

Clarence wanted to share more than that. He reached for a flask in his pocket, until Daniel kicked him. "There's a lady present, not one of Babcock's, ah, ladybirds."

But Susanna wanted a taste, which Daniel disallowed, of course. "They'll sell lemonade."

"And nuts?" Clarence wanted to know, sitting forward.

Susanna was watching out the window, as if her wishing could get them there faster. "Maybe boiled sweets?"

Clarence rubbed his hands together, clacking his rings. "Rum balls are my favorite."

Lord, Daniel thought, was he ever that young?

*   *   *

Susanna watched the horses, Clarence watched the bareback riders in their short spangled skirts, and Daniel watched both of them, who were so entranced, so rapt in the show. Usually he enjoyed the well-trained horses, the sparkling women, the daring male riders. Tonight he felt old, old and jaded.

He wondered what Miss Abbott would have thought about the performance. She was no flighty juvenile, despite being fresh on the Town; nor was she a staid matron, although she tried to look prim and proper. He wondered what she did enjoy, what would bring a smile to her lips. Her soft, warm lips.

Damn, his wits had gone begging again. The intermission had come and Haversmith had gone to fetch refreshments. Susanna seemed more enthralled with the ringmaster's twirled and waxed mustache, thank goodness, than Haversmith's baby-smooth cheeks. While they waited for him to return, Daniel asked, "Does your friend ride? I bought the chestnut in case Miss Abbott wants to accompany us to the park, or perhaps to Richmond to see the famous maze."

Susanna was fanning herself, overheated with the excitement. "She used to be an excellent rider before her accident."

"She had an accident?"

"She does not like to speak of it, but she seldom rides now. Sometimes she walks with her maid, but mostly her father sends her everywhere in a carriage, with a driver and a groom. I'd learn to drive a gig myself. Or a curricle. May I, Daniel? Please? You could teach me while we are here and lend me yours, and then I could cut a dash in the park and . . ."

Squire Abbott did not trust his daughter, it seemed. Daniel had no way of knowing if that mistrust was warranted. For all he knew, she had another soldier in her sights, waiting to make a run for the border. Her father's vigilance might be all that kept Miss Abbott from another elopement, or another affair. Damn, now the watch was on his shoulders. Daniel wondered if there'd been an accident at all.

There was one . . . and there wasn't.

His mother declared they needed one more day of shopping before being ready for company. With his bureau and his clothespress overflowing, Daniel took himself to Jackson's Boxing Parlour. He might be old, but the devil take it if he'd get fat and out of condition, too. He tried to convince Deauville to accompany him, citing the man's paunch, but the valet wasn't about to jeopardize his teeth, or his employment if he managed to land Mr. Stamfield a solid punch.

"Please do not let anyone land you a facer, monsieur," he called after Daniel's retreating back. "Black eyes are the devil to hide, and a split lip will be off-putting at Lady Cora's table."

His mother was planning a small gathering for the following night, an intimate dinner for twelve couples, at least. Most were old friends of hers and her late husband's. Most happened to have young, unmarried sons or daughters. She was not matchmaking, she swore to Daniel, just giving her girls a chance to make new acquaintances before a larger party full of strangers. This way, they'd have partners for the dances, and friends their own age to chat with.

When one of her old beaux from her own come-out conversed with Corie over the predinner sherry, instead of herself, Lady Cora was not concerned.

Daniel was. Stynchcombe was an old fool in a dark brown toupee, as if no one knew he was as bald as an egg underneath when it slipped to one side. Besides, his son was as young and silly as Clarence Haversmith, except Clarence had a chin.

Susanna had insisted they invite Clarence to the dinner party because he was all alone in London and might find himself in low company, otherwise. Low company? Daniel almost mentioned the dairymaid, but still refrained. It wasn't that his sister was too innocent for such talk, since she knew all about Harry now that he wasn't the earl's dirty secret. But Susanna had a good heart, and treated Clarence like a younger brother, betting pennies on who could ride faster on their new horses, or do more tricks like they'd seen at Astley's. Thank goodness she cared too much about making a success in society to try standing on her mare's bare back.

Daniel nodded in satisfaction, watching the brat converse with the gentlemen on either side of her, a tongue-tied, red-haired university student and his garrulous, red-haired younger brother. She was growing into a real lady.

Daniel himself was seated at the head of the table, with a marchioness on one side and a dowager viscountess on the other. The two were so busy pairing one's son with the other's daughter, they let him eat his mutton in peace. He was considered too old, too rakish, too set in his ways for the young chits, thank heavens, and thank the gaming hells, too. A few of the matrons did appraise him in speculation, for their older nieces or a spinster sister. At least he hoped they weren't eyeing him for themselves.

He breathed easier when the women left the men to enjoy their port and cigars, although he had firm instructions not to keep the gentlemen from the drawing room too long, and not to let any of the younger lads have too much to drink. Damn, now he was riding herd on a pack of schoolboys.

The night got worse as the young ladies tortured the pianoforte one after the other. Daniel pitied the poor boys who had to survive without the earl's brandy. The viscountess's daughter was dreadful; the knight's niece was worse. After the third girl had her turn, and Stynchcombe was snoring in the corner, Lady Cora announced an intermission for tea.

Daniel approached Miss Abbott. She was looking lovely and serene, her gloved hands in her lap, smiling across the room at the giggling cluster of Susanna and her new best friends.

"Your turn will come after tea, I suppose," Daniel said, taking a seat beside hers.

Her smile disappeared. "No, I do not play the pianoforte."

"Lud, you're not going to drag out a harp, are you?" There was nothing worse, in his opinion.

"No, I do not play at all. Your mother knows that. She'll not ask me."

"Come, this is not the place for modesty. I thought every chit knows one song by heart, for these occasions. It is expected of every properly educated female, I understand." If he had to suffer through the performances, then she did, too.

"I do not know how to play." Her lips were pursed; her hands were clenched together.

And Daniel's ear started to itch. He could swear he remembered her playing carols one Christmas, when Corie was young and the families were together, Mrs. Abbott proudly pulling her daughter forward to show off her talent.

"I have heard you."

If looks could kill, he'd have a hole between his eyes. "As a child."

"Come, even without practice you cannot be worse than that mop-haired chit who butchered the Bach piece. At least I think it was Bach. You'll be expected to perform at all the dinners and musical-evening parties, you know. Better to get the judging over with now."

She stood, so he had to, also. "Then I shall fail," she said, keeping her voice low so no one else could hear her angry words. "And be deemed unsuitable for a gentleman's bride. That is what you already believe, anyway."

Before he could interrupt, or deny her accusation, she went on, changing the course of the conversation: "Do not worry; my shortcomings will not reflect poorly on Susanna. She plays well, and with passion."

He'd heard his sister. "You mean fast and loud."

"And she will look beautiful doing so. Young Clarence has already asked to turn her pages. You do know he is in danger of being swept off his feet, don't you?"

"No, that is the port I let him drink while the men stayed in the dining room." Then Daniel returned to the topic at hand. "Really, you ought to take your turn and be done with it. It will look odd if you are the only female not stepping forward to perform."

"Not as odd as arguing with my host. People are

watching us, Mr. Stamfield, and neither of us will wish to give them anything to gossip about."

Something did not sit right with Daniel. "Then play."

She turned her back to the company and drew off her lace gloves. For an instant Daniel thought she was about to toss them at his face, an age-old challenge to a duel. Instead she held out her hands. The knuckles were swollen and misshapen, two fingers bent out of line. She hissed at him: "There, are you pleased now?"

No, he wasn't pleased. He felt like a clod again and cruel, to boot, especially when she replaced her gloves, whispered in Lady Cora's ear, and quietly left the room.

His mother said only that Corie had told them she'd had an accident. And yes, she used to play wondrously. Whatever happened did not stop her from needlework or gardening, only from baring her hands in public. "Foolish society frowns on any kind of physical imperfection, you know. We do not speak of it."

Some of them did, unfortunately. Blast, how many times did he have to apologize to the same woman?

Chapter Eleven

The new gowns started to arrive, along with seamstresses for the final fittings. The sister-in-law of the Countess of Royce got special treatment, especially when word went out that the Stamfields paid on time, unlike so many of their peers.

Invitations started to arrive, so many that Susanna's former governess, Miss Reynolds, was rehired as social secretary. Aside from Lady Royce's vast circle of friends, Lady Cora had been popular in her own youth, and had kept up correspondence with many acquaintances who wanted to welcome her and her charges to London.

Miss Stamfield was said to be pretty, pleasingly mannered, and well dowered, the perfect debutante, in other words. There was no title in the family, but the connections could not have been higher unless one counted royalty. Every matron with a younger son to see established sent cards for dinners, balls, or at-homes. Every mother of a less-favored miss sent invites, too, hoping some of Miss Stamfield's prospective beaux would attend their parties and dance with their wallflower daughters.

It was Lady Cora's goddaughter, however, who

drew the most interest. She had no title, either, but Abbott's only child was bound to come into a fortune. Word was, she was a beauty, too, if a bit standoffish. Some said she was shy; that was why her father kept her home. Others said she was selective; that was why she was unwed. The conjectures made her all the more attractive to gentlemen who enjoyed the hunt. They urged their mothers, aunts, or married mistresses to invite the female already wagered to be the new star in the social firmament.

Responses to Corie's letters came, also, from the schoolmates who were in Town and entertaining. They'd be delighted to renew friendships, especially if they had brothers.

With such a stack of invitations, the ladies would be busy beyond imagining. Lady Cora was satisfied. Susanna was ecstatic. Corie hoped the new gowns would give her the courage to face the stares and speculations. She knew everyone was asking how deep was her dowry, how high her resolve to find the perfect match.

Besides invitations, flowers arrived, too, with an apology from Daniel Stamfield—whom she'd been avoiding—and an invitation to ride with him and Susanna. Or drive in his curricle, whichever she wished. He promised not to be as clumsy with the reins as he was with his manners. The note was sweet, and Corie deemed his script neat for such a savage. She wondered if his new valet had composed and written it. She refused.

Not that she blamed him for all her troubles, just most of them: her unsightly hands, her unmarried state, her possibly ruinous history, her desperation to find a husband now. She'd blame the rainy and foggy

weather on him, too, if she could. It was enough to
know the dampness made her fingers ache.

She didn't toss the bouquet out the window, as she
wished she could Mr. Stamfield. The flowers were too
pretty and reminded her of her beloved gardens. Their
scent filled her room, hiding the stench of London's
air. Their purchaser was a donkey's derriere, but the
flowers were lovely. She kept them in a vase near her
bedside. His note went in the fire.

Instead of riding in the park with Susanna and her
brother, Corie drove with Lady Cora in the barouche,
pausing every few yards to be introduced to this dowager, that hostess, two of Almack's patronesses, and
any gentlemen who could scrape up an introduction.
Thus, when they finally attended their first ball, Corie
knew far more men than Susanna, and had nearly
every dance bespoken before the orchestra started,
which meant she did not have to suffer through a set
with Daniel Stamfield.

He'd been practicing, she knew, after Susanna
begged. The minx had even produced a few tears,
wailing he'd step on her new gown at the very first
dance of her very first ball unless he improved considerably.

At last they were ready for the Duchess of Haigh's
ball. The final preparations took almost the entire day
before, but Corie counted the hours worth it. She
knew she'd never looked better than in the gold silk
gown with the gold lace overskirt, her mother's diamonds, and her hair done up in a topknot held with
a gold filigree tiara, with curls framing her cheeks.
Those seemingly artless curls took hours to arrange,
but every minute was worth seeing Mr. Stamfield turn
speechless at her appearance when she followed his

mother and sister down the wide marble stairs of Royce House.

Garbled speech was nothing new for the great lummox. She couldn't imagine how Lady Cora was going to find a match for him, even if he was dressed to the nines and could execute the quadrille. Corie thanked heaven that was none of her concern, except that his mother's efforts might keep his broken nose and big feet out of Corie's affairs.

The man wanted to know all her secrets, to protect his family, he'd said. As if he'd bothered being the man of his house for the past two or three years when he was hell-raking in London. No, all he wanted was to torment Corie, she was sure, when his deep blue eyes looked into her soul—and found her wanting.

Tonight, though, his eyes widened, his mouth opened but no words came out, and Dobbson had to tap his shoulder to hand over his hat and gloves. He did not even speak when all three women thanked him for the flowers he'd sent.

The butler must have reminded him, Corie thought, uncharitably. And his valet must have consulted with Miss Reynolds and the ladies' maids as to styles and colors. And one of the footmen most likely got sent to the flower market to pick the blooms. But she thanked Mr. Stamfield, nonetheless.

Whoever had chosen the flowers did an excellent job. Lady Cora was wearing deep blue lutestring, to match her eyes and her sapphires. Her flowers were white gardenias, which she'd pinned to her gown. Susanna's nosegay was blue forget-me-nots, which her maid threaded through her upswept black hair with a blue ribbon that matched her eyes and her white gown's trim.

As for Corie, she hadn't expected him to order flowers for her at all, since she was no relative. She saw no reason to carry them, but her maid insisted that every other female would be wearing a floral token, so now her ensemble was complete. Tiny white rosebuds in a gold filigreed holder were pinned to her long gloves.

White for innocence? White for purity? She thanked him with a curtsy, but looked to see if he wore a sarcastic sneer. All she saw was admiration in his eyes. She also saw a true gentleman in a spotless tailcoat, white satin knee breeches, a respectable neckcloth fixed in place with a sapphire stickpin. She had to remind herself that clothes did not make the man . . . nor did pretty flowers. Flowery words might have swayed her a bit, but he ruined his gentlemanly pretense by stuttering, "I—I think we should st-stay home tonight. Uh, raining, don't you know."

"What, after all this effort?" his mother scoffed. "The footmen all have umbrellas. Furthermore, no one would get to go anywhere if they waited for a clear evening in London. Do not be absurd, Daniel."

He was worse than absurd. He was pitiable, wanting no other man to see the golden goddess. Give her a magic wand and wings and she'd be a fairy princess. Most likely she'd turn him into a toad. She already had him gasping and gaping like a pop-eyed frog too long out of water. He did not want her, but damn, the idea of another man touching those nearly bare shoulders, fondling those wayward curls, stepping on those gold-painted toes peeking from gold sandals, made his blood run cold.

Except he was sweating. Gads, how did they stand

it, this stifling heat, the close-packed crowds, the watery punch? He stepped behind a pillar holding a large fern, safe for the moment. He'd survived the receiving line, with some resplendent butler intoning their names as they entered and everyone staring at his companions. He wanted to smash a few noses at the haughty inspections, the counting of shillings, the calculating of odds of a grand alliance. And those were the women. As for the men's looks—dash it, he'd told his mother that Susanna's gown needed another inch or two.

Then came the first dance. He had not stepped on Susanna's skirts, knocked over the waiflike debutantes next to them in the set, or forgotten the steps. After that, Clarence claimed Sukey's next dance. He looked like a tailor's dummy to Daniel, but he was harmless in the crowd, and better the enemy you knew.

His mother was surrounded by jewel-laden ladies and manicured gentlemen, some of the latter widowers or old bachelors. She was laughing and blushing like a schoolgirl and accepting who knew what offers, but she did not seem to require Daniel's presence, thank goodness.

Miss Abbott was already on the floor with another partner. He could not see who it was in this damned crowd, despite his height. He had to step out from his safe lair—straight into the searing line of sight of the hostess. The duchess was looking like thunderbolts, as if he'd been caught spicing up the punch. Hell, he hadn't done that since . . . since the last time he'd been thrown out of one of the Haigh balls. He was a different man now, with females to protect. He stopped shaking in his shoes, proper, shiny ones at that.

"Your Grace." He bowed and almost said that the punch was better last time. "Lovely party."

"You, sir, are not dancing," Her Grace stated, as if he were not aware he was holding up a pillar. The swaying fern on top did not count as a partner, it seemed. All he could do was agree with the obvious.

"No, Your Grace." Daniel half expected the duchess to issue an edict, such as "Out" or "Off with your head." He hastily added, trying not to stammer, "I, that is, my mother and I. We're watching out for—"

For naught. Her Grace towed him to the gilt seats lining the walls, the whole while lecturing him on proper etiquette for a gentleman at a ball. The only reason he was included in the invitation, Her Grace informed him, was that his mother swore he was reformed.

Daniel promised himself a few words with his doting mother. He was too reformed to knock down a duchess, that was all. Hell, his fond parent could have warned him that any bachelor who showed he could move two legs in the correct steps was fair game. Unless tossing him to the wolves—the women with daughters—was Lady Cora's plan all along. "I'll go have a word thanking her now, shall I?"

No. The duchess held his arm with a grip that would have made a bear wrestler proud. Her Grace led him to a female in spectacles and too many pink ruffles that looked like they'd been collecting dust in this distant corner. Miss Thomlinson had seen—or squinted at—too many Seasons for her tittering chaperone to worry about his reputation. The featherheaded woman most likely wished some rake would ravish her charge in the garden, because then he'd have to marry the female, frills and all. Daniel felt a trail of sweat running between his shoulder blades. The whole fardling ball was a trap.

At least Miss Thomlinson was not a midget. She wasn't as tall as Miss Abbott, but he didn't feel like Polyphemus next to her. She knew more about steam engines and electricity than he cared to hear, but at least he did not have to make conversation. And she jerked her head to the right or left when he forgot the dance moves, so he didn't look the fool.

He bowed, saw her back to her chaperone, and bowed again before anyone could suggest a cooling walk through the French doors to the lantern-lit gardens. He made his escape to those same blessed doors before his hostess could pair him with another spinster in waiting.

He ducked outside, where a clutch of like-minded men stood on the terrace, claiming they needed the fresh air, but blowing smoke and draining glasses of punch a uniformed waiter passed out from his tray.

One of them wheezed, and Daniel saw Lord Morgan Babcock and his nephew. Jeremy held up a monogrammed flask and offered to make the punch more palatable. Daniel gulped the punch—at least it was wet and cold—but turned down the alcohol. He needed to keep his wits about him tonight in order to watch his sister, and watch his own back.

"I say, old man, how about an introduction to your family?" Jeremy said, slurring his words a bit.

Daniel said no. "You are already foxed."

"Nonsense, I'm just a bit on the go. So are most of the gents here tonight, and half the ladies. You don't think those biddies on the sidelines keep a spot of spirits in their reticules? Why else do so many of them fall asleep in those spindly chairs? By the time the duchess trots out the champagne, even the shyest debutante will be babbling like a brook. How do you think so many engagements are made at these affairs? The little darlings get compromised, that's how."

Daniel's escort duty suddenly got harder than guarding the supply lines against French scouts, Spanish spies, and starving peasants. Maybe he should have a drink, a real drink, after all.

"Later," he told Babcock, and himself. He took a step back to the doorway, where he could see over most of the heads to the dance floor. If Susanna was dancing, she was safe. If his mother was surrounded by middle-aged Romeos, she was safe. Where the deuce was Miss Abbott? Not that she was his responsibility, precisely. He almost went back to the ballroom when Babcock's words penetrated his addled wits.

"Everyone is talking about the Stamfield women, you know. I'd get Her Grace to make the introductions, but she'll snare me for one of her debutantes."

Daniel doubted that. Not even the duchess was desperate enough to let a womanizer like Babcock dance with any of the susceptible young misses. Even females like Miss Thomlinson deserved better.

"So will you make me known to the ladies?"

Daniel would not. He grabbed Jeremy by his padded shoulders and spun the smaller man around. "If you so much as speak to my baby sister, I will squash you like a bug."

Jeremy brushed his clothing back into place. "Here, now, all I want is an introduction to the other gal, the gilded lily. Not even a relative of yours, what? Every other heiress or beauty has all her dances already spoken for, ages ago. Miss Abbott might have a waltz free, since she's so recently come to Town."

A waltz? Daniel vowed he'd see Babcock in Hades before he let the dirty dish have that intimate dance with his mother's goddaughter. Everyone knew the waltz was nothing but a standing seduction, set to music.

Jeremy was going on, pressing for an introduction. "I won't have a better chance, not once all the hunters catch her scent."

It was lilacs. Daniel did not know if Miss Abbott's card was full. He should know those things, he thought, if he was in charge. Was he in charge of the female? Could he actually refuse to allow a rake to dance with her? No, he was not her father, and not like her father. And she'd be furious at him, again.

He looked into the ballroom and thought he saw a woman in a gold gown float by. "Sorry to disappoint you, but the lady is dancing."

"She'll have to return to your mother's side when the music stops. I'll have a few minutes before her next partner claims her."

"I'd like an introduction, also," Lord Morgan said. "And to your lady mother, of course. No harm intended to either lady, you understand. Paying respects, is all. Gentlemen, you know."

Did he know that? Daniel doubted any man could be trusted around Miss Abbott. Hell, he did not even know if Miss Abbott could be trusted.

Lord Morgan was going on: "You might as well perform the service, my boy. We're bound to meet the ladies sooner or later at one ball or another. I'm even thinking of stopping in at Almack's next week. See if anything appeals to me."

Like pastries in a shop window? Daniel grimaced at the image and at Lord Morgan's tobacco-stained lips, but he knew the way of this world, and he knew he couldn't refuse.

He couldn't leave after those introductions, either, when Jeremy started spouting nonsense about Miss Abbott's beauty. Golden sunrise, his big foot! The man hadn't seen a sunrise in ten years.

Then Lord Morgan recalled meeting Lady Cora years ago, and told her she was more handsome today. All the other gallants gathered around them vied for a dance, a smile, to fetch a cool drink, to wave a fan, to recite bad poetry. Hell, half the cabbageheads were declaring Corie—Miss Abbott, that is—had stolen their hearts with her grace and beauty and dignity and intelligence. Et cetera, ad nauseam.

Worst of all, Daniel felt, was he couldn't claim they had to leave the ball because of a rash. He wasn't feeling the least itchy. They all spoke the truth.

Chapter Twelve

Corie's current partner had possibilities. He dressed well, danced well, and spoke well on varied learned subjects. One of those interesting topics was his estate in Cornwall, which was as far from her father as Corie could hope to get. She thought he was in his forties, and knew he was unmarried. Other than that, she'd ask Lady Cora about his prospects. If her godmother did not know his income to the shilling, his past indiscretions, and his future intentions, then Dobbson would, in the morning. For now, all Corie had to do was recall the gentleman's name and reply to his request to call at Royce House. There was a fraught line between looking too eager, which could make a bachelor skittish, and acting sophisticated and blasé, which might discourage him. She settled on needing to ask Lady Cora if they were receiving.

On the way to where her godmother was holding court, Corie spied one dark head above the rest. She stopped in her tracks. "Would you mind escorting me to the refreshments room? I'd like something cool before the next dance."

No, she would not prefer a walk out to the fresher air of the gardens. She was not that warm, not that

eager. She had no intention of causing gossip or welcoming physical advances. Or letting her potential
suitor speak to Daniel Stamfield.

Daniel was torn. Should he follow Corie to whatever trysting spot that cad Chadwick had found, or
stay and defend his mother and sister from the Babcocks and the rest of the horde of admirers Lady Cora
and Susanna had amassed? Granted, some of the
swains were waiting for Miss Abbott's return, but Susanna had a following of her own, including Clarence
Haversmith. Susanna had adopted the dolt, it seemed,
the way she would a lost puppy.

Daniel's mother had two older noblemen sitting on
the spindly chairs to either side of her. One had a
cane, one had a hearing trumpet, but together they
owned half the land in Lincolnshire. Other slightly
younger, slightly less-highly titled gentlemen of a certain age and dignity were not far off. Lord Morgan
had to be content with leaning on his nephew and
waiting for his turn at a seat near the wealthy, well-
placed widow.

Daniel decided his relatives were safe enough, but
Miss Abbott couldn't know what a practiced seducer
Lord Chadwick was. The scholarly fellow appeared
dull as ditch water, but he kept a string of expensive
mistresses at a love nest in Kensington. Or maybe
the determined female did know of Chadwick's lustful
nature and hoped to wrest a proposal out of him that
way, down some secluded garden path where they just
might happen to be seen.

Chadwick was not a good choice, Daniel told himself. Aside from his mistresses, the man was more than

twice Corie's age, was boringly bookish, and had buried two wives already.

Daniel started to cross the dance floor, keeping a wary watch for the duchess, but he spotted Corie and the viscount coming back from the refreshments room. Then he had to pretend he wasn't on the lookout for them, so he decided to fetch himself another cup of punch, as dull as it was.

Daniel thought he'd bring a cup back for Miss Thomlinson, too, while he was at it. No one else was going to, that was for certain. The space around her chair was filled with nothing but disappointment.

Just as he was about to find the woman and her chaperone, both of his hands full, the orchestra started up the next dance, a waltz. Zeus, he'd almost walked right into the pitfall. If he showed up at Miss Thomlinson's side now, he'd have to ask her to dance. There was scant chance of another fellow bespeaking the set before him. Two dances with the same female in one night, and one of them a waltz? He'd be expected to declare himself before the end of the evening.

He declared himself suddenly parched and so he drank both cups of overly sweet punch and headed back to his family.

Susanna was wheedling permission to waltz, but his mother was having none of it. If such a young girl waltzed without permission from one of the patronesses of Almack's, that holiest of holy shrines to manners and the matchmaking art, she'd be barred from its sacred precincts. Which meant, in those rarefied circles, social death to a debutante.

The rules were not as strict for women past their first blush, but Corie said she was just as happy to sit the dance out . . . until she saw Daniel Stamfield headed toward them. She looked to Lady Cora for approval and, at her nod, accepted the first gentleman she saw. She placed her hand on Mr. Jeremy Babcock's slightly frayed coat sleeve and let him lead her out.

Daniel almost coughed up the insipid punch at the sight. Jeremy winked at him over Miss Abbott's mostly bare shoulder as he whisked her into the first turn on the less-crowded dance floor. She followed his lead gracefully, her gold skirts swirling around her legs, around Jeremy's legs. Daniel cursed.

"What the devil were you about," he whispered into his mother's ear, "letting Miss Abbott go off with Babcock, for a waltz, no less?"

"Why, dear, I thought he was a friend of yours."

"Exactly. That should have told you he was an unsuitable partner. No friend of mine is proper company. They all drink and gamble and associate with fast women. Besides, Babcock needs a wealthy bride."

"Every man does, dear, even the rich ones. Why don't you find some nice heiress to dance with yourself?" She tried to dismiss him so she could go back to flirting with her aged beaux. Lord Morgan appeared to have all his teeth, at any rate.

Daniel thought about the spectacled female he'd narrowly escaped, then thought he'd find the cardroom until the ladies were ready to leave. He was on his way, knowing the duke was bound to provide brandy and gaming for his own cronies somewhere in this huge pile.

Oh hell, the Duchess of Haigh was headed in his direction. He was too large to hide behind his mother, too slow to dive out the window, too bound to the truth to claim a sudden indisposition, although all that punch was not sitting kindly in his stomach.

The dragon was scowling at his mother this time, though, so he stayed where he was, more out of curiosity than loyalty. His mother had gotten them into this wasp nest; she could get them out. Then he'd go find the necessary.

Bravery seemed in short supply among her new suitors, and Susanna's, too. Half the gentlemen faded away, rather than confront the Gargoyle of Grosvenor Square. Her Grace was a higher stickler than any on the Almack's committee, and as loud in her righteousness as a cathedral bell. The oldster with the ear trumpet led the one with the cane as fast as they could go. Lord Morgan took one of the vacant seats, only because he was wheezing too hard to rush away.

One side of the duchess's upper lip curled when she spied the aging rake, but she turned to address Lady Cora. "A word, my dear?"

Daniel's mother nodded graciously, for no one refused a duchess, and Susanna quickly relinquished her seat.

"Word has reached me of a disturbing nature," Her Grace began, once she had adjusted her shawl and her skirts and her ostrich-plume headdress.

Both Lady Cora and Susanna frowned in Daniel's direction. He shrugged his innocence.

"I do not refer to the jackanapes this time. Tonight I am concerned about Miss Abbott."

Daniel looked over to make sure Babcock had not lured his mother's goddaughter out to the darkness. No, they were still waltzing and chatting companionably, the bounder.

The duchess leaned closer to Lady Cora. "Not that I put credence to idle gossip, you know."

Daniel knew nothing of the kind. Her Grace was as big a scandalmonger as any *on-dit* columnist. She considered it her duty to unveil society's sinners. That was why her invitations were so coveted. One of her cards meant the recipient had passed muster.

She sniffed, reminding Daniel of a hound on the scent, except no hound had such a beak of a snout. "My husband's cousin's valet used to be in the employ of a certain Sir Neville."

Now Daniel wished he'd made his escape when he could. Or that he still had a cup of punch to accidentally spill on the old harridan, sending her to the ladies' retiring room before she could say another word.

"Sir Neville?" his mother asked, her brow wrinkled. "Is he still alive? Why would anyone listen to anything that man said? His brain was corrupt, when he still had the use of it."

Lord Morgan, bless him, added, "Don't see why anyone would hire his valet, anyway. Fellow might be as diseased as his master."

The duchess waved her fat, jeweled fingers, brushing both of their interruptions aside. "Haigh's cousin thought Miss Abbott's name sounded familiar when he looked over the guest list."

"Of course it is familiar," Lady Cora acknowledged. "Squire Abbott used to be a member of the Commons from our borough."

"Argued with his own party, he did," Lord Morgan said. "Neither the Whigs nor the Tories wanted him on their side of the aisle."

"I am not speaking politics, sir." Nor, the duchess made clear by turning her back, was she speaking to an asthmatic old sot. "Miss Abbott's name came up in reference to an unfortunate incident several years ago, Lady Cora, before Sir Neville was, ah, incapacitated."

"Locked up, I heard, for going at his physician with a meat cleaver," Lord Chadwick muttered, drawing the duchess's wrath at yet another interruption to her inquisition. Chadwick stepped back, but not out of hearing. He was too interested in listening to disclosures about Miss Abbott's past.

"Yes?" Lady Cora asked in calm, almost bored tones. Only Daniel noticed her fan waving faster. "What unfortunate incident might that be?"

"One that, if true, proves your protégée not the type of female who should be mixing with genteel company."

"My goddaughter is everything admirable."

Chadwick agreed, but not nearly as vehemently as he might have moments ago.

"Are the stories true?" Her Grace demanded. She had other ladies to browbeat, other young misses to bring to tears, other miscreants to cast out of her house.

"I told you," Lord Morgan whispered to Daniel, but not low enough for the others to miss. "Everyone will recall sooner or later that Abbott tried to marry his daughter off to that pox-ridden reprobate."

"Oh," Lady Cora said. "That story. Yes, it is regrettably true. I am certain Squire Abbott no longer holds the misguided notion that his daughter is no different from one of his prize sows, to be offered to the highest bidder."

"Not that story." The duchess curled her lip and sniffed again, both. She'd seen her own daughters wed advantageously, if not with affection. "Such alliances are commonplace. I do not hold with this modern method of letting a silly goose, that is, a school-yard miss, choose her own mate, no more than Haigh would let his milk cows select the bull to—" She looked at Susanna, who had edged closer so as not to miss a single word.

"But that is not for polite company, either. No, Haigh's cousin mentioned to me—and to a few close friends, I suppose, as the valet might have done, also—that Miss Abbott ran off rather than wed the old goat, that is, Sir Neville. If so, Miss Corisande Abbott is no better than she ought to be."

Daniel was wondering how best to murder the duke's cousin. The valet could be impressed into the navy. Her Grace could—

"She did run off," Lady Cora blandly admitted, languidly waving her fan as if bored by the topic. "As any woman with two wits to rub together would have."

"But with a soldier, my dear. With a soldier."

A crowd had gathered around them, knowing the duchess's conversations were often tastier than the food she served. A woman gasped. "A common soldier?"

Her Grace frowned the female into silence. "That is not relevant."

Daniel was ready to grab his mother's hand, sling his sister over his shoulder, and head for the exit, or the East Indies. Matters grew worse with each sentence the duchess proclaimed, louder than Daniel's thudding heart.

"They say she fled to Gretna with her soldier lover, and your own son rode to bring her back. Is that true?"

Daniel held his breath. Now he knew how the captured French officers must have felt when they faced him and his cousin Rex: Death would be an easier fate.

Susanna looked confused.

Lady Cora's eyelid twitched. Then she smiled and said loudly and distinctly, so everyone nearby could hear, "Dear Corisande did leave her father's house rather than marry that wretched old rake. She came to me, her beloved mother's best friend, just as she ought. I do believe a courteous young man escorted her, to ensure her safety. She was barely seventeen at the time, after all, too young to travel even a short distance unaccompanied. Far too young to marry a man so much older than herself, as you may rest assured I told Squire Abbott." She touched her eye, as if in thought. "Now that you mention it, I recall a scarlet coat. A viscount's son, if I remember correctly."

Susanna rose to the occasion, seconding her mother, defending her friend. "She shared my bedchamber that night and kept me awake with her weeping."

Daniel could feel the itch start at his toes and spread up his legs. It was going to reach his nethers in another three seconds.

In two seconds the duchess turned to him. "Did you or did you not ride with Abbott to bring back the lovers?"

He gulped and said, "I did ride north with him." Daniel prayed that the truth would satisfy the gorgon and delay the spread of the rash. "He was too incensed to listen to reason. I hoped his anger would cool before he spoke to his daughter."

"Nasty temper, that chap, don't you know. Why, I remember one time when a footman at White's dropped a dish and he—"

Her Grace swatted Lord Morgan with her lorgnette, sending him into a paroxysm of wheezing. She waited for Daniel to continue.

He had not intended to add any more rash, that is, revelations. Her Grace appeared ready to wait for doomsday, which was not far off as Daniel saw it. He chose his words carefully: "Both Abbott and Sir Neville had a change of heart when they realized how unhappy the bride must have been, to go to such lengths. Miss Abbott was back at her own home the next morning."

The duchess looked from one Stamfield to the other. "They say your family honors the truth above all things."

Now, that was one statement Daniel could gladly affirm. "That is true. Royce family motto and all that. My cousin Rex even named his dog Verity."

"And the gal is better off, I say," Lord Morgan wheezed, although no one asked him.

Daniel would have given the old tosspot Lady Cora's hand on the spot, he was so grateful. Not grateful enough to hand him Miss Abbott, of course.

"And brave," Clarence found the courage to say. He could have Susanna.

"She'll make some man a deuced fine wife," Lord Chadwick added. He could go to hell.

The duchess pasted on a yellow-toothed smile and heaved her considerable bulk out of the chair, which meant everyone else had to rise to their feet, also, and bow and curtsy and try to hide their relief at her leaving. "Then I shall put an immediate end to the gossip and continue to welcome Miss Abbott into society. A lovely girl, as you say. Abbott's heir, is she? That rather expensive cousin of my lord's is still unwed. I shall introduce them."

She sailed off to save society from another encroachment of indecency.

Daniel's mother's eyelid had developed a tic. Susanna's nose was suddenly dripping. And Daniel needed to find a private place to scratch his private parts.

But they'd survived.

Chapter Thirteen

"May we leave now, Mother?"

"Not until after the supper, which should be soon after this dance. We shall *not* retreat."

They all watched Corie return to them with one of the worst rakes in London, which could not be doing her reputation any good amid the gossip.

Lady Cora sent Daniel a look of censure. He sent her one back. She was supposed to be the chaperone, wasn't she?

Lord Morgan beamed. Maybe his impoverished nevvy had a chance at the heiress if the starched-up sticklers wouldn't try. Then Jeremy would stop asking for loans.

Susanna frowned. Mr. Babcock was far more dashing than any of her own suitors, and no such interesting, dangerous gentleman was going to look at her if she kept blowing her nose.

Corie knew something was wrong by the whispers behind her back and the stares and the silence as Jeremy Babcock led her to Lady Cora's seat. Daniel Stamfield was scowling at her, which was nothing out of the ordinary, but she had no choice except to return to his mother's side. Supper was announced and she did not wish to sit with Mr. Babcock, whose conversation was slightly warm, and who'd tried to hold her too close during the waltz.

Once in Lady Cora's circle, Corie noticed fewer gentlemen were hovering nearby, and fewer still were waiting to ask for dances. Lady Cora's left eyelid was fluttering like a butterfly's wing, Susanna was borrowing her mother's handkerchief, and Daniel was grimacing, shifting his weight from foot to foot as if his last partner had stepped on his toes, instead of the other way around.

"Is something wrong?" Corie asked.

"Nothing."

"Not a thing."

"What could be wrong?"

Then all three of them groaned at once. Susanna sneezed, Lady Cora held her hand over her eyes, and Daniel stepped behind his mother's chair.

"Just a bit of old rubbish," the bit of old rubbish called Lord Morgan said. "All resolved now. May I escort you into supper, Miss Abbott?"

They claimed a large table in the corner and Lady Cora demanded champagne. "Now. A lot of it."

Clarence, Jeremy, and Lord Chadwick, who had attached himself to their party, left to fill plates for the ladies. Daniel sat when the women did, and thanked heaven for the trailing tablecloth that hid his frantic scratching.

Lord Morgan asked the waiter with the champagne to fill a plate for him. "Oysters if you've got them." Then he held up his glass in a toast. "To weathering the storm."

"What storm?" Corie sipped her wine but still wanted to know what had her friends and Stamfield so overset.

"Later," was all her godmother said, emptying her own glass in one long swallow. Then she smiled for Corie, albeit with effort, it seemed. "Are you enjoying yourself, my dear?"

"Prodigiously, ma'am. I cannot thank you enough for bringing me to London with you and Susanna."

While Miss Abbott unknowingly expounded on her gratitude for landing them all in the bumble broth, Daniel stood. He felt able to leave the tablecloth's concealment without embarrassing himself or his mother, or bringing Duchess Haigh's wrath down upon them again. He did not feel able to sit near Miss Abbott without putting his hands around her throat and—well, he was not entirely sure what he would do with the wretched woman once he had her, but he doubted Her Grace would approve. Besides, he was hungry. Dinner at home had been a hasty affair, with the females anxious about their gowns and their hair. Ninnies, all of them, he thought, worrying about their appearances more than their appetites. Hell, they should have been worrying about some maggot's former valet.

As he went to the long serving tables to make his selections, he passed Miss Thomlinson and her duenna on line. The younger woman's plate held one lobster patty, two asparagus spears, and a roll. The older one's was filled, as was her bulging reticule. A poor relation, he guessed, or a widow fallen on hard enough times to hire herself out as a paid companion. He filled two plates, choosing a bit of everything as if he did not know what his mother or sister enjoyed, then invited the strangers to share his family's table.

"Too kind," the duenna gushed. Miss Thomlinson took another roll.

"No, sit there, next to Lord Chadwick," he told the spectacled miss when they returned to the table in the corner and he'd made introductions. "The two of you have much in common."

Daniel set both brimming plates in front of his place and started to eat. His mother, nearly recovered by now, raised one nontwitching eyebrow and whispered to him, "I thought you did not approve of matchmaking."

He jerked his head toward Corie. "More like unmaking a mismatch. Chadwick would bore her to death."

Corie did not seem to notice the defection of her favored suitor, as Jeremy Babcock had her laughing and tasting the delicacies he'd chosen for her.

"You'll have to do something about that one, next," Lady Cora said from behind her napkin. "Abbott would never release her dowry to such a gambler as Babcock. And the rogue would make dear Corie's life a misery with his wild ways."

"You do not think she has enough sense to see through him?"

"Of course I do. It is your friend I do not trust to take no for an answer."

Which ruined Daniel's appetite after all.

They left the ball soon afterward, Lady Cora pressing her hand over her eye and claiming a headache. She fell asleep in the carriage, more likely from all the champagne than the pain. Susanna yawned and chose her bed over taking tea with Corie and Daniel, who was still hungry.

Dobbson wheeled in the tea cart and stood nearby, waiting to hear how the evening went, Daniel supposed, and why it ended so early.

"That will be all," Daniel said. He was not about to make excuses to the puffed-up servant, not when he had to think of how to tell Corie of the near disaster.

She poured out the tea. She performed the ritual as gracefully as his mother, he noted, without spilling a drop or clattering a spoon. Crooked fingers did not hinder her perfect handling of the delicate china cups. "Sugar?"

"Please." He went to the sideboard and lifted a cut-glass decanter. He recalled the last time he'd taken tea alone with her and asked, "Would you like a dash of brandy in yours?"

"Will I need it to hear what happened at the ball?" He poured a generous amount into her cup.

Between toast fingers with jam, macaroons, and several slices of poppy seed cake—none of which was as enticing as the uneaten tidbits he'd left on his plate at Haigh House—he told her about the valet, the Haigh cousin, and the duchess. Then he told her what had been said, in case she had to repeat it for anyone else. They should all tell the same story, of course.

She'd gone pale and her lower lip trembled. What was the matter with women, that at the first sign of a crisis, even if the catastrophe was averted, they turned into quivering watering pots? First his mother and her eye twinge, then Susanna and her stuffy nose. Now Corie. He'd hoped she was made of sterner stuff, because sure as Hades he wasn't. He poured another measure of brandy into his own cup.

"You aren't going to cry again, are you?"

She shook her head no, which let one tear fall. "All of you did that? You lied for me?"

"We couldn't tell the truth, now, could we?"

"But no one in your family ever lies."

"We do now, I suppose, although I cannot say I enjoyed the experience."

"I imagine it must have rubbed you wrong, having to compromise your beliefs to defend me."

He hoped she never knew how much. "Well, let us hope the necessity never again arises."

She brushed at her wet cheek and stared into her cup, as if trying to read her future there. "I cannot ever repay you for what you've done."

He moved to the sofa where she sat. "We had to do it, you know. We'd all have been tossed out on our ears, otherwise."

"No, only I would have been ostracized. Your family would have been welcomed back without me."

"I doubt my mother would have gone anywhere you weren't welcome. Or Susanna."

"They are good friends. Loyal." She fumbled in her reticule, but she'd loaned her handkerchief to Susanna.

Daniel handed her his, the one Deauville insisted he carry. Now he knew why.

She dabbed at her eyes. "As you are loyal to your family. I do appreciate your sacrifice."

"Don't think of that. It was no great deal." The rash was almost gone by now. A cool bath, perhaps with oatmeal in it, would cure the rest. Deauville might wonder, but he valued his position too well to ask questions. Daniel need only say that the gritty bath was for his skin, and let the man think he was primping for tomorrow.

Devil take it, tomorrow. They still had to face the public, after tonight.

"Will you ride with me in the morning?" he asked. "You ought to be seen out and about, not in hiding as if you had something to be ashamed of. And you won't have to face any of the curious quizzes if you are not home. We'll have a groom along for propriety, of course. And Susanna if she wishes."

"She seemed to be coming down with something."

Some reason to leave Haigh House, Daniel suspected. "She'll be fine."

"Then yes, a ride would be lovely, far better than waiting for callers to ask awkward questions. That is, if you are not busy."

"No, I like a ride in the morning when the park isn't so crowded." And he had no intention of facing his mother's guests and the ladies' admirers any sooner than he had to. Which reminded him: "I'd like to say a word or two about Jeremy Babcock."

She sat back on the cushions, more relaxed now. "A charming gentleman."

"Too charming, if you ask me. He needs money, badly. The devil goes through it like a hot knife through butter."

"Yes, I guessed that. He wouldn't be in the ballroom if he was not looking for a rich wife, would he? He'd be in the cardroom with the other men, the husbands and fathers and confirmed bachelors."

Which was where Daniel was going to be at every ball he had to attend from now on, but not Babcock. "No, he'd be at some low gambling den with higher stakes, trying to stave off his creditors with a big win."

"I suspected such was the case. But he is an amusing companion, and your friend."

"He might be my friend, more like a companion at cards, but I do not intend to marry him."

"Neither do I."

Relieved, Daniel sat back, too, with his arm resting on the top of the sofa. If he reached a little farther, he could just touch one of the trailing curls at her neck. He brought his hand back to his side, where it was safer. "Chadwick?"

She did not misunderstand his question. "I fear I am not learned enough for his lordship. Listening to him and Miss Thomlinson conversing made me realize how inadequate my education was. A gentleman might not care that his wife's brain is not as well developed as his, but I'd hate feeling so inferior to my own husband."

"And bored."

She smiled for the first time. "And bored."

Daniel's hand twitched to touch that nearest curl. Damn, his mother's affliction must be contagious. Forgetting his own intentions to see the women settled within a few weeks, he said, "Ah well, it is early days yet to be thinking of marriage."

She looked away. "Unless the whispers continue."

He could not deny the possibility. Too many people had heard the rumors. That cousin of Haigh's could dine out for days on what he knew. No one wanted the mother of his children to be steeped in scandal. "Have you other prospects? A gentleman back home? Perhaps someone your father refused in the past? I could see about improving his circumstances, if that would help."

Corie shook her head, then took the necklace from around her neck. "These are my only prospects." The diamonds were hers from her mother, not part of her

father's estate. He'd kept them in the vault and re-
leased them only when Lady Cora insisted Corie
needed the jewels to make a good impression, meaning she needed them to attract a wealthy man. Corie
worried her father would give them to the Rivendale
woman if he married her. Her father, she knew, worried she'd use the money the gems could bring to run
away, which was exactly what she intended to do if
she did not find a husband.

"I'll sell these, for one thing, and my pearls. I have
a few other trinkets your mother has given me over
the years. Then I will find a little cottage or something.
Or a position if the jewelry does not fetch enough
money. Would you consider taking them to be ap-
praised, so I know how much money I might expect? I
fear women do not get treated as fairly as gentlemen."

She handed the heavy necklace to Daniel, and
started to take off the earbobs and the bracelet.

The necklace still felt warm from her skin, and at
first he thought that was why his fingertips tingled. He
jiggled it in his hand, but the sensation remained.

"These are yours, you say?"

"Yes, my mother's gift from her own father."

The prickle was strange, and growing stronger. He
didn't think a rash was coming on, but something felt
distinctly wrong. He handed the diamonds back. "You
keep them for now. I'll take care of it if there is a
need."

His fingers brushed hers as he handed the necklace
over. Now, that tingle felt different. And a lot better.

They rode in the morning, Susanna and Clarence,
too. Daniel was correct in thinking not many members
of the beau monde were out and about so early, but

enough gentlemen were exercising their cattle. They'd go home to their wives and daughters and report seeing the young ladies from Royce House in elegant new habits, on highbred new horses, gaily welcoming the new day. Daniel sat proudly on Gideon's wide back. He'd picked the horses. He'd paid for the gowns. He'd brought a smile to Miss Abbott's beautiful face.

When they got home, the drawing room was filled with flowers and callers, so society had accepted their story. Miss Corisande Abbott was still an eligible heiress. She was still to be wooed.

If Daniel was not quite as relieved as the ladies, it was because he didn't want to keep tripping over bacon-brained mooncalves and their bouquets. That was what he told himself, anyway.

Morning calls actually took place in the afternoon, for no lady was expected to rise before noon after a night of partygoing. A gentleman was expected to visit each lady he'd danced with, which made no sense to Daniel. He said thank you, didn't he? But his mother, his sister, and his valet all reminded him of the foolish convention, so he sent a bouquet to Miss Thomlinson, along with a note from his mother inviting the dowdy bluestocking to go shopping with her and Susanna. The spinster needed a stylish gown far more than she needed a galumphing gentleman in her drawing room. She also needed friends.

Well satisfied with the day's work, Daniel took himself off to practice his boxing techniques. With all those suitors in the house, he might need them.

Chapter Fourteen

Corie felt Daniel did not understand. He'd given back the diamonds as if they were nothing, like one might give a child a pat on the head and say, "There, there. Everything will be fine." Like they'd tried to tell her nothing was wrong when Duchess Haigh accused her of being a wanton.

Daniel Stamfield had shown her a great deal of kindness since then. He acted for his mother's sake; Corie did not fool herself into thinking he had any other motive than seeing his kin happy, and happily out of his vicinity. He was still a thickheaded dolt.

He actually believed she could, and should, simply go home to her father if her plans did not work out, if no gentleman came up to scratch. Susanna could. She'd always be welcome at her family home, no matter the scandal, no matter if her needs and desires were not what her mother or brother shared.

Just look at the way Mr. Stamfield accepted Clarence Haversmith in their midst, although he obviously disapproved of the very young man for his sister. And he went to all the sights Susanna wanted to see, despite being bored, except at the Royal Menagerie, the Egyptian Rooms, and the steam engine exhibition where Miss Thomlinson acted as guide. In fact, he was not half as bored as he pretended to be, Corie decided. He even enjoyed the opera, once everyone switched seats so Miss Thomlinson could translate for him.

Corie wondered why he was so obviously fostering a match between that woman and Lord Chadwick, when he admired her himself. Miss Thomlinson looked almost pretty, too, now that Lady Cora had taken her under her wing. Corie supposed Daniel would like a learned wife as little as she wanted to marry a scholarly gentleman. Although Corie told herself she would, if he was kind and made her an offer. So far, no one had.

Not that she lacked for partners at the dances. Lady Cora insisted Mr. Stamfield have the second dance with her at every ball they attended, after he led Susanna out for the first set, to show that Miss Corisande Abbott was under his family's care, and thus above suspicion. He was too busy watching his steps to make conversation during those dances, and afterward he disappeared into the cardroom, if there was one, but he'd done his duty.

His show of approval kept an uninterrupted flow of gentleman callers coming to their at-homes, plus offers for drives in the park, visits to the theater, and private dinners. She had plenty of those last invitations and refused them all, along with picnics, garden tours, and masquerades, anywhere Lady Cora was farther than a few feet away. She knew she had a reputation for being hard to please, but that was better than one for being easy to seduce.

She supposed those gentlemen on the lookout for a wife were waiting to see if there was any truth in the old rumors, despite the Stamfields' statements and shows of support. Or they were waiting for more young women to arrive for the height of the Season, to have the widest selection.

Lady Cora said not to worry; it was early days yet; Corie would find the perfect, loving match. If not this year, she said, then next year.

She did not understand, either.

Corie could not go home. Her father had forbidden her to go to London, relenting only when Lady Cora insisted. Corie had accepted against his wishes. He'd make her pay for her disobedience, one way or another. She was not going to give him the chance. She'd learned years ago never to cross the squire's will.

She'd rent a room in a boardinghouse attic before going back to Abbott Grange. She'd mop floors in the boardinghouse, too, if she had to, until she came of age and claimed her portion from her mother's settlements. She thought about asking Daniel to recommend a solicitor for her, to read those documents, to verify the terms of her dowry, and what recourse she had if her father refused permission for her to wed whichever man she chose.

Then she'd have to explain too much that was too shameful. Besides, Mr. Stamfield was doing enough on her behalf, suffering through those dances, taking her for rides. And as with the diamonds, he'd merely tell her not to worry. She wished he could tell her how to accomplish that.

Meanwhile, she was going to try to enjoy herself. The flowers and compliments were lovely, but the chance to experience new things, meet new people, see plays and paintings she had only read about—that was almost worth the fears. Reestablishing friendships with old schoolmates was delightful, even if one of their husbands tried to corner her in a dark hallway, and another had two screaming infants hanging on her skirts. They'd be no help in her dilemma.

She needed a husband, plain and simple. Naturally, Corie wanted one who was comely and bright, but she'd take what she could get. She vowed to be more agreeable to every clumsy dance partner, every incompetent whip, every gentleman with wayward thoughts and roving hands. Except Jeremy Babcock. He might be a friend of Mr. Stamfield's, and in need of a wife's dowry, but she could not trust him.

No one else could, either, it seemed.

"Daniel, Clarence wishes to speak to you. I suppose I should be calling him Mr. Haversmith."

Daniel looked up from his correspondence, glad for the interruption, but not the cause. "Why should you? You've been 'Sukey' and 'Clarence' since the day you met, and why Mother permits that is beyond me. And the answer is no, so I do not need to talk to the gudgeon. Now go away and leave me to the accounts." Then he noticed Miss Abbott in the doorway and lost the use of his tongue and his wits, as usual with the confounded woman.

"Uh, begging your pardon, Miss Abbott. I did not see you at first." In a bright yellow gown? "Didn't mean to shoo you out, too. That is, I was speaking to my sister. Not that it's a private talk, or anything."

Corie still hovered at the doorway, waiting to see if Susanna was ready to return to the parlor.

She was not. She marched herself closer to her brother's desk in the library and pounded it with her fist. "How do you know what he wants to say?"

Daniel sighed. "Because I have had the same conversation with scores of gentlemen already who want my permission to pay their addresses. No, I will not let any of them offer for you, Miss Abbott, or, heaven help me, Mother."

Corie gasped and came closer, too. "You have been turning gentlemen down on my behalf?"

"Of course I have. Not one of them is a serious suitor, except for your money. I told them I would not entertain any proposals until you have appeared at Almack's in two weeks. By then, you might know which gentleman you prefer. It is absurd to think you'd make a choice on a single waltz. Or who knows? You might fall head over heels at Almack's. Love at first sight and all that rot."

"Is that what you are waiting for before choosing a bride," Susanna asked, "a lightning stroke?"

"No, I am waiting for you to become another man's headache."

Now Corie felt like pounding something, too, but not the desk. That wasn't as hard as Daniel Stamfield's thick skull. "That's outrageous."

"I think so, too. I thought I'd have this whole mare's nest cleaned up by now, but I've come to see it takes a bit more thought."

"But you . . . you are deciding for me? For us?"

"No such thing. I'm only giving you all a bit of breathing room. You wouldn't want chaps falling to one knee everywhere you went. Embarrassing for everyone, that's what my mother said. And dangerous. Someone might trip over one of the moonlings."

"You already said no?"

"I said they could call again after Almack's. You'll tell me which chap you want, and I'll take him aside and ask his intentions. After Dobbson and Deauville confer with his servants about his finances and his character, of course. They both assure me that's how it's done."

Corie collapsed onto a nearby chair, overwhelmed.

Daniel turned toward his sister. "I can't say I'd be best pleased if you settled on Clarence, though, puss."

"Don't be silly, Daniel. I am not going to marry anyone yet. Or Clarence ever. But you think to have us betrothed in two weeks? Why, I intend to dance every dance with every available gentleman, until there are no more."

Daniel groaned. "That could take months!"

She grinned at him. "You might have to purchase a new pair of evening shoes. Deauville will have you carrying a quizzing glass yet. Don't you think he'd look magnificent, Corie?"

Corie thought he looked like a monster, with his black hair falling over his forehead, sitting in his shirt-sleeves like some stone giant behind his vast desk. Who did he think he was, discouraging her suitors before she had a chance to weigh them? What if the cabbageheads were like him, wanting to settle on a bride and go back to their comfortable lives in two weeks? Two weeks could see them select a different woman, one who did not require courting or cotillions. The newspapers were already full of betrothal announcements. Oh, how she hated Daniel Stamfield. The man was determined to ruin her life!

She opened her mouth to tell the ogre what she thought of his high-handed, overbearing, idiotic ways, but Susanna started first.

"So will you speak with Clarence? He is in a fret, and I did not know what to tell him. I think he is embarrassed to ask you, so I said I would."

"If his problem is that personal, he should speak to a clergyman, or a physician. I warned him to stay away from the orange sellers at Drury Lane."

"Daniel, it is nothing like that!"

"Very well, send him in. I am sick of going over the accounts and the reports from Stamfield, anyway. Mother is better at it than I am, but she and that governess of yours, Susanna—what is her name? Miss Reynolds?—are always gadding about the shops and museums with Lord Morgan. And no, I will not accept an offer from him yet, either."

"I should hope not," Susanna said, wrinkling her nose. "His linen is not clean and he smells of smoke. And he wheezes."

Daniel shrugged. "Mother seems to enjoy his company. There's no accounting for tastes. Speaking of which, send in your beau, Sukey, and we'll see what trouble the bacon-brain found for himself."

Lord, if the fool fathered another brat, Daniel thought, he'd see him gelded.

This was different. Clarence had a voucher in his hand, an IOU written out to Jeremy Babcock. Clarence was scarlet-faced, but he placed it on the desk in front of Daniel.

Daniel whistled when he looked down and saw the amount. "Now, that's flying too high, my lad. You've got, what? Eight sisters in Ipswich depending on you." He tapped the ledger in front of him. "Bringing out one of them is deuced expensive."

Clarence turned redder, if that was possible, and hung his head. "That's five sisters, and I do know my responsibilities, sir."

"Good." Daniel hoped one of those responsibilities was the female carrying Clarence's babe. "Can you make the payment? Gentlemen usually give a debt of honor a month, but I know Jeremy is hard-pressed these days. He's asked me for a loan." He frowned. "That's not why you're here, is it?" He tapped the ledgers. "I'm no banker, you know, and this nonsense of having three women loose on Bond Street is making inroads."

Corie sat up at that. "You are supposed to be keeping a record of my purchases so I can repay them."

Daniel shuffled some papers. "Um, yes, that page must be here somewhere." Then he rubbed his ear.

Susanna nodded to Clarence, who tried to square his narrow shoulders. "I can pay my debts. I'll have to sell some investments and give up my rooms in Town and go home. My mother will be disappointed in me, but a gentleman always plays and pays, as they say."

Daniel told him he had the right of it. "A loss at the tables is considered a debt of honor, and not a bad lesson to learn, either. At least you're not in the hands of the cent-per-centers, who will bleed you dry with the interest they charge."

"No, I know better than to get involved with them."

"Then what is the problem? Dashed if I can see anything I can advise you on this. If you need more time, talk to Jeremy."

Clarence stared at his feet until Susanna cleared her throat and told him to go on. "The thing is," he said, "I don't recall losing so heavily. I never bet beyond what's in my pocket, like you told me. I think I fell asleep, so how could I sign a voucher like this?"

"Being foxed doesn't excuse the debt. You ought to know better than to play when your head's all muddled."

"No, I wasn't drunk. At least I don't think so. Susanna convinced me not to drink so much, you know."

"My sister? The one who had so much wine last night I had to carry her out of the carriage?"

"Daniel!"

Clarence nobly defended his friend. "She's not used to spirits, is all. She told me to look at Jeremy and his uncle, and see what drink can do to a man."

Daniel shoved his glass of cognac, his first of the day, to the edge of the desk. He'd been looking at Lord Morgan and Jeremy Babcock, too, and drinking far less than usual. It was half for the sake of his mother and sister, that they not have to see him being carried in by two footmen. The other half was because he didn't want to end up like a lonely old drunk or a ruined gambler.

Clarence didn't want to, either. "I shouldn't wish to grow as hard as Jeremy, or all red-nosed like his uncle."

"Clarence has all those sisters to set a good example for, you know," Susanna put in.

"If that is a hint, I have not stayed out all night drinking since you came. I haven't passed out once, unlike your friend. And I never did fall unconscious during a high-stakes card game."

"But I wasn't drinking, I say," Clarence insisted. "And I don't play for that kind of money, truly. The thing is, I don't think it's my signature."

Daniel stared at him. "Be careful what you are saying, because it sure as Hades sounds like you think Jeremy Babcock slipped something into your drink, then forged your signature while you were asleep. Is that what you meant to imply?"

"I cannot be certain. That's why I didn't say anything to him. I know an accusation like that would be cause for a duel. I've never shot at a man, nor ever learned how to fence. And there's my mother and the girls to think of. How would they go on without me? Most of all, I have no proof."

Corie came to investigate the scrap of paper. She pulled another sheet from a pad on Daniel's desk. "Write your signature."

Clarence did, and they looked similar.

"They are close enough to be a match," Corie decided, "especially if you were inebriated at the time."

Susanna got insulted on Clarence's behalf and said, "He said he wasn't. I believe him."

"Sick, then, or sleepy."

He hadn't been any of those things, Clarence swore, and now Daniel believed him, too.

"It's a dilemma, all right." Daniel picked up the papers to compare the two signatures at closer range. The moment he touched the gambling chit, his fingertips started to tingle, the same way they had with Corie's diamonds. Something just felt wrong; that was the only way he could explain it.

But he couldn't explain it, not to this audience. He wished Lord Royce were here, or Rex, even Harry, to see what they thought about the situation. If he was right . . .

He tore off small squares of paper. He looked around and of course noticed Corie's yellow muslin gown again. Daffodil yellow. Springtime yellow. Sunshine.

"What are you doing?" Susanna wanted to know.

Daydreaming. He shook his head and said, "Everyone write 'I am wearing a yellow gown.'"

Clarence protested. "Dash it, I am not writing that!"

"Very well, everyone write 'I am wearing gloves.' "

Corie blushed. She was the only one wearing any.

"Go on. It's an experiment."

They did, and tossed the three scraps into a pile. Daniel picked them up one by one. "This one is Corie's, Miss Abbott's, that is."

"Silly, you've been calling her Corie for days, if not in public. But Daniel, you know my handwriting, and you've just seen Clarence's."

Ah, but both of them wrote lies, and his fingertips knew it! He felt no itch, no rash, but he knew which was true! Neither Rex nor Harry could do that. They needed to hear words, not see them on a piece of paper. He almost scooped Corie into a jig around the room. He was better at something than his cousins, finally.

He tried to hide his grin by saying Susanna was right; it was a foolish experiment that proved nothing. "I'll go ask some questions." He could discern the truth in the answers, but that wouldn't count as evidence. He couldn't confront Jeremy Babcock on a tingle or an itch, not even if he claimed it was intuition. "Where were you gaming? Someone might have seen something. Or recall what you were served, by what waiter."

"McCann's. They are supposed to be honest."

"They are. I'd bank my life on that. Cousin Harry always did. If something is crooked there, it's Babcock, not the place."

"What shall I do in the meantime?"

"Stay away from the tables, the bottles, and Babcock. Especially Babcock until I've had a chance to look into this. Jupiter, you are here half the time, anyway. You might as well take your meals here, and go to whatever evening entertainment we're attending. I hate being the only male escort, anyway. Or you can go in my stead. That's the ticket! I'll straighten out this hugger-mugger, and you get to go to Lady Clutterbank's musicale. Her daughter plays the harp. And sings. It couldn't be better."

Susanna kissed his cheek and Clarence pumped his hand far more than necessary, out of gratitude.

"Do not thank me. I haven't pulled your chestnut out of the fire yet. Besides, I should be thanking you." Daniel couldn't wait to do more experimenting, to see what his clever fingers could do.

"For escorting the ladies to the musicale?"

"That, too."

"I don't understand."

"Neither do I, but trust me, it's fine. Excellent, in fact. I can feel it in my bones." He laughed, and Susanna and Clarence smiled.

Corie looked at the glass on his desk—assuredly not his first, and breakfast hardly over—and shook her head. Daniel Stamfield was kind to help the younger man, but he was still a drunk. And dense. And the devil incarnate.

Chapter Fifteen

Daniel was good at asking questions, not so good at receiving wrong answers. As a result, he seldom got lies—not twice, anyway. His size alone scared most strangers into true replies, and his reputation did the rest. Luckily, no one at McCann's Club had anything to hide.

Harrison, the manager, was incensed anyone would use his premises to pluck a tender young pigeon. The club's success depended on the integrity of its dealers and the honesty of its bank. If patrons were drugged, robbed, or swindled, if the cards were marked, the dice weighted, the wine diluted, there'd be no customers.

Mr. Harrison did not ask how Daniel knew. If Stamfield said a signature was wrong, then it was wrong. After all, Daniel's cousin Harry was like a brother to him, and half owner of the club, besides. Harry'd come to the Harrisons as a toddler, when his opera dancer mother passed on, so they knew—and protected—the family secret. The club manager had also protected and sheltered Harry's spy network before Harry retired as the Aide.

Now all he did was ask a favor. "An experiment, if you will. We've been having a bit of a problem collecting some debts."

Daniel stretched his fingers. Harrison took a pile of bank drafts from a locked drawer in his desk, and another, smaller stack of check payments from a different drawer. He shuffled the papers and handed them over without giving a clue as to his concerns. Harrison tried to offer Daniel a magnifying lens, too, so he could read the signatures better, but Daniel shook his head.

He straightened the checks written on five different banks, some from outlying cities, some from London. Then he counted them out onto the desk, one by one, letting each rest in his fingers a bare moment or two.

"I'd guess that these three"—he placed those in a separate pile—"are forgeries, closed accounts, or made-up names. I don't know how to explain it, but they feel wrong."

Harrison looked at the names on the three Daniel discredited, then whistled. "Damn, you got every one correct! Those are the ones the tellers at the bank refused to cash. I can try to locate the Captain Sharps, or at least not take any more of their money if it's not gold. You're a marvel, all right. Anytime you want a job, you'll be welcome here, room and board included."

Daniel was grinning. Harrison wanted to pour him a drink, but he turned him down, asking to speak to the serving staff and the dealers before they got too busy.

One waiter recalled bringing a bottle and two glasses to Mr. Babcock's table. He'd looked over occasionally to see if the gentlemen required another, but the younger man playing piquet with Mr. Babcock kept holding his hand over the top of his glass.

The floor guard, Hocking, who was Daniel's size but not half as well mannered, remembered seeing the greenling slumped in his seat. He'd shaken the boy awake and sent him on his way, telling him not to come back until he learned his limit. "We don't want no one what can't hold their liquor, gov. They makes a bad impression. And waste seats at the tables."

A serving wench was still mad at Jeremy for shoving her off his lap midgame, none too gently. She'd been expecting a more profitable night from one of her usual customers, who always let her watch the play and keep the small change that fell.

No one saw large amounts of money change hands, no one saw the wine tampered with, and no one brought pen and ink and paper to the table.

"Circumstantial evidence, at best, I'm thinking," Harrison told Daniel when they'd spoken to everyone they could who was present the night in question. "I can't toss Babcock out on such slim proof."

"No, and that wouldn't help the boy, anyway."

"So what should I do? I can't let it get out that one of the regulars is a cheat. The club could pay Mr. Haversmith's debt, on the sly, but that would set a bad precedent and still leave Babcock free to gull another flat."

Daniel flexed his knuckles. "I'll have a little word with the gentleman, shall I?"

Harrison groaned. "Just don't throw any chairs over the bar. That mirror cost a fortune, and there's a week's supply of liquor back there."

"I have no such intentions. Just a friendly chat, gentleman to gentleman, don't you know."

"Bloody hell, I'll go move the bottles now."

At McCann's, Jeremy Babcock sat down at Daniel's table without invitation. Babcock was wearing less-fashionable attire tonight than he had been recently, unlike Daniel, who was still dressed befitting his mother's dining table. Jeremy raised his hand to catch the eye of a waiter to order a drink, which Daniel fully expected to be added to his own bill.

"Evening, Stamfield. Surprised to see you here so early. I thought you'd be attending Lady Clutterbank's musicale."

"The gods were merciful tonight. I got out of it. What about you?" Daniel asked, tossing dice from hand to hand.

"I wasn't invited, and no regrets there. No heiress is worth sitting through an amateur recital."

Daniel sipped at the tankard of ale that had been in front of him all night while he waited for Babcock to arrive. "You are still looking for a rich wife, then? I guess wealthy women aren't as plentiful as poor ones. And rich men do tend to be protective of their little lambs, don't they? Perhaps you should look to the merchant class if you are so badly dipped. I hear bankers and mill owners are willing to buy well-bred husbands for their daughters to make them ladies."

Jeremy grimaced. "I'm not that far below hatches yet that I'd take a tradesman's filly."

"Just as well, I suppose. They want a title to go along with a pockets-to-let son-in-law."

"No matter. I have plans to come about until I find the right woman."

"Do you?" Daniel took Clarence's voucher out of his pocket. "Might this be one of your plans?"

Babcock licked his thin lips, his eyes shifting around the room. "So the whelp ran to you, did he? And you agreed to play banker for the boy? I never took you for a fool, Stamfield, but you have to know what a bad cardplayer he is. You'll never see a farthing of your blunt. Ah, but I suppose he must have secured your sister's hand after all to have you sporting the brass for him. I wish I'd heard it before, so I could put my money on the boy in the betting books. I thought your sister would do better for herself. She's a taking little thing."

Daniel had taken enough of the whole unpleasant conversation. "Susanna will do better, and I am not paying. No one is, I'm thinking." He wondered how he ever called the man a friend.

Babcock called for another glass of wine. "I do not take your meaning. A debt is a debt."

"Unless it's a rook. You don't pay someone to rob your house, do you?"

"You are making no sense, man. A gambling loss is a debt of honor. If you call yourself any kind of gentleman, you know that."

"There is no honor in paying an extortionist."

Jeremy wiped his thin lips with the back of his sleeve.

"What are you saying?"

"Did Clarence sign this IOU?"

"Of course he did. That's his name, ain't it?"

Daniel's toes burned. "It's his name, but I don't think it's his signature. I think you wrote it."

Babcock looked around to see if anyone had heard. He leaned closer to Daniel, breathing stale wine and tobacco stench in Daniel's face. "You are accusing me of forging a gaming debt? To let some country lumpkin weasel out of paying his rightful dues?"

"I would see justice done," was all Daniel said.

"In that case, I swear it was an honest game, an honest debt."

Daniel kicked his shoes off so he could rub his feet together. "I believe you are lying. I do have proof, of course. I wouldn't accuse a man without evidence." The rash starting up his ankles was all the evidence Daniel needed, so that was no lie on his own part.

Babcock looked around. "You cannot have proof. No one was watch—" He caught himself, but too late.

"No one was watching you pour a draft of sleeping powder into the lad's drink? Watching you pull a paper out of your pocket, one you'd practiced at home to get the signatures passably alike?"

"I did not, I say. It's his word against mine. He was castaway drunk."

"Give over, Babcock. You are finished in London."

"Wh-what do you mean?"

Daniel traced the circle his tankard of ale had left on the wooden tabletop. "I mean no one will ever play with you again. The doors to every decent club and gaming hall will be closed to you. You might even go to prison if young Haversmith decides to lodge a complaint with the magistrate's office. Unless . . ."

Babcock leaned forward. "Unless?"

"You rip up this forgery, for one thing, and forget the debt."

The gambler stared at the chit, knowing he'd lost. He'd never see a ha'penny of the sum now, and it could be used against him if the damned cub took his case to court. He tore it into halves, then quarters, which he put in his own pocket. He stood. "There, the debt is satisfied."

"But I am not. You'll leave London. No, England. My family has property in the Indies. They'll find you a post or something there."

"I cannot leave my mother and sister. What will become of them?"

"Oh, you've been providing well for them, have you?"

"They've been managing," Babcock grumbled. "They need me."

Daniel knew that Lord Morgan had been paying the bills for his dead brother's family. "Your sister will be better off without you. She might even find a suitor, once there's no wastrel brother to keep pulling out of dun territory. If you stay, she'll be ruined. A card shark is a large blot on the family escutcheon."

Jeremy sneered. "You've got a bastard in your family, and you still survive. I won't go. No one will believe you or the boy now that the voucher is destroyed."

"Are you willing to bet on it?"

"Cards?" He was ready to call for a deck, until he saw the bouncer, Hocking, watching them, a short wooden cudgel in his hands.

Daniel took another sip of the tepid ale. "No, I won't play with you," he said, although that was precisely what he was doing. "I'm no foolish young sprig. I had another kind of wager in mind."

"You mean bet my life? A duel? I—I will challenge you, then. For the insult. That's right. You'll have to apologize and eat your words. No one will blame me for shooting you, or running you through with my sword. A gentleman has the right to protect his good name."

"I won't duel with the likes of you."

"I never took you for a coward, Stamfield."

"You misunderstand. I never took you for a gentleman. I will meet you in the rear courtyard, though."

He cracked his knuckles.

Babcock blanched. "That is unfair."

"So was drugging an innocent boy."

Babcock's eyes kept darting around, looking for an ally, or a way out. "I thought you were my friend."

"Clarence thought you were his friend. So which is it to be? The rear court or paid passage on a ship? Of course I could leave you to the mercy of Ham Hocks over there."

Hocking was stroking his cudgel as if it were a woman's leg.

Babcock gulped. "If I meet you out back, then you'll let me alone? I'll be free of you and this wretched place?"

"Oh, no. Then I'll pick up your remains and carry you to the ship. The other way you get to pack and call on your banker, and tell your family you have an opportunity to make your fortune. Maybe they'll go with you. I'll pay their passage, in fact."

"That's no choice!"

"Did you give Clarence any choice?"

Jeremy licked his lips again; they were that dry. "I know what this is about," he said. "You don't care about the halfling or your sister. You want me out of the way so you can pursue the Abbott doxy for yourself. You want the jade and her father's blunt for your own."

Daniel almost forgot his promise to Harrison about

the mirror over the bar and all those bottles. He had his hands on Jeremy's shoulders; Jeremy's feet were inches off the ground. "Never, ever let me hear you mention the lady again. She is no doxy and I do not want her. I do not need her money, and I am not looking for a wife. She'll find a better man than either of us. Now, what is it to be, you go quietly home to pack, or you go in pieces?"

"You'll give me a fortnight to get my affairs in order?"

Daniel put him down, about as gently as he'd lower a sack of coal. "A sennight, no more. Less if I find a ship leaving sooner."

"Very well, I'll go."

The rash did not go away. Daniel didn't think anything of it, only that he needed more time to wash the ichor of lies away. He refused to consider that half the spots were because he himself had spoken half-truths about Corie being a doxy.

He stayed at his corner table for supper and a bit of flirtation with a blonde, a redhead, and a black-haired wench, to prove that no starchy brunette held his interest. None of them appealed, so he paid his bill—and Jeremy's—and left the club's public rooms. He went down to the kitchens to visit with Miss White, as he always did these days, and to see if the cook had anything left over. Then he left by the kitchen entry, also as usual.

He quickly realized this was one of his stupidest acts. He was growing soft and careless. Then again, he wasn't a soldier, England wasn't at war, and he didn't have any enemies.

Until tonight. Babcock was waiting in the dark alley

that led back to the street, hiding behind a stack of crates. He leaped out of the shadows before Daniel's eyes adjusted to the darkness, and brought a bottle down on Daniel's head. The bottle broke; Daniel's head didn't. For once, he was glad to have such a thick skull.

Dripping with gin and blood, he staggered but stayed on his feet. He barely had time to wipe his eyes before Jeremy came at him with a long, narrow knife.

Babcock was smaller, lighter, and less fit, but he was wiry, and he held the weapon. The knife slashed out. Daniel offered a large target, and the alleyway was too narrow and too cluttered with the fallen crates for much evasion. Daniel roared and threw his arm up to deflect the lunge. His coat front got slashed, then his collar, and his sleeve gave way at the seams as he ducked and dodged. He'd told Deauville the blasted coat was too tight, and now look. He could hardly defend himself against this puny caitiff and his blade. He pulled the sleeve off to wrap around his arm.

The next time Jeremy came at him, Daniel fended him off with his padded shield, then used his foot to trip him, sending him sprawling onto the crates, which spilled cabbages and potatoes and turnips.

Jeremy grabbed for Daniel, who lost his own footing in the gin-soaked, vegetable-strewn alley. Soon they were rolling on the filthy ground, with Daniel having to hold Babcock's knife hand and avoid his knee, while trying to catch hold of the man's throat. The dastard bit him! Now, that was dirty fighting.

So Daniel stopped playing fair. He bent Jeremy's hand with the knife backward until he heard bone snap.

Jeremy screamed, but still tried to claw at Daniel's

face with his other hand, until Daniel could throw his weight behind a solid punch to the chin for cheating Clarence, then another to the man's ugly nose for insulting Corie. And one to the jaw for his ruined coat.

Hocking was standing nearby, with his cudgel and a towel.

Daniel took the towel, but didn't know where to start; he had so many cuts and scrapes starting to be felt now that the fight was over. "Why the hell didn't you help, dash it?"

"And spoil your fun? You was doing fine. And I'm not paid to keep the alley clean. I'll put the crates on your tab, though."

Harrison was there, too, watching. "You're getting soft and careless, Stamfield. Harry taught you better than to fight fair." He and Hocking dragged Jeremy off to a locked storeroom behind the kitchen. They agreed to keep him until a ship was ready to sail.

The tut-tutting cook cleaned Daniel up as best she could. She nimbly set a couple of stitches to the back of his head, as capable as any sawbones from all her years at the club. She dabbed the bite mark and the lesser cuts on his arm and his neck with brandy, which would likely go on his account, too, so he drank the rest of it to dull the pain. His coat was nothing but rags, his tattered neckcloth was torn to bind the back of his head, and his trousers were covered in the muck from the alley, and blood. What was left of his clothing reeked of gin and the gutter.

That was what he looked and smelled like when he half fell to the pavement getting out of the hackney coach at Royce House. That was what the ladies saw as they descended their own carriage after their evening out. That was what caused enough shrieking and shouting to rouse everyone on Grosvenor Square.

His mother started weeping. His sister swooned into Clarence's arms. Dobbson came running with a blunderbuss, yelling for the footmen to lock all the doors and windows. And Miss Corisande Abbott stepped around Daniel, pulling her skirts aside, and said, "I will not be riding out with you in the morning. Or ever again."

That was what hurt worst of all.

Chapter Sixteen

There was pain, and more pain. And there were tears.

First came Deauville, when he helped Daniel into a bath, and then into a nightshirt, one that must have been his father's, because Daniel never owned one of the voluminous shrouds. He hurt too much to complain about the fabric encompassing him. But the valet's sniveling was too much to bear with a headache.

"Dash it, man, if you are going to blubber like a baby every time I get a scrape or a cut, you're no good to me."

"You? No, monsieur. It is the coat. That beautiful coat that Deauville pressed this very afternoon. A work of art, a masterpiece, ruined."

His arm ached too much to lift to point at the door, but Daniel managed to shout, "Get out."

Then his sister arrived at his bedchamber, along with Clarence. Daniel had explained as much as they needed to hear before he dragged himself up the stairs. Now they wanted to thank him.

"Not necessary," he tried to say, hoping they'd leave, but Susanna threw herself against his chest, exactly where the corner of a wooden crate had left a massive bruise. Then she hugged his neck, right where that bastard Babcock had bitten him. Then she wept all over the dratted nightshirt.

Even Clarence had tears in his eyes when he tried to express his gratitude. He was free of debt, and free of having to confront Jeremy. He was exonerated of being a fall-down drunken gambler, too. "How can I repay you?"

Daniel groaned. "Marry the brat and get her off me."

Clarence tugged at Susanna's shoulder. "Come on, Sukey, he must be concussed if he wants us to get hitched."

That brought a giggle from Susanna, at least. It brought another groan from Daniel when she climbed off the wide mattress and jostled his aching head.

His mother was still mopping at her tears from before when she came in to assure herself that her baby boy was not at death's door. "Are you certain I should not call a physician? A surgeon? The Watch?"

"Lud, no. We want to keep this as quiet as possible for Lord Morgan's niece and her mother. I'll be fine after a night's rest. I've survived far worse, you know." In fact, he was almost embarrassed that such a weakling as Jeremy Babcock had done so much damage. He really was getting too old for this nonsense.

Lady Cora insisted, between blowing her nose and wiping her eyes, on staying the night with him. "In case you need anything, dear."

He'd drown before he asked his mother for the chamber pot. "That's Deauville's job."

"The man told me you'd just dismissed him."

"For the night, blast it, not permanently. He's good with a neckcloth. Lud knows I'd never be able to tie one right. Go offer him a raise in salary. And more if he stops caring for the clothes more than the man in them."

"Are you certain, dear? I wouldn't mind sleeping in the chair, here. I used to do it when you had the measles. And that time you broke your arm after stealing those apples. But we won't speak of that, will we, dear, how a mother's love is stronger than any sacrifice?"

Now he felt like a child again, a particularly troublesome urchin who caused his mother pain. He sighed. "I really do not need anything except rest, Mother, but thank you for the concern."

She headed for the door, but first said, "Your father was the same way, until he died from not letting me send for the doctor."

"He died from falling off his horse. The doctor could not have saved him."

She wept some more. "But I would have tried."

There were more tears at the opposite end of the corridor.

Corie was huddled in her bed, curled with all the blankets she could pile on top, and still felt cold; she still saw that broken, bloody body in the street, in her mind.

She cursed him soundly, employing words he'd used when a thief tried to pick his pocket at the British Museum. The would-be bandit ran off before Daniel could catch him, because he had to stay with the ladies rather than give chase.

Corie did not know what half of the words meant, but she was sure Daniel Stamfield deserved them all. Lady Cora's son was no hero, as his family and Clarence were proclaiming. They put him on a pedestal, like some marble statue of an all-powerful god to be worshipped and adored. Bah. The man had the proverbial feet of clay. He was nothing but a man, and a sorry excuse for one at that. He was a drunkard, a brawler, a man who took the law into his own ridiculously large hands and twisted it to please himself. Certes, he had solved Clarence's problem, but he'd done so like the uncivilized ape he was.

And this was the man who was rejecting her suitors. That alone was worth crying over. Corie was currently dependent upon the goodwill of an overgrown ape who'd set himself up as the arbiter of her future. He was a bully, a tyrant, a menace. He was like her father.

Susanna said he was brave. Corie thought he was a fool.

Lady Cora said he was loyal. Corie decided "obstinate" was a more fitting word.

To Clarence, Daniel Stamfield was a lifesaver. To Corie, he was a stumbling block. She wouldn't even trust him with her diamonds after tonight. He was just as liable to lose them in a hand of cards as get her a fair price. A woman could not rely on a man in his cups.

The worst part of all was she was coming to like the big baboon. He could be pleasant company when he forgot to be shy and awkward. He laughed a lot, and at himself sometimes, too. He was intelligent enough to know where his knowledge was scant, and he sought advice and information from those better-informed. He was honest. And handsome, with his extraordinary black-rimmed blue eyes. Dressed right, he was turning into the gentleman his mother always said he could be.

Unfortunately, Corie reminded herself, he had all the faults of the worst London gentlemen, the town bucks and dandies and rakes: wine, women, and so what if people were counting on you?

So she cried there in her bed, alone with her despair and disappointment, and the pain of losing something she never had.

Pain, and more pain. It came to Daniel in waves, from his chest to his skull to his neck and arm, and everywhere else he'd been kicked or shoved or struck by falling crates. And that female thought he'd be able to go riding in the morning? What did she think, that he was made of marble that never got a headache? He had the devil of one now, enough to keep him awake.

He wasn't sorry he'd refused the sleeping powders his mother offered. He'd seen enough poor souls addicted to the stuff. He was sorry he hadn't asked for some lemonade, or some ice for his bruised knuckles, a cool cloth for his head . . . and a soft, gentle hand to place it there, not Deauville's heavy fist. And not his mother's hand, either.

He thought about tugging the bellpull, but the servants were all asleep by now and he saw no reason to bother them, not when his own stupidity had let him walk into a trap. He considered going down to the kitchens himself. A bit of cheese and a slice of beef might make him feel more the thing, to go along with the lemonade for his dry throat, but his sore muscles protested the idea of getting out of the bed. And what if anyone saw him stumbling around like a rum-soaked sailor?

He ought to get up in the morning—no, at dawn—and have a hearty gallop in the park, just to show the woman he was neither jug-bitten, dissolute, nor pining for her company. Then he worried his head would crack open with Gideon's first hoofbeat and what was left of his brains would fall out. Hell, she might laugh at the sight.

He could still see that look on her face when she walked over him. She didn't believe he wasn't drunk or that he hadn't picked the fight with Babcock, or enjoyed it. Well, he might have gotten satisfaction in seeing the man's nose gushing blood, but who could blame him after being ambushed in an alleyway? Miss Corisande Abbott could blame him, that was who. She did not believe for an instant he'd carefully considered the best way to handle the cheat without resorting to violence. The mayhem was of Jeremy's making, but she did not accept that.

She didn't think he had any business dealing with her suitors, either. Fine, he'd let every fortune hunter in Town fall at her feet. He'd give every libertine leave to seduce her. And good riddance to a responsibility he'd never wanted nor asked for. Why, he should have let Babcock ask for her hand. They could both have sailed to the Indies, for all he cared.

The worst thing was, he did care. He wanted her to like him. He admitted to himself, here in his dark, pain-filled misery, that his efforts to look and act like a gentleman—all that cultural blather, the dance practice, exercise, and primping—they were for her. Oh, he'd convinced himself he was being a dutiful son and brother, but he was trying to impress Corie. He acknowledged it now, when it was too late.

She was beautiful, so beautiful he wished he could paint a picture to keep forever. She'd be smiling in the portrait, and he'd have to smile back every time he passed by. No painting could capture her prickly, standoffish nature that thawed when she relaxed, nor that lilac scent that stayed in his memory.

And in his body. Corie had all the right curves, at just the right height. Just thinking about her gowns, so temptingly revealing in front, so temptingly clinging in back, made him wish he had spent the night with one of the females at McCann's after all. So what if a much younger Corie'd given herself to that muckworm Snelling? No female was perfect. Hell, he was the last man on earth to demand perfection from a woman. Besides, she acted with the utmost circumspection these days, playing the role of prim and proper lady for all of society to see.

She was a lady, with one blot on her copybook. Well, he had a few himself.

But she hated him, and there wasn't a damn thing he could do about it. A grown man, a real man, a true British gentleman, did not cry.

He was not worth crying over. Corie gave herself a mental shake and got out of bed. She laid more coal on the fire and found a warm woolen shawl. She thought about fixing herself some hot tea to take away the chill. Then she thought about seeing if Daniel needed anything. That was only polite.

What if his head wound had opened and he was bleeding to death? Or if one of the cuts had become infected and he became feverish? She knew the sapskull had sent his mother and his valet off to their own beds, out of some ridiculous stoicism, which she felt was nothing but misplaced male pride. He most likely agreed with his doting mother's belief he was some kind of lesser god, an invincible hero. He was not.

He'd be unattended and possibly too weak to reach the bellpull, or too ill to call out for help. Besides, his room was down the farthest corridor and no one would hear him. If she was already going down to the kitchens, she might as well ask if he needed anything. For all his faults, she supposed Daniel's intentions were good: rescuing Clarence, trying to protect her and his sister from fortune hunters and adventurers. The least she could do was see if he was still breathing. She tied a knot in the shawl and opened her door as quietly as possible so no one else was disturbed.

He couldn't sleep. All because of a woman? Hell, no. It was the nightshirt that was strangling him, and all the blankets his mother had tucked so tightly around him. She seemed to feel that a wounded man needed a raging fire in the hearth, a mound of coverings, and all the windows shut tight. He was used to sleeping naked with one thin quilt, and fresh air to breathe. How could he recover when he was drenched in his own sweat?

He kicked the blankets to the floor but he was still too hot in the confines of his father's night rail. He tried to tug the blasted nightshirt off, but the collar buttons were too small for his swollen knuckles to manage, so he just ripped the thing down the front and tossed it aside. He banked the fire, then found where Deauville had left a carafe of water and a plate of macaroons. Maybe he'd been too harsh with the chap after all.

He ate the macaroons, drank the water, relieved

himself, and, naked, climbed back in bed, his sore muscles protesting the effort. He lay on his stomach to protect the stitches on the back of his aching head and felt a great deal better. Now he could sleep.

He wouldn't think about a woman, any woman. Any brown-haired woman. Any brown-haired woman with lovely breasts. Any breasts with brown hair. No, that didn't seem right. Any woman . . .

He snored. Corie added that to the long list of the man's faults. She could hear him from halfway down the hall, and remembered his sister saying that was why they placed him so far away from any of the occupied rooms. Well, if he was sleeping so soundly, she wouldn't disturb him to ask if he wanted tea or anything. She'd just shield her candle and peek in to see he wasn't lying in a pool of blood. He'd said some cook stitched his head, but really, he should have seen a surgeon to have it done properly. He should have—

He should have a sheet over him, by heaven!

And she should leave, but she didn't. Corie stepped closer, for a better look. That was when she decided perhaps his mother and sister were right, that he was indeed some kind of deity. From this angle, he sure beat those marble museum gods to flinders.

Chapter Seventeen

Lady Cora believed Daniel ought to stay in bed until he felt better. Deauville, back in Daniel's employ, believed he ought to stay in bed until he looked better. Judging by the sudden flush on Miss Abbott's cheeks, her averted eyes, and the way she pushed her breakfast plate aside, his appearance must be worse than Daniel thought.

No matter. He had business to attend to. Deauville applied a bit of powder to cover some of the scratches and tied his cravat higher to cover the bite marks on his neck. Daniel refused a bandage around his head, but he did agree to wear a hat—a hat, by Jupiter!—so as not to scare women and children with the stitches on the back of his skull. And he put on gloves—gloves, by Zeus!—to shield his bloodied knuckles.

His first call was to the Royce and Stamfield solicitor. The two families, plus the earl's other son, Harry Harmon, kept Mr. Marcus Glessing so busy and well paid that the man did not need many other clients. Of course he had time to spare for Mr. Stamfield, even without an appointment. He had time to congratulate him on his excellent appearance. Why, he was a regular Beau Brummell, Mr. Glessing said with a chuckle, a new man.

"I'd wager it's the influence of a special lady, eh? Your mother must be delighted. She was just telling me she wished—"

So Daniel took off his hat and his gloves and loosened his neckcloth, to prove he was his own man, the same man.

"Ah. I see. So what may I help you with today, sir?"

Glessing accepted without a qualm Daniel's need to arrange secure and speedy transport and a livelihood for a gentleman who had proved an embarrassment to the polite world. He should not return, not speak of the past, and not be trusted. But he shouldn't be left to starve, either.

If one of his special clients said the moon was made of green cheese, the solicitor would have accepted the statement as fact, so if Mr. Stamfield said the man was guilty, then guilty he was. "I'll get on it immediately."

"Excellent, Glessing. I knew I could count on you. Whenever you have the arrangements finalized, send a message to McCann's Club. Harrison will see the dastard delivered, under guard."

Mr. Glessing eyed Daniel's bruised knuckles. "Will he be, ah, needing medical attention aboard ship? The captain will want to know."

"Oh, Harrison must have called for a surgeon. I don't think the cook had time to set a broken wrist, straighten a broken nose, which might have improved the maggot's looks, or shove back a dislocated jaw. She had a roast in the oven, for the evening dinner rush. But don't worry; Babcock isn't going to die. And I have witnesses who know he attacked me first."

"I never doubted that. I've seldom known you to

start a fight." So spoke the man who'd had to pay damages at more taverns than he'd known existed, and replace enough windows, tables, and chairs for the queen's castle.

"Thank you." Daniel's business was finished, except for one last request. "Oh, there is another small matter I'd have you look into. That goddaughter of my mother's who she brought to Town?"

"Yes, a Miss Corisande Abbott. I look forward to meeting the young lady."

"Could you find out the terms of her mother's marriage settlement, to see if a dowry was left for the young lady, and under what conditions?"

Glessing beamed. "It will be my pleasure."

"Great gods," Daniel almost shouted. "It wouldn't be my pleasure we're talking about. Not that Miss Abbott isn't acceptable, if I were accepting leg shackles, which I'm not. Not at all. The female is attracting suitors—that's why my mother brought her to London in the first place—and I need to know what to tell them."

"Oh. Of course."

Daniel could hear the regret in Glessing's voice, but couldn't imagine why the solicitor was disappointed in a client's contented bachelorhood. Then he remembered that Glessing had a wife and a cricket team of children. Misery loved company, they always said.

His next call was to Lord Morgan's town house. Daniel did not want the old gent to hear of his nephew's disgrace and imminent departure from the servants' grapevine, or to wonder at the circumstances.

The house was small, with weeds where a flower path used to be. The brass door knocker was tarnished, and the windows were so covered with soot that Daniel couldn't see any light coming from within. A surly butler answered the door, the onions on his breath enough to discourage any less-insistent visitors.

At least the room where Lord Morgan sat was warm. He sat near the fire wrapped in a blanket, a bottle of medicine beside him, the newspaper in his lap, an old spotted hound sleeping at his feet. The dog opened one eye, saw that Daniel had no food, and rolled over.

Lord Morgan was surprised at Daniel's visit to his house, but not at his news. "I knew he'd come to a bad end sooner or later, the way he was headed. I'm only glad for his mother's sake that no one ran him through or shot him in some alley. I appreciate your giving him a chance and keeping his reputation, such as it was, out of the filth. You're more generous than most men would be, especially after he broke a bottle over your head."

"He got worse. But tell me, if you will, did you know about his scheme to hoodwink Haversmith into paying a sham debt?"

"No, I swear. Outplaying a green 'un at cards is one thing. Even loosening his purse strings with liquor. But signing his name after poisoning him? That's the devil's hand, none of mine."

Daniel believed him. If he'd felt the slightest itch, he'd have left instead of staying to hear the older man out.

"I only knew Jeremy was badly dipped. I thought he'd find a rich wife, although that would satisfy his creditors for too short a time. He'd keep losing, and keep gambling until the money was gone."

"Which every father, brother, or solicitor in the

country knew. No one with a care for his daughter, or her fortune, would let her wed a man like him."

"True, all too true."

They both thought about that for a bit, how neither one of them could pass muster in a father's eyes, or, in Lord Morgan's case, a son's eyes.

The older man sighed. "I think he hoped to seduce some woman who had control of her own fortune, but your Miss Abbott was too downy a bird for him."

"I would have been the one to run him through."

"Yes, well, that's what I told him."

"What about his sister?" Daniel asked.

"Lud, you can't be interested in my niece. Ugly as mud, and mean as a snake."

"No, I meant her future. Will she and her mother be in dire straits without Jeremy's support?"

"What support? I've been paying their bills since my younger brother died. Asthma, don't you know. Runs in the family," Lord Morgan said.

"I am sorry to hear that."

"Not as sorry as I am. With a family like that, though, I doubt my brother was keen on staying around." He wheezed and pointed to his cordial, so Daniel poured him a glass. "They'll manage. If they weren't both foul-tempered shrews, I'd have them here." He looked around, then cleared his throat, embarrassed. "Place could use a woman's touch, I suppose."

It could use a maid, at any rate. Dishes and old newspapers and dog hair covered every surface. Lord Morgan hadn't shaved. His slippers had holes in the toes.

"If you won't have them here, would they want to go with Jeremy?"

"What, to some heathen country where they'd be too poor for the British gentry? No, they keep busy with their church committees and friends in the country, I suppose. No reason to banish them, too."

Daniel stood, his mission completed. He hadn't been offered tea or spirits or anything to eat, which worried him on Lord Morgan's behalf. "Will you be all right?"

"Without Jeremy sponging off me here? Do you think he cared about his old uncle? Only what he could borrow or steal. It was the gambling and the drink together, you know. Like a disease, it was, worse than the asthmatics. He could not fight both. No backbone, just like his father."

Daniel did not know what to say to that. He fiddled with the gloves he still carried, not putting them on, but edging toward the door.

Lord Morgan did not expect a reply. "I'll be fine. Thank you for asking. In fact, I've decided to mend my ways before they kill me. Haven't had a drink in days, and no cigars, either. Early nights, not such rich food. I'm breathing better already. Can you tell?"

The fact he was still breathing at all was a miracle to Daniel. "I wish you continued improvement."

"It's your mother's influence, don't you know."

Daniel ripped the seam of one of the gloves by cramming his hand into it. "Yes, I do know."

He left, after putting a flea in the butler's ear about taking better care of his master and the house, and putting a gold coin in the man's hand to encourage him.

His next stop was at McCann's. He went around the back to look at the alley, but the club's staff had cleaned up.

Cook insisted on checking her handiwork, and feeding him. Now that was more like it—good food, a good cat on his lap, no one nattering about a fellow changing his ways.

Harrison was glad to hear of the arrangements for his bothersome guest. Luckily the surgeon left enough laudanum to keep Babcock drugged, because his moans were disturbing the paying guests. Harrison thought he might be trying to shout for his release, but who could tell, with his jaw held together with a wide bandage around his head? The club manager knew Mr. Glessing and would deliver the unwanted baggage in person. The crime and the assault happened at his club, so he felt as if he were responsible.

Daniel asked to look at a couple of checks while he ate the plentiful, and free, meal. With all the crime in the city now, and gentlemen being attacked right outside their own clubs, some of the swells were afraid to carry so much of the ready with them. Some of them forgot how much money was in their accounts, too. A few forgot their names.

Daniel could help them remember.

Corie had errands that morning, too. Lady Cora blinked a time or two, but she did not say anything when Corie took one of the maids along and asked Dobbson to hire them a hackney.

The butler raised his eyebrows, but did as she requested. After all, she was not a daughter of the house, and not a flighty young miss, either.

Corie told the maid she wished to purchase a trinket or two for Lady Cora, who had been so good to her, and directed the driver to Rundell and Bridge. The jewelry shop was a favorite of the upper classes, and known

to be reputable. Corie had no intention of taking the
first price she was offered, having learned to bargain at
the village fairs. In fact, she hoped she never needed to
sell her mother's gems at all. But their worth was a
starting place, so she'd feel more in command of her
own life again, so she could plan for disaster if it came.

The clerk was polite, but no more, after he inspected her clothing to see if she was worthy of his
minimal attention. He turned into a fawning lackey
when she mentioned she was a guest at Royce House.
The countess was one of the establishment's best customers. What could he do to assist?

Corie waited until the maid's back was turned to
look at the other customers; then she opened the velvet pouch she carried and spilled the contents onto a
velvet cloth the clerk provided. "I need to know how
much these are worth. For safety purposes, of course.
I know I should not be carrying them casually, but I'd
like to know their value."

"Of course." Ladies were always selling their jewelry, and always using some excuse or other; the toffs
never wanted to admit they were living above their
means. He maintained his polite air while he fixed a
jeweler's loupe to his eye, then held the necklace up
close. Then the earbobs, and the bracelet.

"I think you can carry these anywhere you wish,
miss. They are worth less than ten pounds."

"Ten pounds!" she cried, then lowered her voice.
"Ten pounds?"

"They are excellent fakes. A pleasing design, an attractive set, but they are glass for all that."

"Glass?"

"Oh, yes." He took a strand of diamonds from the
case behind him, a necklace that was similar in size

of the stones. "Do you see the difference, the depth, the clarity, the sparkle? And see?" He used a sheet of glass set aside for just that purpose to etch a line with one of the real diamonds. He tried it with one of hers, from the bracelet. The stone—the piece of glass crystal—cracked.

So did something inside Corie.

"Miss? Are you ill? Shall I fetch a glass of water? Your maid? Do you have a carriage waiting?"

"No. No, I shall be fine. The, ah, surprise, you know. I—I suppose my father felt the real ones were too valuable to chance in London. All the tales of crimes, you know."

" 'Tis better to be cautious with family heirlooms, I say. No telling when a robber will break into your own house these days."

"Frightening, isn't it?" Worse to know one's own father was the thief. How could she admit it to anyone? It was embarrassing enough the Stamfields knew he was courting Alberta Rivendale like some besotted swain. The whole neighborhood was laughing behind his back. It was mortifying the tenants feared him for his temper, the tradesmen disliked him for his cheeseparing ways, and the local society no longer invited him to their parties because of his nastiness when drunk. But this? This was beyond humiliating. Now she was ashamed.

Her own father cared so little for Corie that he stole from her. She wondered when he'd made the copy, if he'd sold the originals or kept them somewhere.

She wondered what she should do now she had no money to fall back on.

"Miss, did you find a gift for Lady Cora? There's a pretty brooch she might like for that new turban."

"No, there are too many choices. I cannot decide. We'll come back another day."

She thanked the clerk, who had discreetly restored her imitations to their pouch. She tucked the pouch back into her reticule, in the guise of searching for a handkerchief. "I do believe I am feeling the chill that had Miss Stamfield sneezing last night. We ought to return home."

She looked so pale, no one questioned her decision to stay home that afternoon and rest.

No one except Daniel, that was. He worried. His mother and sister went off to pay calls and spend more of his money on fripperies, but he didn't like Corie's pallor. First that flush this morning; now she'd gone ashen-faced. He told himself he'd be stuck with her forever if she turned sickly. That was why he was concerned.

Perhaps a physician should be called. He forgot he distrusted the entire profession, and almost sent a footman off to find one. Then he decided someone should see if she needed more than an afternoon's rest, and where the devil had his mother gone that was more important than the health of her guest?

He knocked softly on her door in case she was sleeping.

The door opened immediately. She was still wearing the green gown of the morning, but her hair was down, loose around her shoulders, and lower. He hadn't realized how long it was, that sun-touched brown, how smooth, how soft it looked. How much he wanted to run his fingers through it.

"What do you want?"

"Uh, to see if you were well."

"No, I am not well. I am poor."

"Do you mean poorly? Should I send for a physician?"

"No, I mean poor as in penniless, poor as in no means of supporting myself if I cannot find a husband or a paying position. Poor as in my diamonds are made of paste. Did you know that?"

He did not want to have this discussion in the hallway, where passing servants could overhear. "May I come in?"

"I am not that poor I would accept carte blanche from you."

"Lud, I wasn't offering . . . That is, right. It would be wrong for me to enter your bedchamber. I, ah . . . ."

"Did you know?"

He wavered. She'd hate him with the truth. He'd have hives at a lie. "How could I know? I'm no jeweler."

"But you suspected, didn't you?"

That he had to admit.

"And you never told me."

"I saw no reason to. They are pretty baubles, and only an expert could tell, especially at night, at the theater. You know."

She clenched her fists. "Yes, I know now. I asked a real jeweler, someone who wouldn't lie to me."

Daniel stood his ground in the doorway. "I never lied. I never said one way or another. It did not matter."

"It did to me."

She slammed the door in his face.

Chapter Eighteen

A maid screamed and dropped her bundle of sheets. A footman ran, tripped over the sheets, and bumped into Dobbson, who came to see what gust of wind—or, woe betide, servant—dared shut one of the doors forcefully enough to awaken the resting Miss Abbott, or the dead.

"She did not want a doctor," Daniel told them. He stepped over the sheets, helped the footman to his feet, straightened Dobbson's powdered wig, and left.

Miss Abbott did not leave her room until dinnertime, where she appeared her usual self, in a high-waisted, rose-colored silk gown. She wore pearls at her throat and silk roses in her upswept hair. She spoke of Lady Cora's afternoon visits. She spoke of the evening ahead. She did not speak to Daniel.

As usual, Daniel addressed his meal instead of the feminine chatter about fripperies. Lady Cora and Susanna shared glances and shrugs, but did not ask any questions. They'd heard all they needed to know from the servants.

The ball was hot, crowded, and noisy. In other words, it was a success. Susanna's hand was solicited for every dance, with Clarence offering to sit out the waltzes with her. Daniel noted the boy did not have to be coerced by their hostess to take other partners, including the erudite Miss Thomlinson, who looked almost pretty waltzing twice with Lord Chadwick. Luckily Chadwick was a superb dancer, for Miss Thomlinson could not see a thing without her thick spectacles, but she did look worlds better, and happier. No one at White's would bet against that match.

Daniel also noticed that Corie, Miss Abbott, danced every set, strolled the perimeter between dances, took supper with a different group of acquaintances, and seldom returned to Lady Cora's side. She laughingly declared herself too old to need such careful chaperonage, and too much in the way of Lady Cora's own beaux. One time when she did come to see how his mother fared, Daniel tried to engage her in conversation. She quickly asked if he might fetch her a lemonade, since she'd become thirsty from all the dancing. She was gone when he got back with the drink.

Daniel handed the cup to his mother, who handed it to Lord Morgan, who hid it behind a potted palm tree. Daniel wished he could hide there, too, to avoid their looks of concern at the blatant insult. They both, undoubtedly, believed he deserved it. Maybe he did. Who could tell what a woman was thinking?

Daniel looked for Corie on the dance floor, something he did far too often for his own comfort. He saw her smiling at her current partner, twirling in the dance fast enough to show her ankles. Damn.

She flirted more, laughed more, stood a little closer to her partners. And, Zeus, was her rose bodice more revealing, too? Or was it just that the pearls caught his eye, and his glance at the gleaming white orbs— that is, the pearls—lingered.

She was obviously more determined than ever to snag herself a husband. If that was a crime, every other young female attending these tedious affairs was just as guilty, but Corie seemed more blatant about it than the others tonight. Or maybe he was just more observant, or was more aware of her motives.

Didn't she understand gentlemen grew nervous when a female was too eager? They were supposed to be the hunters, not the prey. Like a canny old fox, a bachelor could see his pursuers coming for miles away. He'd either outrun the pack or go to ground. The London gents had a lot of practice avoiding capture.

And yet, Daniel had to admit, Corie's strategy seemed to be working well enough. More and more men begged him for an introduction, or a private appointment to discuss their prospects. No one had prospects, he repeated time and again, until after Almack's, if then. A great deal of talcum powder in his unmentionables permitted him to say the ladies, including the world's most determined huntress, were merely enjoying themselves for now.

He was not.

How could he stand around watching his friends drool over her, call her the Toast of the Town, the Belle of the Beau Monde? And how could he watch her assess each potential victim with the scrutiny of a housewife buying a trout for dinner? Revolting, that was what it was.

She showed no affection for any of them, never danced twice with the same man. Yet she was going to choose her life's mate, and soon. How? Pick the richest? The one with the highest title, the finest estate, the best looks? Maybe she'd never seen an example of a good, lasting marriage, like his own parents' had been, filled with affection and devotion and friendship. Or seen that syrupy tenderness between new parents, like Rex and Amanda. Or felt that hunger that burned between the newlyweds Harry and Simone. No, she was a coldhearted shrew, seeking a cold alliance.

Her admirers thought she was warm enough, obviously, because they took her flirting as a challenge. Her lack of favorites seemed to increase her popularity, instead of sending a warning to the crowd. Sheep, that was what they were, following the herd after the newest, greenest grass. Miss Abbott was no longer hard to please; she was simply too much in demand, which made her all that much more appealing, more of a game to the beaux.

Daniel went to the gaming room.

And heard her name mentioned on every side. Bother it, couldn't a man escape that drivel in a smoke-filled room of older gentlemen? At least there was no betting book in the host's study, like there was in every club, with a certain wealthy commoner's daughter and her marriage prospects mentioned on every other line. The last time he'd looked—very well, this afternoon, again—the wagers were evenly spread among ten men, all respectable, all acceptable. His name was not in the running.

No one would dare, Daniel told himself, getting satisfaction where he could. No one would speak discourteously of her, either. He'd seen to that. One look at his face and his hands, combined with snippets of Babcock's downfall and Daniel's reputation, silenced any disrespectful prattle before it began, no matter what the rakes were thinking.

They all knew by now that, in loco parentis, he

would not entertain any honorable proposals until after Almack's. They knew, too, he'd pummel any man who dared issue the other kind of offer. Still, nothing could keep them, even the older, married men in the cardroom, from commenting that she was a beauty, and just as lovely inside as out, according to their wives and daughters. Miss Corisande Abbott was a true gentlewoman, a charming addition to London society.

Ha! They didn't almost get their noses slammed in a door. They didn't get stepped on when they were injured. They didn't get turned down for a ride, a drive, a blasted museum visit, or a dance. They didn't get left bringing a blasted cup of lemonade to an empty space. They didn't get shouted at for trying to protect her, by God.

He wanted to shout at them, loudly enough to be heard by her horde of smooth-talking, smooth-dancing, smooth-skinned, rash-free suitors in the ballroom, that she was *not* a desirable bride. Miss Abbott was not a gentle lady, not by half. She was not the complacent, amiable female she pretended, not at all. She was grasping and greedy and coldhearted, out to make the most advantageous match, with love or affection being no advantage at all.

She'd make a man's life a misery once he realized she'd wed him only to escape her father's rule and the doxy Abbott might marry. She wanted to come into her own funds, have her own house, and rule her own roost, and she'd marry Attila the Hun to get her way.

If the poor fool loved her, if he expected her to return his fondness, nay, if he expected to be the king in his own castle, he'd be all the more wretched.

Almost as wretched as Daniel was now.

After several more days of this, of seeing his fellow bachelors make gullible fools of themselves—and watching his mother's and sister's collections of suitors grow, too—Daniel put his foot down.

He was not going to any more balls, Venetian breakfasts (although the food was usually good and plentiful at those absurd afternoon events), routs, or dinner parties. The ladies did not need him to fetch and carry; they had too many willing slaves as it was. They did not need him to fill empty spaces on their dance cards, for there were none. And they did not need protection. No one dared step over the line with any of the ladies from Royce House after word got out how readily and how permanently Daniel Stamfield defended his friends and family.

Since Daniel had stepped on the ruffled hem of his latest hostess's hopeful daughter, leaving the twit in tears, her petticoat showing, and her mother screeching for his blood, Lady Cora accepted his defection—as long as he promised to escort them to the all-important Almack's next week.

The problem was, he was no happier at his old haunts. His new clothes and tidier appearance made him the target of jokes, which were not half as funny now that he drank less. The cards held no sport, not when he had to tally all those dressmakers' bills, extra servants' wages, and food and drink for the incessant callers.

Not that Daniel was near to being hard-pressed, but somehow money was more valuable these days. Going over the estate books his mother used to handle made him realize his funds were not endless, nor easily earned. He'd always known it, of course, but seeing Corie and her diamonds made him appreciate what he had, and how stupid he'd been to risk losing any of it for an evening's mindless pleasure.

His old friends were not as friendly now, either. He wasn't one of them anymore, up to any rig or wager. And to be honest, they smelled bad.

The world was a different place when one didn't spend it in an alcoholic haze, he realized, and not half as much fun.

Women? Lud, now he saw the desperation in their eyes. Maybe that was always there, too, and he'd ignored it for his own peace of mind. The serving girls, the dealers, the women who worked at Lydia Burton's bordello—all had so few years to earn a livelihood, with so much danger, so much degradation and despair. He couldn't enjoy their favors anymore, knowing they had no choice. Instead he bought them dinners, and paid for their time without asking anything back but a bit of companionship.

"You're a real gent, Danny, you are," one of the girls told him. "You've got heart."

And remorse and a restlessness that kept him awake at night, wanting who knew what. Not anything he would put a name to, at any rate. He took to spending more of his time with Miss White and McCann's cook than with the dealers and drinkers at the club.

Harrison tried to console him. "The women will be settled soon and out of your hair. The word is that the Diamond will have more offers than any female this Season, with your sister a close second. They're wagering on the number of offers, since the number of suitors has filled the betting books. I've been asked to request for you to keep a tally."

Daniel's growl was his only response.

"No? I thought you'd say so. Not kind to the rejected suitors and all. At any rate, odds are in favor that Lord Morgan, that old rip, will come up to scratch for your mother. It's not a bad match, now that he's trying to reform. We haven't seen him at the club since Babcock left. So cheer up, my friend; you'll have your own life back soon enough."

"I was thinking right after Almack's, possibly. Now I'm hoping for after my mother's ball next month. The end of the Season at the worst."

Tomorrow was too late.

Corie knew she'd have at least a dozen gentlemen to choose from. They were not speaking of their intentions—thanks to that dolt Daniel—but a woman knew. Certain callers held her hand longer, left her side with regretful looks, competed to send the largest bouquets, the biggest box of sweets. If she mentioned a certain book, she'd have a dozen copies. A lost fan? A dozen replacements.

She could have at least two dozen less-honorable offers, she knew, if Daniel—who was not such a dolt when it came to a rakehell's intentions, curse his wild ways—were not such an intimidating presence.

None of her admirers caught her fancy. This one was so handsome every other female sighed when he walked by. That one was known to be as rich as Golden Ball. Lord This danced divinely, and Sir That had a ready wit. A baronet had a charming little motherless daughter; a banker had a beautiful house on the Thames. None of them had her undivided attention.

Corie could not imagine confessing to any one of them she had once broken every rule of polite society. She dreaded seeing their faces when she showed her broken fingers. How could she explain her diamonds, her mother's beautiful diamonds, were as fake as her claim to respectability?

Corie knew she could not enter a betrothal under false pretenses. The Stamfields were not the only ones who honored the truth. Besides, Daniel and his mother knew about her past. That valet knew. Sooner or later, others might. A husband had to be informed first.

She'd meet privately with the suitor she decided upon, after Daniel approved him, the self-important simpleton. None of the gentlemen she was considering could be faulted or they would not have gotten past Lady Cora or Dobbson, but Daniel had to feel important and all-powerful, the prig.

Then, before she accepted the proposal she was sure was coming, she'd have to reveal her secrets. Her hands were ugly, but uglier were the facts a suitor was entitled to know before plighting his troth: Her father might not release her dowry without a fight; he would not throw her a fancy wedding or purchase her bride clothes. He, that unknown future fiancé, had to be told why her own host considered her too impure to be trusted.

Then her chosen match would hem and haw—she could hear it now—and the proposal would never come. He'd swear not to reveal her private revelations, but what gentleman held his tongue after a few rounds with his cronies at his club?

She thought about holding her silence and her secrets until after the engagement was announced, perhaps at the ball Lady Cora was so busy planning. No gentleman worth that title ever reneged on a betrothal, so she'd be safe. But no man liked being sold used merchandise, either. She'd have to live with the man, and live with his disgust and anger at being lied to, although by omission.

How could she do that? She had a hard enough time dealing with Daniel Stamfield, and she did not even like him. Well, not much, anyway. Not as much as she liked her last partner, she swore to herself, whoever he was.

She was glad Daniel wasn't watching her every move now, not at the parties, not at home when callers came. She did not miss his frowns, not at all. Now she could concentrate on getting to know her suitors better, instead of avoiding Mr. Sneerfield.

Her only hope was to form a real relationship in the short time she had, to build on affection that could last through her confessions.

So she stopped accepting every offer, and kept her partners to that select dozen, granting each two dances apiece, or a dance and the supper, a dance and a drive in the park. She even let some of her favorites steal a kiss, to see if they were daring enough to face Daniel's wrath, and to see if she could tolerate their touch. Mostly she had to know if they wanted her enough to accept her for what she was.

Which was miserable.

Chapter Nineteen

Almack's, at last. An invitation to the assembly was the be-all and end-all of a young girl's aspirations. The queen's drawing room didn't matter half so much. Her own come-out ball, the most lavish her parents could afford, meant nothing, for it would be empty of guests if she stumbled at this summit of acceptance. Here she could make a brilliant match. Here her dreams could be reduced to rubble.

Who the devil were these hawk-nosed witches deciding who qualified to join their elevated ranks? Daniel wanted to know. Who the deuce allowed a parcel of stiff-rumped prudes to make the rules for the rest of them, anyway? Knee breeches only, no admittance past the designated hour, no waltzing until the potentates gave the nod.

And what made anyone care? There were no beverages worth mentioning, barely enough food for a family of undiscriminating mice, parsonage stakes in the cardroom, and the most lackluster collection of insipid girls in pale colors he'd ever had the misfortune to—

"How many did you say I had to dance with, Mother?"

"Hush, and be happy they let you in the door. After last time . . ."

Happy? That was like saying be happy the knife was in your back and not through your heart. Last time, when he was on leave from the army and his aunt dragged him here, one of the old besoms told him how pleased they were to see him in their sacred precincts. Another told him how glad he'd be to dance with her niece, one of the stupidest, silliest chits he'd ever met, a pink, pig-faced girl who called him a noble hero in his regimentals. The next miss they chose for him was half his size, so horrified to be presented with so large a partner that she could barely speak. What she said was how delighted she was.

He hadn't heard one word of truth in the pack of social lies. Polite fibs? No lie was polite when it caused him hives on top of hives, so he scratched them.

"And, dear, you must not itch your, ah, your—"

"My arse, Mother."

Lady Cora took a deep breath. "That. Please, dear. You know how much this means to Susanna. And to Corisande. Oh, and you must dance once with her. It is only proper, with me as her sponsor and you as her escort."

He was willing, he supposed, to make the sacrifice for his mother, except— "She won't dance with me."

"Yes, she will. I have arranged it. The first waltz. She is old enough to dance without permission."

"A waltz, Mother? You know I can never keep from bumping into another couple. And this dance floor is so small and crowded, I'll make a hash of it."

"You will not tonight, dear. Corie is graceful enough

to make any partner look proficient, and you have improved considerably. I shall be proud, as always."

He should have broken out in rashes at that, but his mother spoke the truth as only a mother saw it, through eyes clouded by love. He'd do his best not to disappoint her, although she was bound for a letdown either way. Corie was as unwilling as he was, and she'd likely be as stiff as a broomstick in his arms.

"Well, arrange for her to smile, too," he told his mother, "so no one thinks we are about to murder each other on the dance floor. Oh, and tell her not to say how delighted she is to be my partner."

His mother smiled. "I doubt she will say those words, dear. In fact, I had to admonish her for the words she did use when I told her about the waltz. I do believe she must have overheard the grooms in the stable."

So if he stepped on her foot, she was liable to utter a blasphemy certain to get them all tossed out on their ears? Now Daniel did not have to worry about rashes, only the perspiration trickling down his neck under the blasted tight, high, and starchy neckcloth.

"After that, I am for the cardroom, no matter what anyone says or who they tell me to dance with. Nothing untoward is going to happen in this musty crowd, so you will be safe without me. Ah, I see Lord Morgan headed your way. Shall I take him to the cardroom with me when I go, to give your other beaux a chance?"

"Daniel, I do not have any other—that is, I do not have any beaux. I simply feel sorry for Lord Morgan, with his nephew gone and his own son and grandchildren so far away. He must be lonely, and those smoky clubs and late nights cannot be good for his lungs."

"What about Susanna? Shall I dissuade Clarence from sitting in her pocket all night?"

"He does his duty by the other young girls while she partners as many young men as there are dances. And why would you send him away? Susanna has said time and again she is not looking for a match in London this Season, and I believe her."

Daniel had heard his sister say the same thing, so believed her, too. He did not believe he could survive another Season. "Still, if Clarence weren't nearby, she might get to know the other chaps better and one of them might catch her fancy."

Lady Cora shook her turbaned head. "A determined suitor will quickly see they are merely friends. They are both young and miss their companions at home. That is all."

"Clarence Haversmith is not the steadiest influence, you know." Daniel never did have that conversation about sowing one's seed around the countryside. Somehow the idea of lecturing an unwashed cub like Haversmith made him feel paternal, avuncular, old.

"Susanna has a level enough head for both of them," Lady Cora replied. "Both my children do. You will do what is right, I know. So will Susanna. And Corie, who is like a daughter to me."

So Daniel bowed to the patronesses. He kissed the air over their gloved hands without crushing them, presented his sister and Miss Abbott, then found seats for his party. He wiped the sweat off his forehead and sang bawdy tavern songs under his breath so he'd miss most of the false flattery and the insincere welcomes. No amount of talcum was going to help him tonight.

So this was Almack's. Corie did not think it looked all that impressive for such an important place. Some of the assembly rooms at home were decorated more festively, and most offered better refreshments than bread and butter. Yet this was the pinnacle of the polite world, and thus the center of her world, tonight.

She knew that few gentlemen of the aristocracy married outside their own ranks, and few wed anyone unacceptable to their peers. Even among the upper ten thousand, not every female was deemed a suitable bride. Here was where the self-appointed arbiters decided what was suitable or not, which of this Season's crop of debutantes, spinsters, and widows were marriage material.

Corie was on trial here, the same way her suitors were being tested. If a man could put up with this stuffy atmosphere, with all the punctilio of a foreign court, if he could maintain his poise and his politeness in the heat and the crowd, then he moved up a notch on her list. If he acted the buffoon, embarrassed his partners, stood tongue-tied—then he was Daniel Stamfield, with whom his mother insisted she dance.

She'd avoided him for days and concentrated on her admirers. She eliminated two, one for letting his horse stand outside too long, another for shouting at a war veteran begging in the street. She almost wished she could ask Daniel's opinions about some of the others, but wouldn't give him the satisfaction of seeking his counsel when he so disapproved of her quest for a husband. Lady Cora, Dobbson, and the servants' grapevine had to suffice.

According to her sources, the remaining bachelors— and two widowers—who had shown the most interest in her were not known to drink heavily or wager excessively or indulge in sporting activities beyond the usual. One or two might keep a mistress, and some were known to visit houses of accommodation, but they were all expected to mend their ways once their vows were spoken.

In other words, they were not Daniel Stamfield.

If Corie had to choose tonight, she thought she might pick Lord Whiting, a widower with a small daughter, whose portrait he carried around with him. He was obviously a loving father, which was important to her, and she'd like to be a mother, the sooner the better.

Or she might accept Sir Jamison, a banker who was older than she wished, but not as old or dissipated as Lord Morgan. He was not going to be in attendance tonight, he'd told her, because his ties to trade made him ineligible for Almack's. Not for Corie's hand, she let him know as discreetly as possible. She cared little enough for the world of dukes and earls, and respected a man who made something of himself, unlike Daniel Stamfield. Besides, Sir Jamison wouldn't care about her father's money, according to gossip about his fortune.

Then there was Lord Alexander, a second son who thought she was the most beautiful woman in all of England, and made her feel beautiful with his compliments and sighs. He wouldn't care about the diamonds, but he might find her bent fingers unattractive.

The others were all pleasant gentlemen, or so it seemed on such short acquaintance. She realized she had no overwhelming, convincing basis for selecting a lifelong partner in this analytic fashion, so she'd do her best to fall in love with one of them tonight . . . right after the waltz with Daniel Stamfield, if he did not step on her gown or her toes or spill punch on her skirts. Or scratch his arse.

She couldn't help the giggle that escaped her at the

picture she'd imagined, just as she was paying her respects to another of the patronesses.

"So pleased to be here, my lady. Thank you."

Daniel got through the opening dance with Susanna
in fair form. He was used to starting balls with her,
and she chattered throughout. If he forgot a turn, she
was quick to remind him, without criticism.

Then he danced with Miss Thomlinson, who'd had
the first set with Chadwick, and was promised for
more dances to a Latin scholar down from Oxford and
an amateur botanist. Her modest success was thanks to
him and his family, she told him. She'd never had such
an enjoyable Season.

Daniel was glad for her. He knew what it was like
to be an outsider. "Happy to oblige," he said, wishing
his next partner was as easy to please. Then Miss
Thomlinson's hair ribbon caught on the button of his
coat sleeve. She stopped dancing to untangle herself,
the couple behind them turned to the side, and the
next couple in the line tripped over them, until the
dance was a shambles.

Miss Thomlinson blamed herself. She should have
worn her spectacles, and the quadrille was such a complicated dance, wasn't it?

"Nice gal," Daniel told Chadwick as he handed her
over before heading back to his mother's seat, where
Corie was waiting for her waltz, tapping her foot, and
not in time to the music, which hadn't started yet.

The quadrille wasn't half as complicated as pushing
a reluctant partner around in the waltz was going to
be.

"What do you say we sit the dance out?" he asked

Corie moments later when the orchestra struck up the first notes.

She readily agreed, to protect her toes, her hair, and the flounce on her peach-colored sarcenet overskirt.

They found an unoccupied alcove, in view of the assembly, of course. Heaven forbid a young lady and her beau found a private corner at Almack's.

At first, neither spoke. Both realized they were being watched, though, and so both spoke at once.

"Miss Thomlinson is a lovely woman, don't you think?" Corie said. "Thank you for introducing her to me."

While Daniel said, "What do you want me to tell the gentlemen who will call tomorrow?"

They looked away from each other and stayed silent again. Then Daniel cleared his throat and said, "I told them they could after Almack's. Have you decided which poor fool—uh, which prospective husband—you want me to accept on your behalf? That is," he hurried to add, "I'm not accepting, just passing him on to you to decide. Unless you want to hear a dozen proposals."

"Heavens, no. But I . . . I have not quite decided."

"I can see why not. It's only the rest of your life, but I thought you were in a hurry. If it's any help, Lord Whiting's precious daughter has gone through eight governesses and she's barely seven. A hellion, I hear, spoiled unmercifully by her papa."

"Thank you. I suppose the child's nature should be a consideration, as well as the father's."

He nodded, smiling in case anyone was watching, and because of the look of dismay on Corie's face. "You get two for the price of one wedding. Oh, and

Lord Alexander hasn't a feather to fly with. His father expects him to live off his heiress bride. The duke's got one picked out for him, in Scotland.''

Oh dear. Corie wished she'd consulted Daniel after all, and not wasted her time on poor choices. Then she saw his smile. "You are not just saying that to discourage me, are you?"

His grin grew broader, showing dimples. "I do not lie."

She supposed even a lummox had a few redeeming traits. "What about Sir Jamison, who owns his own bank?"

"His longtime mistress owns her own house next door to his."

"I see." She named a few others on her dance program.

The baronet relied on sawdust to fill out his stockings.

"That's not so bad."

And his trousers.

"Oh." She blushed and he laughed out loud.

The retired naval captain lived with his battle-ax mother, the reason he joined the navy in the first place. The undersecretary once assaulted a housemaid, although she disappeared before she could press charges. One of the knights played with a marked deck; the other played with boys.

"How could you possibly know all this when the servants don't?" He seemed so sure, Corie wished she had half his confidence. Unless it was arrogant pride that made him smile at her disappointment, and everything he said was a parcel of lies. "You could be making it all up."

"I told you, I don't lie, and no one lies to me. I

know people who don't go to fancy affairs like this
but serve the swells who do. They tell me what I want
to know. And it's always true."

Which made as much sense as two incompatible
combatants smiling in an alcove for the world to see.
Two gentlemen remained on Corie's list, so she asked
Daniel about them. He did not know anything to
their discredit.

"That's a relief."

"Why? Do you like either one? Should I give both
permission to ask for your hand?"

To be honest, Corie could barely remember what
either gentleman looked like. "I am to dance with
Lord Harcourt next. I'll know better after that, I
hope."

Lady Cora and Lord Morgan waltzed past their corner, smiling and seeming to enjoy themselves. "I wonder if that is my mother's plan, too. Do you think they
will make a match of it?"

Corie waved to the passing couple. "I think she just
wanted to dance again. And she feels sorry for him."

"I suppose pity is as plausible a reason as any to
base a marriage on. Of course"—he looked directly
at Corie—"there are worse reasons."

She turned her back on him. "We cannot all have
the luxury to wait for the perfect match." She started
to walk back to where Susanna and Clarence were
sitting with some other young ladies denied the waltz.

The dance ended as they reached the seats, but before Corie could look around for her next partner, a
short, florid-faced woman rushed in their direction.

"I just had to greet you," she squealed before they
were close enough.

By heaven, Daniel thought, he remembered dancing

with the piggy chit, one of the patronesses' nieces, three years ago. Some of the gentlemen who stood nearby waiting for a word with the Diamond or Miss Stamfield smiled in sympathy. But no, the female wanted to meet Corie, thank goodness.

"Do you remember me from Miss Meadow's Academy? I am Jane Wardley."

Daniel could swear she snorted as she spoke.

"I heard the most diverting tale, my dear. Of how you refused the man your father wanted you to wed, in favor of a handsome soldier."

Corie stepped closer to Daniel. He gallantly reminded Miss Wardley of their dance some years ago, but she was not to be denied.

She clutched her hands to her plump chest, almost worshipfully. "And you, noble creature, have stayed faithful to his memory ever since."

"Would you do me the honor of standing up for the next dance?" Daniel offered, although calling it an honor might kill him.

She ignored the hand he extended, but squealed again and sighed. "Let that be a message to all of us females looking for suitable marriages, to hold out for True Love. I told my father I would not wed without a Grand Passion."

Who could love her, much less feel an iota of passion for the sow? Better yet, who could shut her up? He looked around for help, but all he saw was interested faces, curious looks, especially from Corie's admirers.

She was trying to convince Miss Wardley that what she'd heard was all a hum. "It was nothing of the sort, I promise you. A schoolgirl's infatuation for a dashing uniform."

"Oh, but everyone knows that's why you never accepted another suitor."

Corie's suitors were looking uncomfortable now. If she was bent on a love match, they had no chance, except maybe Lord Alexander, whose adoration could not overcome his appreciation for the finer things in life he'd never afford on his own. Besides, who wanted a wife to be the heroine of some novel, pining away for a dead soldier? For that matter, who wanted such an emotional, clinging wife?

They stepped closer, to hear better, except the ones who had heard enough. Those faded into the crowd.

Then Lady Cora was at Corie's side, with Lord Morgan trailing behind, wheezing from the exertions of the dance, or to drown out Miss Wardley's shrills and snorts.

"But do you still love—"

Lord Morgan collapsed on the floor at her feet, gasping for air. Miss Wardley squealed louder still, and grabbed on to Daniel's arm. He pushed her away to kneel at Lord Morgan's side, to raise the older man's head. His mother was at the man's other side, loosening his neckcloth.

While women cried and men rushed in every direction, shouting for water, a surgeon, a vinaigrette, Daniel leaned over and whispered, "Thanks, old man. Great diversion."

Lord Morgan grabbed his hand, murmured, "Not . . . pretending," and gave his last gasp.

Chapter Twenty

"You are not going to die, old man!" Daniel swore, shaking him. Daniel did not feel any heat on his own skin, so shook him again.

If Lord Morgan was not going to die, his heart seemed to decide, he better start breathing. So he gave another gasp, then another. Women fainted; men cheered. The patronesses clapped for the orchestra to begin again; such high drama was unseemly.

Daniel was all for scooping the man over his shoulder, bundling him into his carriage, and, with misgivings, taking him home. He recalled that slovenly, sullen butler and the mess in the house, though, and worried what kind of care Lord Morgan was going to receive there.

Lady Cora was having none of that nonsense. Leave a man at death's door at his own doorstep, to be tended by indifferent servants? Not while she had a breath in her body, which was more than Lord Morgan seemed to have a moment ago.

She directed a footman to have her coach brought to the front door, then three more footmen—not her son in his tight-fitting, elegant evening clothes—to carry his lordship to it, and yet another footman to run and fetch a doctor to Royce House. Lord Morgan would be far better off there.

"Are you certain, Mother?" Daniel asked as he watched the three men carry the moaning man through the gawking crowds, while he could have done it himself with far less commotion in half the time. Instead he had to wait while his sister and Corie made their excuses to their dance partners and their fare-wells to the hostesses. Which he could also have done in half the time. At least Lord Morgan was breathing easier, and his color had returned some. The crisis seemed passed. "Perhaps he simply suffered a weak spell, and he'll recover as easily at his own home, with familiar surroundings. I know he has some kind of restorative some physician prescribed for him."

Lady Cora gathered her fan and her shawl and her beaded reticule. "We are taking him home and that is final."

"It will give rise to more speculation, you know."

She started toward the exit, the girls following be-hind. "Bosh. He is too ill to ruin my reputation, even if I were willing to permit it. The girls will not be left unchaperoned by me or Susanna's former governess."

"Having him stay will be a great deal of work."

"And my brother employs a great many servants. Furthermore, Eugenia Reynolds has nothing to do. My new secretary, which I never truly required, will be happy to sit by his bedside and read to the old dear or play piquet with him. They've become good friends during our jaunts around the city."

"Matchmaking again, Mother?"

She hid her blushes by hurrying after the footmen to direct the placement of the invalid. "Lord Morgan needs someone to look after him, and Eugenia needs to be useful. We'll see. And you'll have to ride up on top with the coachman and the groom. Make sure they do not race through the streets. Lord Morgan does not need to be jostled."

So they brought him home, all of them relieved he was breathing better, some of them also relieved to be leaving Almack's.

The next morning, the house was still at sixes and sevens. Physicians and apothecaries were running up and down the stairs; footmen were being sent hither and thither with notes to Lord Morgan's son in the country, canceling his appointments and those of the ladies. Meanwhile, dozens—no, scores of gentlemen clutching bouquets gathered in the hall, while the women of the house were neither coming down to breakfast nor receiving visitors.

And the current master? Mr. Stamfield went out early to fetch, of all things, a dog! A dog, in Royce House. How Dobbson's standing would fall in the local pub.

His wig was so askew he tossed it aside and powdered his own gray hair. Mr. Stamfield left instructions to placate the gentlemen with food until he got back, so now Cook was having apoplexy of her own in the kitchen. Suddenly she had to satisfy an army of hungry males instead of feeding ladies with dainty appetites. On top of that, she was expected to provide invalid food.

With another gentleman to look after, Deauville also threatened to give notice, except the master was not in to receive it. He was out—out of his mind, half the household believed.

Daniel couldn't leave the old relic at that near-derelict house. Or his dog, either. So he went himself to fetch the spotted hound.

The butler was snoring, a maid was sloshing dirty water around the front hall, and the dog was whining. No one had missed Lord Morgan except the old bitch, who likely hadn't been fed or walked. Daniel threatened to pound the butler into dog food if the house was not clean, with all its belongings accounted for, when his lordship returned. Or else he'd have the majordomo replaced.

Then he asked the butler for the dog's name.

"Go to Hell" did not seem appropriate for such a sweet old thing, so Daniel called her Helen. She followed him out, since he had a thick sandwich of ham and cheese to share.

After letting the dog relieve herself, Daniel picked her up—he wore one of his old, loose coats for just such a need—and placed her carefully beside him on the curricle's driving bench.

Helen whimpered a little when they left the familiar neighborhood, so Daniel fed her more of his sandwich. Then he had to stop at a coffee shop and have his tiger run in to fetch him another breakfast.

"Can't face the suitors on an empty stomach, can I?"

He'd run out of excuses not to face the cork-brained crowd. He thought of throwing all of them out, saying that the ladies had decided not to marry. He'd be lying, but he could blame the instant welts on the dog's fleas.

Corie never got the chance to talk with the rest of the gentlemen on her list last night, so she couldn't be smitten with any of them. Which did not mean the ambitious female wouldn't grasp at the first offer she received. She might as well pick names out of a hat, for all she seemed to care about any of the men. He wondered why he cared about her finding a happy marriage.

He also wondered if he was honor-bound to tell the goddess's chosen sacrifice about her past.

He took himself into his uncle's library, with its rows of special bottles on the sideboard. He did not pour any because his poor head was muddled enough thinking about Corie and her marriage, Corie and her happiness, Corie and her enchanting green eyes.

Dobbson gave him a minute to settle into the chair behind his uncle's desk, where Daniel thought he might feel wiser, or look more confident and in command than he felt. Then the butler started bringing in the supplicants—the suitors, that was—in order of rank.

The Russian prince fought too many duels. The earl had buried too many wives. The duke's heir had no hair on his head but a mustache full of crumbs. None of them was worthy of any of the females.

Daniel gave up. He was not his stately, Solomon-like uncle, who should be here where he belonged as head of the family. Daniel told Dobbson to send in all the rest of the men at once, and serve Lord Royce's finest.

There weren't enough seats, but they weren't staying long, not if Daniel had his way. He looked around while Dobbson and a footman served various wines and liquors. Some of those present surprised him. He didn't think such confirmed bachelors were in the marriage market. Some of the absentees surprised him, too. A few of Corie's suitors must have gotten wind of last night's news, her supposedly broken heart. He doubted they'd heard more, or no one would be here.

Clarence was not among the petitioners, either, Daniel was relieved to see. Dobbson informed him that Master Haversmith and Miss Stamfield had taken the dog to the kitchens, for breakfast.

Better Helen having another meal than Haversmith asking for Susanna's hand, Daniel decided. He had strict instructions to turn away any offers for his sister until the end of the Season.

So he dismissed most of the youngest suitors. "You"—he pointed at one of them—"come back in two months."

"You"—the youngest—"come back in two years."

To one with a vacant, opiate-induced smile, he said, "Do not come back at all."

He told the older gentlemen what his mother had instructed him to say: that she was honored by the attention, but she was not considering a courtship at this time. She was too busy preparing for the ball next month, chaperoning her charges, and caring for Lord Morgan. Daniel tempered the mature suitors' disappointment by adding, "He is her secretary's particular friend, you see."

They left happy after draining their glasses in a toast to Lady Cora.

Few men were left, far fewer than Daniel expected from the names in the betting books. All were sober and well dressed, some in riding attire with high-topped boots, some with high shirt collars. Some were at ease; some appeared anxious; some looked as if they'd come simply because it was all the fashion this week.

The banker kept consulting his watch. Like Daniel, he must have thought getting a female hitched was a matter of moments. Daniel couldn't reject a chap for being impatient. Not a rich one, anyway. If Sir Jamison was late for a tryst with his mistress, that was another matter.

He cleared his throat to get their attention. "As you must know, Miss Abbott is not receiving callers this morning. Nor do I speak for her, except to ensure no unsuitable gentlemen are permitted to call on her. Therefore, if you are persona non grata in polite circles, I'd be grateful if you left before I have to rearrange your facial features. The rest of you are free to pursue your suit, as you will." Then he added, "Within the bounds of propriety, of course."

Which caused hoots of laughter, that Daniel Stamfield was preaching correct behavior.

He laughed along with them. "I know, I know; there's nothing like a reformed rake for hypocrisy, but we're talking about a lady. I'll have to consult with Miss Abbott's father, of course, before making any formal announcements, but it is not I you have to convince of your worth; it is Miss Abbott herself."

He tipped his glass, his first of the day, and muttered, "And heaven help you."

They filed out, patting one another on the back, laying more wagers, bragging of their prospects.

He poured himself another glass.

Before he could drink it, someone coughed. Daniel looked over toward the cushioned window ledge, where a gentleman was getting to his feet.

"Sorry. I didn't notice you in the crowd. Lord Trowbridge, is it?" Daniel vaguely recalled the distinguished-looking gentleman had something to do with the government, from when he helped Harry. Trowbridge was older than most of Corie's admirers, although not as old as the banker. He hadn't been at Almack's, but

Daniel never got to visit the cardroom. Nor had Trow-bridge called at Royce House before, as far as Daniel knew, so he must have come upon Miss Abbott at one of the functions Daniel had escaped. The unfortunate chap undoubtedly fell silver-templed head over well-shined boots the moment Trowbridge saw her beauty and heard her lilting voice.

The problem, though, other than his resenting the man for being so perfect, was Lord Trowbridge wore black ribbons trailing from his sleeve.

"It is a little soon to come courting Miss Abbott, isn't it? That is fairly brazen while you still wear mourning for your first wife."

Trowbridge came closer to Daniel's desk. He touched the ribbon at his sleeve. "Yes, it would be disrespectful, but you mistake my reason for calling today."

"Lud, you are not interested in my sister, are you?"

Trowbridge frowned. "Are you always so quick to jump to conclusions? I worry about my mission, then."

"Your mission?"

For answer, the man reached into his inner pocket and pulled out a ten-pound note, issued by the Bank of England. He put the largish paper on the desk in front of Daniel.

"I don't recall any debts. I don't even recall seeing you at the clubs."

"I seldom have time. And, as you said, I am in mourning. And you are making hasty judgments again."

Daniel looked at the bank certificate. "Then . . . ?"

"Pick it up."

Daniel watched Trowbridge's face, watching him. "Not trying to bribe me or anything, are you?"

Trowbridge shook his head and clucked his tongue, so Daniel knew he'd guessed wrong again.

Daniel picked up the banknote with two fingers, and dropped it quickly. He looked at his fingers, then at Trowbridge, and grinned. "Who are you exactly and how did you know to come to me?"

The older man smiled back. "So they were right. You can tell a counterfeit bill by its feel."

Daniel stretched his fingers, still sensing that bit of heat at their tips. "It seems I can, which is a surprise to me, too. I think you better sit down and tell me how you got here. More important, who else you are going to tell." The whole family could be in jeopardy if word got out that the Royce men dabbled in what appeared to be magic.

Trowbridge explained that he was an undersecretary at the royal exchequer, answerable to the minister of finance. He worked with various other branches of the government, ones seldom in the public eye.

That answered one question for Daniel. "You know Harry, do you?"

"I have had that pleasure, yes. Very closemouthed, your, ah . . ." Trowbridge was not sure what to call Lord Royce's baseborn son.

"My cousin. My friend."

"You are fortunate. As we all are, to have had him working for England in the late war. No one quite understood his function, or his talent, of course."

Which was meant to reassure Daniel that whatever Trowbridge was, he wasn't a talebearer. "Of course."

"Or your other cousin's talent, Lord Rexford."

Which in turn meant Trowbridge was well-informed. "Rex was a brave soldier, an officer, don't you know."

"And much more." While Daniel waited to find out

how much more Trowbridge knew, the older man added, "I understand Lord Rexford has been a major assistance to Bow Street and the magistrate's office."

Those facts were common knowledge, after Rex helped solve a highly publicized, sensational case, then married the accused murderess. "You still have not answered how you came to be on my doorstep this morning."

"Mr. Harrison of McCann's Club thought I might have need for one of your skills. He still has ties to the Intelligence Division, you know."

Daniel decided he'd have to murder Harrison, even if the man was his friend, and like a brother to Harry.

Trowbridge must have seen the fury on Daniel's face, or else remembered Mr. Stamfield's own reputation for violence. He quickly said, "I assure you, Harrison told no one else, and only spoke to me for the sake of England's safety. I told no one, either, and would not even if I had not given my sworn word, since I did not half believe what Harrison said. Here." He tossed five more government-issue notes on the desk, two five-pound and three one-pound denominations.

Daniel touched each one. One of the five-pound notes was fake. He held it to its mate and studied them for differences. "Very good. No one would know without careful scrutiny."

"Precisely. The forgers managed to duplicate the watermark the bank added to discourage copying. Neither that nor Parliament's making counterfeiting a capital offense seems to be working currently. Do you know what a flood of these can do to the entire economy of the country?"

Daniel could imagine. The poorest Englishmen

rarely used the paper currency, not trusting its value. Now the wealthier, more knowledgeable citizens might want to see the gold the flimsies represented. There would be panic at the banks, shops closed, and businesses bankrupt. The government would be blamed. Prinny was already so unpopular there could be rioting in the streets.

"It's not a pretty picture."

"Then you'll help?"

Daniel did not hesitate an instant. "Of course."

Trowbridge nodded and gathered up the banknotes. "Mr. Hase, the head teller at Threadneedle Street, is expecting us."

"Now who is jumping to conclusions?"

"Harrison said the Royce men never fail their country."

"Well, that may be true"—his lack of the slightest itch told Daniel it was—"but I don't see how I can help much other than picking out the fakes. I cannot trace them back to their maker, and I sure as the devil cannot stop them from being circulated."

"But you can ask people where they got them."

Daniel forced himself not to squirm like a schoolboy. "I much prefer to stick with the paper money."

"But no one lies to you."

Daniel stared across the room at the portrait of one of his Royce ancestors. He couldn't remember if that was the earl who could literally smell out a lie, or if he was the one who heard buzzing in his ears. They'd all done their duty. He found a clean glass and poured Trowbridge a drink. He raised his own glass in a toast. "To King and Country."

And to old dogs with fleas.

Chapter Twenty-one

The Bank of England took up most of Threadneedle Street. As Daniel and Lord Trowbridge were escorted by guards through the building to the head teller's office, Daniel could not help thinking that Miss Abbott could be interested in a tour of this place. Miss Thomlinson might know what all the men were doing, rushing around, silently moving ledgers and folders and boxes from one place to another, but Corie was more appreciative of a new spectacle. He'd seen the two women in the art museums, where Miss Thomlinson could recite the artist's place of birth and year, and the entire provenance of the painting. Corie was more like Daniel. She'd given soft little "Oh" sounds when something impressed her.

He should not be thinking of Corie now, nor her murmurings. This was business, state business, Daniel's new trade. Counterfeit Detector? Inspector of Currency? None sounded as dashing as Harry's being the Aide. Not that Daniel wanted the public to know what he was doing, but he did wish, for an instant, that some people—Miss Corisande Abbott in particular—could see he was not just a here-and-thereian.

Trowbridge definitely was no idle town buck. He

seemed at home here, nodding to this man or that as if he understood their functions, every one of them. He received a warm welcome, almost one of relief, from the head of the vast accounting office. Mr. Hase was willing to listen, but he showed a degree of skepticism that Daniel was the expert found to assist them with their "little problem."

Daniel could not blame the man. He knew he did not look like any counterfeiting expert, not in his rough clothes covered in dog hair, but if he were Hase, in danger of seeing the whole British Empire go bankrupt on his watch, he'd sure as hell welcome anyone with a plan to help.

Trowbridge must have warned Mr. Hase that Daniel used special methods, which were not to be viewed or discussed. Mr. Hase, however, refused to allow Daniel to sit alone in the vault room he led them to.

It was tempting, all right. Not that Daniel needed the blunt, not that he'd think of stealing a shilling, but damn, there was a king's ransom in this room alone, and it was only one of many.

Trowbridge explained the bound stacks of government-issued currency were from various private banks—Child's, Coates, Lloyds, and lesser ones in the countryside—sent to London in exchange for coins. With each pile labeled, they might discover the counterfeits' origin, if one pile held a higher proportion of sham bills. It would take the bank's own team of professional examiners, including the extra men hired once the trouble was discovered, days to inspect just these, with more coming and going every day. Besides, the fewer people who knew of the country's finances being tampered with, the better.

Trowbridge said he would stay with Mr. Stamfield,

to vouch for his honesty. Not that such steps were necessary. "Stamfield here is a Royce, don't you know."

In that case, the head teller acknowledged, no committee of bank officers and guards was required.

When the man left, Trowbridge handed Daniel a bundle. Daniel riffled through the bills, as if he were counting out a deck of cards, only the pound notes were thinner than pasteboards. He found one counterfeit, of a low denomination. Those were not as potentially damaging as the larger designations in the short run, but over any length of time, and with enough of the false flimsies changing hands, they could be catastrophic. A smart counterfeiter would know that. A patient one would not try for a huge windfall all at once, which would alert the authorities that much sooner. Smaller bills were easier to pass around, and less likely to draw attention. According to Trowbridge, the government had no idea how long ago the current scheme had begun.

The next pile revealed nothing out of the usual, nor the one after. After that, Daniel detected a few notes that gave his fingers prickles, but not many. Trowbridge consulted with a minor official waiting by the door.

Then Daniel started to riffle a pile of banknotes that came from Chimkin's Bank in Oxfordshire.

"Got it!" he yelled, blowing on his fingers. Nearly a fifth of the bills were as crooked as a shepherd's staff.

"Good job!" Trowbridge shouted, bringing their escort into the vault room, then hurrying to fetch the director back. Now they could withdraw the tainted bills from circulation before they caused more problems, and go after the source. Trowbridge considered that setting up shop near the university was a brilliant move on the part of the counterfeiters. Students seldom held their money for long, had no reason to inspect each pound note, and went elsewhere for holidays. Of course Oxford may have been the testing ground, to see how easily the counterfeits passed among the students, shopkeepers, and landladies. More were coming to London now.

Trowbridge was already writing memos to send examiners and investigators to Oxford on the instant. Would Daniel care to accompany them?

To interrogate swindlers? Not for all the money in the room. Daniel was glad he had the excuse of his mother's ball, a sick houseguest, two young ladies who could not be left without an escort. He'd plead on behalf of the old dog if he thought that could keep him from playing at Bow Street Runner again. The last time had left his skin raw from scratching.

He went through several more bundles of banknotes, but none of the other rural banks held as many counterfeits as some of the London banks. The scheme was definitely spreading into London, via lesser denominations, which were less likely to be scrutinized as carefully.

Of course they did not know about the Bank of England's expert inspector. Daniel rolled that on his tongue while Trowbridge and Hase conferred. "Expert inspector" sounded a lot better than "Inquisitor." He liked working with the money far more than with spies and criminals. Money did not cringe or cry when he came near.

Meanwhile a clerk with a magnifying lens examined the notes Daniel said were forgeries. The head teller wasn't ready to believe that a civilian, not even a banker or a clerk, had found so many counterfeits in twenty minutes. The clerk found the discrepancies.

Now Mr. Hase shook Daniel's hand. What an eye he must have! What an uncanny knack.

Trowbridge hustled them out before anyone could ask questions. "Yes, isn't it?"

Daniel promised to return later in the week for another inspection.

Daniel left the bank and Trowbridge with a lighter step, a lighter heart. He bought himself a meat pie from a vendor on the corner and licked his fingers afterward, his excellent, artful fingers.

He wished Harry were here, to brag to about his new skill. Or Rex, who'd be glad Daniel was working with the government again, doing something rewarding. Speaking of rewarding, Daniel wondered if shaved playing cards would affect his fingers. What a boon that could be when he went gaming in the stews. Not that he wanted to visit his old low haunts, not while his mother was in Town, anyway. He pondered what else he could do.

He did regret having no one to tell, no one to help him figure out what other lies he could uncover with his new truth-touching fingers. Here he was, not gaming, not wenching, not drinking—well, not to excess—and no one seemed to notice that, either.

So what was the point of reforming oneself?

For oneself, of course. He knew it all along. He liked having a clear head in the morning, and waking up in clean sheets. He enjoyed not depending on his gambling winnings, and seeing his mother's smile when he bought her and the girls flowers. He bought three bunches of violets from a flower girl, and gave her an extra coin, one he was positive was real.

He liked doing what no one else could do. He did not like having no one to share it with.

Everyone at home was too busy, even if he wanted to discuss his amazing day.

His mother and Susanna were at a waltzing party for the youngest set, according to Dobbson. The afternoon functions were intended to give the debutantes experience with the dance steps and varied partners for when they were finally granted permission. Daniel couldn't see much difference in dancing in the daytime versus at night. In fact the whole pother over a dance made as much sense as reading Shakespeare to a sheep, but his mother thought someone from Royce House ought to be seen in public after last night's hurried departure from Almack's. Everyone would be coming to their door otherwise, feigning interest in Lord Morgan's welfare, but wanting to know the truth about Corie's supposedly broken heart.

They dragged Clarence Haversmith along with them, since there were never enough willing males at these afternoon gatherings. Who could blame the poor cubs for making excuses?

Miss Reynolds was playing piquet with Lord Morgan when Daniel stopped by his room. He was better, she was blooming, and the dog was banished to the hallway outside the door. The physician had prescribed rest, no cigars, no late nights, no strenuous activity, and no pets in the bedroom. Besides, Miss Reynolds was afraid of dogs, and this one kept scratching her ears and licking her feet. Helen's feet, that was, not Miss Reynolds's, or the dog would be sent to the stables.

The hound's name was Pip, Daniel learned, for the black spots. Daniel preferred Helen, and since she was nearly deaf anyway, he continued to call her by that name. She answered to it, or to the smell of the kidney pie on his fingers. Which reminded Daniel he hadn't eaten in a while, so they followed the scent of raspberry tarts and tea.

Helen started scratching again.

So was Miss Abbott, scratching with a pen in the morning room on yet more letters to old friends. At least that was what he guessed, from the addresses on the other letters. He wondered if she was asking them if they had any brothers or unwed cousins, now that the ranks of her suitors were thinner, and she could not depend on her diamonds.

He'd never met a female so determined to land a husband. He should be grateful, he supposed, that he wouldn't be responsible for her much longer, but it was not as if they were throwing her out of Royce House anytime soon. They'd been good hosts, he thought, and his mother more than generous, so Corie's haste to leave was almost insulting.

He knew they had to go out this evening so she could flirt and show the world she was not pining for any dead soldier. His mother expected him to go, too, he knew, instead of finding his own pleasure—which hadn't been all that pleasurable recently, anyway—in case they needed another diversion. He thought he'd just interrupt Corie to assure her of his support, in case she was worried. But if she yelled at him like Cook when he tried to bring the dog into her kitchens, he was leaving, and she could face the *ton* on her own. Corie never had a problem finding fault with him at the best of times.

Miss Abbott did not yell, but she was pale, with dark circles under her eyes. She looked sad. Daniel knew she'd been keeping late nights; now she had to worry about losing her status as the most popular female in Town, and losing her suitors.

"Am I interrupting? I thought I'd see if you wanted to drive in the park. You know, so you'd be seen acting merry, not like a woman wearing the willow for a dead soldier."

Her lips turned down. "They'll think what they want no matter what I do. You know me, and still don't think I'm worthy of becoming someone's wife."

"I don't think that."

"You did."

And she'd think him a wastrel no matter what he did. Daniel wished he could tell her about his work with the Finance Ministry, but that was to be a close-held secret for now. It was too hard to explain, too easy for the counterfeiters to hear of an investigation, especially with Daniel's reputation.

On his way home he'd considered some hypotheses: that an operation of this magnitude needed more than one man, an artist, a printmaker, a pressman; that a gentleman was in charge, someone of stature who could pass bills the easiest, without being questioned. Perhaps he held a title, so did not fear a public hanging. Peers had to be tried in Parliament, where the lords would rather wear donkeys' ears than accuse one of their own. But he remembered Trowbridge chiding him for leaping to conclusions. It was too soon to speculate.

"A drive?" Corie asked, bringing him back to the morning room and his offer. "It is pouring out."

It was? Daniel hadn't noticed. He'd been so intent on his new discovery and his theorizing, it could have been snowing. When Deauville handed him a fresh coat, Daniel had thought the dog hairs bothered the valet, not that it was damp.

Still, he did not think Corie ought to be sitting here by herself. "Um, they are playing cards upstairs."

Corie picked up her pen again. "I do not wish to lose what pin money I still have. And Miss Reynolds seemed comfortable enough with Lord Morgan."

She seemed more than comfortable to Daniel. He tried again. "I thought I'd visit one of the print shops, you know, look at the artwork."

That got her to put her pen down. "You? That is, go to an art exhibit without being forced?"

He bent down to give the dog a bite of pastry. "I, uh, didn't intend to look at paintings, just some engravings for sale. I thought I'd take a look." He wanted to see if any felt wrong, to test his new skill.

He must have looked guilty, because she turned back to her letters. "There is nothing in those places but scurrilous cartoons of the prince and his brothers. Or salacious ones." She looked up and frowned at him.

So there'd be no drive, no galleries, nothing to cheer her up. As much as the woman aggravated him, he hated to see her blue-deviled. "Anything you'd rather do this afternoon?"

"Yes, I'd rather not be the center of gossip."

He fed the dog some more of his raspberry tart. "I'm sorry, but that can't be helped. It's a story straight out of some novel, a beautiful damsel, a forlorn love. You'll have to show them tonight."

"By being merry as a grig," she said, scowling at the idea.

"I don't know what entertainment my mother has planned."

"Whatever it is, I will be on display again." Corie was tired of being onstage, always acting. She was writing to Lady Cora's man of business, asking if she might call on him to ask for legal advice.

With the tart all gone, the dog started itching again.

Daniel looked at Corie, her green eyes all shadowed, her shoulders slumped with the weight of the world on them. Then he looked at Helen. "I know just the thing. Let's give the dog a bath."

She did smile, faintly, as one would for a babbling infant.

"It's great fun, and you look like you could use cheering up."

She was surprised he noticed, or cared. She was not altogether surprised a dolt like Daniel Stamfield would think bathing an old dog was fun. "I cannot imagine enjoying that."

"Neither can Helen, but she'll feel better after. We'll all get wet and look silly. Come."

"I thought the dog's name was Pip."

"She's deaf, so it doesn't matter. The vermin on her do."

That made the job sound less appealing, if possible. "Surely the grooms in the stables can give her a wash."

"They are busy, and she doesn't know them. They don't know her, so mightn't care about getting the temperature of the water right, or not getting soap in her eyes, or drying her off right. I took her away from her comfortable digs, not that she was well cared for there, so she is my responsibility. But it's definitely a two-man job. Or a man and a woman. Two people."

Corie tilted her head, as if looking at him for some kind of trap or sarcasm. "Daniel Stamfield spouting responsibility. Wonders never cease." But she got up, petted the dog's head after letting the hound sniff at her hand. "A bath it is."

They decided to use the bathing chamber upstairs, where there was piped hot water and plenty of towels. Neither mentioned what a breach of propriety this was, with his mother not at home and Miss Reynolds not free to chaperone.

Daniel took off his coat and neckcloth. Corie tied on an apron borrowed from the broom closet. Soon both of them were sopping wet, along with the floor, the walls, and parts of the dog. Soap suds were everywhere, and laughter.

Daniel was right: She was happier. So was he, except that he couldn't help noticing how the wet apron pressed against her breasts.

Corie couldn't help noticing how gentle he was with the dog, how his big hands stroked the old hound and calmed her.

He dragged his eyes from her bosom and noticed her hands, her bent hands scrubbing Helen's back. "What happened to your fingers?"

Corie couldn't hide them in her skirts, not when they were full of soap and water. Besides, she was more in charity with Daniel than ever before, so why not tell him? Everyone else was discussing her; he might as well, too. He hadn't given away any of her history yet.

Mostly she decided to tell him because he'd already seen what she kept hidden, and seemed only curious, not repulsed. She could not keep the bitterness from her voice when she started: "It was when my father dragged me away from that inn."

He did not need to ask which inn. "You fell down the stairs? Your hand got caught in the carriage door?"

She did not answer until they rinsed Helen off and wrapped her in towels in front of the fire in Daniel's bedroom. "I suppose she'll be sleeping there now that she's been evicted from Lord Morgan's room," he said, then took up a dry towel to wrap around Corie's hands, carefully patting them dry so he did not hurt her. "Your fingers?" he persisted.

She said it all at once: "My father slammed a book down on my hand when we got home."

"You mean he dropped a book? That was the accident?"

She laughed. "Oh, no, there was no accident. He picked up the family Bible, a heavy, ancient volume, from its place on the book stand. I thought he was going to pray for me, or read me some edifying passage. Instead he said I'd broken his dreams, made him break his word to Sir Neville. I'd broken the chain of life inscribed in the Bible because he'd never let me marry or bring forth tainted seed. So he broke my hand with the book, to show the world. I suppose if he had a flaming brand he would have marked my forehead the way they used to do."

Daniel stared at her crooked fingers, the enlarged knuckles. Her own father had done that? "And no one straightened them for you?"

"He would not permit anyone to call for a surgeon. He locked me in my room until there was proof that

I was not breeding. By then it was too late to repair the damage."

Daniel still held her hand, still could not look at her face.

"That was not the first time my father grew violent, only the worst. Lady Cora says I may stay with her, but he'd have the right to reclaim me at any time. I will never be safe without another man's name to protect me. That's why I went with Snelling, even knowing him for a scoundrel. He had to be better than my father. So now you see why I cannot go home, why I need a husband so badly."

Now he saw why she hated him so much.

Chapter Twenty-two

Corie felt better for the telling.

Daniel felt worse for the hearing. He let go of her hands, to pace the length of his bedchamber, where the dog was no proper duenna. He did not care.

She hated him, and with reason. He'd thought she despised him for keeping her from eloping with her lover. Instead he'd helped Squire Abbott, without knowing about Sir Neville, without knowing about the squire's cruelty. Daniel was the one who condemned her to life with a sadistic bastard. And all without asking a single question. That was what he felt guiltiest about. He'd accepted his neighbor's frantic call to save his daughter from ruination at the hands of an unscrupulous fortune hunter.

One question, one simple question, and he would have known the truth the way he always knew the truth: Why? Why did she go, and why didn't he ask?

Because, as always, he'd jumped to conclusions. Fool he was, he'd rushed in, where the proverbial angels were fearful enough to ask for more information. He did so now, three years too late.

"You said that was not the first time."

Corie untied the strings of the wet apron and

draped it over the back of a chair. "No. He is a violent man."

The idea of a man striking a woman was repugnant to Daniel. Any man, any woman. But to lift one's hand against a child, a young girl who could not defend herself? One's own flesh and blood? He thought of the tiny infant he'd held at his goddaughter's christening, his cousin Rex's baby daughter. Rex could hardly bear to see her in another man's arms; he'd kill anyone who threatened her in any way. So would Daniel, the mite's godfather. Now he wanted to murder Abbott.

He kept pacing, rather than putting his fist through the wall of his uncle's house. "Was that the last time?"

"He never wanted me near him, and I made sure to keep my distance, especially when I knew he'd been drinking."

Which did not entirely answer Daniel's question. Abbott was always drinking, as far as he knew. He was always looking for new servants, too, for few stayed long in his employ. A child had no such choice. Daniel was furious at himself. Why hadn't he asked, damn it? Granted, Abbott hustled the girl away at the inn, while she was screaming and crying.

Not because she was leaving her lover, he knew now, but because she was returning to her father. "Hell and damnation."

Corie mistook his anger. "He never hurt me so badly after that, although he threatened to. I—I took to carrying a small knife in my pocket."

He looked at her. She was tall for a woman, but light-boned, almost delicate, except for her impressive bust. Now was not the time to be noticing that the dampness from the apron had seeped through to her thin muslin gown to outline her breasts. If he stared, he might be able to see her nipples, hardened with the chill. He turned his back. "Can you shoot?"

"Shoot? A pistol?"

"Not a bow and arrow, by Zeus. They make tiny pistols that fit in your pocket. A man would have a knife out of your hand before you could shout for help. Then he'd use it on you, for thwarting him. At least you could do more damage with a gun. I'll get you one."

Corie was not sure she could actually shoot someone, much less her own father, but she was touched by Daniel's concern. Then again, she could trust Daniel Stamfield to know the best way to injure a man.

He was still pacing, still angry, but not with her, she was certain. Even knowing his reputation, even alone in a room with him and his fury, she did not feel afraid. He was outraged on her behalf, for once, instead of being angry at her. Remembering his gentleness with the dog soothed her, took away the trembling when he asked about her mother.

"I cannot prove he killed her, if that is what you are asking. When I was young, she always claimed she was clumsy, that she fell a lot. As I grew older and felt his hand, I suspected she was not clumsy at all, but she would never say anything against him. Then it was too late for me to help her. She took to her bed and died."

"There was nothing you could have done. The authorities would not have stepped in between a husband and wife."

"Or a father and his daughter."

He nodded. Such were the laws. "So you ran away."

"So I tried to run away."

"And I helped stop you." Now he did pound the mantel, sending the ormolu clock bouncing into a small, carved wooden chest that held flint and tinder. "Lord, I am sorry. I realize now I did not know half the facts of the matter. I just knew your father was distraught, and Snelling a scoundrel. His reputation followed him throughout the army in the Peninsula. He would have gone through your money and left you at the first chance."

"But he would not have left me until we were married, because he had hopes of getting my dowry. He said he was going to take me to his family on the way back from Gretna, to stay there while he conducted business in London. I knew Francis had no business but to get his hands on my money, that he'd sold his commission, but I reasoned that his father, Viscount Snelling, would have to keep me, if only out of shame when his son abandoned me. If I could get my diamonds or my dower money, his lordship might even welcome me. If they all despised me, living with Snelling's family had to be better than life with my father."

If the family was anything like that sniveling worm, Daniel had his doubts.

"How the devil did you meet a loose screw like Snelling, anyway?"

Corie tried to smooth her skirts, rather than meet his gaze. "I was young and foolish, and just out of Miss Meadow's Select Academy for Young Ladies. My father sent me there to make me more attractive on the marriage market. I was to go to the highest bidder, it seemed."

"That could not have been Lieutenant Francis Snelling. He never had a shilling to his name, other than what he stole or borrowed or won in rigged card games. He was another Jeremy Babcock, an unscrupulous cheat. He sold out when no one would play with him, and before the army could toss him out for all the duels and fights he was embroiled in."

"But no one tells those things to young women, do they? I do not know that anyone nearby knew about his past, anyway. He was visiting friends in the neighborhood, and they weren't about to admit to harboring a villain. They were renting the old Mahoney estate. Do you recall it?"

He and Rex had raided the orchards there in earlier days. "I suppose he was still wearing his uniform?" Even intelligent females turned into peageese at the sight of scarlet regimentals.

"Yes, and he looked strong and brave and handsome. We met at dinner there, and again at church, and a dance at another neighbor's house. Handsome young officers were always welcome."

"He was stalking you. He must have known your father had no son, that you'd be well dowered."

"Perhaps. But he said he cared for me, enough to ask my father for permission to pay his addresses."

"After what? Three meetings?"

"More like five. I was thrilled, even though I knew he'd be rejected."

"I do not blame your father for that."

"No, but the lieutenant's attentions spurred my father to make the match he wanted, to save himself the expense of bringing me to London. He accepted Sir Neville without consulting me."

This time when Daniel hit the mantel, the wooden chest fell off and spilled its contents all over the floor. The dog left her nest of towels to investigate, but nothing was edible, so she went back to sleep.

Corie went on, to finish the tale she'd never told anyone else. "When I heard about Sir Neville, I argued and I pleaded and I wept, to no avail. So I sent Francis a note. He was appalled at the wedding plans, and declared himself my knight, my savior, my future husband. We left three days later, with what moneys I could scrape together. Unfortunately it wasn't enough to hire prime cattle or faster carriages. You know the rest of the story."

"Did you love him?" He did not know that, and now it mattered.

"I was grateful and glad to be gone. If I did have any affection for Francis, it died after the first few hours in the smelly coach. He complained about my baggage, my lack of funds, my needing to stop occasionally. And he drank. I would have gone through with the elopement, anyway, just to be married to anyone but Sir Neville."

Daniel recalled the scene at the inn, with Corie's nightgown open at the neck, its hem up to her waist, her legs bare, and Snelling on top of her. The bounder was guaranteeing that Abbott couldn't stop the marriage, not knowing the rabid squire cared more about his vengeance than his daughter's honor. If she'd been with child, Daniel supposed, she'd have disappeared somehow, with a visit to a distant relative to satisfy the neighborhood. The infant would never have seen the light of day.

"At least you could have been a widow when he died at the war."

"I never wished for his death. I never imagined he'd rejoin his regiment or go to the front lines."

Neither had Snelling, but that was another story. The rotter was dead, they'd never reached Gretna

Green or a border blacksmith to conduct a legal ceremony, and Daniel had helped place Corie back in her father's clutches.

"Did you try to escape again?"

She shrugged. "I had no money, no beaux. My father saw to that. He kept up the public pretense, parading me out at assemblies and church on Sunday, but always under his watch. He said he would break my arm the next time I shamed him, or else he would make my face so ugly no man would look at me."

Daniel took a deep breath to keep from saying words that could only shock the woman who was now sitting on the floor, rubbing the dog's head with a fresh towel. She was so lovely, even with her hair in damp curls, that he could not imagine anyone wanting to mar that beauty. It would be like taking a knife to those masterpieces in the museum, like making an angel cry. He swallowed, hard.

"Did you tell my mother?"

"That my father was a brute, that he was cruel to me? I think she knew from talk in the neighborhood. Heaven knew what the servants told their friends in the village. But I could not bring myself to speak of such things to Lady Cora. Admit my own father was a vicious bully? How could I, when I was too ashamed of my own actions? I still have not found a way to tell her he stole my diamonds. Besides, what could she do? I thought of going to your uncle, Lord Royce. I'd always heard what a wise man the earl was, how he helped people find justice. But he was living as an invalid who never left his home. How could I call on him when I was seldom permitted to leave the grounds of the manor?"

"Uncle Royce will do something now, I promise. If

he does not, the countess will. No one crosses Lady Royce, not ever. But you are right; the earl was weak three years ago, with a congestion of the lungs that never went away. He hardly spoke to me, except to hear news of Rex. We all worried for his health and wondered if he was going to survive until Rex returned from the war. All is well now, though. He'll know what to do about your father. And your mother's death."

"No, I do not want to involve your family any more than I already have. Besides, you said it yourself, that a father has the law on his side. The courts would not intervene unless he killed me, I suppose, but a surgeon could be bribed to lie. That's what happened with my mother, I have no doubt."

Two questions to the squire and no male Royce descendant would have any doubt: How did your wife die? Did you do it? Daniel intended to put those questions to the blackguard before too long. Now he had to atone for his own sins against a helpless young female.

She was going on: "No one could help. A daughter belongs to her parent, the same as a horse, a piece of farm equipment, only she is less valuable than a horse and plow. A daughter is her father's to use as he sees fit. He can marry her off, keep her as unpaid housekeeper, throw her out onto the streets to starve."

Daniel knew there were vicars who did not quibble at the bride's tears, not when their fee was doubled or tripled. No doubt Sir Neville and Abbott had one waiting nearby, with a special license to keep the repugnant marriage ceremony private until its conclusion. He also knew the streets of London were filled with girls whose parents threw them out because they had disgraced themselves and their families. Others sent their daughters to the city because they simply could not afford to feed them. A woman's lot was not an easy one.

What he said was, "My mother would not let you go hungry." Which reminded Daniel of the tin of biscuits Deauville kept filled on his dressing table. He handed one to the dog, and one to Corie. "Eat it. You are too thin."

She nibbled on the edge of the biscuit. Daniel ate two. Helen ate three and looked for more with her pleading brown eyes. Corie's green eyes were prettier, Daniel thought. And just as soulful, to be recounting the dreadful events.

"My father wanted Sir Neville's money, estate, and a title in the family," Corie continued, giving her biscuit to the dog. "He wanted obedience. When I gave him none of those, he had no use for me."

"I am so sorry."

"You said that already."

"And I know it does not change anything, but I feel it."

"I believe you. But do you believe me?"

He never thought to wait for an itch or a prickle. He knew she spoke the truth without resort to any mystical Royce powers. He knelt beside her and took both of her hands into his, the fine-boned elegant one and the twisted, mangled one. He brought them both to his lips. "I believe you." He wanted to brush the damp tendrils of hair away from her cheeks, to smooth the worried lines on her forehead, but he was already daring more than he should, especially if she had that knife in her pocket. "And this time I swear I will help you."

"You'll get me a pistol?"

"Better. I'll get you a husband. Someone who will treat you with the respect you deserve. Someone who is kind and caring, with no bad habits. A steady fellow. Reliable. Honest. Dedicated."

She smiled, finally. "While you are conjuring up this paragon, could you make him wealthy and handsome, too?"

"Of course. Nothing is too hard for us Royce men, you know. Or us Stamfields. Miracle workers, all of us."

So he invited Lord Trowbridge to take dinner with them that evening.

Chapter Twenty-three

First, Daniel asked Dobbson and Deauville. Neither knew anything to the man's discredit. Dobbson confirmed that Viscount Trowbridge was a proper gentleman of excellent lineage and promising future in the government. Deauville reported that his valet had been with Trowbridge for decades, a sign of a good employer and a generous wage.

Next Daniel asked his mother when she returned from the waltz party. She felt she deserved a sip of sherry after an afternoon of giggly girls and awkward boys, so Daniel joined her in a glass. The invitation to dinner ought to come from her, anyway, but mostly he conferred with her because she knew everything about everyone, although she'd been away from London for most of her marriage. He wondered how she kept so well-informed.

"My loyal correspondents, you know, dear. And the London papers your father always subscribed to for me. I do like to keep up with the social and political news, no matter how far away I am. Why, when you were in that dreadful war, we had five newspapers delivered every day. We had the London *Times*, the—"

Daniel cleared his throat. The invitation ought to go out well before the dinner hour.

"Oh, yes, you wanted to know about Viscount Trowbridge, didn't you? I believe I knew him from my own come-out days, before he succeeded to the title. His family has been close to the court forever."

"He's that old? I mean, he appears far younger." Daniel had thought Trowbridge was in his forties, not really too old for a mature miss of twenty summers. Still, he kept fit enough for a younger wife.

Lady Cora patted her son's cheek. "Clean living, my dear, clean living." She did not refer to Daniel's former carousing, only that Lord Morgan looked older than his age, from all his drinking and smoking. "And other wildness that adds years to a gentleman's looks, like brawling."

Daniel touched his many-times-broken nose, then asked, "How is the invalid, by the way? He was resting quietly when I peeked in, with Miss Reynolds reading at his side. His breathing seemed normal."

His mother smiled. "The physician thinks he is ready to return to his own home, with proper precautions, of course. I convinced him that Lord Morgan needed a few more days of bed rest and attentive nursing."

"How much did you have to bribe the doctor?"

"Not much. Not as much as I saw Lord Morgan hand him."

"So your matchmaking is bearing fruit?"

"I don't believe I smell orange blossoms yet, but I have hopes. By the time he leaves, Lord Morgan should appreciate a woman's tender touch too much to give it up."

"And you won't let him leave until he does. Is that playing fair?"

Lady Cora countered the unspoken criticism with, "Was he happy before, alone in that run-down house with no family or friends to help him?"

"No, he'd been considering finding another wife." Daniel did not mention that Lord Morgan had been considering Corie, while Daniel thought he might suit Lady Cora herself. "Um, about Lord Trowbridge?"

"Why this sudden interest, Daniel? You are not thinking of doing a little matchmaking of your own?"

He wasn't about to lie to his own mother, so he told the truth, what he wished her to know, at any rate. "I am thinking of taking a minor post with his office. Not for money, of course, and not a full-time position. Just a gentleman-adviser type of thing. I wanted to get to know him better before I decide."

His mother's brow furrowed as she sipped her sherry. "But, dear, he works with the Finance Ministry, does he not? You hate settling your own accounts."

"Oh, I don't intend to shuffle papers and figure sums like one of his clerks. Lord, no, although I am getting better at the estate ledgers, you know."

"Yes, and I am glad to see you taking over. But what in the world could you be advising Lord Trowbridge about, dear? Not that I doubt your abilities, of course."

Now he avoided her quizzical look by refilling her glass. "He's asked me to assist with some technical business about finding errors, that kind of thing."

"Similar to what you did in the army?"

"Not half as fraught."

"Ah, you'd be more of an investigator, like Rex was, or Harry."

"Something like that, I suppose. We haven't exactly settled on my role. What do you know about him?"

"He used to be handsome. Is he still?"

Daniel wasn't in the habit of judging a man on his looks. His character, his skills, his speed of reaction, maybe, but not the arrangement of his features. He pictured the viscount in his mind: upright posture, trim waist, full head of hair. Eyes and nose and mouth in the right places. "I suppose you could call him handsome." Trowbridge was good-looking enough to meet Corie's requirements, anyway.

His mother took a few moments to search her memories. "I met his wife a few times. A lovely woman, a shame she died so young. Annabelle? Mirabelle? Something like that. She was an Armitage, I believe. An arranged marriage, of course."

"Of course?"

"His family was very political. Hers was a powerful force in the government. They were not about to let their progeny marry all willy-nilly without advantage. Trowbridge is in line for a cabinet post, I hear, so the alliance must have been successful. By all reports the marriage was, too. I never heard of an affair or a scandal on either side. I believe she bore him two sons, just as she ought. Both should be at university by now."

"When you say 'just as she ought,' did you regret not giving Father the heir and the spare?"

"I regretted not having more children, of either gender. But it was not to be, so I never fretted over it. Neither did your father. We had Susanna for him to spoil unmercifully, and you were enough to make any father doubly proud. Besides, it was not as if Stamfield Manor was entailed or there was a title to pass down.''

While his mother was being so talkative, due either to the sherry or the exhausting afternoon, Daniel mentioned something else that was bothering him: ''You know, I always wondered about that. You spent part of your early years in London, and you knew everyone.''

''Of course I did. Everyone who mattered, at least. My father was an earl, you know. That meant I was invited everywhere.''

''So you could have had your choice of any beau you wanted?''

''More or less. An earl's unwed daughter was always popular, especially when her dowry was substantial.'' She used her napkin to pat her lips. ''And I was considered quite a beauty in my day.''

''You still are beautiful, Mother,'' her loyal son said, and meant it.

''And you are still my darling baby boy.''

He had to smile at that, towering over her as he did. ''But why, if you had so many men to choose from, did you choose Papa? I've always wondered. Was it because he lived nearby and you could stay close to your parents?''

''It was no such thing, Daniel. I would have followed Peter Stamfield to Scotland if he lived there. I would have followed him to the ends of the world. We grew up together, you know, and neither one of us ever thought about marrying another.''

''Even though Father was no London swell? No polished gentleman? Papa was a farmer to the core, and your other beaux must have been the sons of dukes and earls."

"And one foreign prince, I'll have you know. But your father did not precisely walk barefoot behind the horses plowing the fields or eat with his fingers. He loved the land—I hope you will find that same sense of belonging once you settle down—but he was educated as a gentleman, and had more honor than many of them. Yes, he was hearty and bluff and plainspoken, but he never lied to me." She dabbed at her eyes with the napkin.

"I am sorry, Mother. I did not mean to disparage my father in any way. A boy could not ask for a better sire. I would have hated a London puffguts. I did not mean to make you cry."

"I know, dear. It's just sad to recall that I lost my best friend. But let us not dwell on the past, not today. The future lies ahead, does it not?"

"It's this marriage business. Deuced hard to comprehend, you know."

"No, dear, it is the simplest thing on earth." She found the pad and pencil she always kept nearby for her endless lists. "Now, is there anyone else you would like me to invite besides your Lord Trowbridge? Perhaps some duke's daughter?"

"Mother!"

"Quite right. It really is too short notice. But we are to attend the theater tomorrow night. Do you think Lord Trowbridge might like to go with us if he is already engaged for this evening? There is nothing exceptional about that for a gentleman in mourning, you know, not unless a comedy or a farce is on the program. They are performing Shakespeare tomorrow, I believe one of the tragedies. Only the highest sticklers can find fault with that."

Daniel far preferred the farces himself, but he considered that Trowbridge must have few diversions, with no balls or card parties and such. He might be ready for company. Ready to consider his own future. Ready to look about him for a second wife. "Please invite him, Mother, as long as we're not seeing *Romeo and Juliet*. It won't do to give the gabble-grinders a reminder of that preposterous story of Miss Abbott's tragic love affair."

Miss Abbott, meanwhile, was in her bedchamber changing her damp clothes and having a good laugh. She'd laughed more this afternoon, washing the dog, than she had in ages, in fact.

But what a joke, Daniel Stamfield promising to find her a husband! The man thought "marriage" was a curse word worse than any he'd let escape his lips, an utter blasphemy against the male race. Yet he was sweet enough to say he'd try.

He was intelligent enough to know what to look for, too. The qualities he mentioned were those she'd look for in a husband herself: kindness, honesty, respectfulness, and no bad habits.

She doubted Daniel knew anyone like that.

As she brushed out her hair, she thought of their conversation. He'd been more than kind, listening to her and believing her. He'd treated her with respect. His eyes had wandered where they oughtn't a time or two, but he never took advantage of the close quarters or the secluded corridor. Heavens, they were in his bedchamber. He had every right to think she could be treated more familiarly than with a kiss on the hand.

His honesty had never been in question, only his

intelligence, which she now knew was sharp and knowing, when he chose to use it.

No bad habits? Ha!

The dinner was perfect, neither too large nor too small, with no fussy or demanding guests, and no single females of marriageable age other than Corie and Susanna, who did not count. Neither of them was a threat to Daniel's freedom.

Lord Morgan managed to totter down the stairs, leaning on Daniel on one side and Miss Reynolds on the other, listing more toward the former governess, Daniel noted, than toward his own, far more muscular, arm.

Clarence Haversmith and an older married couple, neighborhood friends of Lady Royce's, dined with them, too.

Lord Trowbridge was the perfect guest, polite and conversant, knowledgeable about whatever topic was under discussion without being forcefully opinionated. He was a true diplomat, Daniel considered, while he himself found little to speak about with the neighbor lady on his right other than to pass the dishes. Miss Reynolds on his left was too busy helping Lord Morgan select the healthiest foods to bother with Daniel, which was fine. So were the beef, the turbot, and the braised lamb.

Lord Trowbridge sat at Lady Cora's right, with Corie on his other side. They seemed to be dealing well, sharing anecdotes and smiles along with the wine and side dishes.

Trust his annoying little sister to ruin a promising relationship. Susanna asked, across the table, no less, how Lord Trowbridge came to know Daniel. Which had Trowbridge explaining he'd come to Mr. Stamfield for assistance in some banking matters.

Susanna almost fell off her seat in laughter, the wretch. "But, Daniel, Mother did your banking for years."

Daniel could feel the embarrassed color creep into his cheeks. He looked to see if Corie was laughing, too. She was too busy cutting her meat.

His mother was nicer. "I think it's excellent your brother is finding a way to be useful. Thank you, Lord Trowbridge, for recognizing my son's sterling qualities."

Lord Trowbridge raised his wineglass to Daniel. "Sterling and gold, indeed. We intend to rely heavily on his expertise."

No matter what Corie decided, Daniel liked the fellow, especially when his lordship turned the conversation so no one asked what expertise Daniel could possibly bring to the Finance Ministry.

After the meal, over cheese and fruit, Lady Cora said they were having such a delightful evening that it would be a shame to leave for Lady Barre's ball after all. Lord Morgan was too ill to attend, Lord Trowbridge was in mourning, and the neighbors hated traveling through London's streets after dark. If Corie and Susanna did not mind, of course.

Susanna said she was content to play spillikins and charades with Clarence. Corie was relieved that she would not have to be on exhibit tonight. "Not that I care about the gossip," she told them.

Daniel's big toe started to feel warm. His mother's right eyelid twitched. Susanna sneezed.

They all decided they'd be happy to stay in another night. The neighbors left for their own home.

Lord Morgan suggested cards, which Lady Cora ve-
toed. She wanted a musical evening instead, like the
ones she used to enjoy with her children and neighbors. She played the pianoforte until Miss Reynolds
took over, with Lord Morgan beside her to turn the
pages. Daniel got back at his sister by asking her not
to play. Corie and Susanna sang together; then Clarence surprised them with a resounding tenor voice.
Daniel joined in with his baritone.

They weren't half bad, Daniel considered, enjoying
himself far more than he would at a dance or a gaming den.

Trowbridge couldn't carry a tune in a bucket, but
he was an excellent audience, obviously enjoying this
moment of simple pleasure. He called out requests,
and supplied words when the vocalists stumbled over
the lyrics. He even rubbed the dog's ears while they
performed.

After tea, he thanked them all and kissed Lady
Cora's hands when he left, in appreciation of a delightful evening, he said. He gladly accepted her invitation to join them for tomorrow's theater party and
offered to host dinner at the Grand Hotel afterward.

"What do you think?" Daniel asked when he'd left.

Corie was sipping at the last of her tea. Daniel was
eating the last of the poppy seed cake. Lord Morgan
and Miss Reynolds had gone upstairs, perhaps on account of the dog's presence, perhaps on reasons more
personal. Lady Cora was conferring with Dobbson, and
Susanna and Clarence were squabbling over jackstraws.

"What do I think about what?" Corie wanted to
know.

"About Lord Trowbridge, of course. He seems perfect to me. Couldn't ask for a nicer chap. He's smart,

pleasant, polite, and knows his own limitations. He likes dogs, too, which says a lot about a man, I always said."

"Yes, he seemed quite nice."

"He'll be in mourning for another few months, but that's not to keep him from making his intentions clear."

She stirred her tea. "I suppose not."

The tea was tepid; so was her response. Daniel pressed her for a shade more enthusiasm. "Then you think I should encourage him?"

"Most definitely."

That was better, but now Daniel could not tell if he was relieved or disappointed or just suffering indigestion. He fed the last slice of poppy seed cake to the dog.

"I'll speak to him in the morning when I see him at the bank."

"Oh, there is no need for you to say anything that might prove embarrassing to both of you. I think Lord Trowbridge made up his own mind already. And I believe she gave him enough encouragement herself."

"She? Herself?"

"Why, your mother of course. Didn't you notice the way they were recounting old stories and comparing mutual friends? How she showed so much interest in his sons? Why, they will be perfect, and the delay for his mourning period will not matter. Your mother swears she is not going to think about her future until Susanna is settled. He will be ready by then. Lady Cora will make him the ideal hostess as he rises in the government, and she will be thrilled with the London scene."

"My mother?"

Corie patted his hand. "They'll make a fine match."

"Uh, of course. That's what I was thinking all along, why I invited the man, naturally."

He went upstairs to soak his feet.

Chapter Twenty-four

Corie loved the theater. She'd seen plays, but not many truly professional ones, nor any with actors of this stature and renown. The building's interior alone was a marvel, all gilt and crystal and towering tiers. The architecture's opulence was rivaled only by that of the audience members in their private boxes, in their satin and jewels and feathered headdresses.

Everyone stared at everyone else, with their opera glasses, no less, so Corie did the same from the Royce box. With her own sight focused across the vast theater, she escaped feeling that every eye was on her. It did not matter where the spectators gazed, because the party from Royce House had purposely arrived too late for visitors to their box, and too late to overhear gossip from the nearby seats.

Corie sat in front at Lady Cora's direction, where people could see her enjoying herself. Even so visibly situated, she felt far enough away that no one could tell her diamonds were fake. She was reassured no one could find fault with her gown, either. One of Madame Journet's masterpieces, the gold satin made her feel like a fairy-tale princess.

It made Daniel Stamfield go speechless or stuttering

again, so Corie knew she looked her finest. He did that, she realized, only when he was overwhelmed or feeling trapped. Since they both knew she had no designs on him, he must find her gown and elaborately twisted coronet of hair pleasing.

He hadn't said the bodice was too low-cut, either, which Corie had feared he might, since she'd complained to the dressmaker herself. Madame Journet had laughed. Daniel licked his lips and swallowed a few times before getting a single word out. That was compliment enough.

Lord Trowbridge gracefully complimented all the ladies, including Miss Reynolds, proving what a gentleman he was. Daniel should take lessons, Corie decided, but then he wouldn't be as much fun to tease by leaning forward, taking longer strides so one's gown clung, or fluttering one's darkened eyelashes. Too bad he was seated behind her, except that her back was nearly bare in the low-cut gown. Let Mr. Stamfield swallow that!

Through her opera glasses, she surveyed the audience the same way they were inspecting her before the lights were turned down. She recognized many of the faces, but not one held her interest as much as Daniel and Trowbridge sitting behind her. They were talking about their morning at the bank, and how successful, how interesting. At the bank?

Then the drama began and Corie was lost in the magic of the play.

She was still bemused and in a different world, a different era, at intermission when the present intruded all too swiftly. Lady Cora's friends stopped at the box to show their support. Lord Morgan's acquaintances wanted to congratulate him on his recovery. Government officials sought a moment of Lord Trowbridge's time, now that he was out and socializing. Susanna's suitors were too awed by the presence of such eminences to intrude, but not so Corie's older, more sophisticated admirers. They were too needy to be deterred.

She knew the baronet who brought her a glass of champagne was spending borrowed money to woo a bride. She suspected the knight who brought her an orange would likely go home with one of the orange sellers. The high-level clerk who was ogling her while speaking with Trowbridge had no manners. The finance minister had manners, but held her hand far too long.

The entire intermission lasted too long for Corie's taste. The wine, the carefully peeled orange, and the gentlemen were not to her taste, either. She tried to lose herself in the play again, putting worries of her future aside for now. Somehow she was more aware of the man behind her than she was of all the men on the stage, all the heroes, all the villains. Now, that was a tragedy.

The women recited half the play in the carriage on the way to the Grand Hotel for Trowbridge's dinner. The viscount went ahead with Clarence to see that everything was arranged to his satisfaction, although he'd made reservations, selected the menu, and chosen the wines before meeting Daniel at the bank in the morning. They found more counterfeits, but no information had come back from Oxford this soon, so Daniel kept shuffling through the stacks of banknotes.

Trowbridge was an efficient bloke, Daniel thought, and not just at the bank or his own office. He was jealous of the man's polish, his elegance, his damn smooth tongue. No matter what Corie said, she had to have her head turned by the paragon. Half the women in the audience did. Even with the theater lights turned down, Daniel could see the calculating gleams in their eyes as they wondered how long before they could get their claws into the wealthy new widower.

Half the men in the audience ogled Corie. The other half had their wives or mistresses with them and feared for their lives, or their evening's pleasure, if they showed too much interest in Miss Corisande Abbott. He couldn't blame any of the gawkers, either. She glittered more than her diamonds, and she was for real. Really, she ought to be wearing more clothing! Just looking at her back, the smooth skin, the planes of her delicate bones, the graceful way she held her head, made him go as hard as those glass diamonds she wore so valiantly.

Thinking about the stolen gems made him want to go buy her genuine ones, diamonds and rubies and sapphires, to see her wearing them and nothing else. Hell, just breathing in her lilac scent made him glad he was sitting in the shadows. Thank heavens he could not see her front, or he'd be like a stag in rut.

To get his mind off such inappropriate desires—he'd been without a woman too long, that was all—Daniel tried to select a few gentlemen he might invite for the next gathering of candidates at his mother's. Looking at the nearby boxes, though, he could not find one man he'd like to dine with, much less see wed to his mother's ward.

The government types who pretended business with Trowbridge in order to scrape up an acquaintance with the beauty were prigs. They'd bore her to death in a week. And they were so stupid they started talking about a counterfeiting ring where anyone could overhear. Those were the men running the government? Maybe he'd go help Harrison and his friends with forged checks instead.

His friends—well, he'd shoved a few out of the box before being forced to make the introductions. None of them was good enough for her, or met her standards. By Jupiter, none of them met his standards. Some of the actors were more respectable. Then again, some of the actors were his friends, too. No, none of them would do for Corie.

He came back to the present while the women were going over the play, act by act, scene by scene, monologue by monologue, in the carriage. They each had to choose their favorite part, the actor they thought performed best, the most elegant costume. They compared this enactment to other versions they had seen or acted in at school, then to the original as written. They all knew the blasted tragedy by heart.

Daniel couldn't remember which play he'd sat through.

The Grand Hotel was one of the more recent additions to social London's favorite haunts. Facing Green Park, the hotel boasted a French chef known for his genius and his volatile temperament. Sometimes the charlotte russe was set aflame; sometimes the hotel was, although the chef swore that was an accident. Recently rebuilt, the establishment was gloriously elegant, except for the buckets of sand and pails of water under every table.

A magisterial majordomo led them to their table, where Lord Trowbridge and Clarence were waiting.

Every other table in the place was filled, some with distinguished theatergoers like themselves, some with wealthy families visiting the capital, some with gentlemen and their—

"Do not stare," Miss Reynolds hissed at Susanna, falling back into her role of governess in the face of painted women.

As if Susanna did not know such females existed, Daniel mused, since they'd been outside the theater, soliciting customers for a private show. The women inside the hotel were higher-caliber courtesans, the ones Susanna must have seen in the park or shopping on Bond Street.

They were dressed as fashionably as the ladies of Royce House, perhaps by the same modistes. The dashers wore more jewels, which were probably more authentic than Corie's. But their manners were far freer, their laughs louder, their cosmetics more heavily applied.

One table in particular was more raucous than good manners or wisdom allowed. From what Daniel had heard, the unpredictable chef was liable to come threaten the revelers with a meat cleaver for distracting the patrons from his creations.

Trowbridge's table was as far as possible from the lords and their ladybirds, Daniel was relieved to see. It was all well and good for him to associate with such females—he even caught the wink from one courtesan he recognized from the Cyprian's Ball—but his mother and sister should not be subjected to such low company. Or Miss Abbott, he quickly added in his mind. She might not be as pure as driven snow, but she was not covered in the mud of a mistress for hire.

She'd had motives for her actions, Daniel reminded

himself, good reasons for acting the way she had. He supposed these females did, too, hunger being the primary cause for a woman's fall from grace, but Corie was still a lady. These trollops never had been, never would be.

The meal was one of the finest Daniel had ever tasted, at least since last evening. Dish followed dish, each more delightful to look at, better to savor. Wines, china, silverware, and strolling musicians changed with each course. For once, Daniel did not have to think of anything to say, because the entire party was more interested in their food than chattering. Even Corie ate more than her usual bird pickings.

The only bar to Daniel's total enjoyment of the dinner was the noise coming from that far table. The violinist was drowned out; the harpist in the corner could not be heard at all, which wasn't entirely unfortunate. The talk was getting more risqué with each glass of wine, however, and the women more blatant about their business. Trowbridge was frowning and Daniel knew he was thinking of complaining to the waiter, which might have led the chef to take offense, which might deny Daniel a taste of the hotel's famous flambé desserts.

So Daniel stood, excused himself to his party, and walked toward the roisterers. He recognized several of the men, none of them friends of his, and a few more of the women. He did not think any of them were former lovers, since he seldom employed such high-priced prostitutes, except perhaps for the one who called out, "Hallo, Danny. Want to join our fun instead of that sobersides group?"

"I'm sorry, but they're my family. I'd like to suggest this is not the place for such, ah, licentious behavior."

She giggled. "What, do we need a license to have a good time?" Some of the others laughed, too.

"I merely meant there are ladies present."

"Ooh, real ladies. Now, ain't you come up in the world, our Danny?"

"Even fall-down drunks have famblies, Sophie," a yellow-haired woman told her, trying to act prim and proper, with her gown half undone. "Why don't we go somewhere we can dance and let these nice folks have their dinner in peace?"

Daniel thought that an excellent idea. He placed a pound note—a good one—on the table and said, "And have a bottle of champagne on me."

Sophie and the blonde were squabbling over the blunt when Daniel turned to go back to Trowbridge's party, but one of the men lurched to his feet and followed him. "Who the hell are you to tell me where to drink and what to say?"

Daniel did not want any trouble, not with his family and Corie looking on, so he kept walking. The man followed him.

Daniel didn't know the fellow, but he was dressed like a gentleman and his accent was educated, albeit loud and slurred, so Daniel apologized for his intrusion. "I merely wish everyone to enjoy their dinners."

The maître d' was looking anxious. The rest of the restaurant was hushed. The harpist stopped plucking the strings midchord.

"Hurry back, Stamfield," Lord Morgan called across the room. "They're about to serve dessert."

"Stamfield?" the drunk bellowed. "Daniel Stamfield? The cur who killed my brother?"

Daniel did not want to cause a scene, not now, not here. He tried again. "I assure you, sir, I never killed anyone's brother, not even a Frenchman's. My aim was never that good."

But the man was looking past Daniel, toward his table. "You are as guilty of murder as if you pulled the trigger yourself. You and that harlot with you!"

Gasps broke out everywhere, especially among the members of the *ton*.

"If you are referring to Miss Reynolds," Daniel said, still trying to defuse the situation, "I assure you, she is a respectable governess and my mother's loyal secretary."

"Here now," Lord Morgan said, failing to see the humor.

The waiters were lining up, ready to start evicting customers. It was obvious who the troublemaker was, but their job was to protect the china and the chairs.

Lord Trowbridge took out a quizzing glass to survey the intruder in their midst, a superior gesture in itself. "I say, Snelling. Why do you not rejoin your friends? They are waiting by the door."

Snelling? Godfrey, Viscount Snelling? The brother of that scum who'd run off with Corie three years ago? Daniel looked over at her. Her face was as white as the tablecloth.

He blocked Snelling's view of her and said, "Ah, now I see where you get your manners. They must run in the family, or stumble, as the case may be. As for your brother, he died a hero, I understand, keeping England free."

"He died because you sent him to the front," Snelling shouted. "After he'd sold out, damn you. You pulled strings, with your family's influence and paid-for power, to make my brother cannon fodder."

"Your brother would have been killed by some father or brother or cheated cardplayer sooner or later if not in front of an army firing squad. At least he died for a purpose."

"What, so you could tup Abbott's ewe lamb?"

Daniel would have sent him to join his friends across the room, through the air like a badminton shuttlecock, but Trowbridge was on his feet now. So was Clarence. Lord Morgan was wheezing.

Trowbridge spoke before Daniel could act. "You are speaking of a lady at my table, Snelling."

Snelling sneered. "That is no lady. She ran off with my brother. Spent the night at an inn, didn't you know, before this mountain of manure ruined their plans."

Now Lady Cora stood. "We have heard this calumny before." She spoke loudly enough to be heard by everyone in the room, including a mustachioed man in a tall white toque, with a flaming brand in one hand and a platter of brandied peaches in the other. Two waiters stood beside him, each with a bucket of water.

"As I explained once, and will once more, and never again, your brother brought Miss Abbott to my house."

"Where she shared my bedroom," Susanna added, like before, before she wiped her nose.

"So you say. That is not what my brother wrote."

"You are doubting the word of a lady?" Trowbridge placed his own napkin on the table, ready to toss it or his goblet in the man's face in challenge. Clarence was trying to decide if he should issue a call for a duel himself, on Susanna's behalf. He handed her his handkerchief instead. Lord Morgan was on his feet, still wheezing.

"Oh, sit down, you glorified clerk," Snelling told

Lord Trowbridge, "and you, too, you old tosspot. It's him I have issue with." He pointed at Daniel. "Did you or did you not follow my brother to an inn and break his nose before hauling him to some naval port and throwing him aboard a ship?"

Daniel stood firm. "I did, and I am damned proud of it. The man was a menace."

"You see?" Snelling asked his audience, holding his arms out in a theatrical gesture more overblown than any they'd seen onstage that night. "He followed the lovers to bring back the doxy."

"You heard my mother say Miss Abbott was not with your brother by then." That was what they all heard, so Daniel was not telling an untruth. "No, I went to keep Squire Abbott from murdering Francis for asking her to elope. Abbott had already rejected your brother as a suitor for her hand."

"And you found him with the whore in his bed."

Daniel could not look at Corie. If she was crying, if she was trembling, he'd have to kill Snelling after all. He faced her accuser and said, "I found your brother attacking an innocent young girl." Daniel expected his skin to burn for that lie, but he felt nothing, most likely because he was too angry for anything as insignificant as a rash.

"What girl? You are making that up."

"Unlike you, I would not sully a respectable female's reputation by saying her name. She was wealthy, and that was enough for your brother. He was nothing but a fortune hunter and a would-be rapist."

"I'll call you out for that!"

"I'm sure you would, after I just admitted what a poor shot I am. But dueling is illegal. I will meet you at Gentleman Jackson's Boxing Parlour, however, anytime you wish."

Before Snelling could reply, a high-pitched voice rang out. "*Moi*, I will meet you behind zee kitchen, with my sharpest knife. Now leave, *chien*, before I put you on my spit"—the chef waved the burning torch for his famous flaming dessert—"like I do zee capon."

Snelling's friends dragged him off. "This is not over yet," he called over his shoulder.

But the dinner was. No one except Daniel was in the mood for dessert.

Chapter Twenty-five

Corie was ready to start packing, without a plan, without a destination or funds. She'd leave to save the Stamfields, the loving family she never really had, from further disgrace.

Lady Cora debated whether that was a smart move. People would remember, next year, and the next. Corie might be happier in the short run, not having to face the stares and the speculations, but in the long run? Well, if she left now, there might be no long run at all. Although Lady Cora could ask the earl and the countess to look about the countryside for a likely husband.

"Who?" Daniel wanted to know. "The vicar's curate?"

"What's wrong with the curate?" Susanna demanded, jumping from her seat near the fireplace.

Lady Cora ignored them both, and Corie, for that matter. From her reclined position on the sofa, cucumber slices covering her eyes, she supposed out loud that they could consider a trip to Bath or Brighton, where the London news was not as fresh, not as important. They could not leave until after Susanna's come-out ball, of course. The invitations had gone out, with a gratifying number of acceptances already. The orchestra was hired, the lobster patties were ordered, and their gowns due for final fittings next week.

"She is not going," Daniel stated. "Gossip always reaches ears you least wish it to. That's a rule, or seems to be. And where would she go until the blasted ball? Not back to that miserable excuse for a father, I swear. Would you hide her in a broom closet?"

Corie did not like being ignored. This was her future being decided. Broom closet, indeed! "I thought I might ask Lord Trowbridge for a position at the bank. Heaven knows the place is big enough. If Daniel can do the work . . ."

She let her voice trail off rather than insult him. Then she wished she had completed the sentence, that whatever he did there, she was certain she could do as well. The oaf was laughing at her.

"Do not be daft. No one but men work at the bank or in Trowbridge's office. And I promise, you cannot do the assignments I am given. Furthermore, taking a post means taking yourself off the bride market."

"Who would marry me now?"

"More than would wed a female doing men's work," he countered.

"That might be true, dear, but if Corisande remains among the *ton*, she might have to face Snelling and his venom again. And what if that dreadful man meets up with the sniveling cousin of the Duke of Haigh, or, worse, that cousin's valet who used to work for Sir Neville? Everyone will doubt our refutations, and Corie's reputation will be just as damaged."

Daniel brushed that aside. "What are the chances of those two meeting?"

"Excellent, I'd guess, especially if that law you mentioned is true, that what you least wish to happen usually does."

Now Susanna added her thoughts: "That awful man might search out the valet, Daniel. He seems to hate you so much."

Daniel glared at his sister, but Corie said, "Susanna is right. Snelling will not simply go away or let his thirst for vengeance fade. You heard him say he was not finished, and why should he be? His brother did die because of me."

"Francis Snelling died because he was a despicable swine and a miserable officer. Lud knows how many good men died needlessly with him in that battle. Their blood might be on my hands for sending him back to Portugal, but Snelling brought his death on himself. And no one will listen to his brother. Everyone knows what a rotter Snelling was."

"Not everyone," Susanna pointed out, to Daniel's disgust. Where was her sense of loyalty? "Mother has been trying to say he was kind enough to bring Corie to our house."

Lady Cora moaned from the couch. "You see what happens when you lie?"

Daniel knew very well what happened when he lied, and he was not going to discuss that in front of the women. "That is a minor detail. With all of us united, we can dismiss any garbage the brother spews. Corie will stay right here where she belongs, until the end of the Season unless she gets married before then."

Corie thought that was a vain hope of getting rid of her gracefully. "But you will all have to keep lying for me."

Lady Cora removed the cucumber slices from her eyes and finally looked at Corie. "I doubt it will be necessary. We can take a page from my sister-in-law's book and stare down anyone who questions our respectability. After all, Lady Royce lived separately from her husband for years, and he was suspected of subverting justice while serving on the courts. No one ever cut her from their invitations list. In fact, I shall write to dear Margaret in the morning. I am certain she won't mind arriving a few weeks early for Susanna's ball. No one—I repeat, no one—doubts her propriety or dares to challenge her authority. Not the Almack's committee, not the prince regent."

"That's the ticket, Mother. We'll scrape through, and Snelling will return to whatever hole he crawled out from."

"Oxford," Corie said, touched by the lengths these Stamfields were willing to take for her.

"What?" Daniel forgot where he was and shouted loudly enough for a battlefield or a tavern brawl. "What did you say?"

"I said Oxford. A small town outside, actually, but I never knew its name. That is where the Snelling family seat is. The estate is called Silverwoods. Francis said his father seldom went to London because he had so many interests and investments in the area. Since Godfrey is viscount now, he must have taken over all those properties and duties."

"Oxford," Daniel repeated, more quietly this time as he considered the counterfeits. "Now, who would believe that coincidence?"

"A lot of people live near Oxford, dear," his mother said, doubt shadowing her face.

"Yes, but few of them are as scurvy as Snelling and

his brother." He kissed his mother's cheek. "I need to go out."

"Now, at this time of night? Whatever for?"

"I, ah, need to see a man about a, ah, printing press. That's what."

His mother shook her head and *tsk*ed. "And here I thought you'd given up overindulging in spirits, dear."

"These are good spirits, Mother. Do not worry." He kissed her cheek again while he straightened his neckcloth. Then he kissed his sister's cheek, headed for the door, came back, and kissed Corie's cheek. "Everything will be fine, without a doubt. You'll see."

He left a world of doubt in Corie's mind. Where was he going if not to continue his low-life carousing? A printing press? Good grief, he was mad! How could she trust a Bedlam-bound clunch like Daniel to rescue her? Daniel was a fool. And why did he kiss her good night?

Daniel almost forgot where he was going, thinking about that kiss. Lord, he wanted to kiss her soft pink lips so badly he'd slay a dragon, or Snelling, for her, just to see if she'd reward him with a smile.

Stupid, stupid, stupid. She needed a safe, sober husband. Someone like Trowbridge. Maybe the man had a brother.

Trowbridge's butler was not certain the master could be disturbed at this late hour. The butler seemed the one most disturbed by the visit, hastily adjusting his wig. His lordship was retired, the butler claimed, and might be asleep. Whatever Mr. Stamfield wanted could wait until the morning, when civilized people conducted business. After all, this was not the War Office,

England was no longer at war, and officials of the Finance Ministry did not have midnight emergencies.

So Daniel stepped around the sputtering servant and shouted up the stairwell, "Trowbridge, I have news. Snelling is from Oxford."

Ten minutes later, they sat in Trowbridge's office, the viscount in a brocaded robe and slippers, his hair tousled from sleep. The butler brought ale and cheese, all he could find in the deserted pantry.

Trowbridge was not pleased to be awakened, not impressed with Daniel's latest theory.

"You are going off half-cocked again, Stamfield. Just because the man insulted your ladies does not make him a criminal. I realize that if you cast doubt on his own character, people will be less likely to believe his hogwash about Miss Abbott, but you cannot hang a man for spreading lies and unfounded gossip."

Well, they weren't all unfounded, or lies, but Trowbridge did not have to know that. "I am not suspicious of him because of his rudeness, but nastiness is a common thread through traitors, thieves, and spies. I know, for I've met my fair share of all of them."

"Backwards logic, lad. Not all dastards are criminals; not all criminals are ill-mannered. Why, some of the MPs I have to deal with are foulmouthed devils, but they are honorable men. And some of the most softly spoken, courteous gentlemen would stick a knife in your back while they are smiling. No, your notion does not ring true."

"I still say it's worth making some inquiries."

"Which my men are doing in Oxford even as we speak. We'll know more when they return with their reports, next week at the soonest."

Daniel was pacing, a tankard of ale in one hand, a wedge of cheese in the other. He cursed at the delay.

Trowbridge studied him over the rim of his own tankard. "Of course you could still go to Oxford yourself. You could ask the right questions, look over the contents of that bank's vaults."

"And leave this mare's nest behind? I could not abandon Corie—that is, my mother and Miss Abbott—at this time. You must see that."

"Of course. They need our support."

Which was tacit assurance of Trowbridge's interest in Daniel's mother. "Good, but our escort is not enough. I want to ask Snelling a few questions myself, and he is right here in Town. I don't suppose you know where he stays in London?"

"There's no town house I know of. Perhaps he took rooms at the Grand Hotel, and that's why he was dining there. But before you go charging off to confront the dirty dish, remember we need evidence to charge a peer of the realm, not just your . . . intuition, let us call it. Not telling the truth does not constitute a confession. This is not the army."

No, in the army lives depended on Daniel knowing truth from lies. French spies were shot on his say-so and nothing else, to save English soldiers. Daniel swore to get Trowbridge his proof, once he found Snelling.

Trowbridge was right: Daniel's best chance of finding his quarry was back at the Grand Hotel. First he bribed Matthews, the maître d', for a table in the still-crowded restaurant; then he ordered three desserts for himself and handed Matthews another gold coin. For his largesse, he got the best the chef had to offer, and answers to his questions.

No, the unruly gentlemen were not staying here, nor their bits of muslin, either. The Grand Hotel did not accept such lewd and licentious guests. No, Matthews had no idea which direction they took upon leaving. Yes, they had paid in paper currency, not coin. No, Daniel could not look at the receipts drawer! Not for any price.

"Not even if I suspect his party gave you counterfeit bills?"

Merciful heavens, the management might take the money out of Matthews's own salary, if not out of his hide.

Daniel pulled out two false pound notes. He had no way of proving they belonged to Snelling and his friends, not mixed in with the rest of the week's earnings. But he knew.

He showed Matthews what to look for on the bills, rather than explain how his fingers acted as counterfeit dowsers. Then he switched the unsanctioned flimsies for good ones from his own pocket. He added another pound note to safeguard his secrecy. "King's business, don't you know."

The man was thrilled with his gratuities, delighted to assist in aiding his country, and not half surprised the mad king was issuing false certificates.

Daniel was glad he got to taste the chef's specialties.

Daniel stopped at the Clarendon and the Pulteney next, the two premier hotels in London for wealthy nobs. Snelling was not staying at either, but one of the biggest gossips in town was having a solitary late supper at the Clarendon. No one ever wanted to dine with the overdressed tattlemonger, who was said to sell his gleanings to the scandal sheets. Lord Hebert was just what Daniel needed, so he accepted the dandy's invitation to share his meal.

Daniel ate, and fed Hebert the story of the Grand Hotel and Snelling accosting them.

"Grief for his father and brother has made the man go mad," Daniel explained. "Or drove him to drink. Of course the brother was no gentleman, either. An embarrassment to the army and all. Still, Snelling had no right to go slandering a lady with an old tale no one believes, not after my mother told the right of it. I'd like to explain to Snelling, when he's not in his cups. Do you know where I can find him?"

Hebert did not know. But now he knew the correct version, and he also knew Daniel Stamfield and his cousins were not men to offend without expecting retribution, usually in the form of one's own blood staining one's elegantly embroidered waistcoat. If the earl's nephew said the exquisite Miss Corisande Abbott was a nun, then Hebert would pray with her.

After checking a few more hotels where gentlemen stayed, Daniel paid a call at Lydia Burton's house of convenience. Lydia's girls didn't fly as high as Sophie and her yellow-haired friend, but they might know of them. The frail sisterhood was a close-knit group and the better-paid courtesans could find themselves at a bordello between protectors.

He had greetings and offers aplenty when he walked into the elegantly appointed brothel. No shabby sofas or unwashed bodies at Lyddie's establishment. The girls were healthy, well fed, and well treated, or else.

The else was Little George at the door, who was larger than Daniel. Daniel himself had stepped forward to protect a few of the girls when Little George was busy, or to give a lesson on how to treat a woman, no matter her circumstances. That was why he was a favorite with the ladies here, at least. He was gallant and generous, and he knew how to please them.

"Of course he does," Lydia told one male guest who complained of all the attention the newcomer was receiving. "I taught him myself. As a favor to his cousin, my friend Harry."

Lydia did not know who had Sophie in keeping currently, or where she was living. Females like that, out on their own, lived the life of luxury, but only for brief periods unless they were the few lucky ones.

While she went to ask if any of her employees had better information, she left Daniel with two pretty girls, a drink, and a sandwich. Lydia's kitchen did not make the puny, crustless affairs his mother had for tea, but great slabs of bread filled with cheese and ham and beef.

Lydia knew how to please a man, just not where to find that one in particular. When she returned to her front parlor and sent the girls off to entertain other gentlemen, she said, "I can't say I'd like having him come here. Last time he tried to get rough with one of the girls. The brother was no better."

Now Daniel had another reason to find Snelling.

He wiped his chin and said, "Send for me if he does come, and don't take any paper money from him if he pays before going upstairs."

"Paper money? Pound notes? Daniel, my girls are good, but not that good."

He left her a real banknote so she could compare

any that came her way; then he kissed her hand. "Your sandwiches and your smile are worth more than gold."

Which was why he was a favorite with the abbess, too.

He was almost too full for Cook's pastries at McCann's Club, but he ate them, anyway, so as not to hurt her feelings. Miss White must have smelled the hound dog on him, because she kept her distance. Daniel shrugged. "Females."

Seated across from him at the kitchen table, Harrison agreed to send men to find where Snelling stayed, who his friends were, what bank he used in London. "If you are sure this is intelligence department business?"

"Who else's? The man is a counterfeiter. I'd put money on it. I already did, a small fortune in bribes. Tell your men to see what kind of investments he has, too. That might be the key, if he has shares in a newspaper or a book publisher or an art gallery, any place with access to a printing press. Oh, and have your men look for a ladybird named Sophie, or another with yellow hair. They might know where he is."

Harrison had heard about the contretemps at the Grand Hotel. "Seems to me the scum will come looking for you."

"All the better."

Harrison worried that he ought to send a bodyguard after Daniel, who was too valuable to the country to lose. So was his own life, if Daniel found out. He settled on warning him to watch his back. "It makes too big a target."

"I always do."

"No, my friend, you never do. You just wade right in to whatever melee you see. Or create. Are you sure this is not personal?"

"National security," Daniel mumbled around a cream-filled pastry. "Ask Trowbridge."

Daniel intended to ask Snelling himself. When he found him.

By the time he got home, Daniel stank of Lydia's girls' perfumes, smoke and wine from McCann's, the sewers from his walk back. He was a lot poorer from all the bribes, and bilious. It had been a good evening, except for his upset stomach, with a good chance of having results—Snelling's whereabouts—by morning.

Corie watched him amble into the parlor, humming some tavern ditty. He poured himself a glass of brandy, then belched. She stayed tucked back in the window seat where she'd been contemplating her choices.

Daniel Stamfield was not one of them.

Chapter Twenty-six

All the king's men and all the underworld informants could not find Snelling. Of course not. It was a race week at Epsom and every sporting gentleman, every betting gentleman, every gentleman who could beg, borrow, or steal off from his wife, was there. Daniel wished he could be, too, and not just for the thrill of the race and the glory of the highbred horses.

What better place to pass counterfeit notes than at the racecourse? Vast sums were wagered and lost on each heat, sometimes through a bookmaker, often on private bets between men, either strangers at the rails or boon companions. Snelling was there, Daniel believed, and spreading the counterfeits around like the plague.

Daniel was certain; Harrison considered it probable; Trowbridge thought it possible. They all sent men to Epsom, but no one had proof Snelling was involved, so they had no cause to arrest him, if they found the gallows bait amid the huge crowds at the track.

A message had come from near Oxford, saying Trowbridge's agents found a large number of the forgeries at Chimkin's Bank, right where Daniel told them to go. Chimkin himself, the owner of the bank, denied knowing anything about how the counterfeits arrived at his establishment, who had deposited which bills, or which one of his tellers had not looked carefully enough to detect the frauds. He was willing to show them his books, but not until they showed him a warrant to invade the privacy of his customers.

Chimkin was so outraged that anyone might be using his bank as a clearinghouse for criminal profit, he was coming to London himself to speak to the home secretary, the finance minister, the prime minister himself, to prove his own innocence of any misconduct. The reputation of his bank depended on it.

They hadn't known about Snelling before the investigators left London, so no one thought to ask if he held an account there. Chimkin would know. Daniel would know if the banker spoke the truth. Next week, at the soonest.

Daniel hated the wait, the not knowing, the damned letting other people ask the questions. He hated being the only one—one of a handful, anyway—who could judge the answers. So why couldn't he go? Why couldn't he be the one to settle this quickly, faster than any clerk from the ministry could? Because, by all that was holy, he had to take the ladies to Almack's again.

Corie was still a toast, although with several fewer suitors than the last time they attended the assembly on King Street. No one could tell if the lessening of admirers was due to the gossip or the horse meet. She never lacked for dance partners, not with Trowbridge, Haversmith, and Daniel himself standing nearby to make sure. Daniel also scoured the clubs and Trowbridge's office for likely candidates for Corie's hand. To what ungodly, unmasculine, traitorous-to-his-gender depths had he sunk?

His mother gave him odd, worried glances, but she entertained whomever he brought home for dinner.

Corie tried. She really did. She wanted to find a gentleman to like, to love, to trust, to share her concerns. Susanna made fun of every one of the bachelors so obviously on exhibit, but Corie tried to find good qualities in each of them.

This one had a strong chin and lovely blue eyes. But ordinary blue eyes faded next to Daniel's black-rimmed, sky-bright ones, with their long, dark eyelashes.

That one was well-spoken, but his words were too polished, too practiced. He must use the same phrases on every heiress. Somehow, Daniel's sputters were more charming, because he hadn't planned what to say.

Some of the gentlemen he brought home were well built, but most were shorter than Daniel. She did not feel as comfortable dancing with them, even if they were better dancers. Next to Daniel, she felt graceful and almost petite. Who wouldn't, aside the great lummox? The ones who were as fit as Daniel had likely been dragged out of the boxing parlors, the last place she would look for a match.

She would not look for one at the tailors, either. Some of the gentlemen who stayed in London were too foppish, too concerned with their clothes and hair to take a chance of mussing their looks, or traveling without their wardrobes or servants. Daniel brought only one or two of the dandy set to meet her, most likely because he knew so few of them, or respected so few. Corie disliked the idea of a husband who cared more for his appearance than for her. She loved her new apparel, and felt like a princess in the silks and satins, but she could not go gardening in them, or help in the stillroom. She thought Daniel's casual attitude to clothes made far more sense.

Botheration! The men who had not gone to the races were the steady sort, not gamblers, not ones to leave their wives and children and responsibilities to jaunt off with their cronies. She did not want one of those sports-mad Corinthians who went to cockfights, foxhunts, and fishing trips to Scotland to kill things for pleasure, with ladybirds along for more pleasure. She told herself to pick one of those who stayed in Town to oversee their investments or conduct government business, or look after their families. That was what she wanted, so she had only to decide, then charm an offer out of the lucky man.

So why hadn't she done so? It wasn't as if she were waiting to fall in love with one of these serious-minded gentlemen. She did not have the leisure or the luxury to hold out for love. She wished only to like her future partner, and perhaps feel some physical attraction. How could she kiss a man she did not like, or share the more intimate aspects of marriage? Some women did, she knew, considering the act a duty, a fair exchange for a home and family. Corie could not imagine taking a stranger to her bed, a stranger who owned her, body and soul.

The very thought made her pull away when a gentleman became too familiar. That stiffness was not going to win her any proposals, she knew, but she couldn't help her reaction. She'd survived the wondering looks; she could survive being considered standoffish and cold. The problem was, finding a position or settling in a cottage by herself did not have the appeal it used to. Marriage to a stranger was not so attractive, either. Which left . . . ?

Which left showing their faces at Almack's again, as the missing gentlemen returned from the races with their pockets empty enough that finding a rich wife was critical. A fortune hunter was not what she wanted, especially with her dowry in her father's greedy clutches.

She did not know what she wanted.

Corie told herself that was because she had not met him yet. She wouldn't listen to that niggling voice in her head that said she was lying, a great sin in the Stamfield household. That was why, the pinching, pulling ache inside told her, she compared every man to that dunderheaded Daniel.

No, she insisted to her own inner self. She had not felt that heart stirring, that world shattering, that first glance of a Grand Passion. That was how Susanna described True Love, straight out of a silly novel or a bad poem, where the beloved was always perfection personified. Daniel Stamfield, perfect? Ha! She'd just have to put all thoughts of him out of her mind. He set her aside easily enough as soon as he found enough partners for her at whatever dance they attended. One duty dance with her, at his mother's insistence, and he was off to the cardrooms, or outside for a cigarillo, or in the corner with Trowbridge and some of his official-looking friends.

She'd wash her hair again, that was what she'd do, and put on a pretty gown, with her pearls, not the diamonds that made her feel cheapened each time she wore them, cheapened and betrayed. And she'd go to

Almack's to find her true love. Or the next best thing, a willing husband.

Almack's was easier the second time around. The introductions were not as long, the names and faces coming together. The ladies all had friends now, other women they could converse with without the fears of wallflowerhood. They all had partners without needing one of the patronesses to intercede on their behalf with some hapless youth dragged in by his mother, the way Daniel was.

Before he could escape to safer grounds, he was dragooned into spending a set with a rotund little sparrow who laughed like a crow and danced like a two-headed chicken.

He'd done so well with Miss Thomlinson, seeing her established with his friend Chadwick, that Princess Lieven told him, "You might even steal a bit of our thunder, making so many matches." She inclined her befeathered head toward his mother and Trowbridge, Susanna and Haversmith, Lord Morgan and Miss Reynolds, Corie and—who the deuce was that man with the hair parted in the middle slobbering over her hand? If he squeezed her poor fingers too hard, he was dead.

"Him? Oh, that is the Duke of Haigh's cousin Haggerty. The duchess called him back from Epsom just to meet your Miss Abbott."

"Not my Miss Abbott," he grumbled, "my mother's goddaughter."

"But you're the one looking after her, aren't you, scrutinizing her suitors? He will come up to scratch— excuse the expression—if Her Grace tells him to. She holds the purse strings in that family, you know."

"He's not in line for the title or anything. I don't see why he's still living at their sufferance, on their financial support. A grown man ought to be self-sufficient, doing something besides keeping his hair part straight."

The princess waved her hand at the gathering. "How many men here actually work for a living, Mr. Stamfield, other than military officers, some well-connected clergy, or cabinet undersecretaries? Our bachelors are mostly younger sons, or cousins like Haggerty, whose job is to make his tailor look good and marry well."

Daniel excused himself before they could reach the next ugly duckling someone thought he could turn into a swan. "I see my mother beckoning to me. That is my commission for tonight, keeping her content."

His mother hadn't raised her hand or her eyebrow, but she sat stiffly, listening to the duke's connection while Corie and Susanna went off with their next partners. Trowbridge was nearby speaking to his government counterparts, and Lord Morgan was dozing on his chair, forbidden to drink, dance, or smoke.

"Ah, Daniel, I was hoping you were free," Lady Cora said. "Mr. Haggerty has been telling me about his trip to the racecourse."

His mother wouldn't give a groat to hear about what horse finished first. After brief introductions and briefer bows, Daniel said, "Yes? What news from Epsom?"

"I was trying to tell Lady Cora about a tale I heard from an old friend of yours, Viscount Snelling."

"The man is no friend." Daniel must have spoken louder than he intended, because Lord Morgan woke up. Trowbridge looked over from his discussion and stepped back toward Lady Cora. Susanna and Clarence Haversmith returned to the group of gilded chairs when they realized the dance was a waltz, and she had still not received permission to take part.

A few other heads turned to see what new delicious disasters the Stamfield contingent caused tonight. Daniel lowered his voice. "That is, I met him once, which was enough."

Haggerty raised a scented handkerchief to his nose and chuckled. "So I gathered. But the viscount did mention a troublesome tale, one that especially concerns me, now that I have met the delightful Miss Abbott."

Daniel wanted to say that nothing about Miss Abbott concerned this mincing prig. Instead he folded his arms across his chest and put on an affected, bored look.

His sister giggled. "You look like you swallowed a worm in your apple."

"Hush, Sukey," Clarence whispered to her. "He's trying to look nonchalant."

"Thank you, Clarence," Daniel said, frowning both of the youngsters into silence. "I am glad you pointed that out to everyone. Go on, Haggerty. What Banbury tale did Snelling spout now?"

"Well, he was in his cups, so I disregarded him at first. But the man kept losing, and I felt sorry for him."

Now, that got Daniel's interest. He looked over to make certain Trowbridge was not missing any of the conversation.

The older man nodded. "Lost a lot, did Snelling?"

Haggerty laughed, almost as high-pitched a cackle

as Daniel's last dance partner had. "A fortune. I've never seen a man so unlucky. It was as if he picked the slowest horse in every race."

Of course he did. Daniel asked, "What did he say, that he was playing the odds?"

"Why, yes, in fact. That's just what Snelling said, that he was hoping for a big payoff."

"And he paid right there, I'd wager, in pound notes."

Now Haggerty began to look uncertain. "Why, yes, how did you know? Most other chaps wrote vouchers, to settle when they returned to London. Thirty days is usual. But not Snelling. He came rich and went home poor."

"Oh, I'd guess he has plenty more blunt where that pile came from."

Trowbridge tried to signal to Daniel, reminding him that this was not public information yet. And they still had no proof. An unlucky, foolish bettor wasn't necessarily a counterfeiter.

Daniel ignored him. "Go on," he said to Haggerty.

"Well, he started bandying Miss Abbott's name around, and yours. Now, I had just received orders—that is, a suggestion—that I return to Town in time to meet Miss Abbott. So I asked him about that unfortunate event my valet swears took place three years ago when he worked for Sir Neville—the event Her Grace decided to consider a pack of nonsense, considering Sir Neville's age and condition. Snelling swore he had a letter from his dead brother, which gave credence to my valet's version."

Daniel's bright blue stare was fixed on Haggerty's puce waistcoat, as if wondering which embroidered hummingbird covered his black heart. "Were you one of the gentlemen fortunate enough to win from Snelling?"

"Why, yes, but what has that to do with Miss Abbott?"

"I suggest that you inspect those pound notes. They will prove as worthless as the lies he spoke."

"What?" Haggerty squawked, which drew even more attention to their conversation.

Trowbridge coughed and glared at Daniel.

"The man is a swindler and his brother was a snake."

"You say his coin is false?" Haggerty went pale. "I used it to pay my tailor and my boot maker."

"Then you could be charged with the same crimes as the counterfeiter when we catch him, passing forged documents. It is a hanging crime, you know."

"But I didn't . . . I never . . . Snelling? You are accusing Snelling?"

"Not at all." Trowbridge stepped in front of Daniel. "We've noticed some slight imperfections in a few of the recent bank issues. The Finance Ministry is looking into it, I assure you, as is the royal exchequer. The Bank of England stands behind its currency."

Haggerty wiped his forehead. "Well, that is a relief." Now he sneered at Daniel. "There was no need to start a panic about the bills. People will stop using them and demand gold or silver instead."

"Quite, " Trowbridge confirmed, with another glare toward Daniel. "No need for the least concern." He placed his arm around Haggerty's thin, padded shoulders to lead him away.

The man was willing to go, anxious to inspect the remaining bills in his inside pocket, for the high-stakes card game he intended to join later. Before he left, however, Haggerty felt he had to excuse himself to Lady Cora. "If my winnings are good, my debts are not as pressing now. That is, I do not feel I can offer for Miss Abbott until this elopement story is settled one way or the other. Her Grace would not want any dirty laundry hanging on the ducal family tree."

"I do not believe I gave you permission to address Miss Abbott," Daniel practically spit out, coming between Trowbridge and Haggerty. "In fact, I do not. Not for a dance, not for a glance."

Haggerty stepped back, farther from Daniel and his clenched fists. When he reached what he thought was a safe enough distance, he warned, "I'd be careful were I you. When Snelling gets back, he'll demand satisfaction for the slurs you cast tonight. And you don't have to warn me off the wench. No one will offer for the Abbott female, anyway. There are too many doubts about her whereabouts that night."

Daniel growled. "You are doubting my mother's word?"

"N-not at all." Haggerty bowed in Lady Cora's direction. She turned her head away, the cut direct. Trowbridge reached down, as if for a sword at his side. Lord Morgan wheezed something about calling out the impudent puppy himself, while some smooth-skinned youth held back Lady Cora's daughter from clawing his eyes out. Stamfield was growing all red in the face, and Miss Abbott herself was returning to her party.

Haggerty tried to smile as if he had not just offended every one of them. "I—I am just withdrawing the offer I made to Lady Cora, when you were not available, Stamfield. Your pardon, Miss Abbott, but I do not wish to wed at this time."

Corie raised her chin. "And I would not marry one who lets his cousin select his bride, sight unseen, or who proposes marriage after one dance. For that matter, I will not wed a gentleman"—she did not try to keep the sneer from her voice—"who does not ask me himself."

A few more steps and Haggerty felt he'd escape with his skin intact. He was confident enough to call back, "Well, you won't be so particular when no man offers."

Princess Lieven and the other patronesses hurried over, likely to evict the Stamfields and their friends from the premises. It wouldn't be the first time for Daniel, but he'd be damned if anyone was going to treat his womenfolk so poorly. Hell, if they were thrown out here, now, Susanna might have to marry Clarence after all.

So he rose to the occasion, took Corie's hand in his, and loudly proclaimed, "Miss Abbott needs no other offers. I am pleased to announce we have an understanding."

That was no lie. He understood she needed a husband. She understood he was insane.

"An understanding?"

Daniel didn't know who asked the question, Haggerty, a hostess, or Corie herself. He took a deep breath to get ready for the welts he knew were coming. "I am honored she has accepted my proposal of marriage."

It was a good thing he held her hand—as gently as he could—to keep her on her feet, or to keep her from slapping him, or to keep him from scratching his arse again, right in full view of half the *ton*.

Into the stunned silence that followed, his mother, bless her, stood and smiled. "I was hoping to keep it secret until the end of the Season, you know. Or at least announce it at our ball, which the rest of the family will be attending."

Daniel watched, but his mother's eyelid did not twitch, the manipulative, matchmaking . . . mother. She'd planned this all along. Corie hadn't, he could tell by her trembling, and now he had the rash to prove he hadn't. He rubbed his nose.

Then someone screamed. And pointed, right at him and his poor face. "The pox! He has the smallpox!"

Women fainted; men almost trampled them on the way out the doors. Others climbed out the balconies. The orchestra decamped, overturning the refreshments tables. Glasses shattered; sickly punch spilled everywhere. Females screamed as they slid into one another and across the floor.

Well, at least he'd never have to go to Almack's again.

Chapter Twenty-seven

"A toast to celebrate the happy event?" Lord Morgan suggested once they returned to Royce House.

Silence met his cheery effort. "I, ah, see. Plenty of things to discuss, what? I'll just toddle off to bed, then, shall I?"

Daniel had ridden up with the driver to cool his flaming cheeks. Corie had ridden in a huddle, biting the inside of her cheeks. A look from one to the other had Susanna and Lady Cora also excusing themselves.

"It has been a tumultuous evening. I propose"— Lady Cora almost choked on the word—"that is, I think we should all make an early night of it. Tomorrow is bound to be equally as fraught." She intended to hide at her dressmaker's, then go on a tour of the Bank of England that Lord Trowbridge had promised. From now on, Daniel and Corie could handle matters without her. She deserved a rest, if neither of them smothered her in her sleep.

Once everyone but Corie and Daniel had left the front parlor, Dobbson inquired if tea was required. He was answered with the door slammed in his face. And locked behind him.

"Now, that is highly improper," could be heard from inside the room.

Someone, possibly one of the footmen who had attended their coach to Almack's and heard of the debacle there, said, "It's all right. They are betrothed now."

"About time, I say. And pity the poor woman."

"What woman'd that be, then? Her ladyship who threw them together, or Miss Abbott?"

Daniel could not hear the butler's reply. The former butler, if he had his way. And the former footman, too.

He touched his face, hoping the welts had faded, hoping he wouldn't be called upon to tell any more clankers, like how happy he was with the engagement. Judging from the look on his bride-to-be's face, any happiness would be short-lived. Her eyes were narrowed so tightly he couldn't find that pretty moss color. And if she sucked on the insides of her cheeks any harder, she'd look like a carp. For that matter, he was glad Dobbson had not brought the tea cart. There might have been a butter knife for her to stick through his heart.

"Uh, about the betrothal." He was wondering if she wanted him to get down on one knee to make it proper. Females set great store by that kind of thing, he'd heard. Or maybe she wanted a ring to show her friends.

She wanted him to go to the devil. "We. Are. Not. Betrothed." Each word had a space around it, as if he were deaf. Or dumb. Her fists were clenched, he could see, but thankfully empty.

Keeping his distance, and nervously eyeing Aunt Royce's prize Ming vases scattered around the room, he tried to use a comforting voice, the one he used for Miss White, or a frightened horse. "I am sorry, my dear, but in the eyes of society, we are as good as promised, which is all that matters. No one will be bandying your name around, or caring about your reputation."

"I am not your dear, and I care."

His effort at softness and endearments failed, so he went back to blunt honesty. "Well, you'd have no reputation left if I hadn't done what I did."

"For that, I am supposed to thank you? You are the last man in the world I would wed."

Daniel thought that, yes, she should have thanked him. Wasn't that the form ladies were taught from birth? Something about being grateful for the honor or drivel like that. She did not appear honored. She was almost trembling with rage. Or was that horror at the idea of wedding him? Neither made Daniel happy. "I believe I am the last man on earth who is liable to ask you."

"Now, that is a certainty if the gentlemen think I am already bespoken."

She had not said "the other gentlemen." Damn. Stung, Daniel said, "Do not work yourself into an apoplexy. If I am such a bad bargain, you can cry off in a few weeks. After Susanna's ball, so there'll be less gossip on her big night."

"What, you think I should become known as a jilt besides a loose woman?"

"Well, no gentleman"—he emphasized the title—"is permitted to end an engagement. Doing so makes the female look no-account. So I cannot cry off. I can always irritate you past bearing, until you call an end. No one will blame you, I daresay. And I seem to succeed at that, at any rate."

She did not contradict him. Her brow stayed furrowed while she thought. "We could agree we do not suit, I suppose."

"That's the ticket." He tried to sound enthusiastic about being the scorned suitor, no matter what they said.

"How long must we pretend?"

It could not be a pretense or he'd break out in hives every time someone congratulated him. "It has to look official, and last long enough that people believe I really did offer for you. And you accepted." He'd better get a ring tomorrow.

"I won't hang on your arm."

She disliked him so much? He brushed at his coat the way the dandies did. "Lud, I'd never want a woman creasing my sleeve."

"I will not show affection in public. Or private." Her arms were crossed in front of her chest so he could not even see what he was forbidden to touch.

"You might have to bend a little, to make the thing look convincing."

"How much bending?"

"Dash it, how should I know? I've never been engaged before, have I?"

She turned her back to him. "And you are not now."

He ran his hands through his already-disordered black hair. "Well, I am feeling married, all right, to a shrew. I thought you'd be grateful I pulled your chestnuts out of the fire."

"But I wanted to find—"

"The ideal husband, who will cherish and adore you. Yes, yes, but what if his parents never met? What if your missing soul mate stays missing, in India or Jamaica? I am here, dash it."

He heard a sniffle. "You aren't crying, are you?"

She said no, with a catch in her throat. "Just saying we are affianced out loud made you break out in spots."

"The spots had nothing to do with you. It was the lie. That is, the, ah, situation. Nerves, don't you know."

"You are not itching now, and this must be one of the most anxious conversations of your life, forcing yourself to pretend you don't mind being tied to me."

"I don't mind, and that is the truth, so, no, I am not covered in hives."

She turned to face him, inspecting his neck, his ears, his hands that stayed loose at his side, not squirming to scratch some unmentionable part of his anatomy. "So it's true; you do get a rash from a lie. And yet you did that, for me?"

"Tonight's was the most sudden, spectacular rash of my lifetime, but how did you know?"

She kept staring at him, but not in fright, not in disgust. "Some things your mother and sister said. They react to lies, too, only differently."

He sighed. "So I have come to realize, although I don't understand it. The truth thing was supposed to be a Royce legacy, which somehow came to me through the distaff line. I never heard of any females being truth-knowers. It is all very secret, you understand. It could prove dangerous and disastrous if anyone found out."

"No one would believe it, anyway. I've seen Lady Cora's eyelid twitch too many times not to put credence in your family's talent. No one else noticed."

"No, but now you'll have to marry me, of course."

She sat down on a high-backed wooden chair, her spine as rigid as the slats. "Why?"

He took a seat opposite her, but close enough for him to reach out for her hand. "Because a wife can't bear witness against her husband. And that way I'd know you wouldn't betray me."

"I wouldn't betray my godmother or my dear friend Susanna."

"It is not the same. Besides, why not? Why are you so set against going through with the betrothal, the marriage? You'd be mistress of Stamfield Manor, and we could find a small place here in Town for visits if you want. I can provide whatever you wish, and you'd never have to fear your father."

She looked down, studying their linked hands, hers still in gloves. "Because you are too much like him."

Daniel dropped her hand and jumped to his feet, almost knocking over a piecrust table that held a jade horse, likely worth more than he and his own horse combined. "Like hell I am. Pardon my language, but I resent being compared to a man who would strike a woman. Or steal from her, or force her into a marriage against her—" He'd done just that. "Well, only if it is necessary."

"You are a man who acts first and thinks later. You are a man who drinks and wenches and gambles."

"I am a bachelor! That's what we do. But that's not to say I would continue on that path if I had a wife waiting for me. And I have not indulged half so much since my mother's come to Town."

"But as soon as she leaves?"

He glowered at her. "Men can change, can't they?"

"Only if they want to. You want to be in charge,

to make decisions. You ride roughshod over those who don't act the way you want."

He wanted a drink, but he would not prove her point for her. "I am not such a wastrel or as much a ruffian as you think. I am working for the government now, doing paperwork." Inspecting currency was just that, and more than she needed to know.

Corie was not impressed. "I saw Trowbridge shaking his head. You must have ruined whatever investigation he is conducting by mentioning the counterfeiting in public."

"No such thing. He asked for my services, and he would be months behind if not for me. I am solving the mess for him."

"By blackening Snelling's name?"

"I'll find proof."

She found her handkerchief and blew her nose. "I still won't marry you."

He came back close to her chair and knelt in front. Then he tipped her chin up so he could look into her eyes. "I don't see why not. I don't care about the money or the jewels. You like my family. I, uh, I like you."

She started to lay her hand against his cheek, but then thought better of it. "Marriage is more than that, more than liking. You . . . you are a fighter."

"No, I—" He couldn't deny he'd been in more drunken brawls than there were years she'd been alive. Or that his reputation in the Intelligence Division wasn't partly well earned. Or that he liked to follow the Fancy, or how he'd wallop anyone who threatened her or his family. "I'd never hurt you."

"But you'd teach our sons to be bullies."

Sons? He'd have sons? Daniel wasn't used to the

idea of having a wife yet, and he'd have sons? Little boys with golden brown hair and moss green eyes? Or would they have his black hair and dark-rimmed blue eyes? Would they carry on the Royce tradition or be normal boys, telling fibs and getting caught instead of telling fibs and getting measles?

Now she did reach out to touch his nose, his many-times-broken nose. "I wouldn't want my sons to be hurt."

He took her hand again. "I'd teach them to defend themselves, no more."

"What of our daughters? They'd cower in fear from you."

Daughters? Tiny little fragile birdlings? Afraid of him? "No! I am not a brute. I can be gentle."

He leaned closer and brought his lips to hers. He meant to show her just how gentle he could be, how light his touch. He intended nothing more than a quick brushing of lips, to show her how harmless he was, how not threatening.

He couldn't help himself. One touch and he was lost. She tasted so sweet, her lips so soft, her skin like silk, her distinctive scent enfolding him like a velvet mist, the sound she made so encouraging. Or was that him, purring?

He deepened the kiss, and touched her lips with his tongue. Corie jerked back, as if startled. Daniel put his hand behind her head, kneading her neck, and brushed his lips across her eyelids, over her cheeks, then back to her lips. "Nothing to fear."

Breathing heavily, sighing softly, she let her tongue flick out to meet his. She relaxed into the kiss, in his arms, with her hands coming up to caress his neck, to clutch his shoulders as if she might fall off her chair otherwise. He kissed her neck, her ear, her chin, wishing he could start at her toes and kiss every inch of her. But he could not, not here, not now. He ended the kiss and stood, helping her rise, and smiling when he saw that her knees were wobbly. "See? We do suit."

She slapped him, hard, smack across the face. "I am not a loose woman."

He rubbed his cheek, which was all red again. "And you accused me of being violent."

She started crying for real. She sobbed, "I am not like my father. I am not what he says I am. You had no right to treat me like a harlot."

"Damn it, I treated you like a desirable woman, nothing more. And I stopped, didn't I? I know you are chaste, and you will stay that way until the day we are wed." Even if it killed him.

"You believed Snelling was my lover."

He handed over his handkerchief. "I don't now."

She looked at him through eyes welled with moisture. Her misery almost brought tears to his own eyes, and shame and guilt to his heart.

"Why do you believe me now?" she asked. "Did I kiss so poorly?"

"You kissed well enough to—" He did not mention how well. All she had to do was look. He blamed the dratted rulers of Almack's for insisting on knee breeches, and his tailor and Deauville for making them so blasted tight. His breathing was labored, his skin was flushed, and all he wanted to do was tear her clothes off with his teeth. And she thought she was a bad kisser? "I would not care if you and Snelling had anticipated your vows, because it no longer matters to me. You were young; you were in danger. But I believe you did not, despite his efforts, because you said so, because you are a true lady."

"And you trust me? Oh, no, you trust these odd instincts of yours."

"Whatever the reason, I know you are no wanton."

She stared at him, considering. "Then why did you kiss me like that?"

"Because I wanted to, by Jupiter. Because I have been wanting to since you got here. 'Like that'? Sweetheart, like that and a great deal more, besides. Why, if you only knew the ways I want to kiss you, you'd be wearing a permanent blush. As it is, I'll be wearing a permanent—" He did not complete that sentence, either. "Now are you satisfied?"

"No."

Well, hell, neither was Daniel.

Chapter Twenty-eight

C orie came to accept the temporary proposal. She did not like it, but she accepted it, and Daniel, for a while.

She felt as if she were a deer at a river, with the wolves behind her, and the water too wide to jump, too deep to forge. She'd just have to trust that the raging currents would carry her to safety.

If Daniel were the river, he made her feel safe, but the tides were notoriously unreliable. If he were the wolf, she was in desperate trouble because he was stubborn enough to follow. Now that he felt responsible for her, he would not rest until she was settled, to his satisfaction if not her own. Most dangerous of all, she found him far too attractive.

His kisses proved to her she was not entirely the dispassionate woman who shied from a man's touch. She liked Daniel's touch very well indeed, and wanted more: more than was safe, more than was wise, and more than she wanted anything else in the world. Dangerous waters, for certain.

His kisses and caresses, his handsome looks and beautiful blue eyes, weren't the only aspects of Daniel Stamfield that Corie admired. She knew other women noticed his strength and virile size, but she alone saw his gentler side. At first, he'd stood by her through all the congratulations, the penetrating looks to see if the couple really meant to wed. He bought her a ring, in addition to the one his mother passed down, the one Peter Stamfield had given to Lady Cora on their betrothal. Daniel said he wanted Corie to have something all her own, so he picked a diamond for a Perfect Diamond, his note said. Or Deauville wrote for him.

He gave her the pleasure of going to dinners and dances and the opera without having to please anyone but herself—and him, who always did his best to appear cheerful and happy with their betrothal, despite all the teasing from his bachelor friends. He still grew hard of talking when she came down the stairs before an evening out, so she knew he admired her.

He still grew hard when they kissed good night—for the benefit of his mother and the servants, she supposed—so she knew he wanted her. She wanted him, too, so perhaps she really was a harlot at heart. She'd never succumb to such base emotions, of course, not when the engagement was a sham.

Speaking of shams, Daniel took her to art galleries and print shops. "You really do not have to do this for me, you know. I adore the museums, but I like drives in the countryside just as well."

"Happy to please you."

Corie looked for the telltale signs she was getting to know, and saw nothing to show he was feigning enjoyment. But his interest in the artwork turned out not to be on her behalf, anyway. He was happy she was knowledgeable about the artists, but he wanted only to hold the pictures, or touch them, just to see what they felt like.

"You are not supposed to touch paintings," she whispered when the shopkeeper's back was turned.

So he waited until her back was turned, too. One framed print felt wrong. So he could do it!

"This one," he said, smiling, indicating the fake. "Do you know the artist?"

She was not as well schooled in current artists as in past masters, but she recognized the name on this print of a mother and child. They'd just seen the signature of the artist, Noel Edel, at the previous gallery they'd visited, on a number of pen-and-ink sketches of horses, some of the winners of the past week. She'd noticed them particularly, because Daniel admired one he thought might be his cousin's horse. He wanted to purchase it as a gift for his goddaughter until Corie pointed out the child would probably enjoy a doll more. Corie thought how lovely it would be to afford to purchase the drawing for Daniel himself, as a betrothal gift. She did not have the funds; they were not betrothed.

This Noel Edel print appeared to be in a style close to the horse drawing, but with less-bold lines and more-subtle shadings, but a portrait would have been done indoors, at leisure, not at the trackside. "The subject alone might explain the differences in technique. I'd have to compare the handwriting."

"No, it's a forgery. I am certain of it."

The gallery owner hurried over when his clerk heard Daniel's comment. The owner was horrified that one of his works was of dubious provenance. "But . . . but how can you know?"

"The lady is not only beautiful; she knows her art,"
Daniel explained. He could not say it felt wrong, just
as he couldn't say that the man's shock did not raise
a rash.

A new customer of his had brought it in that very
morning when he came to purchase artwork for the
new home he was building, the gallery owner, Mr.
Findley, explained. Since the customer and his wife
had not been blessed with children, the mother and
infant drawing upset them. Findley'd taken the Edel
print, because the artist was so popular now, and the
customer's order was so large. He proudly showed one
back corner of the gallery, where all the paintings and
prints were marked sold and a worker was building
crates to transport them.

Findley asked Corie if she'd mind looking these
over in case he'd missed another fake. She looked,
but Daniel touched each one, to the man's horror.

Findley was relieved when Daniel put his hand
under Corie's arm, and more so when she declared
everything seemed aboveboard, and quite beautiful.
"Your customer has excellent taste."

The paintings were some of the most expensive in
the shop, the gallery owner admitted, and he'd hate
to give the customer anything less than the quality he
paid for, especially when his lordship's house, on one
of the new squares being developed as London grew,
was bound to be a showplace for the *ton*.

Daniel was ready to leave, now that his experiment
had proved successful, but Findley's next words
stopped him. The man studied the questionable Edel
print, wondering aloud if he should mention it to his
customer, then decided against it. "After all, he paid

full price for the lot of these"—the ones on the walls and the ones already crated—"and paid cash, too."

"Cash?" Daniel asked.

"Oh, yes, to my delight. Now I have no need to send a bill, then wait to collect, like with some of the other no—" He started to say "nobs," then recollected that the couple in front of him were well dressed and educated, and the lady had a maid waiting outside. "Other notable customers. I did not have to accept a bank draft, either, only to find the account is closed when one goes to collect."

Daniel was tallying up the number of crates. "Cash, you say? That must have been a substantial pile of coins. I hope you took it to the bank immediately."

"Oh, no. Who walks around with that heavy a purse? He paid by notes issued by the Bank of England itself. They are all safe and sound in my own vault until closing time."

Daniel smiled, a slow grin that showed a dimple. He looked younger, mischievous, and proud, all at once, Corie thought. She mistrusted that look.

He asked, "Was your extravagant customer perchance a gentleman from Oxford?"

"Gracious, how did you guess?"

Now Corie gasped. "Snelling?"

The owner looked at her. "How did you know?"

"We're old acquaintances," Daniel said. "In fact, I believe I can cancel his order, except for this one."

He took the fake Edel out of the man's suddenly limp grip. "Which I will see delivered as soon as you tell me where."

"But . . . but . . . the money?"

"As false as the print, I regret. And the government

will want to collect it as evidence. But you will not suffer, since you haven't delivered any of the artwork or tried to deposit the funds."

They left Findley in tears, but with the print wrapped in brown paper, and the address of the house being built, most likely on a foundation as shaky as the payments.

Daniel was walking too fast for Corie to keep up. "Sorry, my love. I need to get you home and send messages for Trowbridge. I was right! The bill of sale, the counterfeit bills, and Mr. Findley's testimony will prove Snelling's guilt. Then we can find out where the imitations are being printed, and the artist who dared copy the banknotes." He held up the wrapped picture. "Likely whoever turned this out, too."

He was so excited, Corie did not want to mention they had not exactly proved the painting was a forgery yet. She wasn't entirely comfortable with the idea that a wrong feeling, after one touch, was a valid judgment. "Lord Trowbridge will be pleased," was all she said, figuring the distinguished viscount would know best how to proceed.

Daniel turned and kissed her, right in the street. "I am pleased, and I couldn't have done it so easily without you. Do you see what a good partnership we'll make?" He kissed her again, to the amusement of passersby, and her maid's blushes. "You are a gem, my love. And I will show my appreciation tonight at Mother's dinner when we make the formal announcement of our betrothal."

"Not another gift, Daniel. You are too generous, and we are not . . . partners."

"Not yet, but we need to show everyone it's a love match, you know. Besides, Deauville and Dobbson both agree it's proper for me to give you gifts now that the notice has been in the paper. I . . . I like buying you presents. I like seeing you smile, Corie."

That raging river? She jumped right in.

Daniel left her off at Royce House, sent footmen off to Trowbridge's home, his office, the bank, and his club, then went to Layton Square. He left his groom with the horses a few houses away from the one under construction, and decided to walk past, to reconnoiter, until reinforcements arrived.

Some of the window openings were still empty; the exterior was half painted, the entry not yet bricked. Scaffolds and ladders surrounded the outside, but only one man seemed to be working on the house, and he was loading an already-full wagon.

"I have come to see Lord Snelling," Daniel said. "I hoped he might be here surveying the progress."

The man spit a few inches from Daniel's boots. "Ain't no progress and ain't like to be. They've all gone to find the rotter. Sorry iffen he's a friend of yours." He waved vaguely at the stacks of tiles, the tools, and the piles of wood. "Sorrier for us, getting paid with ass wipes."

"Ass wipes?"

"Paper money. All it's good for. That's what we heard, anyway. Some toff said it right out at one of them fancy dos. Now the banks is lookin' at the flimsies with magnifiers and half the shops won't take 'em in trade. The boss went to find out for hisself. T'see if he can't shake some gold or silver out of him."

"Do you know where he's staying?"

"He were out of town, but word is he's back, staying with his brother-in-law. An artist or something."

Daniel could not picture the viscount in any artist's garret, but he found it intriguing that Snelling knew an artist. Everything was coming together nicely, except the mention of the growing concern among the banks and their customers. Trowbridge wouldn't be happy.

For a silver coin the man recalled the artist, Eden or something.

"Edel?"

"I s'pose. Must be successful, has a house in Kensington."

So Daniel left more coins with the man, to direct Trowbridge and his men to the new address. He was too busy thinking about why Edel was putting his name to inferior work to notice the worker was loading the wagon faster, to get away before any official types came near. It would be just like the magistrate's men to haul away the tools and supplies as evidence. There'd be nothing left for the work crew.

Unaware his message was not going to be delivered, Daniel collected his curricle and went to find his quarry in Kensington this time.

What he found was a mob outside a small row house, shaking their fists, tossing pebbles at the windows. Concerned neighbors were standing across the street, debating about calling the Watch.

"Do that," Daniel told them, although he doubted any street patrol came this way. "And Bow Street, too. I don't know who guards the Finance Ministry or the Bank of England, but they'll be here soon."

Which effectively thinned the crowd of those who wished to have as little to do with the authorities as possible. Then Daniel approached the workers in their rough shirts and one, the boss, he assumed, in a leather vest. Two merchants in dark suits waved bank-notes; one big chap held a pail and shovel. It was his lumps of coal, not stones, that were being tossed at the upper stories of the artist's house. It was not a pretty picture, and the landlord, who lived in the lower half of the house, was in the street, too, shouting at the crowd to go away.

The workmen were ready to attack Daniel, until they saw the package in his hands.

"Iffen you're expectin' payment, get in line. We all found out 'is blunt is worthless."

"Is Snelling inside? What about the artist? The fellow might have nothing to do with the cheat."

"The landlord says the dauber's gone to Epsom. 'E don't know if Snelling's here or not, and the painter's manservant won't say."

"Let me ask."

He was the biggest man, so they let him rap on the door. "Is Snelling in there?" he yelled through the wood when it did not open.

"No," came back. "Go away."

"He's inside," Daniel told the building foreman. That was what the back of Daniel's neck told him, anyway.

One of the carpenters decided that was invitation enough. He had a hammer in his hand, and he used it to batter down the door while the landlord tried to fend him off. A brickmason and the coal hauler rushed inside.

Daniel followed them, but more slowly. An aproned servant rushed past him on his way out. Then another servant, in a large cape.

"It's him!" someone shouted. "Snelling!"

All the men raced back down the stairs and outside, joining the rest of the angry creditors in attacking the fleeing man. So many bodies were piled on top of one another that Daniel couldn't tell if they'd tackled Snelling or some hapless cook. So he waded in, pulling off one man after another. He tried to avoid punches and a few kicks meant for Snelling, but some were aimed directly at him, for interfering.

It was Snelling, all right, bloody and battered at the bottom, rolled into a ball. "You!" he screamed when Daniel dragged him to his feet. "You're the one who's out to destroy me and my entire family!"

"I just saved your life!"

"You killed my brother. Now you set these hoodlums on me. For nothing!"

For the rash, Daniel almost let the builders have Snelling again. Four of them did not see why they couldn't finish what the others started, so Daniel had to give them two good reasons: his right fist and his left. After all, he needed Snelling to confess and give up the name of the artist and the location of the counterfeit originals. Otherwise someone else could take over the operation and England's economy could still be in peril.

Besides, they were four muscular workers against one puny lordling. Daniel never could stand to see an injustice, or miss a good melee. This one turned into a free-for-all, with the builders turning against the coal deliverer, and the merchants against the landlord, who had a musket now to keep them from destroying his house.

Somehow, Daniel never noticed that Snelling crawled away. Nor could he go after him, not with the Watch and Bow Street's finest holding him down, under arrest.

*   *   *

The treacherous waters turned into a sweetly babbling brook. Corie's mock engagement was turning out to be more pleasant than any real betrothal she could imagine. Now she realized she couldn't imagine her life after Daniel left. Her bedroom was filled with flowers, a silly little bonnet with forget-me-nots on the brim came from a millinery shop, and all of Lady Cora's friends kissed her cheek and smiled their approval.

How sweet it was . . . and how short-lived.

Corie had to accept the congratulations by herself.

Lady Cora had to start the dinner without one of the guests of honor before it was entirely ruined.

Fifteen couples had accepted the impromptu invitation; the cook had outdone herself; the Grand Hotel delivered three kinds of desserts Daniel had ordered. And his seat stayed empty. Lord Trowbridge was there, looking confused when Corie asked if he'd seen Daniel. By the time he got the message about Snelling, no one was at the house on Layton Square, no Daniel, no Snelling, no workers, with no one in sight to say where they'd gone. No, he doubted Snelling had shot Daniel. No, he didn't believe Daniel was lying in the road somewhere.

Toast after toast was made—but not to the engagement, because there was no happy couple. The guests were restless, having other parties to attend after dinner. Lady Cora was looking thunderclouds; Susanna shredded her napkin. Clarence Haversmith volunteered to go to McCann's to look for Daniel, or Lydia Burton's, which earned him a sour look from everyone.

Just as they were about to leave the dining room, Daniel staggered through the door on the arm of a red-vested Bow Street Runner. Daniel's lip was cut, his eye was blackened, his clothing was torn, he smelled like a sewer, and he had no Snelling to show for it.

Corie jumped from her chair, threw her wine in his face, then his ring, then his mother's ring, then the necklace he'd bought her, then the pretty fan painted with lilacs he bought because she always smelled of them to him, then the flowers from her hair because he'd sent them. Finally she slapped him before fleeing the room.

"I suppose that means there's not going to be any champagne toast again," Lord Morgan said to no one in particular.

Chapter Twenty-nine

"**B**ut I won!"
"Go away" came from the other side of Corie's locked, latched, and barricaded—as far as he knew—bedroom door.

"Don't you want to hear that we already have enough evidence to see Snelling hang?"

"No. It is the middle of the night, Mr. Stamfield. And I do not want to hear anything whatsoever from you. Not ever."

That "Mr. Stamfield" was hint enough; so was the "not ever," and his sister's giggles from the next room. His mother's snores were so fake, she might develop a permanent tic in her eye. But Daniel was not giving up.

It had taken him so long to come to talk to Corie because of briefing Trowbridge, helping him send messages to all the toll keepers, the militia captains, the Horse Guards, Harrison's underworld, and the navy. They'd get Snelling before he could sail away, ride away, or disappear into Seven Dials. And then they'd find the printing press and the engraver. Other, legitimate presses were already printing a picture of his likeness, from a sketch they found at his brother-in-law's. Nothing else about the artist's rooms seemed suspicious, but Runners left for Epsom to apprehend Mr. Noel Edel, anyway.

Daniel's job was done until they had someone to question. Now he had to ask a more important one, for his own future. He looked somewhat better, thanks to Deauville, a raw steak, and a change of clothes. He stood with flowers, her fan, and her rings outside her door, long after the ladies had sought their beds.

"Please, Corie. We need to talk."

The door stayed shut.

"I bought you a house."

The giggling stopped. So did the snoring. The door opened an inch. "You did what, you buffle-headed baboon?"

Corie was wearing nothing but a thin white nightgown. Daniel could almost see through it, with her hearth fire glowing behind her. He knew her hair draped her shoulder in a long braid, tied with a silly blue ribbon, but he couldn't keep his eyes from the outlines of her breasts, the dark circles of her nipples, the darker shadow between her legs.

"Well?"

"Ah, very, thank you. I think."

She stamped her foot, which was bare. She had tiny pink toes. He'd never wanted to lick a woman's toes before now. To suckle them, to fondle them. Maybe if she liked the house, she'd let him.

"I bought you a house. A perfectly nice one, brand-new, going to waste with Snelling a fugitive. The builder was happy enough to let me take over the costs so his men won't be out of work."

"You bought me a house? Without asking?"

"Well, there wasn't a lot of time before Inspector

Dimm from Bow Street got to the magistrate's office to vouch for me. And the apothecary coming to set the builder's nose. Oh, and settling with Noel Edel's landlord for damages to that place before they let any of us go. You can go look at the construction tomorrow and tell the workers about any changes you'd like."

While Corie stood, dumbfounded, Daniel pushed past her so he could dump the flowers and jewelry down on the bed. There weren't any beds at the Layton Square house. He'd have to order some, tomorrow. Lots and lots of beds. And thick carpets. Maybe a billiard table. A dining table, too, he supposed.

"You bought me a house?" she repeated, ignoring the dog who padded into the room behind Daniel.

"I, ah, was hoping you'd share it with me. You know, as my wife."

"We are not getting married. We never were."

"But I've been thinking how nice it would be. Maybe it was getting hit on the head with a coal bucket that did it, but I thought you'd like a place in Town, with a little park of its own, not close to all the traffic, but not far away from the shops. I want to help at the Finance Ministry or the museums when we're not at Stamfield Manor, so we'll need a more permanent place than staying here with my relatives, and rooms at McCann's won't do for a lady."

"No. No house, no rooms, no marriage. I will not marry a man such as you. I told you before—I'd never ally myself with a man of violence, a street brawler. Besides, you could have been killed. I worried all night. I will not go through that again, wondering if Snelling or some other miscreant killed you. It would be worse than being wed to a soldier. And there had to have been a way of settling the disputes without your fists."

Daniel sat on the bed, an even worse trespass than entering a lady's bedchamber uninvited. Pigs would fly before he was invited. He sighed. "I was afraid you'd say that. I couldn't think of a way to avoid a fight, and there was no time to have a polite discussion. The crowd was out for blood after they realized they'd been cheated. I had to save Snelling."

"You saved . . . Snelling?"

"They would have torn him apart, not that they'd get a ha'penny from him, but no one likes to be the pigeon that gets plucked that way."

Corie looked around for her dressing robe, but the oaf was sitting on it. "I thought you must have fought with him."

"The man's not much for using anything but words. He must have crawled away while I was holding the gang off. He's a coward."

Without her robe, Corie felt cold. Or else the idea of Daniel battling a mob gave her a chill. She went to stir up the fire. "So was his brother. He tried to jump out the window rather than face my father."

Daniel shrugged. "Both men got to live another day." He tried not to look at the back side of her thin gown as she bent over the coals. He mightn't make it through the night. He stood and joined her at the fireplace and took the poker from her. "Let me do that."

When he had the fire blazing, and the fire in his blood under control, he said, "Um, the house is yours, anyway. So you never have to go home to your father. You can tell people you bought it with your mother's inheritance. Nothing improper about that. Of course you'd have to hire a respectable female to live with you. But if that is what you want . . . ?" He stared at her, waiting.

Corie looked at his poor battered face, the hope there, and almost, almost said all she wanted was him. A man who fought, to save a loathsome criminal? A man whose family was touched by a magic she could never understand? A man who bought houses while in jail, for a woman who never agreed to marry him?

"I cannot—" she began.

"You don't have to decide tonight," he interrupted before she could ruin all his dreams of a new life in the new house, with Corie in the doorway, holding a babe like in the forged print. His baby. "But you ought to know we need to stay betrothed until Susanna's ball. I invited your father."

Now she screamed loudly enough to wake Lady Cora, if that woman hadn't had her ear pressed to the connecting wall.

"It was the only proper thing to do if we were making a formal public announcement of the betrothal. Why, Trowbridge already asked permission to pay his addresses to my mother when his mourning period is over. He's bringing his sons to meet her over their summer holidays."

"What did you tell him?"

"That my mother was a dab hand with boys. They'll love her."

"Not Trowbridge, you ninny. What did you write to my father?"

"Only that I was marrying his daughter. I didn't ask his permission. I could not bring myself to do that, no matter the conventions. I just said my mother was announcing it at her ball, and you ought to be wearing your diamonds then. Your real diamonds. Oh, and he could discuss your dowry with the family's solicitor when he arrived in Town. Our man Glessing will not let Abbott cheat you of that, either."

Corie had to sit down because her head was spinning. She chose the bed because it was closest. "I thought you didn't care about the jewels or the dowry."

"I don't, but you do. This way the solicitor can tie the money up for our daughters. Or for you, to have money of your own. Of course you'll have to marry me to get it. And to get daughters."

"You are only offering for me out of pity, and we both agreed that was no basis for a match."

He came to the bed. "Pity? Pity me, trying to do this up right when I know I'm making a hash of it." He took her hand. "Lord, Corie, I'll do my best to make you happy. I know I'm no nonpareil, no true gentleman, but I do love you." He waited, but felt no itch. "I do! Yes, I do love you. I wasn't sure, never having fallen before. I won't live in that house without you. I'll never want to share it with another woman. Only you."

Now he did get down on his knees. "Please." But he looked down and saw her perfect pink toes, so he kissed them instead of pleading his case.

She laughed. "That tickles. Get up, you looby."

He did, and sat beside her on the bed, taking her hand back.

She let him, too concerned with her father coming to London. "Do you really think he will attend the ball?"

"I may have mentioned I'd call on him when I returned to the manor if I did not see him before. With my cousins, big, sturdy chaps, you know. And my uncle, the earl."

He could threaten the squire with a regiment of warriors, a raft of nobles. They were not enough. "No, I cannot stay here. I cannot see him. I'll go visit a friend or—"

"Hush, sweetheart." He put his arm around her and pulled her close. "No one will hurt you. You'll never be alone with him. I'll see to that. And you won't have to say a word, either. I have a few I've been saving for him, though. You cannot disappoint Susanna on her big day, can you? Or my mother. She planned for us to be thrown together, you know."

"She was wrong. We'd never suit."

"We suit perfectly." He took her into his embrace, breathing in the intoxicating scent of her. He cursed his clothes, all the layers Deauville thought proper for an improper midnight visit. He cursed his cut lip, which ached, and his privates, which ached worse.

He forgot it all—his name, his honorable intentions, his mother in the next room—when Corie kissed him.

"You are the nicest man I have ever known, Daniel Stamfield," she told him when they had to breathe.

"But can you love me, just a little?"

She showed him how much, with her eager kisses.

He was lost. The time, the place, everything was wrong except the woman. She was kissing him with a hunger he recognized, a need to be needed, a passion to become one with the only one who mattered.

"I love you," he kept whispering, when he could. "Too fast," he panted when he couldn't bear any more. In an instant his shirt was off, her nightgown was across the room, and his shoes—had he been wearing shoes?—Daniel couldn't recall, and did not care. Corie was naked beside him, and she was the most beautiful thing he had ever seen in his life. "All those paintings, all those masterpieces. They cannot compare," he murmured, thinking he could just look at her forever and die a happy man. No, he could not. He had to touch her.

He started with her toes—and worked his way up to her trim ankles, her firm calves and luscious thighs, then her belly, which made her laugh, and her breasts. Oh, he lavished his attention on her beautiful breasts for hours—well, enough for her to squirm and pant and pull at his hair. So he moved on to her neck, her ears, her eyelids. Then her mouth again.

"Oh, Daniel, I never knew. Francis—"

He stopped her with a tiny bite to her lower lip. "The man was a cad. He cared nothing about the treasure he held. I do, and mean to cherish you forever. I never want to hear Snelling's name again. Certainly not in my bed."

She laughed. "This is my bed."

"Not tonight, it isn't. I wish it were a garden bower. No, there'd be prickers and ants. A grotto is too cold, the beach too sandy. This is perfect until we have a bedroom of our own to share, the way my parents did. None of that separate-chambers twaddle. Unless you hate my snoring. You'll have to tell me, honestly. And also if I do something that distresses you, or touch you in a way you do not feel pleasurable. I would never force you or embarrass you or—"

She reached out for the closure on his pantaloons.

"I see. You're not shy. That's good." She cradled his manhood in her hand. "Oh, that is very, very good."

He touched her, every silken petal, every dewy bud,

and followed with hot kisses that had both of them burning.

"More," she urged.

"No, you greedy wench. Not until you agree to marry me. There have been enough babies born early in this family. And if I begot one out of wedlock altogether, Harry would murder me."

But Corie could not say it in words. She could not trust herself to a man. She'd gladly give her body to Daniel tonight, because he gave her a woman's pleasure she never knew existed, and he made her understand there was so much more. Yes, she could give her body, despite the risks, despite her principles. But her heart and soul? Her very existence?

"I need time."

Daniel did not know how long his mother, or Dobbson, was going to leave them alone in Corie's bedchamber. They both must want the match badly, to allow this much leeway, although Daniel decided to throw Dobbson down the stairs if he interrupted with anything less than a fire bell. Still, he knew he could not stay until dawn, when the maids were about and footmen carried coals to replenish the fires. Corie's reputation was too important to her. Her answer was too important to him.

But he did his best to convince her in the few hours left. He might not be a swordsman of note, or a member of the Four-Horse Club, an orator, or a poet, but at loving a woman? His best at that was very, very good. He'd been practicing half his life for just this moment, just this woman.

Chapter Thirty

Corie woke with her muscles like meringue, her bones like butter, and a smile like a satiated woman. She was alone except for a rose on the pillow beside her and her nightgown tucked into the bed under the covers. How thoughtful he was, to think of her embarrassment when the maids came in, in the morning.

She rolled over, hugging her pillow that smelled like him.

Last night had been magical, and not to be repeated. They both agreed on that. They disagreed on last night's results.

Daniel felt they had to be married now. If he hadn't looked so smug by the candle's last light, she might have considered his proposal. But he had, as if he'd planned to seduce her, to guarantee her consent. Just like Francis Snelling.

"No. I am still a virgin, so no harm was done to an already-tarnished reputation. I doubt any of the servants will speak, since they are loyal and like working here."

Daniel laughed. "You might be a virgin, technically speaking, but only because I managed to keep my wits about me. There is no doubt that you are my virgin. My bride. You have my fingerprints all over you. Hell, you have my saliva all over you."

She was glad the candles were so low that he could not see her blushes. "Do not be vulgar."

"Do not tempt me to make you mine entirely. We both know I could do it, the way you were begging for more."

Gracious, her cheeks must be glowing. "Do you think me a wanton for enjoying your attentions?"

He kissed her, which led to more wantonness on her part, then said, "I think you are wonderful and will make the perfect wife, lover, and friend."

So Corie agreed to keep up the engagement, at least until after Susanna's ball. She had no place to hide, and had no desire to leave this house, this room, this bed, this man, but the thought of facing her father alone had her shaking. Daniel held her then, and he would protect her at the ball. But who would protect him from her father's filth?

She agreed to the betrothal, but not to a wedding, not until Daniel heard what lies her father told, how many ways he'd cheat her of the dowry money and a future he felt she did not deserve. Only then, if Daniel still wanted to marry her, would Corie feel really promised, really able to marry in good conscience.

Now, by the light coming through the curtains, she smiled to herself, and kept hope nestled inside her like a tiny seed. Daniel would know her father's words were false. Somehow, by some miracle, he believed what Corie said about Francis Snelling. He believed everything she told him, except the lie she did not love Daniel enough to marry him.

*   *   *

The house started to fill up days before the ball. The earl and countess's rooms were readied, and a suite for both cousins and their wives. The nursery was cleaned and aired for Rex's twins, and more rooms for the additional servants.

Lord Morgan offered to move back to his own house, but no one listened. He was part of the family now. Besides, Miss Reynolds was too busy with the invitations, acceptances, and seating charts to worry about him alone in that shabby place. He helped Dobbson select wines, without sampling too much of the earl's collection.

A surprise visitor was the vicar's assistant from St. Cecilia's Chapel near Stamfield Manor. The Reverend Mr. Barnaby Choate's arrival was a surprise to Daniel, at any rate. Lady Cora had written to the young curate that Lord Trowbridge had a living coming open at his estate, if the bishop approved, and if Mr. Choate agreed.

The way Susanna flew down the stairs and into the curate's arms was the real surprise to Daniel. The curate? That was why she didn't care about any of the men she met in London? His mother smiled.

Susanna was babbling about how a vicarage suited her to a cow's thumb, and her darling Barny could look as high as a bishop, and now Daniel would accept his offer for her hand without misgivings.

"He would have loved you, anyway," she said, then wiped her nose. "I am just so happy to see you, I cannot help crying. London wasn't half as much fun as it would have been if you were here. And waiting until the Season is over was forever!"

"What about Clarence Haversmith?" Daniel whis-

pered to Corie, while a beaming Susanna introduced
Barny to Lord Morgan.

"Oh, he is to wed his Maisy this summer."

Daniel watched his sister skipping across the room,
the curate's hand firmly in hers. He'd never seen her
look so happy. "The preg—that is, the dairymaid?"

"From what I understand, Maisy is no servant. She
is the daughter of his head tenant farmer. They raise
cows, very successfully. She is no milkmaid, and the
family is very respectable."

"Until Clarence got his hands on her. Why aren't
they wed already? I am surprised her father did not
insist."

"Mr. Haversmith told Susanna that Maisy wanted
time to gather a trousseau, and she wanted Clarence
to see some of London, so he does not regret settling
in the country so young. There is plenty of time before
the baby comes."

According to Mr. Choate, there was less time until
Squire Abbott arrived in London. "Lady Royce
thought I should ride ahead and tell you." He bowed
toward Corie. "What can I do to help?"

Daniel decided he liked the lad, even if he had no
chin to speak of. A beard could fix that. Very biblical.
"I will handle Abbott myself."

Barny was to stay at Royce House. Abbott was not.

"Sorry," Daniel told the older man when Dobbson
showed him into the library, "but the house is full,
what with the entire Royce family coming. And Miss
Abbott is far too busy helping with preparations for
the ball to stay with you at a hotel. I recommend the
Grand. Excellent meals there." He handed over his
solicitor's card. "Mr. Glessing is expecting you."

Abbott was getting red in the face. "This is the welcome I get? This is how my daughter greets me?"

"Why, no. She will greet you at the ball, of course. She'll look as fine as fivepence in the diamonds, too. The real ones given to her in her mother's will. You did bring them, didn't you?"

Abbott handed over a velvet pouch. Daniel let the jewels slide through his fingers once before smiling at the man he'd left standing. Something about Daniel's smile made Abbott natter about keeping them safe. "Girls can be flighty, don't you know."

Not his sister, it seemed, not Corie. "Excellent. I'll see you in a few days, then." He stood, knowing that his height alone would intimidate the smaller man. "Oh, and you'll keep away from Corie until the ball. I expect you to be proud father, nothing else. Do you understand?"

Abbott understood he had no choice, and was furious. "You know you're getting used goods. You saw it yourself back at that inn. What, did the Jezebel trap you, too?"

Daniel kept his temper, but just barely, for Corie's sake. She hated physical violence and he already had a black eye. He took a deep breath, thought of her naked, and smiled. "With her loveliness. But you should be glad I am taking her off your hands if you feel that way about it."

Now a crafty look came over Abbott's beady eyes. "I'm not sure she couldn't do better, with Lady Royce backing her. A baronetcy, at least."

If Abbott thought he'd get a better settlement, he hadn't met the family's solicitor. Daniel changed the subject. "Are congratulations in order for you, too? We heard rumors of a match with a certain widow."

Abbott scowled. "Some busybody said something to turn her away from me. The jade won't let me near her. You wouldn't know anything about that, would you?"

"My mother might, or Lady Royce." Neither of which was an outright faradiddle.

"No matter. I still aim to get me a young wife and a son, so don't you go thinking you're getting any heiress. The wench was always a disappointment to me." He sneered at Daniel. "Not even a knighthood. Well, you two deserve each other."

"Let us shake on that," Daniel said, holding his hand out.

Abbott winced when they shook.

"Sorry about that. Sometimes I don't know my own strength."

Daniel was sorrier he didn't hear any bones crunch; Corie hated violence.

The next arrivals were his cousins, Harry and Rex. While the ladies exclaimed over Rex's twin infants and Harry's wife's increasingly evident condition, Daniel related news from Oxford about the counterfeiters.

The government inspectors had, as expected, not found much, but Harrison's men, Harry's old spy network, were more successful. Having far fewer scruples than glorified bank clerks, they looked in windows, broke into houses, bribed informants. No one found Snelling, but they did discover one of his holdings was a wallpaper manufactory.

"I thought the stuff was painted," Rex said.

"The coverings put on earls' walls are, most likely," Daniel answered with a laugh. "We lesser folks buy printed wallpaper. Sometimes the details are hand-colored after the designs are printed out on rolling presses. Snelling's wife does the artwork. Word is, she could have been an artist of note, like her brother, but Snelling decided a viscountess ought to stick to dabbling with her watercolors like a proper lady, not go into trade."

Harry whistled. "So instead of showing her work at galleries and museums, she almost destroyed the British banking system."

Unfortunately, with all the government men asking questions and Chimkin closing his bank, Lady Snelling had warning. By the time the men got to the printing plant, the woman and the press foreman had blown it up. A great fire it was, too, according to the locals, what with all the stores of paper. Lady Snelling and her lover— also according to the nearby villagers—fled together while the workers tried to save their lives and their jobs. The wooden presses were destroyed, but the metal engraving plates were not.

"We've got the evidence, on its way to London under guard, so the bunch of them are out of business. And I doubt they'll get far, with every port or road being watched."

Rex and Harry slapped his back, congratulating Daniel.

"She's a beauty, isn't she? And a true lady."

Both men laughed. "Not the female, old son, although Miss Abbott is a prize indeed. But this new talent of yours is amazing, too. Does your lady mind your sensitive fingers?"

"Hell, no," Daniel said, then blushed, which had England's brilliant former spymaster almost falling off his seat and the country's most promising legal mind spilling his brandy laughing.

The females would be doing nothing but cooing over babies and making wedding plans for hours, so the earl's two sons, one legitimate, one not, took Daniel out to see what he could do. They went to banks and art galleries and jewelers and gambling dens to test his touch. Neither of the others could tell a glass ruby from a real one, even when Daniel told them which was which. So they went to look at the new house, then to several pubs, to see who could tell if the wine was watered. As Rex told Daniel, he might as well stay gone, because Lady Royce was such a high stickler that Daniel'd be lucky to be in the same room with his beloved before parson's noose was firmly around his neck.

So Daniel had to explain the circumstances of the betrothal, and some of Corie's history, so they'd help keep a watch on her father. Later he had to explain it again to his uncle, the Earl of Royce, too. After all, the earl would know the truth as soon as the engagement was mentioned. Lies were sour notes in his head.

Reconciled with his beloved wife after a long separation, Lord Royce was happier and healthier than he'd felt in decades. He wished such joy for Daniel, and pledged his support, even if it meant dealing with that reprobate Abbott. "We'll celebrate the engagement and worry about the wedding later, all right?"

Knowing his uncle Royce's reverence for honesty, Daniel was relieved. He was proud, too, when his uncle told him how pleased he was that Daniel finally found a use for the family gift. Between the banking establishments and the art world, Daniel had enough work to last a lifetime, without rashes.

And now he had the chance to bring more little Royce-Stamfields to life, the earl applauded, and who knew what ways they could find to serve their country and their fellow men?

Thinking of babies, Daniel went to find his goddaughter in the nursery. She and her twin brother were surrounded by women, so he stood outside the door, listening. They were all laughing and cooing and getting acquainted, Corie right in the middle, with one of the infants in her arms.

Later his aunt Royce privately declared Miss Abbott just what he needed, which was high praise indeed. The countess never heeded gossip, and never liked mealymouthed females who did not fight for their rights. She liked Miss Corisande Abbott very well. That was why she was moving Corie's room closer to her own, to protect the dear girl's reputation.

And if that man—Corie's father—dared to make trouble, Lady Royce would comb his hair with a footstool.

Between the cousins, the bank business, and the babies, Daniel and Corie had no time alone. That vast empty house on Layton Square was looking better and better in his eyes. Family was all well and good, and he was glad they approved of his choice of bride, but he wished they'd go home soon, so he could get on with his courtship. Hell, with the wedding. One taste of Corie's lips, of her enchanting body, left him wanting more, and soon. He never had been a patient man. Besides, Rex and Harry kept laughing at him, so he took them on at Gentleman Jackson's Boxing Parlour. Rex was the finest marksman, Harry could defeat anyone in a fencing match, but Daniel could box.

So they were all in the females' black books, with their black eyes and swollen lips and empurpled jaws, just in time for Susanna's come-out ball.

Chapter Thirty-one

The receiving line for the affair could have filled a small ballroom on its own. The earl and the countess stood at the head of the line, of course. It was their home, after all. Then came Daniel's family, since Lady Cora was throwing the party in her daughter's honor and had issued the invitations. Daniel insisted on having Corie at his side, what with her father coming, so Susanna claimed she could have Barnaby Choate at hers. Rex and Amanda, Harry, and Simone also joined the welcoming party, to show their support and greet old friends and accept congratulations on their own good news. Lord Trowbridge hovered nearby, and Lord Morgan and Miss Reynolds sat on chairs just inside the entry.

Squire Abbott was one of the first to arrive. Daniel could feel Corie tense beside him, then start trembling. He quickly touched her, behind her skirts. Startled, she turned to him, away from her glowering parent. When Abbott would have taken her hand to pull her aside, Daniel stepped forward.

She was gorgeous, in a blue gown selected, his mother swore, to match Daniel's eyes. It matched Lady Cora's eyes, too, and Susanna's, and those of all the other men on the receiving line except Barnaby, whose eyes were brown. Everyone commented on what a handsome family they were.

Daniel thought Corie was the most beautiful of all, especially with her hair done in curls trailing blue ribbons, and diamonds at her throat. Real diamonds. She touched them, in anxiety.

"Lovely, aren't they?" Daniel prompted his prospective father-in-law. "But not as lovely as your daughter."

The man made a *hrumph*ing sound. "I would speak with you, girl."

"We cannot leave the receiving line," Daniel said, including himself in whatever conversation Abbott wanted with Corie. "My mother would flay us alive, then toss us to Lady Royce."

"Later," the squire grumbled, ready to pass to the next in line.

Corie stopped him. "Are you happy for me, Father?"

"Is this what you want?" Abbott did not look at the loving family closing ranks around Corie, the elegant house, the renowned guests. He just looked at Daniel, the largest man there, the one whose neckcloth was askew from playing with the babies and who had dog hair on his coat and a bruise on his cheek that no cosmetics could cover. "This shabrag of a poor relation to an earl?"

Before Daniel could protest, or his mother, or the earl, Corie spoke out, clearly, loudly, with no tremor: "Yes. This is what I want. Daniel Stamfield is the man I want to wed."

"Then I am happy for you, I suppose."

Daniel raised his hand to scratch the back of his neck, but he took Corie's hand instead and brought it to his lips. He kissed her fingers, glove and all, then held his hand out to Abbott. Again, he shook the older man's hand, a bit too hard. "Sorry." He scratched his neck again.

After what seemed like hours, Lady Cora ordered the hired orchestra to begin the dancing. Lady Royce stayed behind to welcome latecomers, but the rest joined the hordes in the ballroom. By numbers alone, Susanna's ball was a success, with few invitations not accepted. No one wanted to miss the latest Stamfield set-to. Surely there would be one.

Daniel led off the cotillion with his sister. The earl followed with Corie, setting his seal of approval on the match. Daniel heard whispers and sighs, but he was concentrating on his steps, on Corie behind him, on Abbott's location, on Trowbridge dancing with his mother, the viscount's first dance out of mourning. So what if he was a few months early?

Harry's wife, Simone, added her mite to the next morning's *on-dit* columns, gracefully tripping down the line, or as gracefully as she could, with her babe due to be born soon.

Lord Morgan and Miss Reynolds even took their turn on the polished wood floor. He wheezed a bit at the end, but seemed pleased with himself and his partner. The two younger men, Haversmith and Choate, danced with less-favored young misses, and without any prompting from Lady Cora that Daniel could see. They were good lads, both of them.

Then it was time for his dance with Corie, a waltz. Either Susanna had finally been given permission to dance the suggestive steps, or she did not care anymore, for she took Barny Choate by the arm and led him to the floor. They must have had a lot of practice, for they performed admirably. Choate was a better dancer than Daniel. Hell, everyone was a better dancer than Daniel, but he held the world in his arms, the world and the sun and the moon and everything good. He kept waltzing, watching Corie's eyes smile at him, even when the music stopped.

It was time for the announcements.

"Past time, if you ask me," he heard one starchy matron comment. "If he held her any closer, we'd have to throw a bucket of water on them, like we do with the cats in season."

The family gathered in front of the raised orchestra stage, and someone dragged Abbott forward while servants wove through the crowds with trays of champagne glasses. First Lord Royce welcomed everyone to his home, to help rejoice on this festive occasion, his niece's presentation. They all sipped a toast to Susanna, who blushed adorably.

Then the earl bowed toward Corie's father.

With a few glasses of the earl's cognac in him, Abbott's complexion was redder than ever. He started, "I am honored . . ."

Now Daniel's face turned red, too.

Someone nudged Abbott. "I am proud . . ."

The earl slapped a hand to his ear to stop the din of discord. Harry screwed up his face at the sour taste. Rex blinked to clear his eyes of the red haze. Lady Cora's eyelid twitched and Susanna borrowed Choate's handkerchief.

Daniel pushed the older man aside. Ignoring the hives, he raised his champagne glass to Corie. "I am the happiest man alive. Miss Corisande Abbott truly wants to marry me."

Amid the applause, Susanna pulled Barny forward. "I am the happiest man alive, too," the young cleric said, a bit incoherent with nerves and joy. "Miss Susanna Stamfield has agreed to be my wife."

"And I, too," Lord Morgan shouted from the side. "Never been happier. Miss Eugenia Reynolds has done me the honor of accepting my proposal. She saved my life; now she gets to spend hers with me."

Lord Trowbridge was next, holding his hand up to quiet the shouts of congratulations while the servants refilled the glasses. "I am not the happiest man on earth, yet"—he glanced toward Lady Cora—"but I am pleased to announce that with the assistance of Mr. Daniel Stamfield, the Bank of England has destroyed a counterfeit ring. The British currency is safe."

That got the loudest cheers: to England, to the Crown, to the lucky couples, to the Royce family.

Daniel made sure to shake Abbott's hand where everyone could see. No one noticed the man wince. Daniel passed his future father-in-law on to Harry, the master swordsman, who shook his hand, harder. Then to Rex, who raised and trained horses, who shook his hand, harder still. Then Clarence Haversmith, by prearrangement, led him off to the little room set aside for waiting tradesmen and the like. He left him with a decanter of Lord Royce's finest port, and a bucket of ice for his hand. Never mind that the ice had been packed around the oysters.

Clarence nodded to Daniel when he returned to the ballroom, so Daniel was able to reassure Corie that she'd seen the last of her father. He'd drink himself into a stupor; then someone would see him into a hackney. Once he signed papers at solicitor Glessing's office in the morning, she never had to see him again. "You don't have to invite him to the wedding if you don't want."

Corie was about to say she was the happiest female in the universe, and that, yes, she wanted that wedding as much as—

"Gentlemen, ladies, your pardon," Dobbson said, looking as if he was about to cry. "The constables are here. And Bow Street. And the militia, surrounding the house. They have Lord Snelling."

The Stamfields had not failed the gossip columns after all. The crowds parted to allow a line of blue-eyed men and Lord Trowbridge to file from the room as unobtrusively as possible for four distinguished members of Britain's upper class—an earl, two viscounts, a bastard who was about to be knighted—and Daniel Stamfield.

They all went to the servants' hall, which was empty now with everyone busy at the party. Uniformed men stood around the edges of the room, watching their prisoner less carefully than they watched Harry's former spies, cutpurses, and pickpockets.

Snelling was slumped in a chair, looking far more battered than when Daniel lost him, and far more dispirited. His wife had run off with her lover, his own brother-in-law had turned him in for the reward and for forging his name, and now he was facing a sure death sentence, after he faced the united Royce family.

"She did it all, the cheating bitch," he cried. "My wife planned it all so she and her lover could live abroad. I swear I had nothing to do with any of it."

Trowbridge looked at the Royce men. Every one was cringing and looking ill, except for Daniel, who was scratching his backside.

"Guilty," they all declared.

All that was left was to decide what to do with the poltroon. Counterfeiting was a hanging offense, but it would be a scandal for Parliament to convict one of their own. "We can make good on the bad currency," Trowbridge told them, "but that a viscount almost bankrupted the country? The regent will look worse than he does now."

They all nodded. The only decent solution was a gentleman's exit: one room, one pistol, no way out.

"I'll take care of it," Trowbridge said, "so you can go back to the party. No one needs to know. Just tell the orchestra to play louder. I'll station soldiers outside and guards inside."

After the men left, and a hasty conference with Dobbson, Trowbridge and some of the uniformed men led Snelling to a small side room, one with no carpet to get ruined. There'd be a desk, if Snelling wished to write his last thoughts, and a bottle of brandy. Trowbridge left him at the door, with the loaded pistol one of the soldiers handed him. "There is no other way."

Trowbridge returned to Daniel and the party and signaled that the distasteful affair was almost concluded. Snelling was in the tradesmen's receiving room, where his body could be taken directly out through the service entrance.

"But . . . but isn't that where Clarence said he sequestered my father?" Corie asked.

They all raced through the dancers, past the refreshments room, down the stairs, back across endless corridors to the servants' stairs, and over to the farthest corridor.

Daniel kept shouting for Corie to go back. She kept running. He was about to throw her over his shoulder and hand her to one of his cousins when they heard shouting from that small, seldom-used room.

Abbott was ranting about his broken fingers, and how Snelling's brother ran off with the squire's daughter, ruining all Abbott's plans. He almost had a title for his grandsons, and a fortune in his own pocket.

Snelling was screaming that the doxy's lover killed Snelling's brother, and ruined all of *his* plans. Francis was going to take the false script abroad where no one would notice.

Daniel shoved a confused guard aside and broke the door down. There was Snelling, aiming the pistol at Abbott, and Abbott wielding a broken bottle.

"Stop, both of you," Daniel shouted.

Both men looked at Daniel, and both aimed their weapons in his direction. Corie leaped in front of him. "No!"

One of the men decided she'd make a good shield. Her own father held her in front of himself, daring Snelling to shoot. Now Daniel shouted, "No!" He pushed Corie aside, knocked Abbott down, and then rushed Snelling, throwing his aim off.

The squire shrieked and fell to the floor. He threw his makeshift weapon at Daniel, but Trowbridge was there ahead of Rex and Harry, and only his sleeve got sliced. Meanwhile, Snelling used his empty gun to break the small window in the room and leaped through it, leaving shards and threads and blood behind.

"It's Snelling," Trowbridge shouted out the window. "He is escaping."

The soldiers in the grass outside were not gentlemen. They did not care about the party going on, or a viscount's dignity. They knew only that a crime against their country had been committed. They fired, all five of them.

Corie was on the floor beside her father, while Daniel and his cousins ripped off their neckcloths to stanch his wound.

"Will he live?" she whispered.

"Yes, unfortunately," Daniel told her, his hands covered in Abbott's blood. "But I doubt he'll be fathering any son, not where he was hit."

Abbott groaned. "All I ever wanted was a boy to carry on." He looked at Corie with loathing. "And a title for my grandchildren. Not a puny female who disobeyed every order I gave. Now see what you've done, you—"

So Daniel clipped him a sharp right to the jaw, knocking the man unconscious. "So he doesn't feel the pain," he told the audience, which seemed to be half of his mother's guests, all crowded in the hall.

The party was officially over. One gunshot could be explained as an accident in the kitchens. A firing squad on the lawns, below the ballroom windows, was cause for panic, chaos, and running to see.

"At least I got some champagne this time," Lord Morgan commented, holding up his glass.

Miss Reynolds took it out of his hands.

"Do you still want to marry me?" Corie asked hours later. Her father had been stitched and sewn and drugged—and carted back to his hotel, where his own valet could listen to his caterwauling.

Daniel'd had a bath, a change of clothes, and a conference with his cousins and the earl about the best way to handle this latest social debacle. They decided to return to the country. Susanna did not need to complete her debutante Season, Lord Trowbridge could bring his sons to Stamfield Manor for the summer, Harry's wife wanted to be at her own home for the lying-in, and Lady Royce and Lady Cora had weddings to plan. They'd given him twenty minutes, with Dobbson watching the clock, to name a date. Twenty minutes? Hell, he couldn't even—yes, he could, maybe twice, but he wouldn't. Corie deserved better, and longer, and a bed. Although the chair they shared did have possibilities. . . .

He laughed. She was sitting on his lap. Surely she could tell how much he wanted to marry her.

"There will always be talk about that elopement."

He kissed her and said, "There will always be a fight that needs winning."

Corie stroked his bruised jaw and traced the outlines of his fading black eye. "As long as you don't go looking for trouble."

"As long as you don't rush into danger. I thought my heart would stop when Snelling pointed his pistol at you."

"He was pointing it at you—that's why I had to run in front. You are my heart. I could not live without you."

"*Mi corazón*," he said in Spanish. "My heart. My Corie."

A lot of the twenty minutes flew past on kisses and caresses, until they heard a cough from the slightly open doorway.

"You still have not said you would marry me, you know."

"Ask me again."

"I'm not getting down on my knees this time because I'd have to let go of you, which I don't intend to do until Lady Royce calls the militia back." He kissed her lips, then her hands, each in turn. "My darling, you already have my heart, my ring, my family's adoration. Won't you take my name?"

Corie tried not to cry; she really did. He kissed away her tears. "I love your name, and your ring, and your family. I love you, Daniel Stamfield, and I will as long as I live. I will be honored to be your wife. Proud to bear your sons. Ecstatic to be your lover. When?"

They both laughed, but Daniel brushed at a tear of his own. "As soon as possible, because I could not survive a long engagement. According to my mother and my aunt, they need almost a year to do the thing up right. I say let them plan Susanna's wedding. We can elope to Gretna."

Corie smiled, there in his arms. "Do you think anyone will ride after us to stop the marriage?"

"No. It won't be much of a scandal, after all. Hardly worth the inconvenience. Bad meals, damp sheets, hired horses."

"And your family will be disappointed. Susanna wants to be a bridesmaid."

"Aunt Royce will be furious that another of the Royce line married in a harum-scarum haste. What would you think about a special license? Susanna's curate can perform the ceremony as soon as we are back at Stamfield Manor. Then we can honeymoon at our new house in London."

"Will it be ready in time?"

"It will be ready if I have to pawn your diamonds, my love."

She took them off and handed them to Daniel. "Take them. Everything I have is yours."

He pulled her closer. "Everything I need is right here."

"Truly?"

"As true as it gets, just like my love for you. You can bank on it."

Read on for an excerpt from
Barbara Metzger's

The Scandalous Life of a True Lady

Available at penguin.com or wherever
books are sold

He needed her.

No, he needed a female *like* her. Otherwise he could take one of Lyddie's girls and be done with it. He'd have a pretty bit of fluff on his arm with less effort, less money, and less on his conscience. He'd also make less of an impression as a connoisseur of women, a man with exquisite taste and deep pockets. He needed a ladybird who was almost a lady, one who would have everyone talking, to create a stir heard back in London. For once, Harry sought the publicity, the notoriety, with everyone and his uncle knowing precisely where he was and with whom. Then Major Harrison, Harry's alternate identity, could die.

Miss Ryland was perfect; too perfect, unfortunately. No matter that every head would turn when she walked into a room—he could not turn a well-bred woman into a whore. If he didn't, though, Lyddie would, so what would his scruples and sacrifice have accomplished? Nothing. Furthermore, Miss Ryland herself seemed determined on the course. She had problems, too, and lofty principles could not outweigh bare necessity. She needed money; Harry needed a mistress. Both of them were in a hurry.

As she watched him, Harry watched her, wishing he knew what she was thinking, how she wanted him to decide. Then he recalled that he was done making decisions for others. His half brother had pummeled the fact into him that he was not always correct in what he thought best for everyone else. No matter that he thought himself omniscient, he did not have the right to play god with anyone else's life. Rex had said so while Harry lay bleeding on the canvas at Jackson's Boxing Parlour. Of course, Harry had let the younger man win the match; Rex was lame in one leg, after all.

He could make provision for Miss Ryland and the brother. That was no problem. He could even leave her as chaste as he found her. That might be a problem, for the woman was exquisite. Her reputation would be destroyed, though, and he knew how precious that was to a female.

But, damn, she was stunning enough to make headlines in the gossip columns, and smart enough to listen to whispered conversations in whatever language.

Harry wanted to be done with this scheme, with all intrigue, for all times. The war was over; his days as spymaster in the Intelligence Division of the War Office were almost at an end. He wanted to retire, by Zeus, not live in shadows and disguises and under aliases for the rest of his life.

He saw how happy his half brother, Rex, was, with his lovely wife, Amanda, helping him recover from his war wounds, both mental and physical. Why, they had twins already, a boy and a girl, that Rex doted on. Harry was jealous, not just of the infants, but of the peace he felt surrounding the viscount and his wife at the christening.

Harry hadn't wanted to attend the event at all. What, the bastard brother waving his bar sinister at the church for all to see? His presence would have embarrassed everyone. But Rex had insisted, and their father, the Earl of Royce, had written his hopes of seeing all his family, sons and grandchildren, together. Even Lady Royce, his father's wife, had written a polite letter of invitation herself. The countess, Harry knew, felt guilty for keeping the half brothers apart so long. Some women would have taken their husband's by-blow into their home to raise. Not Lady Royce. She'd left the earl and her own son, instead. Now that she and Lord Royce were reconciled, secure in their own marriage at last, she could be forgiving of the boy—a man now, of over thirty years—for coming between them through no fault of his own.

Harry might still have refused the invitation to the family's ancestral home, where he would never be part of the true family, but Cousin Daniel had insisted they'd all be offended otherwise. Daniel reported that his own mother wanted to meet her new nephew, and his sister was excited when she heard he was as handsome as the other Royce males, with the same dark coloring and unique black-rimmed blue eyes. She wanted to show him off to her girlfriends, which would have been enough to keep Harry in London, except Amanda, Rex's wife and the sweetest woman he knew, had asked him to stand as godfather to the boy. He could not refuse.

Daniel was godfather to the girl. He started weeping the instant that tiny scrap of lace and love was placed in his arms. Everyone laughed except Harry, feeling the tears well up in his own eyes, to see them reflected in matching blue ones with the dark rim. A baby, born in harmony, wanting for nothing, his future assured. Oh, lucky Rex, and oh, how Harry wanted that peace, that promise, a son, for himself.

And that was the truth. It was as sweet as honey, as sweet on his tongue as nectar.

Miss Ryland coughed, and he came back from his woolgathering to wonder what her lips would taste like.

He sighed. Such thoughts were for another tomorrow. Today was for finding out the truth, the way the Royce men always had, always could. Rex saw colors, true blue for honesty. The earl heard notes of discord for lies. Poor Daniel got rashes at untruths. And he, Harry, the illegitimate son, could taste a falsehood.

The odd, unheard-of gift of truth-knowing made them all invaluable to the country. Lord Royce acted in the legal system; Rex and Daniel had been the Inquisitors on the Peninsula, interrogating prisoners to find the enemy's secrets, secrets that could keep the generals informed and the soldiers safe. Recently Rex had been a huge help to Bow Street's police force before he left London for his wife's confinement and the infants' births. He'd do more when he returned to Town. They all worked in secrecy, of course, for the talent was too close to sorcery or witchcraft or magic for the public's comfort. Or for Daniel's. He was determined to sow his wild oats in London, then become a gentleman farmer, where only nettles could make him break out in hives. He had no interest in serving the country in time of peace, only in carousing his way through the city's underworld. Harry could sympathize, but he had plans for Daniel, anyway. The gift was too important to waste on barmaids, brawls, or barley crops.

As for himself, Harry was usually tucked away in hidden offices, in wigs and disguises when he went out. He was the Aide, a state secret unto himself. Half myth, half truth, he could sift through all the gathered intelligence and recognize the truth. He had fingers in every aspect of military and political and criminal life, in everything that could threaten his country. Recently he'd dealt with smugglers, embezzlers, and spies, French sympathizers all.

Now Napoleon was gone, and the Aide could be, too. Then Harry might make a real life for himself, as himself. The house party was the key. Harry Harmon, Lord Royce's bastard son, was invited now that he was acknowledged by his powerful father. He'd go, raffish Harry, and Major Harrison would stay behind. An assistant was already fitted for the right clothes, the wig and beard and mustache. The man wouldn't be in actual danger despite the death threats—Harry would not have let another man take a bullet meant for him—but he'd die, anyway. He'd suffer a heart spasm spectacularly, loudly, visible, right there on the steps of Whitehall for everyone to see. He'd be carried inside, physicians sent for, for naught. Harry had the obituary already written.

Farewell, Major, with all your enemies. Welcome, Harry Harmon, rakehell from the wrong side of the blanket. No one could connect the two, not when Harry was conducting a torrid affair at Lord Gorham's party in Richmond. He'd be safe and done with intrigue, ready for the rest of his life.

Also Available from
BARBARA METZGER

Spymaster Major Harry Harmon's latest assignment
requires him to serve as a nobleman at a house party
attended by his enemies. To play the part convincingly,
he needs an intelligent, beautiful woman to act as his
mistress. A woman like Simone Ryland.

Simone and Harry both have their reasons for going
along with the ploy, but they both also have secrets—
and desires…